THE KEY TO THE

Kingdom

Unlocking Walt Disney's Magic Kingdom

THE KEY TO THE
Kingdom

Unlocking Walt Disney's Magic Kingdom

Jeff Dixon

Jeff Dixon
www.jeffdixon.org
www.keytothekingdombook.com
jdixon@touchandchange.com

The Key to the Kingdom: Unlocking Walt Disney's Magic Kingdom
© 2010 Jeff Dixon

Published by
Deep River Books
Sisters, Oregon
http://www.deepriverbooks.com

ISBN: 978-1-935265-24-5
ISBN 13: 1-935265-24-5

Library of Congress: LOC 2010940072

Printed in the USA

Cover design by Joe Bailen

For my Dad

While this story was being written you have regained your sight
and can actually see these words on the printed page. You remind me
to believe in miracles all over again. You are my hero.

This book is built upon the following facts:

November 15, 1965—The Disney brothers, Walt and Roy, met at the Cherry Plaza Hotel in Orlando, Florida for a press conference. Sitting on either side of Florida Governor Haydon Burns they announced to the public their plans to build a new Disney theme park in Central Florida.

December 15, 1966—Walter Elias Disney passed away at the age of 65 in St. Joseph's Hospital in Burbank, California.

December 16, 1966—A private memorial ceremony was held at the Little Church of the Flowers at Forest Lawn Cemetery in Glendale, California. No announcement of the funeral was made until after it had taken place. No staff or executives from Disney Studios were invited, and only immediate family members were in attendance. Forest Lawn officials refused to disclose any details of the funeral or disposition of the body, stating only that "Mr. Disney's wishes were very specific and had been spelled out in great detail."

January 1967—Disney department heads were invited to a screening room at the Disney Studios. Sitting in assigned seats they viewed a film featuring Walt Disney sitting behind his desk and addressing them as individuals, gesturing toward them as he spoke, and laying out future plans. Roy Disney postpones retirement to complete the Florida project.

February 2, 1967—Roy Disney is the host at Wometco's Park Theatre in Central Florida for Project Florida. This invitation-only event screens the film Walt Disney World *Resort-Phase 1* followed by a press conference. The film includes portions of the documentary *EPCOT* featuring Walt Disney filmed just months before his death.

October 1, 1971—The Walt Disney World Resort opens the gates to the Magic Kingdom theme park.

October 23, 1971—Roy Disney dedicates the Magic Kingdom theme park based upon the philosophies and vision of his brother, Walt Disney.

December 20, 1971—Roy Disney passes away at the age of 78, with Walt Disney World being their last great project.

Today—The legacy of the Disney Brothers continues to touch the lives of people around the world.

 *Day One*
Night

HALOGEN HEADLAMPS PIERCED the darkness of the cool central Florida night. The GPS guided the Mustang surging toward the coastal community of Port Orange. Racing along Taylor Road, Dr. Grayson Hawkes approached an unknown destination. Questions swirled in the tornado of curiosity whipping through the preacher's mind. The glow of the dashboard light illuminated the business card propped against the gearshift; "1819 Taylor Road, Port Orange" had been neatly printed in blue ink. Flipping the card he read the name on the other side.

Farren Rales
Imagineering Ambassador
Walt Disney Company

Reading the name of his dear friend brought a slight smile to his face. Rales had been hired by the late Walt Disney himself as an animator at the Walt Disney Studios on Rales's thirtieth birthday. In the years that followed he had worked on animated features, been involved in projects at Disneyland, and eventually became a part of that exclusive group of creative Walt Disney Company designers known as Imagineers. Rales was part Disney historian, part Disney philosopher, and a modern day keeper of the dream that Walt himself had begun.

Farren Rales had given him the business card with an invitation to meet the old Imagineer at ten o'clock this evening. The GPS announced a turn seconds before an inconspicuous dirt road veered to the right. Hawk responded sluggishly and shot past it. He instantly banked his ride into a U-turn that corrected his course. Slowly navigating the heavily wooded, chassis-jarring dirt road, he watched for signage. The headlights threw a glow on a sign that read Gamble Place Parking with an arrow that pointed right. He turned the wheel. A gate immediately came into view, blocking forward progress. Hawk looked over the steering wheel trying to decide whether he had managed to bungle the directions and gotten hopelessly lost. With the car idling, he got out and walked to the gate. Grasping the chain that held the gate closed, he saw the lock had been secured to the chain, but the chain was not fastened. When he dropped the chain, the gate lazily swung open. Hawk slid back behind the wheel of the car and it crawled forward as the dirt became softer below the tires. The Mustang eased up to a parking barrier, above which the headlights shone on a yellow house trimmed in green.

Exiting the automobile, Hawk left the parking area and made his way toward the house. There was a display in front of the walkway to the house that probably explained where he was. The automatic timer for the headlamps clicked off, leaving him standing in darkness. Sensing his eyes would never adjust in the moonless night to read the display, he remembered a flashlight that was hopefully still in the trunk of the car. He retraced his steps. In addition to the soft sound of his shoe steps in the sand, Hawk thought he heard something else moving near him. He came to an abrupt halt. Rales? Listening closely, he now only heard the sounds of the outdoor evening. The trunk popped open, producing a blast of light that momentarily blinded him. He fumbled for the flashlight and flicked the switch. The beam shone strongly as he slammed the trunk shut. He again moved toward the house. Sweeping the beam around him, he saw a large historical marker looming in the dark, over his left shoulder. He refocused the attention of the light on this newly discovered sign.

> Gamble Place
>
> In 1898, James N. Gamble, of the Proctor and Gamble Company and a longtime winter resident of Daytona Beach, bought this land on Spruce Creek for use as a rural retreat. In 1907 he built a small cracker cottage with an open front porch and a breezeway connecting a separate kitchen and dining room . . . In 1938, Gamble's son-in-law, Alfred K. Nippert, completed the "Snow White House," a Black Forest style cottage inspired by the Disney animated film classic, *Snow White and the Seven Dwarfs*. The house is surrounded by a Witch's Hut, the Dwarfs' Mine Shaft, and an elaborate network of rock gardens. Collectively these buildings and grounds form a historic landscape now known as Gamble Place. This property was listed in the National Register of Historic Places in 1993.

Obviously Rales had asked Hawk here because of the Disney connection. It had been a Disney connection that had started the friendship between the two men. Hawk had been introduced to Rales and asked the Imagineer if he would meet with him and his church staff to teach them the art of storytelling. The first meeting had gone so well it turned into a standing appointment each month. However this evening the invitation was for Hawk alone. Sighing deeply in an attempt to relax, Hawk listened closely and his ears tuned in to the sound of water gently playing along an unseen shoreline. The unexpected snap of a branch unleashed a wave of adrenaline spinning him in the direction of the noise. He peered into the blackness of the trees, searching for the maker of the sound, but heard nothing.

"Farren, is that you?" Hawk spoke with a bit more edge than he anticipated.

Silence confirmed Rales was not the source of the sound. "So when did you get so scared of the dark?" he muttered to himself. "And when did you start talking to yourself?"

Out of the corner of his vision he noticed a glimmer of light across the wooded darkness. With a bit of reservation he moved toward it. His shoes cracked sticks and crushed leaves, creating a symphony of sound that shattered the haunting noises of nature that had moments ago surrounded him. His flashlight began to dim. Shaking it violently he resurrected the brilliance of the beam, only to watch it fade into a momentary glow, and then disappear completely.

"Tremendous," he said in frustration at the malfunctioning light. "Still talking to . . . and answering yourself."

The point of light he had been moving toward disappeared as well. Pressing onward, he drew nearer to where it had been. Once again it appeared and this time looked brighter and stronger. Hawk's trudging through the undergrowth yielded to softer ground as he heard a familiar voice cut quietly through the night.

"I began to think you weren't going to make it."

"I was starting to think you were playing a practical joke on me," Hawk whispered back.

"Now, would I do that to you?" Rales laughed softly.

Hawk could now see much better as he approached the place where Rales stood. Farren had brought a lantern that illuminated the place he was standing and cast long shadows in multiple directions. Hawk descended the steps to join Rales on what appeared to be a recently created platform. The sound of the creek was closer and Hawk assumed they were now on the edge of the river. Rales was dressed in a pair of black slacks with a lightweight black windbreaker. Hawk did not miss the stealth attire and was getting ready to comment on it when Rales again spoke in a hushed tone.

"Any trouble finding the place?"

"I suppose not, since it's out in the middle of nowhere!" Hawk decided to satisfy his curiosity. "And could you tell me why we're whispering?"

"Didn't you read the sign? We're in a state park. It closed at dusk. We could get arrested for being here."

"Then why didn't we come here in the daylight?"

"Now, that wouldn't be as much fun, would it?"

"Farren, we should clarify our definitions of fun."

"Breaking into a state park is a story you'll be able to tell for years!"

"I didn't break in, the gate was unlocked."

"So you opened it and drove on in."

"You invited me."

"Shhh," Rales interrupted.

Hawk grew quiet and strained to hear sounds coming out of the darkness. He studied Rales's tense features, trying to decide whether the old man was toying with him or was actually concerned that they might be caught after hours in the park. Rales's face softened and he turned away from Hawk, letting his lantern shine toward a nearby wooden cottage that looked as if it had been plucked off of an animation cell from an antique piece of film. Hawk's mouth opened slightly. Rales moved forward and panned the light across the front of this cottage that did not belong in this time or any other. It was recognizable as the cottage in the Black Forest of the classic cartoon *Snow White and the Seven Dwarfs*. Hawk's eyes followed the movement of the lantern to the carved lintel and a stone trough. Rales moved toward the front door, fumbled with the handle, and then opened it. Looking back to Hawk, he motioned for him to follow him inside. Hawk entered, feeling like he was stepping into a fairy tale as Rales silently closed the door behind them.

 *Day One*
Night

THE FLOOR CREAKED with age as Hawk shifted his weight in the center of the room. There was a fireplace to his left with a rocking chair in front of it. On the mantel above the fireplace was a painting of Snow White taken from a scene in the movie. A staircase on the opposite wall crawled up to a second story of the cottage. Perched on each stair, looking through the banisters, were wooden cutouts of each of the seven dwarfs. Fourteen unseeing eyes peered at the two men as they stood in the cottage.

Hawk broke the silence.

"Unbelievable."

"Not a lot of people have seen this place. I assume you read the historical marker down by the cracker cottage."

"The son of the Procter and Gamble guy built this place because he was a fan of the movie," Hawks recalled.

"Not exactly." Rales walked over to the fireplace and set the light on the mantel. The indirect glow bouncing off the ceiling creating a surreal atmosphere. Specks of light glinted off Rales's eyes.

"You are standing in the real cottage of the Seven Dwarfs."

"The real one?" asked Hawk, realizing that Rales intended to unravel the real history of this place.

"Certainly," Rales continued. "Think about it. The one in the original story is nothing but imagination. The cottage in Walt's cartoon was merely a drawing. But this is where the imagination and the drawing were combined to create the real thing."

"Are you suggesting that there were dwarfs that lived here?"

"Of course not, but what I am suggesting is that this place was here before Walt Disney World came into existence in the real world."

Hawk studied the Imagineer and wondered how many more secret places like this he had discovered through the years. Farren always managed to surprise him. His ability to blend ideas and thoughts in unique ways ignited Hawk's own creativity and curiosity.

"The historical marker gives you part of the history," Rales began. "In 1898, James Gamble bought this property and built the cracker cottage on it. He owned it for thirty-four years and then left it to his two daughters, Olivia and Maude when he passed away. Maude was married to Alfred Nippert until she died unexpectedly five years later. All of this property became his. Nippert was devastated by his wife's death and was having trouble coping with his life without her. One day he took their kids to see the first full-length animated film, *Snow White and the Seven Dwarfs*. The cartoon enchanted him in that darkened theatre, and he found a way to move on with his life."

"He was able to move on with his life because of Snow White?" Hawk asked.

"Yep, he hired a carpenter to watch the movie ten times so he could learn every detail about the cottage from the movie. Look around. He got the fireplace right, the stairway is made of split logs, and there are even headboards for each of the seven dwarfs on the bed in the bedroom."

"So all he was missing was the seven dwarfs."

"But he did not stop with the house. He took an old tree and fashioned a witch's hut and then built the seven dwarfs' mine shaft. This whole enchanted playland is surrounded by elaborate rock gardens and paths. There is even a well that connects to the creek. Isn't it amazing how people will cope with unexpected loss or grief?"

Hawk cut his eyes directly toward Rales, who was staring intensely at him. He wondered whether there was hidden meaning in what Rales had just said or if it was accidental. The two always managed to skirt revealing certain details of their lives. Rales did know that Hawk was not married, but had surmised that at some point he had been. He also had surmised that Hawk had children but something had happened to them. It was a moment that Hawk did not discuss and had never spoken to Rales about. He wondered if Rales had somehow heard about what happened.

Hawk, after pausing longer than he had intended, replied, "People have to cope in many ways when life takes the unexpected turn."

"Of course, you already know that," Rales offered back and then slowly measured his next sentence. "I am sure you deal with that every single day . . . as you minister to other people."

Rales's expression was difficult to read by the light of the lantern. The moment became agonizing. Hawk's past, although a mystery to most who knew him, had shaped and defined his life forever. His friend was moving uncomfortably close to an area of his life that he had no intention of discussing or sharing. The silence in the room was smothering.

Suddenly Rales's face burst in an ear-to-ear grin that Hawk had seen many times before. Shifting into a more upbeat tone, Rales once again turned the conversation.

"That is the power of a good story. It can encourage, it can make you laugh, it can bring you joy. It will make you think, it will tap into your hidden emotions, and it can make you cry. The power of a story can also bring about healing, give you peace, and change your life!"

In the dimly lit room the storyteller's words were dramatic and powerful. Hawk allowed them to sink in and continued to struggle with just how personal Rales had intended them to be.

"Hawk, you want to change the world. You are a storyteller, just like me. You think the story you tell as a preacher is one that is real and powerful enough to accomplish the impossible. I believe it can, but you have to tell it right. You have to share it so it connects with people where they are, where they live, in ways they can embrace it and make it their own. If you do, your listeners' lives will change forever."

Hawk smiled. Rales had done it once again. Hawk had constantly probed for ways to communicate the story of Jesus in more compelling ways. Now Rales had immersed Hawk in a story, a saga, about a man who learned to cope and move on with his life because of the power of a story. By bringing Hawk here Rales had placed him in a larger-than-life example of the way a good story can change others. He wondered if he would ever cease being surprised at the drama and flair this master story weaver used to teach him.

Hawk saw a way to please his friend. "I understand why you brought me here. Thank you."

"You understand?" Rales quizzed, "What do you understand?"

"I understand that a great story, told well, can change people." Yet he felt as if he had been sent hurtling back through time into a classroom where a teacher was testing him. He wasn't sure he had passed the test.

"Hawk, I've told you all those things about telling a great story before. I didn't bring you all the way out here this late at night just for dramatic effect." Rales wryly grinned. "I brought you out here so the story would *impact* you!"

"Impact me? Okay, all of the sudden I guess I don't understand."

"A minute ago you understood, now you don't," Rales playfully chided.

"I suppose I'm just a bit overwhelmed," offered Hawk halfheartedly. "After all, I've broken into a state park in the middle of the night for a mysterious meeting with an ancient storyteller, and I'm talking to him in the middle of a cartoon cottage. You must admit, it is a bit much."

"Point well taken," Rales acknowledged. "Let me tell you why I really asked you to come here." He walked toward the front door of the cottage and looked out the window. Hawk could see his reflection as he began to unpack his chronicle.

"In 1993 this land was finally listed on the National Register of Historic Places. It took nearly fifteen years before the state of Florida finally got the property ready to open for the general public. Before '93 the property was private and what was on it was relatively unknown, except to those who might have had the chance to visit."

"When did you visit this place for the first time?"

"I'll tell you in a minute. But let me tell you what happened after Alfred Nippert finished the work on this cottage. He contacted Walt Disney and invited him to come and take a look at what he had built. When Walt got the invitation he was riding a wave of popularity and had gotten an Academy Award for *Snow White and the Seven Dwarfs*. Then unexpectedly in 1939 Nippert was contacted and told that Walt would love to visit." Rales turned from the window and slightly shrugged his shoulders. "Within the month Walt himself showed up and Nippert gave him a tour. Walt Disney and Alfred Nippert stood right here in this cottage, just like we are now, and talked for hours."

"So Walt Disney actually stood right here?" Hawk mused nostalgically.

"No, he stood about a foot and a half to your left," Rales joked.

Quiet settled across the cottage as Rales allowed Hawk to enjoy this bit of trivia. Rales now pressed into the next chapter of the tale.

"Something happened to Walt while he was here."

"Happened? What?"

"The Oscar was his. He was developing new projects. Fans were writing from all over the world, but this was different. This was a fan that some would suggest had taken his love—or need—for the story to an extreme. But Walt understood for the first time in his life, in a tangible way, that if you tell a story with enough heart, people will do whatever they can to become a part of that story. That is what Nippert did. Nippert may have been Walt's biggest fan ever. He made the story come to life so he and his children could become a part of the story."

"This is not a story that shows up in the Disney history books."

"Of course not, but that makes sense when you realize that Walt was a new celebrity. It was still only 1939. The Walt Disney we all know and love from history was still emerging. Still, what happened here was important. Walt told me the story about this place . . . once."

Rales now walked toward the staircase and studied the dwarfs looking into the room. Hawk had a lot of questions but did not ask them because he didn't want to derail the train of thought that Rales had him riding on. Rales casually leaned against the staircase banister and it creaked as he continued.

"We were building Disney World. I rode over here on my day off and conned the caretaker into letting me walk around and look. I gave him a family pass to the Preview Center that was open while we were still building the Magic Kingdom. He even opened up this cottage and let me in to see. That is when I knew."

Not willing to wait, Hawk asked, "Knew what?"

"This is where Disneyland and Disney World were born."

"I thought the idea for Disneyland was born when Walt was at an amusement park with his girls. He started dreaming about a place the entire family could enjoy together."

"That's true," Rales agreed. "But you know, as Walt started developing that idea his mind came back here, to this place, to the moment he stood here for the first time. Realize that this is the first place he ever stood where his imagination and story had become something real. He could touch it, smell it, and see it. His ideas before he came here had been confined to the theatre screen. Here in this cottage his dream surrounded him for the very first time."

"Did Walt talk about this place a lot?"

"I don't think so. He mentioned it to me only one time. He lived in California and didn't spend a whole lot of time here in Florida until he started purchasing the property for the resort. But you know enough about Walt from his biographies, the legends, the stories, the websites, even the podcasts that he was a genius. You and I both know that he went back to the studio, sat behind his desk, and let the memories that this place created in him spark his imagination, his ability to really understand a story, and eventually how he would touch the world. This place, in the moments he was here, impacted his life and he was never the same. I have always believed that Walt would return here in his mind, and that helped him remember how important his dreams and imagination were to others. It inspired him. It sparked his creativity. History proves that Walt's stories continue to live."

Farren rose up off the banister and slowly walked back to the mantel. Taking the lantern, he moved toward the front door and gestured for Hawk to follow. He opened the door and closed it without a sound after they were outside. Motioning with a tilt of his head, he led the way behind the cottage along a very old rock walkway. Without speaking they walked toward an artesian well just below the cottage. Rales glanced in the direction of the water for a moment and then he spoke.

"Grayson Hawkes, I have thought about this for a long time. I have something for you." Rales now brought his face back to look directly at Hawk. "It is something I believe has great worth. At least it does to me. I'm giving it to you because I think you'll discover it to be just as valuable."

Hawk watched as Rales reached into his trouser pocket and brought out a small piece of wrapped cloth that easily fit into the palm of his hand. Rales slowly opened his palm and studied the package that lay there. He raised his eyes and looked into Hawk's face. He had the pastor's complete attention.

"If you will take this and do the same thing Walt did when he left this place, your imagination . . . your ability to understand a story . . . and how you touch the world . . . even your life will never be the same. And the stories you communicate will become timeless."

Almost reverently Rales handed the package to Hawk. The cloth was soft and aged. Hawk took it, studied it, and began to unwrap it. Once, twice, three times, and then the fourth layer of cloth revealed what was nestled inside. Taking it between his index finger and thumb, he lifted it out of the soft material and held it up in front of him.

"It's a key." Hawk inspected the key held between his fingertips. It was a skeleton key. Golden, heavy, and catching light given off by the lantern, it was obvious that this key was old but had been respectfully cared for. As Hawk looked toward Rales he saw him beaming with pride.

"Not just any key, my friend. It is a very special key. There is not another one in the entire world that does what this one will do. You are holding in your hand the key to the kingdom."

The importance of the key to Rales was obvious and therefore the importance of the key to Hawk was never in doubt. Rales's eyes brimmed with tears in the dim light and Hawk was touched by the old man's sincerity and the love, respect, and trust that this heirloom represented.

"Thank you, Farren. I will treasure it always."

"Don't just treasure it, Hawk." Rales clutched his hand. "Use it."

Rales let loose of the preacher's hand and turned to pick up the lantern. He flicked the switch. The light was extinguished and both men were plunged into darkness.

Blinking away the residue of where the light had been, Hawk heard footsteps on the rock walkway. Finally after a dozen rapid blinks his eyes adjusted to the darkness. Rales was no longer there.

"Farren?" Hawk whispered.

Hearing nothing, he knew Farren's exit had been planned and he had no intention of answering the preacher's calls. Hawk carefully placed the skeleton key back into its swaddling wrap and slid it into his pocket. Angling back toward the Seven Dwarfs' cottage, he knew he was going to have to retrace his steps through the darkness toward the parking lot. He wondered how Farren had gotten to this place. He hadn't seen another car in the lot and hadn't seen any other entrance into Gamble Place. However, Hawk was going to have enough trouble navigating the darkness back to his car without worrying how Rales had gotten in or out of this place. Rounding the corner of the cottage, he stumbled over a raised stone on the rock-covered walk and quickly corrected his misstep.

A voice from the darkness spoke loudly with authority.

"Hold it right there!"

He heard the sound of a gun being cocked.

Hawk turned on his heel and exploded into a full run in the direction from which he had just come. Again the voice cried out behind him.

"I said stop!"

Hawk had no intention of stopping. The sound of footsteps followed him on the rocky path. When he arrived back at the well he had expended his knowledge of the layout of the property. Trusting that the owner of the voice was still chasing him, he decided he would simply loop around the house. Any lead he had could be quickly lost; Hawk cut to his left and raced along the back side of the cottage. The footsteps that pursued him were still trailing and he had no idea how far behind they were. Rounding the house he glanced back over his shoulder to catch a glimpse of any motion behind him. His momentum came to an abrupt halt as he thundered into a large obstruction on his path. The sudden impact drove him backward and sent him sprawling on the ground.

Grogginess began to cloud his brain but his survival instincts forced him back on his wobbly legs as he compelled his body to keep moving. Hands in front of him, he felt rough bark. He'd hurtled headlong into a thick tree set off to the side of the cottage. His pursuer's footsteps gained ground. Stumbling around the tree, he found an opening cut into it. He reached his arm into the darkness and found nothing but empty space. This tree had to be the Witch's Hut that Nippert had built in his enchanted playground. Unable to gather his wits to surge beyond this point, Hawk plunged forward into the void of the hut. He gasped for breath and then held it so he would make no sound in the blackness. The footsteps raced past the opening of the hut. He listened as they headed in the direction of the cracker house near the parking lot.

Hawk's mind began to emerge from the crash-induced fog and he knew that his pursuer could simply wait for him to return to his car. Deciding that whoever was chasing him had not had time to get to the parking lot yet, Hawk commanded his legs to again start churning. He struggled to keep his bearings as he navigated the darkness and purposely tried to make as much noise as possible as he ran out of the Witch's Hut. He hoped he was heading through the trees toward Spruce Creek. It only took a moment and he again heard the pursuit turn back toward his direction. Stumbling across the leafy carpet covering the ground, he blindly reached down, grabbing sticks and branches as he ran. Believing his pursuer could not see him and was chasing as blindly as he was running, he held onto the heaviest of the branches he'd picked up off the ground. A few seconds later Hawk threw the branch sideways in the direction of the water. After a moment of silence he heard the sound he was hoping for. The branch splashed along the shoreline of the creek. At the same moment he heard the pursuer angle away from him toward the edge of the water. Knowing he only had a moment to use to his advantage, he changed direction at the same time and headed toward what he hoped was the parking lot. The footsteps of his pursuer slowed and then stopped. This was the moment he had been banking on. The chaser in the dark was trying to decide which sound to follow.

Indecisiveness ended and the footsteps again headed in the direction Hawk was running. It was then that Hawk's eyes began to see the shape of his car emerging into clarity out of the inkiness of the night. In one motion his car key was out and Hawk pressed a button on the key ring to unlock the car.

The horn blared and the lights flashed. His pulse rocketed and his heart was trying to hammer out of his chest. He'd inadvertently hit the alarm button instead.

Gulping air, Hawk pressed the correct button. The horn silenced and the lights fell dark as he pulled open the door. He crashed in the seat and inserted the key into the ignition. The lights of the car destroyed the darkness anew and Hawk saw his pursuer about to reach the car. He shoved the car into gear and glanced into the rearview mirror. Sand flew and his pursuer disappeared in the billowing cloud created by his exit.

Hawk exhaled loudly and felt his heart still thundering in his chest. He veered to the left and bounced back down the pathway toward Taylor Road. As he reached the end of the dirt trail headlights appeared directly in front of him, blinding him. Not slowing, he shifted the wheel to the right and then back left, sliding past the car and turning onto the main road. He punched the accelerator and the tires churned over the asphalt as he looked in the rearview mirror. He saw nothing but darkness and he put distance between himself and Gamble Place as fast as possible.

 *Day Two*
Morning

EVERY MUSCLE IN DR. GRAYSON HAWKES'S BODY ached the next morning as he trudged into his office at Celebration Community Church. The town of Celebration, a creation of the Disney Corporation, meshed Disney philosophies with small-town stereotypes. Young families with strong values desired the stability of being part of a church congregation featuring relevant non-traditional styles of worship and church structures. The Florida Baptist Convention had targeted this area to plant a new church congregation. That is when Grayson Hawkes, a native of central Florida, entered the picture. He accepted the call to become the pastor and immediately assembled a church staff around him that loved Jesus and Walt Disney World.

The office was free of activity as Hawk was not a stickler for keeping regimented office hours. The emptiness of the office allowed him to think back to the events of the night before. Setting down his briefcase he slumped into his office chair and allowed it to spin aimlessly under the shifting weight. The bookcases bowed under the pages of the extensive library Hawk had accumulated through the years. His debit card confirmed his addiction to visiting booksellers. Books and coffee were the two vices that Hawk readily admitted to having to anyone who would ask.

Some would conclude that Hawk was in denial about his other addiction. Simply stated, he was a Disney fan. His office was stuffed with books, collectibles, animated characters, souvenirs, and trinkets that held deep and unspoken personal meaning for Hawk. Disney purists would call the collection Disneyana. His fondness and appreciation for Disney had given Hawk an instant bond with Rales. Their meeting the night before had unexpectedly left Hawk tired, aching, and with a brain load of questions.

Hawk wondered where Farren had disappeared to in the dark. He wondered who had chased him at the Dwarf House. Thinking restlessly about it through the night, he'd assumed it must have been a security guard at the state park. However, that did not explain the car waiting at the end of the driveway to the main road. As he pondered the blinding headlamps, he created various scenarios that would explain the car's presence: teenagers parking, some type of illegal mischief, someone resting after a long drive, or the gnawing sense that his pursuer had walked in from the parked car and the driver was waiting for him to return. This last thought bothered him more than he wanted to admit. Not normally paranoid, Hawk found himself still on edge at fleeing the park so wildly. And last, but most pressing, he was still trying to figure out the real meaning behind the skeleton key that Rales had given him.

Taking the key out of his pocket, he carefully unraveled the wrapping. Hawk felt the weight of the hunk of molded metal in his palm. Squeezing it between his fingertips, he held it up and spun it around. The key, though old, was incredibly well preserved. Rales had told him, "Don't just treasure it . . . use it!"

"I would use it," Hawk thought, "if I only knew how and where."

The phone rang, clanging him back to the moment. Picking it up, Hawk heard the familiar voice of the church student minister, Albert Shepherd.

"Hey, boss," Shep began, "how are you?"

"I'm good, and you?" Hawk replied. He wasn't feeling all that well, but there would be too much to explain if he hinted he was feeling tired or sore. As Shep covered what he wanted to discuss, Hawk noticed his associate pastor, Juliette Keaton, standing in the doorway with her head tilted. Hawk motioned for her to enter and take a seat. Juliette entered and sat down, staring intently at him as he continued to talk. Her stare became distracting and Hawk lost track of what Shep was saying and had to ask him to repeat himself. They quickly finished their conversation.

He hung up the phone and turned to Juliette. "Are you staring?"

"Yes," she replied. Hawk waited, knowing she would tell him what was on her mind. "You look awful. Have you been in a fight?"

Hawk had forgotten about the cut he'd collected when he smashed his face into the Witch's Hut. "You know better than that. I wouldn't get into a fight."

"Oh, really, most of the things you do don't surprise me." Probably not, considering how well he knew her husband and two children. "Are you hurt badly?"

"No, not too bad, just had a bit of an accident."

"Sure you did." She inspected him curiously. "Can I help?"

"No, but thanks." Hawk didn't need help and he didn't want anyone to know that he had run into a tree in the middle of a state park, after the park had closed, chased by an unknown armed pursuer.

Juliette sighed, apparently admitting defeat. She got up, patted him on the shoulder, and left with a smile. She bumped into Jonathan Carlson, the church worship pastor, coming through the door as she was exiting. As Jonathan saw Hawk's face, his jaw dropped open.

Juliette raised her hand. "He had an accident and he isn't talking about it."

Jonathan nodded and looked in at Hawk, "If I can do anything to help just let me know."

"I will," said Hawk with a smirk. He appreciated their concern but hadn't had the time to figure it out for himself. Picking up the phone again, he dialed Farren Rales's cell phone number. Perhaps Farren would shed some insight on the previous night. Without a single ring he heard Farren's voice mail request him to leave a message and have a magical day. He waited for the beep.

"Farren, this is Hawk. When you get a chance give me a call. I had a rather interesting evening last night. I was wondering if you would like to hear about it."

Breathing heavily, he whirled in his chair to face his desk and opened his calendar to the list of appointments for the day. His schedule was booked solid; he would be far too busy to think about the key or his wild flight through the darkness. His first appointment would be walking through the door at any moment. On cue he heard the door open and he got up gingerly to greet his day.

 *Day Two*
Afternoon

EVERY TICK OF THE CLOCK wearied Hawk more than the one before. The late night, the soreness in his body, and the fatigue of being trapped inside the walls of the office only caused him to feel more tired and spent. His last appointment of the day ended at four thirty, and with a slide of the mouse he shut down the computer.

He wondered why he hadn't heard from Rales yet. It was unusual for Rales not to return his call. Could he have run into trouble last night? Hawk also wanted more information about the key he'd been given. He snapped open his cell phone and hit the speed dial number that connected him to Rales's office in Imagineering. On the second ring the call was picked up.

"Imagineering, Farren Rales's office. This is Nancy speaking."

Hawk knew Nancy Alport well. She was Farren Rales's administrative assistant.

"Hi, Nancy, this is Hawk. Is Farren still in today?"

"He didn't come in today," she said, worry creeping into her voice.

"I tried his cell phone earlier and I haven't heard back from him. Do you expect him in tomorrow?"

"I expected him in today. I've been trying to reach him all day, and as far as I know, no one has been able to. I'm a little concerned," Nancy admitted. "He always checks in, even if he's not scheduled to be around the office."

Hawk listened to the concern in Nancy's voice and felt his own concern for his friend begin to rise. Last night Rales had given no indication that he didn't plan on being in the next day. The worry and wondering over who had chased him at Gamble Place came back again.

"I saw him after your meeting yesterday," Nancy stated. "Did he say anything strange to you or do anything out of the ordinary?"

The day before had been the monthly get together, an opportunity for the church staff and Farren to talk. It had been as that meeting ended that the Imagineer had quietly invited Hawk to meet him and slipped him the business card.

"No." Hawk made a decision not to let Nancy know about the late-night road trip. "Why would you ask about anything strange?"

"I'm not sure, Farren just seemed unusually preoccupied most of the day yesterday. He didn't say anything was wrong. Things just seemed . . . I don't know . . . different." Nancy paused. "But he seemed okay to you, didn't he?"

"He was fine." Hawk reaffirmed his decision not to disclose anything that had happened yesterday. "Is there anything I can do to help you track him down?"

"I don't think so. Hopefully he just forgot to let me know he wasn't going to be in the office. He had a meeting that he missed, but I don't think it was a big deal." Nancy had worked with Farren a long time. Her concern was apparent. "If you hear from him, tell him to give me a call."

"I'll do it for sure. Please tell him the same from me."

"You've got it, Hawk. Talk to you soon."

Hawk hung up the phone, already planning his next move.

He'd been to Farren's home a couple of times for dinner. The drive was about forty minutes from Celebration. Next stop: the Rales residence.

Striding down the hallway, he walked past Jonathan's office.

"Hey there, boss," Jonathan called as Hawk was two strides past the door. "I was serious this morning when I told you if there was anything I could do to help, I would. Are you sure you're all right? You look like you were in a brawl."

Hawk had almost forgotten about the soreness in his face. Rubbing his hand tenderly over his eye, he winced at how painful it was.

"I'm fine."

"I just worry about you sometimes, we all do. You never ask for anything and you don't usually complain. But if you want to or need to, you're entitled, and we can take it. We won't think anything less of you if you want to be human like the rest of us," Jonathan subtly opened the conversation for Hawk to unload.

"Just a long day. I started tired and never got my second wind."

"See you tomorrow, Hawk. Enjoy your evening," Jonathan said.

"I'm planning on it. See you in the morning." Hawk moved back down the hallway. Stepping out into the afternoon sun, he noticed that the only cars in the parking lot were his, Jonathan's, and one he didn't recognize.

He hit the key ring to automatically unlock his door, then swung it open and slid down into the seat. Firing up the engine, he pulled out of the lot and turned toward the interstate.

 *Day Two*
Evening

TRAVELING EAST ON INTERSTATE 4 through Orlando, a driver exited the interstate behind Grayson Hawkes's Mustang and followed the preacher toward Lake Adair and Edgewater Drive. They passed shops and stores, grocery stores, coffee shops, restaurants, and specialty shops of the sort that spring up in prime real estate areas like College Park.

Hawkes pulled up beside a solid wooden gate. He glanced into his side view mirror and waited for the car behind him to pass before opening his door. The driver circled the block and found a secluded place to park and watch. From there, Hawkes could be observed scratching his head and staring up at Rales's house. The home was located above a boutique along Edgewater Drive. The preacher tried opening the gate, which was locked. He then scaled the wooden fence and disappeared behind it. A few minutes later he came back over it and paced the sidewalk for a few moments before driving to Gabriel's, a local sub shop where he ordered a sub, a bag of chips, and a large coffee.

Hawkes slumped at his table apparently not noticing the car that had been following him on his College Park trip. It was the same car that had passed him just before he got out of the Mustang at Farren's house. Now the car sat parked along the street where the windows to the sub shop faced outward. Had Hawkes looked up and out the window he would have seen a set of dark glasses hiding the eyes that closely watched him. The eyes behind the glasses perched on the nose of this person had also watched Rales, Hawkes, and the church staff at lunch the day before. Now with Rales missing all day, the driver of the car decided to keep an even closer surveillance on the preacher from Celebration.

Hawk ate his sandwich and sipped his coffee. Having peered through Rales's windows and satisfied his curiosity that his friend had not fallen ill or had an accident at home, he now pondered other matters. Wishing for the food and caffeine to jump start his brain, he traveled a memory trail along the previous night's activities. He remembered Rales giving him the key. What was it that Rales had said about this key?

There is not another one in the entire world that does what this one will do. You are holding in your hand the key to the kingdom.

He didn't know what that statement meant. It was just a key . . . wasn't it? Rales had tears in his eyes as he presented it to Hawk. While Hawk had assumed the value of the key was symbolic, the things Rales had said hinted at something deeper than mere symbolism. *There is not another one in the entire world.* That would make the key unique, one of a kind, and that would give it great value. An antique key would have some worth, but the real value came from what a key opened. Hawk again remembered what Rales had said. *There is not another one in the entire world that does what this one will do.* An old key would open an old lock. Still, there had been the last part of what Rales had said, *you are holding in your hand the key to the kingdom.* How could it be a key to a kingdom?

He allowed his mind to loop the phrase over and over again.

The key to the kingdom, the key to the kingdom, the key to the kingdom . . . it didn't matter how many times he replayed it, he had no idea what it might mean.

"Excuse me sir, did you hear the announcement?" The clerk smiled as she asked the question.

"I'm sorry, I didn't hear an announcement."

"We're closing in five minutes. Is there anything else you need this evening?" The young lady gathered the remains of his meal to take to the trash.

"No, but thanks. I suppose I should quit taking up your table space," Hawk said.

Hawk slugged down his last gulp of coffee. The coldness of the java bitterly reminded him of how long he had been sitting there thinking. He rewrapped the key in the protective cloth and deposited it into his pocket. Exiting the sub shop, he never glanced at the car pulling away from the street parking area the moment he came out of the glass doors. The observer in the car had sat there for hours as the daylight yielded to the darkness. As Hawk rounded the sidewalk and stepped to his car he had a thought. He knew it wasn't a great thought but at least it was something.

The engine fired to life as he turned the ignition switch. He slid the car into reverse and flipped open his cell phone. Tapping the speed dial, Hawk heard the phone ring twice.

"Hello, this is Shep," answered the familiar voice.

"I have an-off-the-wall question for you," Hawk warned.

"Throw it at me."

"Do you remember telling me about a tour you wanted us all to take out at the Magic Kingdom?"

"I think by this time of the evening they are done for the day," chuckled Shep.

"I was trying to remember one that you told me about that had something to do with a behind-the-scenes look at the Magic Kingdom."

"I remember it," Shep replied. "It's the tour that takes you underground into the tunnel system."

"That's the one. What is the name of the tour?"

"Hmm. It has something about the kingdom in the name. Wait! I remember, the name of the tour is the Keys to the Kingdom tour."

"Perfect, that's it!" Hawk smiled. He was certain he had heard about something with the phrase *key to the kingdom* in it. "Shep, I appreciate it. That's all I needed. Thank you."

"Okay boss, have a good rest of the evening."

"You too, bye." Hawk clipped his phone closed as he accelerated back onto the interstate. Now that he knew the name of the tour, he wanted to see if he could find out more about it. He wasn't sure it had anything to do with the key that Farren had entrusted to him, but at least it was something. As the day ticked away he became more perplexed about the key. His instincts were searching for some deeper or hidden meaning in the gift. The unexpected disappearance of his friend only added to the unease he was beginning to feel. Something deep within him believed that Farren's dropping out of sight was somehow connected to the key. Perhaps it was part of the Imagineer's plan. Deciding to try one more time, he dialed Farren Rales's number again. Just like earlier, he was kicked into the voice mailbox.

CHAPTER SIX

Day Three
Morning

SATURDAY MORNING FOUND HAWK rushing into his office for what he hoped would be a brief visit. Punching the keypad on the phone, he entered the number he had found doing some cyber-searching the night before. He had found what he was looking for on Lou Mongello's Web site. As an author of multiple Disney trivia books and the host of a popular weekly podcast, Mongello would be the sure source of the information that Hawk was seeking. The plan was not complicated; Hawk hoped he would be able to get into the Keys to the Kingdom tour at the last minute.

After a quick phone conversation, he had reservations for the tour beginning in less than an hour.

Growing up in Orlando and taking more trips to the Walt Disney World Resort than he could remember gave Hawk a familiarity with Disney property that would rival any expert's. The Keys to the Kingdom tour was meeting at the City Hall on Main Street, USA. In order to get there as fast as possible, Hawk decided to park at the Contemporary Hotel and walk across to the entrance of the Magic Kingdom. Pulling past the security stand at the Contemporary and heading toward the parking area, Hawk took a moment and looked at the futuristic building rising up in front of him. When the Magic Kingdom Resort opened, the Contemporary was one of the two hotels that were a part of the grand opening celebration. The monorail track that stretched from the Ticket and Transportation Center to the Main Gate passed through the Polynesian Resort Hotel and the Grand Floridian Resort on one side of Bay Lake and through the interior of the Contemporary Resort on the other. Each time Hawk remembered the first time he rode on the monorail as a child it brought a grin to his face. It had almost taken his breath away as he looked out the window when the monorail moved from the outside of the hotel to the interior. It was a childhood memory that was burned into his young mind forever. Parking his car and locking the door, he heard the sound of the monorail pass directly overhead carrying another load of eager visitors to the main gate of the Magic Kingdom.

The short walk from the Contemporary to the entrance bypassed the monorail ride and he strode briskly along the redbricked walkway under the monorail track. In a few moments his walk was complete and he was sliding his annual pass into the ticket turnstile. Below the Train Station, he stepped through the entrance that led to the Mickey Mouse face that was made entirely of flowers. Choosing the tunnel on the left he emerged into the Town Square on Main Street, USA with City Hall right in front of him. Climbing the steps while glancing at his watch, he knew the tour was already gathering and preparing to leave. A cast member working behind the counter at City Hall helpfully pointed Hawk through the door where the tour was meeting just outside. The group of people looked like any other group of tourists ready for a day in the theme park. Hawk noticed that the tour guide appeared as if she had just stepped out of a classic Walt Disney brochure. Dressed in a blue jacket, plaid skirt, and dark hat, she was checking a list and making preparations to begin. Her name tag let everyone know her name was Brooke. With a smile she opened her mouth to speak.

"Hold on just a moment please, Brooke," a pleasant but commanding voice interrupted. Brooke turned and watched the approach of another cast member.

This interrupting cast member was not dressed as a tour guide. She had shoulder-length dark hair and wore a professional-looking black skirt, a white long-sleeved blouse, and a pair of heels. Hawk assumed she held a position of authority and was Brooke's supervisor, or "lead," as they were known among cast members. This woman's name tag revealed her name was Kiran, and she and Brooke seemed to be going back over the list that Brooke had been looking at before. As their conversation continued they would occasionally glance up at the slightly curious crowd that watched their discussion and waited to begin the tour. Both Brooke and Kiran would be quick to smile and then would continue to work. As Kiran glanced up Hawk noticed her green eyes and was struck by how attractive she was. Stepping away from Brooke, Kiran addressed the group.

"Good morning, my name is Kiran and this is Brooke. We are so excited that you have chosen to take the Keys to the Kingdom tour. We apologize for the slight delay but we had some last-minute additions to the tour so we've had to reorganize just a little bit."

While Kiran continued to talk to the group, Hawk realized that he was the last-minute addition to the tour and wondered if he was the source of this problem. He tuned back in as Kiran explained what was happening.

"Because there are so many of you, we'll divide this group into two separate tours. Through the course of the day you'll see the same things, but this just allows us to provide you a better guest experience and give you the personal attention that makes these tours more enjoyable. So if you will listen closely for your name, that would help us tremendously."

Kiran read a list of names clearly and concisely. She stopped and again spoke to the group. "If I read your name, I'm going to ask you to go with Brooke. She will be your tour guide and show you the Keys to the Kingdom. Have a great time!" Kiran watched as Brooke began to speak to the group, and soon their tour was underway. Turning back to the remaining guests, she smiled and read off the list of names of the people who should now be in her group. The last name on her list was Grayson Hawkes. Hawk thought she stared an extra moment at him before she began to explain what their day was going to include. If his last-minute reservation had been the reason that she had arrived and split the group in two, he imagined she wasn't real thrilled that she had to spend a chunk of the day leading them around, especially if she hadn't originally planned on doing so. Regardless, she was a true Disney cast member and was now completely committed to doing her best to create a memorable guest experience for the tour group.

Kiran rattled off facts, insights, and bits of trivia about the background and creation of the Magic Kingdom.

She revealed that if you look closely as you walk down Main Street, USA, you will see a series of discs embedded into the street. These are sensors that identify and locate floats during the Magic Kingdom parades. When a float passes over a disc information is transmitted to "Pageant," which is a central computer that keeps the float synchronized with the appropriate music. Strolling down Main Street the group began to spot these discs easily once they knew what they were looking for.

As Kiran explained how the Magic Kingdom covered 107 acres with a capacity of one hundred thousand guests, Hawk remembered a Christmas Day trip he had taken to the park. It was the first time he had ever been alone on Christmas. He had planned a quiet distracting day but was stunned by the massive crowds.

Kiran often paused and allowed the tour guests the chance to ask any questions they wished. Most of Hawk's questions were different than the inquiries from the rest of the group.

Hawk said, "Kiran, I've heard that Walt kept an apartment above the Fire Station on Main Street in Disneyland."

"You are correct," she responded.

"Did he have anything like that built into the plans for the Magic Kingdom?"

"He certainly did." She smiled. Pointing toward Cinderella Castle, she guided the group to a window that was indistinguishable from the others incorporated into the design of the castle. "Look at those three long windows right up there," she instructed, allowing time for the entire group to get focused on the correct windows. "Behind those arched windows is an apartment that was originally designed for Walt and his family to use anytime they were here in the Magic Kingdom. The plans were changed after Walt's death. The apartment was something that Roy didn't seem interested in pursuing. Apparently even as the castle was designed it became a bit of a sacred subject and no other plans were ever put into motion to use that space effectively."

"I don't understand. Why was it a sacred subject?" Hawk wondered.

"Maybe sacred subject isn't the best way to describe it." She paused. "The designers and builders wanted to be sensitive to building what Walt wanted—after all, this was his big dream. Since he had planned to build an apartment, no one wanted to be the person to knock that out of the plan for the castle. As a result, they did nothing. They just built the space without ever finishing it. Depending on what year you might have been inside the castle, you could have seen it used as a big storage area, a large empty space, a housing area of material used in remodeling, or even a telephone switchboard, but it was never more than just an unfinished room. It wasn't until the Year of Million Dreams celebration that it was finally finished and guests were allowed to stay there as a part of the event."

"Do we get to look at it now since it is finished?" Hawk asked.

"No, that is not a part of our tour . . . sorry," she replied. "But I will let you in on a secret. I have been in it and it is breathtaking!"

"So there is no chance you can sneak us in as an added bonus to the tour?" Hawk kidded.

"Afraid not." She quickly changed the subject with a trivia question. "Does anyone know Cinderella's last name?"

The group chatted among themselves and offered no answers. Hawk's attention was still on the window, trying to imagine what kind of view you would have of the Magic Kingdom, and what the park would look like from that vantage point. Almost as an afterthought he quietly answered the trivia question.

"Tremaine," he said, not intending for anyone in particular to hear him.

"Correct again!" Kiran excitedly replied. This launched her into a follow-up question. "Now here is your bonus question. The restaurant in Cinderella Castle was originally called King Stefan's Banquet Hall. What is one of the reasons it was changed to Cinderella's Royal Table?"

Hawk turned back from gazing at the castle toward Kiran and the group. He waited for someone else to answer. No one did and most of the group was staring at him waiting to hear what he had to say. Kiran was looking at him as well and he assumed that the question had been intended for him alone. He inclined his head.

"King Stefan was actually Sleeping Beauty's father. Cinderella's father was not a part of her story since she lived with her stepmother and stepsisters. So I suppose it was the wrong king's name in the wrong castle," he surmised.

Kiran's face broke into a broad smile as she proclaimed to the group, "This gentleman knows his trivia."

There was a smattering of applause from the band of tour takers. One elderly gentleman patted him on the shoulder in a gesture of congratulations. The tour progressed and Hawk found himself going on his own tour of thoughts that were trampling through his brain. Hawk had now personally bought into the mystery of the key Rales had given him, which was what prompted him to take the Keys to the Kingdom tour. But other than the phrase *key to the kingdom*, he had found no other connection to the key he now possessed. In retrospect, thinking he could find answers on the tour and been foolhardy. However, Kiran's beauty was a pleasant bonus if not a distraction to Hawk as he tried to sort out some of the things rolling around his noggin.

"Notice how Walt and his alter ego, Mickey Mouse, look down Main Street," Kiran was saying as Hawk's attention reconnected with the tour.

They were standing in front of the *Partners* statue situated in Central Plaza near Cinderella Castle. The statue featured a life-sized version of Walt Disney holding hands with Mickey. Disney's right hand was extended as if sharing with Mickey a vision of what the future could hold. It was a powerful visual image of the man whose dreams had changed the world.

"Some people look at *Partners* and think that Walt is sharing his latest dream with Mickey. Others think he is pointing out some of the intricate details of something they are looking at." Kiran gazed up admiringly at the two figures. "Whatever they are talking about, this has become one of the most photographed places in the Magic Kingdom. If you would like I will give you a moment to take a few pictures."

She stepped back out of the way as some of the group gathered their parties for a photograph. Kiran helped some of the guests take their pictures by acting as their photographer. After handing a camera back to its owner she stepped backward, her heel digging into Hawk's foot.

"Oh, I am so sorry, Mr. Hawkes," she apologized as she quickly turned toward him.

"No damage done," he reassured her as a twinge of pain danced across his foot.

"Are you sure?"

"Positive," he confirmed.

"Then let's keep moving." She smiled and moved away to herd up the group.

As she moved away, the pain subsided and Hawk caught a whiff of a pleasant scent. She not only looked good, she also smelled good, and she knew a truckload about Disney World. She was practically perfect, but what else would one expect inside the Magic Kingdom?

 *Day Three*
Noon

THE KEYS TO THE KINGDOM TOUR included lunch, and the group made their way to the Columbia Harbour House to eat. Nestled between the edge of Fantasyland and Liberty Square, it offered a variety of choices at reasonable theme park prices. Hawk allowed most of their party to order before him. By the time he carried his tray toward the upstairs dining area where they were eating, most of the others were heavily involved in consuming their meals. He found a table adjacent to the clump of tables their tour group had settled in. He loaded his soft drink with a straw and took a slug, unfolded a napkin, and prepared to eat.

"Mind if I join you?" Kiran stood next to him holding her own lunch tray.

"No, not at—" Hawk answered before completely swallowing and nearly strangled on his soft drink.

"Thanks," she bubbled as she slid into the chair across from him. Setting her tray on the table, she fixed her gaze on him as if calculating what she was going to say next. "All right, Mr. Hawkes, I want to know why you are on this tour. I have a gnawing feeling that you already know most of the things I am saying."

"Well . . . uh, I always wanted to take the tour and finally decided to do it." There was a bit of truth in the statement. He had thought about taking the tour in the past. "I also heard the tour guides were excellent." Hawk meant the remark to sound complimentary and smooth, but it landed with a silly, dorky thud on their lunch trays. If Kiran noticed she didn't show it.

"You were a last-minute addition to our group. As a matter of fact the tour was already overbooked. We were thinking about dividing it into two separate tours. Our reservation specialist gave you a slot and made our decision for us."

"Normally you don't have to lead the tours, do you?"

"Not anymore. I used to years ago. Now I'm a manager in Guest Relations. So I suppose it's your fault I'm a tour guide today."

"Should I apologize?"

"No," she quickly said. "They gave you a reservation instead of saying the tour was already full. But you could answer my question and tell me why you wanted to take the Keys to the Kingdom tour today."

There was no way he could tell her why he was really there. On some level he didn't really know himself. He paused perhaps longer than he should have.

"It's complicated," he offered.

"Is it now?" She waited to see if he was going to continue. When it became apparent that there was nothing more forthcoming, she lobbed another question toward him. "So, Mr. Hawkes, what do you do for a living?"

"I'm a pastor in Celebration," he told her, relieved to be out of the uncomfortable territory her previous questioning had taken them into.

"A preacher?" Kiran studied him with raised brows. "Somehow you don't strike me as a preacher." Her cheeks colored. "Please don't take that wrong. I didn't mean it like it might have sounded."

"No offense taken," Hawk rescued her. He had heard it before. He didn't look like the stereotypical preacher. Usually in need of a haircut and much more comfortable in denim jeans, he only wore a suit if he was forced to do so. "Please, call me Hawk. That's what everyone calls me."

"Okay, Hawk, tell me about being a preacher."

Hawk began to tell Kiran about his passion for the church. They talked about how hard the church had to fight to carve a niche in the culture and how the church had lost some of its identity in the world. She asked probing questions about why Hawk had become a pastor and why he enjoyed it. The conversation focused for a short time on what made the Celebration Community Church so special. He asked her about her role at Walt Disney World. Kiran revealed that working for Disney was something she had always wanted to do. While in high school she had auditioned for a part in a Christmas parade and had gotten the job. Disney World was the only place she had ever worked. She had steadily advanced through the years and now had a bit of position and seniority with the company. Hawk assumed she also had a bit more authority and power than she was letting on. The dialogue volleyed back and forth across the table until their lunches were gone and the rest of the tour group was growing restless waiting. The touring troop began to file down the stairs as Kiran and Hawk were dumping the remains of their lunch in the trash receptacle.

"I really enjoyed chatting with you, Hawk. I'll have to visit your church sometime." Kiran paused as she waited for him to throw away his trash.

"I enjoyed it as well. Sorry I was the reason you had to spend your day leading a tour."

"I'm not sorry at all." She smiled and allowed her eyes to lock onto his for just a moment longer than he had anticipated.

Returning her smile, Hawk felt a moment of awkwardness over not knowing what to say. She walked away and headed down the stairs to continue the tour. Hawk shook his head slightly from side to side and followed in the same direction. When he joined the reassembled group outside the restaurant, he heard a voice come from over his shoulder.

"She is very pretty, son."

Hawk looked back and saw the elderly gentleman who had congratulated him for being a trivia expert. The man winked, nodded, and then shuffled away to keep pace with the group as Kiran led them out into the street headed toward Frontierland. On their walk they paused in front of Ye Olde Christmas Shoppe. She pointed out that although this was a single store that specialized in Christmas items, it also was a great example of the amazing design that was poured into every corner of the Magic Kingdom.

"Notice that from the outside this looks like three distinct time-period-specific storefronts. But once you walk inside, if you look closely, you will see three very different shops that are tied together with a Christmas theme. The Imagineers created a backstory for each shop. The first is a Music Teacher's Shop; if you look at the decorations, you will see a variety of instruments ready for the holiday celebration. The second shop is a Woodcarver's Shop. It's more rustic looking, as if the woodcarver is making toys for gifts." Kiran pointed to the last shop. "The final shop is not a shop at all. Instead it's like a home decorated for the holidays, warm and inviting for guests and family. The family is identified as the Kepple family. Now here is a question for you trivia buffs." She paused to allow them to listen closely. "Why was the name Kepple chosen for this shop?"

Silence was the answer of choice for the tourists. A few couples whispered to each other, trying to figure out the reason for the name. Eventually a few of the tourists looked toward Hawk, who had proven to be an endless stream of trivia facts throughout the tour. Even Kiran looked toward him and cracked a grin as she watched him try to remember the answer. Momentarily he brought the silence to an end.

"I don't know." He shrugged.

"I'll tell you what." Kiran stepped forward. "If you do figure it out by the time the tour ends, I'll have a collector's pin to give you as a prize."

The remainder of the tour flew by as Hawk watched and listened to Kiran talk about the way the Magic Kingdom had been built and the little-known details of the tunnels located below the park. The Utilidoor, she explained, had been Walt's idea after watching the cast members in Disneyland walk through the park in costume one day. He was bothered by the fact that cast members broke the illusion and continuity of the various lands of the theme park by passing through them in clothing used in other lands. Seeing an astronaut walking the old west of Frontierland was simply unacceptable. The Florida creation was going to eliminate that problem. The solution was to build a series of tunnels that would allow the cast members to move beneath the streets of the Magic Kingdom. These tunnels, or utilidoors, formed an underworld city connected by passageways that featured unmarked entrances and exits at various places into the Kingdom.

Nearly five hours later the group returned to City Hall, where they had begun. Kiran wrapped up the presentation. "I hope you have enjoyed our behind-the-scenes look at the Magic Kingdom. It is truly a magical place created by a dreamer that was one of a kind. If you haven't had the chance, and you get the opportunity, you can find out more about the fascinating Walt Disney by visiting One Man's Dream at the Disney Hollywood Studios. While you are there you can even see Walt's office where he would sit behind his desk, meet with others, and read scripts. In the office you can also see some of the diagrams for various areas of the Walt Disney World Resort. No matter how much you learn there is always something else to discover about this amazing place. I hope you now feel like you have a few more keys to unlock the kingdom."

Hawk replayed what she had just said as the group said their good-byes. *While you are there you can even see Walt's office where he would sit behind his desk, meet with others, and read scripts. In the office you can also see some of the diagrams for various areas of the* Walt Disney World *Resort.* The words had a familiar ring to them and Hawk rewound his memory searching for something that Rales had said to him when they were at Gamble Place. Rales had spoken about Walt's being changed after he saw the Seven Dwarfs' Cottage. *He went back to the studio, sat behind his desk, and let the memories that this place created in him spark his imagination, his ability to really understand a story, and eventually how he would touch the world.* Rales had given Hawk the key. *If you will take this and do the same thing Walt did when he left this place . . . your imagination . . . your ability to understand a story . . . and how you touch the world . . . even your life will never be the same. And the stories you communicate will become timeless.*

Hawk was grasping for something that made sense and this was as close as anything he had come up with. In trying to help guide him in understanding the key to the kingdom, Rales had said to do what Walt had done. Walt went back to the studio and sat behind his desk. It was there that his imagination would spring to life, he would better understand a story, and how he would touch the world. Hawk could go to the Disney Studios and at least look at Walt's desk. He had been certain that the key Rales had given him was just a sentimental gift from a friend. But now there was a relentless sense that there had to be a deeper meaning to the key. Now that Rales was unavailable to ask, he didn't know what else to try.

"Hawk, I must say that you have made my tour much more enjoyable." Kiran was now facing him. "I still don't think you learned anything new, but I hope you had a good time."

"I had a great time, thank you," Hawk graciously responded. "Were you serious about wanting to come to church?" He would like the chance to see Kiran again, but most people who said they were going to visit a church just said it to be pleasant and make conversation.

"Of course I was serious. Are you inviting me?" Kiran was looking at him curiously.

"I am indeed. I know the preacher, and he's a little boring, but if you can overlook him you might like it." Hawk was in a very unfamiliar place as he tried to blend inviting someone to church with a feeble attempt to flirt. If it was awkward, Kiran didn't seem to notice.

"Just tell me where and when. I'll try my best to get there."

Hawk gave her his business card, which had a map to the church printed on the back. Making sure she knew what time the services started, he shook her hand and they said their good-byes. As she was leaving, Hawk called out to her.

"You know about all things Disney, right?"

Spinning, she turned back toward him and tilted her head. "Sure I do."

"What time does the Disney Studios close tonight?"

"It closes at 7:00. Is that your next stop?" She grinned.

"Maybe."

"Have fun!"

"One more thing," Hawk remembered. "You forgot to tell us about the name Kepple."

"No, I didn't forget. I just didn't tell you." Kiran tossed her hair and moved off down Main Street.

Hawk watched as she walked away, then glanced down at his watch. It was two thirty. He considered jumping on Disney transportation and riding over to the Studios to take a look at Walt's office. Lost in thought, he moved back through the tunnel below the train station. As he walked through the exit of the Magic Kingdom he decided to postpone his jaunt to the Studios because he had a sermon to complete if he was going to preach it tomorrow.

As Grayson Hawkes strode back across the redbrick walkway toward the Contemporary Resort, the footsteps of the person who followed him were lost in the background noise of the other people bustling around him.

His stalker, whose eyes had taken in his every movement since he arrived back in the Town Square, paused and watched as the preacher moved toward his car and got in to drive away.

 *Day Four*
Morning

THE FOLLOWING MORNING the parking lot of Celebration Community Church bulged under the crush of cars crammed into the available parking spaces. Parking was a problem during services and today was no exception. Jonathan led the stage band in opening the worship service. The vocal team that led the singing took the congregation through a blend of traditional hymns that had been given new tunes, some contemporary praise songs, and some original pieces of worship music that Jonathan had created.

The singing was spirited and the people at the worship service reflected a variety of emotions as each song was unpacked and presented. The band and vocal team left the stage and Jonathan stood alone and sang a soft soulful song that bridged the block of worship songs to the teaching moment to follow. As the last notes of the song finished, Hawk made his way toward the platform from the side of the front row where he had been sitting. Dressed casually in a pair of jeans and button down shirt, he asked the worshipers to open their Bibles to the text he would be teaching from. Allowing the sound of flipping pages to cease, he then bowed his head and led the congregation in prayer.

With an *amen* the prayer ended and right on cue there was once again the sound of rustling paper as the regular attendees prepared to take notes on what was going to be said. Hawk waited for a moment and then launched into a story that would set the tone for the topic of the morning.

Throughout time, preaching had always been an art form. Each generation and cultural setting might influence the style a preacher might use, but at the heart of every great preacher was the desire to take the Bible and make it come alive in the soul of the listener. Hawk was no exception. While he'd never considered himself a strong speaker, he did have the ability to take the Bible and make it clear and applicable to the people who heard him teach.

The story Hawk told had the desired effect. The audience was now fully immersed in the passage and were once again gathering gems of wisdom as he picked them from the text of the morning. Nearing the end of the message, Hawk slowed down and spoke softer as he began to conclude and challenge his listeners with his final thoughts. He allowed his eyes to move from one person to the next and was startled as he locked eyes with a guest seated near the back. It was Kiran.

Hawk had not really expected Kiran to come to church, and his surprise and pleasure at her presence made him lose his train of thought. The usually steady orator now felt his voice searching for words as he stood with mouth slightly opened but silent. Kiran cut her eyes away and with a slight smile bowed her head. Blushing, Hawk stammered through a few final sentences and asked everyone to pray. As he spoke to God once again he rediscovered his voice. Speaking with the familiarity of being with the closest of friends, Hawk asked God to imprint the words of the text on the hearts of the hearers and allow the words to come alive in their everyday lives. During the prayer, Jonathan had silently drifted back on the platform. The prayer concluded and a closing song dismissed the crowd for the week.

As was his habit, Hawk moved down the side aisle toward the exit to speak to every worshiper who attended. The encounters were brief, usually a handshake or a hug, but each was as personal as Hawk could make it. Some weeks he would stand outside and talk with the church members for as long as an hour after the service had ended.

The line of people waiting to speak with him began to shrink, and he caught himself rushing his conversations to move the crowd quicker. He expected to see Kiran as the next person in line as the previous one walked away, but time and time again the next person waiting was not her. The last person in line gave their pastor a hug and Hawk found himself standing alone at the bottom of the steps leading to the front door. Twisting his head to look at the few remaining people leaving the parking lot, he was disappointed to not see Kiran anywhere. He was confused as to how he had missed seeing her exit, and he ascended the four steps to the small porch that leveled off toward the front door. As he reached for the handle, the door unexpectedly opened from the other side. Stepping back for the swing of the door, Hawk was relieved to see Kiran stride out onto the porch.

Hawk had not thought it to be possible, but Kiran looked more stunning today than she had the day before. He firmly clasped her hand in his, and their hands remained joined together as they spoke.

"I'm so glad you decided to come," Hawk began.

"I told you I would try my best to be here," she said.

"You wouldn't believe how often preachers hear people say that."

"I'll bet people tell you that so you don't pester them about showing up."

"Exactly," he affirmed.

"Well," she cheeringly said, "I'm not one of those people. To tell you the truth I really enjoyed it. The band and the preacher were great."

"I don't know about that." He scuffed his shoe against the floor.

"At least he was doing well until he forgot what he was going to say," she chided.

"Oh, you noticed that?"

"Everyone noticed it. The blushing was a dead giveaway."

"I got distracted."

"By what?" she teased.

Hawk merely smiled but decided to say nothing more on the subject. They ended their protracted handshake and stood awkwardly for a moment as silence fell across the front porch. Attempting to fill the silence Hawk asked, "Can I walk you to your car?"

"Sure, that would be great. It is a long walk though; you really pack 'em in here."

Kiran and Hawk walked down the steps and made their way along the sidewalk toward the downtown area. They chatted about the church and how welcomed Kiran had felt being a guest for the first time. Tiring of the church chat, they rounded the corner on Front Street alongside the movie theatre.

"I have always loved this town," Kiran reflected. "I remember when it was built and wished I could live here."

"It is beautiful," Hawk agreed. "It is a unique place."

Their footsteps echoed on the sidewalk as Kiran slowed. Gesturing toward the corner and taking her keys out of her purse, she let Hawk know they had arrived. Kiran looked down toward the sidewalk and slowly raised her face as she spoke.

"Hawk, I was wondering if you would like to have dinner with me tonight?"

She asked so quickly and unexpectedly that Hawk was completely caught off guard. He found himself at a loss for words for the second time of the day. Recovering quickly he said, "I'm sorry. I can't."

"Oh, I'm sorry, I shouldn't have asked." She looked away as she apologized.

"No, no, please don't be sorry," Hawk attempted to reassure her. "I am flattered you would ask."

Kiran's face flushed at her perceived blunder. Fussing with her keys, she walked briskly as though she couldn't get to her car and away from him fast enough. Hawk almost had to run to keep up with her. He reached out and impulsively, but gently, grabbed Kiran by the arm and turned her toward him. Facing her, he steadied himself.

"I would love to take you to dinner. I just can't do it tonight. Could we plan on it tomorrow night?"

She searched his face. "If you're sure . . . tomorrow would be nice."

"Great!" Hawk was genuinely glad she had agreed. "Where do you want me to pick you up?"

"Why don't I meet you right here?" Kiran was now recovering and her confidence was slowly coming back.

"Here?"

"Right here," she stated.

"You want me to pick you up right here on the street corner?"

"It's safe, isn't it?"

"Of course, but I can pick you—"

Kiran interrupted, "I can be here at seven o'clock if that's okay with you."

"That works for me. I'll be here."

"Great, see you then." Kiran patted him twice on the chest and turned toward her car.

Hawk watched as she got into her car and drove away. Everything within him wanted to have dinner with Kiran tonight, but he had already made plans. He had decided before church began that he would head over to the Disney Studios to look at Walt Disney's office in the One Man's Dream attraction. If he was going to figure out what meaning the key to the kingdom Rales had given him possessed, then he had to follow the one idea he had. The plan was not complicated. He was going to look through the glass window at Walt's old office. Hopefully inspiration would hit.

Hawk walked back toward the church, pulling out his cell phone and once again hitting the speed dial button in an attempt to contact Rales. The call was connected to Rale's voice mail. Hawk did not leave a message. Battling back the growing concern, he reminded himself it would not be unlike Rales to avoid him in order to force him forward into the mystery. Arriving in front of the church, Hawk lifted his head toward the sky and whispered a barely audible prayer for his friend Farren.

 *Day Four*
Mid-Afternoon

HALF THE AFTERNOON had ticked past by the time Hawk headed toward the Disney Studios. No matter how hard he tried, there always seemed to be mounds of things to get done after a worship service. Hawk always tried to track down the guest cards that might have been filled out and turned in by first time visitors. Usually he would send each person or family a short but personal e-mail thanking them for spending their time at Celebration Community Church. The quick contact opened the door for any guests that wished to ask questions about the church if they had them. The one surprise to Hawk was that Kiran had not returned a guest card. Selfishly he would like to have had a way to contact her. Professionally he also wanted her to know that he was glad she had come to church that day.

Hawk flashed his annual pass, prompting the attendant to wave him through into the parking lot of the Studios. Following the directions of the parking lot crew, he pulled into a space much closer to the front entrance than he had anticipated. He once again studied the old skeleton key that Rales had presented him. He was holding the key to the kingdom and he had no idea how to use it. If this key really did open something, Hawk was doggedly determined to find the lock.

Exiting his car, he decided to walk to the front entrance. The walkway carried him past a security checkpoint where a guard stood inspecting bags as guests entered the park. Since he wasn't carrying a bag or pack, she waved him through past guest relations windows and the first of many souvenir opportunities that were a part of any Disney experience. There was a line of people waiting to move through the turnstiles and he chose the shortest of the open gates. Inserting his pass and placing his finger on the biometric sensor, he waited for his ticket to be returned so he could push through. The readout on the mechanism flashed, "Welcome Have a Nice Day," and Hawk entered the park and faced the Crossroads of the World. The Crossroads was an information center right inside the Studios entrance. It was here that Hawk found an information card with specifics about the operating schedule of the studio for the day. Quickly reading, he saw that there were over two hours until the park closed. Satisfied that his timing had been good, he knew there was enough time to visit One Man's Dream.

Straight ahead and to the right of the Sorcerer's Hat, his path took the preacher to Mickey Avenue. Just past the Voyage of the Little Mermaid he arrived at the entrance of One Man's Dream. The cast member cheerfully welcomed Hawk to the attraction as he heard the distinctive voice of Walt Disney say, "I hope we never lose sight of one thing, that it was all started by a mouse." Entering, Hawk was as inspired as he was each time he visited the exhibit. Each step you take allows you to walk in the footsteps of Walt Disney. Tracking his life from his birth in Chicago back in 1901, through his boyhood memories of Marceline, Missouri, and to the dreams that became movies, Disneyland, and Disney World . . . this attraction allows guests to catch a glimpse into the life of Walt Disney like none other.

Hawk took the time to reconnect with the history of Walt Disney as he developed innovative breakthrough after breakthrough to revolutionize not only animation but filmmaking in general. The soundtrack of the attraction features the voice of Walt Disney himself revealing some of the most mean-ingful and emotional moments of his life. This carefully crafted narrative was compiled through a rare collection of audio interviews which had never been heard publicly prior to this experience. The first part of the exhibit yielded to a second portion which captured elements of Walt's life that most people are more familiar with. The doorway separating the two served as the portal between the years of animation only and the birth of Disneyland. The emergence of television and the way Disney used that to capture the hearts of an American viewing public as he developed Disneyland was one of the first highlights featured. It was the medium of television that transported Walt into the American household. His face and voice became a part of the fabric of American culture itself as weekly people would tune in to watch and listen to Walt Disney. This portion of the exhibit included models of vari-ous creations in the theme parks worldwide designed by the Imagineers. An interactive display explaining the way animatronics work always fascinates guests. Still amidst the collectibles, the photographs, and the recordings, the most interesting portion of this section is located behind a big glass window. Beyond the window is the office of Walt Disney himself.

This office was what Hawk had come to see. A small group of three peo-ple were clumped together speaking quietly, looking through the glass into the office. The way the display was set up, viewers were given the perspective of being able to look through a wall from a slightly elevated position. In essence you were looking down on the vacant office that had been set up to resemble the way it looked when Walt had last worked in it. Two empty chairs sat opposite Walt's desk chair. On the credenza to what would have been Walt's left, scripts were neatly stacked and stored, available for reference. On the right side stretched another credenza that was complete with a record player, a collection of long-play vinyl albums, and various other mementos. An announcement notified guests the film about the life of Disney would be starting in minutes, and the three people looking through the window wandered off to another part of the attraction.

Hawk was now alone, intensely gazing through the glass, allowing his eyes to seek some detail of the office he had never noticed before. Opposite where he stood there was a window with blinds closed and a wooden door. Hawk knew this was not the original design of the office. Practicality dictated there could not be a door next to an exterior window on any level above a ground floor. Since Walt's office was not on the ground floor, this must have been added to the design as they set up the display. Hawk assumed that the door opened to whatever was behind the set. He then scanned the credenza from right to left slowly and closely. The rows of scripts were stacked on a shelving unit with various items sitting across the top of the shelf. To the left of that was a small box. In appearance it could have been on oversized music box, although Hawk doubted it was musical. An ornate design decorated the top of the box that at one time might have been used to store a variety of valuables inside. The lid of the wooden box was closed so there was no way to see what might be hidden inside. Hawk squinted, trying to bring the details of the box into clearer focus. He could not be certain but it looked as if there was a lock built into the front of the box. He wondered for a moment if the key he possessed might open that box. It was an unlikely theory to be certain, but it also was unlikely that by looking through the window he would find anything that might give him some insight into what the key would open.

Continuing his scan across the credenza he noticed a model replica of an airplane. Since the model was in the office, Hawk assumed it must be a model of the plane that Walt had owned. There were more items that adorned the surface of the credenza; none of them looked unusual or out of place. He moved slowly toward the far left side of the window and tried to see behind the desk. If Farren was to be taken literally about the key, Hawk would need to take it and do the same thing Walt did. *He went back to the studio, sat behind his desk, and let the memories spark his imagination, his ability to really understand a story, and eventually how he would touch the world.* Then Rales had given him the key. *Take this and do the same thing Walt did.* Looking through the window, Hawk knelt down and tried to get a better understanding about what he might see if he were behind the desk. His eyes raced over the view he had from a different angle. Frustratingly, he could see no more detail than he could when he was standing.

"Looking for anything specific?"

From one knee Hawk looked up into the smiling face of a cast member, dressed in a host uniform, towering above him.

"No, I'm just trying to really see everything," Hawk replied.

The cast member bent slightly forward at the waist and looked into the office, trying to see what could be seen differently from Hawk's point of view. Slowly and deliberately the cast member straightened back up, satisfied the view was not that different, and turned his attention from the office back to Hawk. With a pleasant if not patronizing look spreading across his face, he spoke again.

"I did notice that you have been studying the office for quite some time. Are you a big Walt Disney fan?"

"Sure, isn't everyone?" Hawk attempted to respond like an overzealous tourist. He had managed to completely lose track of time studying the details of the office. A quick check of his watch let him know that the attraction would be closing in a few minutes. "I'm fascinated with the creativity that must have come out of this very office. I've been standing here wondering what it would have been like to sit in there and talk with Walt himself."

"It is fascinating to think about," said the cast member, whose badge identified his name as Jim. "You'd be surprised how many people do exactly what you've been doing. Looking through the window and wondering what if."

"What if?" Hawk asked.

"Sure," Jim explained. "What if Walt were still alive, what if he'd seen Disney World completed, what if he were still running the Disney empire, what if you could sit down and chat with him?"

"That's a lot more thought than I was giving it."

"I'm sure if you stood here long enough you would've gotten there. There's just something about Disney that sparks the imagination in people. But sadly you're not going to be able to stay much longer; we close in just a few minutes. The last showing of the movie is when we clear this part of the attraction."

Hawk feigned a look of sadness. "How much longer can I stay here and look?"

"The film will be starting in five minutes."

"Only five minutes?"

"Yes, I'm afraid so." Jim tapped his watch.

"Then five minutes it is. Thanks for letting me know how long I have left, Jim."

"You're welcome. When the doors at the far end of the exhibit open, you can go through them to see the film."

"Those are the ones at the far end on the right?"

"Yes, sir." Jim walked away to give Hawk another few minutes to spend alone with his thoughts at the window.

The thoughts that Hawk was beginning to have at the window were nothing short of strange. He began to imagine what might happen if he could really do what Walt had done. Rales was very clear as he told him the story. Walt had gone back to the studio and sat behind the desk. How in the world did Rales expect Hawk to do the same thing that Walt did?

The announcement jarred his thinking back to the moment at hand. The final showing of the film was getting ready to start in the Walt Disney Theatre. The lingering crowd began to shuffle toward the doors of the theatre. Momentarily they would open and everyone would go inside to find a seat. Hawk had seen the film before. It was a stirring fifteen-minute overview of Walt's life. The doors' automated mechanism swung them open. Ushered in by a cast member, the people started into the theatre. Hawk moved along with the flow of people and glanced back into the exhibit area of One Man's Dream. It was now deserted. All of the guests were finishing their move into the theatre and the lone cast member that had been in the area had gone in as well. Hawk stopped walking. Standing there, he made an impetuous decision and began nonchalantly backing away from the doors.

Moving very casually in reverse, he faced forward as he drifted to the right side of the theatre's holding area. This movement took him out of the line of sight of the cast member greeting the guests and getting ready to introduce the movie. With a quick step he jutted around the corner and now was standing alone in the exhibit area. He anticipated a cast member would be walking through at any moment. He wildly turned his head from side to side, looking for someplace to duck out of view. An adrenaline wave surged inside his chest and his heart began to beat faster. The automated doors clicked shut, sealing off the theatre as the movie began to play.

In the darkened theatre, one lone movie attendee had no interest in the film whatsoever. Instead, this person's attention was focused on scanning the scant crowd scattered across the spacious seating area. Looking once, then again, and one final time, the viewer concluded that Grayson Hawkes had somehow bypassed the movie undetected. The how, when, and why of the preacher's actions escaped this person, who had been keeping the preacher under surveillance without the slightest notice.

Hawk realized there was no escape from inside the attraction unless he retraced his steps to the entrance. If he retraced his steps, he could exit through the doors that opened back onto Mickey Avenue. A voice somewhere in his head told him this was the best thing to do. Stepping lively, he headed that direction. Off to his right he once again looked into the office of Walt Disney. Abruptly he came to a halt and knew that he was going to have to find a way to get inside the office and look around.

Reversing his course, he heard the sounds of the exterior doors at the main entrance slamming shut. Hawk was certain there would be a cast member charged with doing a walk-through inspection of the attraction once it was closed and secure. He needed to find a place to hide. Moving deeper into the attraction he saw a cutout of Roy Disney and Mickey Mouse in front of a huge background photograph of Cinderella Castle. Getting closer he realized there was no way he could hide behind Roy and Mickey. They were securely fastened to the wall and there was very little room between.

On his right were the hands-on displays of how audio-animatronics worked. Seeing the three different interactive panels for guests to manipulate, Hawk jumped over the rail that held these in place. Now inside the display itself, he moved to an audio-animatronics control panel sitting atop a large red multi-drawer toolbox that stood over three feet high. This would be perfect! Disappearing behind it, Hawk breathlessly used the wheels on the base of the box to move it slightly to the left. Wedging the huge toolbox next to a rack of electronic computer components, he created a completely out of sight hiding place. The only way he could be seen was if someone actually stepped over the railing he had scaled and physically looked behind the box. He was safe for now.

As soon as he had hidden his body he broke out in a nervous sweat as he sat, waited, and listened. Hearing footsteps approach, he knew that he was now committed to what was going to be a criminal act no matter what rationale he used to explain it. He was hiding in the attraction to get into an area off limits to the general public. Hawk assumed the cast member approaching was doing a visual inspection to make sure all was clear inside. He stayed perfectly still and as silent as possible. In his ears his heart was beating ridiculously loud. His breath was coming in quick short bursts that he feared the employee might be able to hear. The anxious wait seemed to last an eternity before he heard the click of the emergency exit door open and then snap to a close. Though the cast member had now finished and moved on, Hawk dared not move for a few minutes, waiting for any unexpected activity in the area. He sat alone, hunkered down and hiding, trying to formulate the next move in his unfolding ad-libbed plan.

JEFF DIXON

 *Day Four*
Evening

HAWK TRIED TO SLOW HIS BREATHING as his legs began to cramp while he held his crouching-pastor, hidden-criminal position longer than he thought possible. Realizing he couldn't remain hiding there much longer, he strained to hear any sounds that hinted of someone who might discover him. He'd dared not look at his watch or anything else since he ducked behind the toolbox. He had been there a long time; too long. Now it was time to create the next phase of his plan. Resting on his knees, he looked up to see if he could spot any security cameras. He saw them carefully placed at various spots of the attraction. He was sure that some of them were merely placed strategically so they could be seen by the guests. They probably did not work and were nothing more than a deterrent to anyone who might try to execute a plan like the one Hawk was now living. He was just as certain that some of the security cameras did work. The problem was he had no way of knowing which ones. If indeed there was an active camera pointing in his general direction, it was unmonitored or he had gotten extremely lucky. He decided it was a little of both.

The sudden click of a lock caused Hawk to tense with anticipation and dread. A cast member had opened a door with a keyed lock. He'd noticed that at the front and back of the attraction were two doors with no knobs, only locks that required a key to open them. His assumption was that these doors opened up to a hallway or working area behind the exhibits. He also had assumed that getting through these doors was going to be the way he'd get into Walt's office—he just hadn't figured out how. Now the door was open. A maintenance man walked into the attraction and past the animatronics exhibit, toward the front. After the man's footsteps passed, Hawk straightened up behind the toolbox. He didn't see the maintenance man and he now moved quietly back over the rail of the exhibit to the guest side. Easing through the open door, he pulled it snugly closed and moved into the backstage area of the

One Man's Dream set. Gingerly he stepped down the hallway as he tried to get some perspective on where he was. The door in Walt's office had to open into a backstage area. In a matter of seconds he found himself looking at a door next to a window that had floodlights aimed at it. These lights created the outdoor light effect behind the closed blinds of the office. The interior of Walt's office had to be on the other side of the door. Reaching down and grasping the handle of the door, he pushed down and released it.

When the door opened, Hawk exhaled loudly. Once he entered the office, he could no longer hide; anyone walking by in the guest area of the attraction would see him. Resigned to the fact that it was now too late to worry about such things, he opened the door and stepped inside.

Standing inside Walt's office, he reverently closed the door. He found himself staring out into the exhibit where he had stood moments before gazing in through the window. Knowing he had to get started, he boldly walked to Walt's side of the desk. He gripped the black leather of the seat back and rolled the chair out of his way, then crouched, peering under the desk. Much to his disappointment, there was not a drawer there. Rales had told Hawk to do the same thing that Walt had done. He took a seat in the chair and rolled it back under the desk just as if he were getting ready to do some work. His eyes rapidly danced over the surface of the desk. There was nothing that required a key to open. Hawk looked across the desk to the far wall and saw the plans, notes, and photographs on display. Swiveling to his left, he remembered the wooden box he had spied perched on the credenza behind the desk. The box sat below a picture of Walt and Roy Disney. He studied the box closely and saw, on the front of the box, there was a keyhole. Hawk thrust his body forward to lunge toward the box. The chair rocked backward. The unexpected motion of the chair threw him off balance and he stumbled forward to one knee. This action sent the chair rolling backward and clunking into the credenza. The noise was not loud but in the quietness of the office it was deafening. Certain that the racket would alert someone to his presence, Hawk turned his attention away from the box and instead reclaimed the chair and attempted to place it back in its original position. Constantly looking back toward the window for any warning that someone might be approaching, he saw no one. The thought hit him that he had just sat in Walt Disney's chair, behind Walt Disney's desk, in Walt Disney's office. Before he drifted too far away, his rational mind reminded him that he was going to go to jail if he got caught.

Ripping his attention back to the box, he pulled the key out of his pocket and placed it against the opening on the front side. He moved it forward, but the key did not fit. He lifted the key in front of his face and examined it closely, then knelt and did the same to the keyhole. Repeating his attempt to insert the

JEFF DIXON

key into the lock, he felt the resistance of incompatibility. His key simply did not open the box. Looking to both sides of the credenza, he saw nothing else that held a lock. His mind raced, trying to figure out what to do next. He had his doubts that this was a wise thing to be doing, but those doubts had been eclipsed by the hope that an answer might be found inside this office.

The murmuring of distant voices shattered his concentration. Beginning softly and growing in volume, the sound told him people were approaching on the other side of the glass window. He was momentarily immobilized by the fear of being discovered. This hesitation stole his chance to get safely back out the door he had entered through. Impulsively he ran toward the window itself and then veered off to the left side of the office. Slamming himself into the corner of the office, he was now to the side of the viewing glass. Positive he could be seen if someone looked closely, he stood perfectly still. The angle of his hiding place drew him out of the direct line of sight; he hoped that would be enough. Posing like a statue flat against the wall, Hawk knew that the attention of most people would be on the desk in the center of the room. Hopefully whoever was coming by would not glance into the office too closely and see him. Now the voices that had started in the distance were right there at the window. Hawk studied the floor in front of the viewing window and saw the distinct shadows of more than one person. These people were looking in the window at Walt's office! From the rapport of the conversation, Hawk could tell that they were not there looking for him. While that thought brought some relief, it also meant that they were likely to spend a few minutes searching the office details and in the process catch sight of him. As terrible as that thought was, there was another realization that hit Hawk as he tried to disappear into the wall. He recognized one of the voices. He distinctly heard the voice of Kiran. She was talking to the people who were standing there looking in at the office, her tone similar to the one she'd used on the tour when he first met her the day before. Earlier in the afternoon when he'd made an excuse not to join her for dinner tonight, he had assumed she was not working today. Now she was here, just a few feet away, and he was hiding inside the office of Walt Disney.

Seconds transformed into agonizing minutes as the group examined the office. Although unable to hear everything, Hawk found himself following Kiran's voice as she pointed out some of the highlights of the office. While she spoke he imagined her saying, "Pay no attention to the idiot hiding in the corner!" Moments passed, Hawk heard laughter, and then the voices moved away from the window to explore further into the exhibit. He did not move. Unsure of how long to wait and uncertain who else might be in the area, he didn't dare give up his hiding place yet.

He tried to think through his predicament. Kiran must be leading a tour for VIPs, since the Disney Hollywood Studios was officially closed for the day. After the tour group looked around the exhibit, it would eventually exit into the Walt Disney Theatre for a private showing of the film. If he could time it just right, this would be the opportune moment to make his escape. He had found nothing and risked a lot. The risk was one he had been willing to take, but he found himself frustrated at the futility of his endeavor. Somewhere in the depths of his being, he'd thought he would find something to unlock the mystery of the key. Sadly, he had not taken the time to formulate a strategy for anything he was doing. He was now trapped inside the attraction. Failing to plan had been no plan at all.

Finally Hawk decided it was time to go. Moving away from the wall with a quick glance over his shoulder toward the viewing window, he stepped toward the door. The door handle moved. It clicked and he backed up as the door silently swung open. Kiran stood in the doorway, hands jammed on her hips, her feet shoulder width. It was apparent that she had no intention of allowing him to escape past her.

"Dr. Hawkes, step out of the office. Right now."

Hawk tentatively moved toward the doorway, not sure how to step out of the office since she was blocking the door. Once he was close enough, she clamped her hand around his arm above his elbow. Roughly dragging him through the door, she wheeled him around and slammed him into the set wall behind them both with a thud. In one motion she closed the door to the office and stepped up in front of him. Eyes flashing with anger, she thrust a finger toward his chin.

"Tell me why I shouldn't call security and have you arrested!"

Hawk blew out a breath. "It's a long story."

"You have sixty seconds to tell it," she threatened.

Nearly melting from the heat of her glare, Hawk gave her a rundown of the events of the last few days.

 *Day Four*
Evening

BY THE TIME HAWK FINISHED the tale he was nearly breathless. He had tried to share every detail and hadn't wasted time by pausing to inhale. Slowing he looked at Kiran, awaiting her reaction. Her eyes did not reveal what she was thinking as she stood silently processing the information. The silence was painfully deafening before Kiran obliterated it.

"Let me make sure I understand this," she said in an angry whisper. "Farren Rales, one of the most respected and legendary Imagineers in Disney history, is a friend of yours."

"Yes," replied Hawk.

"Be quiet!" Kiran snapped. "He asked you to meet him at a real-life Dwarf Cottage and gave you a key that he called the key to the kingdom. He gave you some vague instructions to take the key and do what Walt did after he left the Dwarf Cottage all those years ago. But you weren't clear on what he meant, and Rales seems to have disappeared so you couldn't ask him about it."

She paused for a moment but Hawk knew better than to acknowledge the accuracy of her review. He didn't have to wait long before she launched back into her dissertation.

"Even though you aren't sure what the key is for, you figured you needed to bring it to Walt Disney's office because there was something inside that the key would open. The only way to get to Walt Disney's office was to break into the exhibit, inside a closed attraction, inside a closed theme park. But then I came wandering by leading a private tour and noticed a pair of feet attached to a man hiding in the corner of the office. As I was getting ready to alert security I was able to get a glimpse of the burglar and recognized him as the pastor of the Celebration Community Church, who I was supposed to have a date with tomorrow. Did I miss anything?"

"The date is at seven o'clock." Hawk mustered a crooked smile.

"There is no date," Kiran fired back. "Your story is the craziest one I've heard in a long time. I still haven't heard a reason I shouldn't call security."

"I know it's unbelievable, but I don't think it's crazy," Hawk countered. "For what it's worth, I didn't mess up anything in the office."

"So you were in the office long enough to search it?"

"Yes, but my key didn't fit anything. Walt's desk doesn't have a locked drawer; there is no drawer in the desk. Nothing else in the office has a lock that the key fits."

"You really rifled through the office of Walt Disney?" she repeated in disbelief.

"I was trying to do what Farren told me to do."

"You aren't sure what he intended for you to do! Somehow I don't think it involved trespassing in a valuable exhibit." Kiran dropped her head and looked down at the ground. She drew several deep breaths before she spoke again. "And what did you plan to do after you found whatever you were looking for?"

"I don't know," Hawk said.

"What did you say?"

"I didn't really know what I would do after I was done. The plan was just kind of unfolding as I went."

"Unbelievable." Kiran shook her head.

"See, I told you it was unbelievable. Not crazy, just unbelievable."

Kiran opened her mouth, then closed it. Her hesitation prompted him to fill the silence that hung between them.

"I promise you I am not crazy. I guess after I was chased out of the Gamble Place and Farren disappeared without any word, I thought that if I figured out what the key meant . . ."

"You might figure out what happened to your friend?"

"I guess." Hawk nodded. "So are you going to call security?"

Kiran pressed her lips together. "Let me see the key."

Hawk produced the key from his pocket and unwrapped it. Kiran watched the care and reverence he used as he released it from its bindings. He held it out between them and she reached out and took it from his grasp. Frowning, she turned it over and studied it.

"This key looks extremely old," she stated. "I doubt there was ever anything in Walt's office that this would have opened. The exhibit contains Walt's office as it would have looked when he passed away in 1966. Most of what's in there are recreations of the original pieces. Anything this key might have opened is something that the family would have kept."

"Like I told you, according to what Rales said, Walt went back to his studio and the memories of what he had seen at Gamble Place inspired him in amazing ways. After he gave me the key he told me to do the same. A little while ago it made sense to me that it would unlock something in Walt's office." Hawk knew his thinking had been more emotional than rational. "Kiran, if you'd been there when Farren gave me the key, you would have seen the look on his face and heard the intensity in his voice when he . . ."

"When he what?" Kiran responded with less intensity than she had moments ago.

"When he told me not just to treasure the key but to use it," Hawk said softly.

"So he actually told you to use the key?"

"Yes. That's what has me standing here with you."

Kiran's demeanor was less angry and now more puzzled than before. While Hawk waited for her to decide what to do next, she raised her head and gazed off to her left. With a look that balanced caution and confusion, she focused back on Hawk as if trying to decide to say what she was thinking.

"If Walt was in Florida at the Dwarfs' Cottage in 1939, there's no way he could have gone back and reflected on his trip in his office," she said with conviction.

"So Farren was just telling me a story?"

"I have no idea what he was telling you. I'm telling you that Walt could not have come back and sat down and did whatever he did in this office. This was the office from the Walt Disney Studios that didn't exist until years later. Like I told you, this was what his office looked like in 1966. That would have been twenty-seven years after he went to the Dwarfs' Cottage."

Awareness dawned like a sunrise ending a moonless night. Recreating the moment as Walt sat down behind his desk in this office couldn't happen because it had not existed until years later. Realizing the idiocy of his plan, he nodded.

"You're right." Hawk's voice echoed with a twinge of disappointment. He lowered his face.

"Bad plan, huh?" she said softly.

"Yes, bad plan," Hawk agreed as he looked back toward her.

She cocked her head over her right shoulder. "To do what Walt would have done, you'd have to get back to the office he had in 1939. That building and office disappeared years ago."

"Kiran, will you get me out of here?" Hawk asked and waited as silence fell between them once again.

"I am going to regret this." She shook her head from side to side as she spoke.

Hawk felt a wave of relief that Kiran was willing to help him extract himself from this mess he had created. However, she held up her index finger.

"You can't visit the office Walt had in 1939, but you could still get behind his desk." Her voice took on a conspiratorial tone.

"What?" Hawk's pulse tripped.

"The desk from his office at the old studio is here."

"Here?"

"Yes, it's here, in this attraction. You've walked past it every single time you've walked through it." Kiran clamped her mouth shut again as though realizing she'd offered too much information.

He waited to hear what she was going to say next. Finally Kiran reached out and took Hawk by the hand. She led him forward through the narrow passageway that curved to the right and then made a slight jog behind additional exhibits. Kiran stopped at a wall with a small door that resembled an oversized doggy door. The door was large enough for a person to get through, and like the others, had a keyed lock. Kiran once again faced Hawk and handed him the old skeleton key Rales had given him. In all of their discussion, he'd forgotten she still was holding it.

"Here, you hold your key to the kingdom. I need to find a key to the door. Don't go wandering off," she instructed, then moved away, leaving him standing there.

Hawk looked at the key in his hand. Earlier he had been so sure he needed to get into Walt's office. Speaking with Kiran had shown him how ridiculous his line of thinking was. Now he didn't know what to think. Hearing footsteps, he turned his attention to the sound of Kiran returning from around the corner of the passageway. She smiled triumphantly, holding up a key.

"I'm going to open this door and we're going to crawl through. We only have a few minutes inside. This key is a maintenance key, which means the crew isn't working inside this part of the attraction yet."

"What about security cameras?" Hawk inquired.

She looked at him with astonishment. "You're worried about that now?"

Kiran did not wait for an answer. She knelt down and placed the key into the bolted lock.

"Actually there is a security camera inside this exhibit. Behind this door is the desk from Walt's office in the late thirties and early forties. We used to have the special Academy Award that Walt had received for *Snow White and the Seven Dwarfs* sitting on the desk itself. That was the one with the large statue flanked by seven smaller ones. While that was on display this part of the exhibit was monitored closely. Now that piece of memorabilia is on display elsewhere, so the camera isn't monitored anymore." She paused as she turned the lock and prepared to open the door. "At least I hope it isn't monitored anymore."

Kiran got on her hands and knees and managed to navigate her way through the door opening. Hawk watched with distracted amusement and admiration as she did so in a skirt which made the trek through the door even more difficult to accomplish with the appropriate degree of modesty. Seeing her straighten up and step out of the way through the opening, he heard her whisper.

"Are you coming in here or not?"

Crouching and then moving to his hands and knees, Hawk navigated the path through the door as Kiran had just done. Straightening up, he found himself standing inside a compact display with an old wooden desk as the focal point. Hanging on the back wall above the desk was a picture of Walt Disney receiving the Academy Award for *Snow White* from Shirley Temple. The spotlights that illuminated the desk were intense and Hawk once again looked out at the interior of One Man's Dream from behind the glass of another display.

"This was the desk Walt used in his office when *Snow White* was created. If he went back to his office and sat behind his desk after his Florida trip to the Dwarfs' Cottage, this would be the desk." Kiran's eyes sparkled. "This is what you came for. See if your key fits."

Hawk stepped to the back of the desk. This was what you could see from the tour of the exhibit. Kiran had been right. Hawk had walked past this every time he had been in the attraction. He had never paid as much attention to this desk or the history behind it as he had the other things in the exhibit. With his back against the glass separating the desk from the touch of the tourists, he reached down to the center drawer of the desk. He pulled it toward him. It did not open. Hawk looked up at Kiran, and without saying a word, confirmed for her that it was indeed locked. Standing to the side of the desk, she placed both hands on it and leaned forward to better see what Hawk was about to attempt.

Hawk placed the key to the kingdom that Farren Rales had given him into the lock on the desk drawer. The old antique skeleton key slid into the lock without resistance. Now with the key firmly placed inside the lock, he exchanged a glance with Kiran. She nodded slightly, prodding Hawk to continue. He attempted to turn the key to the right and immediately felt resistance. It would not turn in that direction. He turned the key to the left and held his breath. A satisfying *click* and then another broke the silence as the lock opened, releasing the mechanism holding the drawer closed. Removing the key from the lock, Hawk hesitated, and for a moment, pondered the value of the key and wondered how Rales had managed to come into the possession of it. He slowly rewrapped it and placed it back into his pocket.

Kiran whispered impatiently, "Are you going to open the drawer or not?"

Tensing his arm, he gently flexed and pulled the drawer toward him. After a slight resistance, the drawer of Walt Disney's desk slid open. Hawk stared with disbelief at what he saw inside.

 *Day Four*
Night

HAWK AND KIRAN STOOD STARING at the contents of Walt Disney's
drawer. The elation he'd felt when the key actually unlocked the desk drawer
was now surpassed by the confusion created by what the drawer contained.

"Is that it?" Kiran inquired.

Reaching into the desk drawer, Hawk pulled out the prize that had been
awaiting him. He retracted his arm, clutching a stuffed Mickey Mouse attired
in a dress tuxedo and tails. Holding it in his hand, Hawk looked into the
drawer again, but there was nothing else to be seen. Bending down closer so
he would be sure not to miss anything, he examined every nook and corner
of the drawer. Now that Mickey had been removed, the drawer was completely empty.

"Tremendous," Kiran exclaimed. "Close the drawer, we have to get out
of here."

Hawk slid the drawer back into place and moved around the desk toward
the diminutive doorway. Kiran placed her hand on his back and pushed him
down toward the opening. Complying and repeating his actions from before,
he quickly was back on the other side of the exhibit. In a moment Kiran was
through the opening. Hawk helped her to her feet, and she spun to close and
relock the access door.

"I risked becoming your accomplice in this disaster so we could find a stuffed
animal," she scolded. "Stay right here while I put the key to the door back."

She moved back toward the unseen area where she had found the key earlier. Hawk awaited her return, examining the Mickey Mouse doll. It was ten
or eleven inches tall, had the familiar cute face, a hard plastic nose, but was
slightly different than a normal stuffed animal. At the moment, although
Hawk knew it was different, he wasn't entirely sure what the difference was.
Momentarily Kiran returned, her face a mask of frustration. Hawk wasn't
sure which one of them was the target of her frustration, or if it was both.

"Follow me," she said as she moved past him, retracing their steps. "So this is why you couldn't have dinner with me. Because you wanted to break into a theme park so you could find a stuffed Mickey Mouse?" It didn't seem a question that she wanted an answer to, but Hawk couldn't resist.

"This is not exactly what I planned, but how could you have had dinner with me when you had to be at work?"

"I didn't agree to lead the tour until this afternoon, which is more than you deserve to know, by the way."

They wound past the office where Kiran had found Hawk and continued back toward the maintenance door by the audio-animatronics display Hawk had originally hidden in. Arriving at the door, Kiran pressed up against it to listen for any activity on the other side. Satisfied that she heard nothing, she cracked the door open slightly to make sure the coast was clear.

Turning back to him she whispered, "You're a guest and I'm leading you on a private tour. If we get lucky, we'll get out of the park without anyone noticing us. No matter what happens, follow my lead."

Reaching back and grabbing his shirt, she pulled him through the doorway. Once again he found himself on the guest side of One Man's Dream as he fell in step next to Kiran. Silently they walked back toward the front entrance. Passing the massive window opening into Walt's office, Hawk realized just how risky his stunt had been. As they turned into the early Disney years portion of the attraction, he heard voices in front of them. Without hesitation Kiran launched into a tour guide's spiel.

"Walt was the ultimate storyteller. He was convinced that a great story would connect with audiences of all ages. He also was never satisfied with what he had already accomplished. He constantly was trying to discover better ways to creatively use film as a storytelling medium."

Two cast members who were vacuuming the carpet and chatting nonchalantly paused in their work and smiled as Hawk and Kiran walked past. Nodding at them, Hawk turned back and waited for Kiran to continue her impromptu tour.

When they arrived at the front of the attraction, the noises of the cleaning began again behind them. They hit the crash bars on the doors and stepped out onto Mickey Avenue. Standing outside the main entrance to One Man's Dream, Hawk felt a vibration in his hand. Looking down, he realized Mickey Mouse was the source. He glanced toward Kiran, who was looking in both directions trying to decide which way was going to be the best exit strategy. The vibrating stuffed animal stopped shaking and emitted a high-pitched *ha-ha!* in the distinct voice of none other than Mickey Mouse.

"Did I just hear Mickey Mouse?" she demanded.

"Yeah." Hawk frowned at the toy. "He started shaking and then laughed."

"I'll bet that's a Pal Mickey," Kiran stated. "That's what they do."

"A Pal Mickey?"

"Yes, a Pal Mickey. It's an interactive tour guide we used to sell here at the Disney Resort. No matter where you went on Disney property, your Mickey would talk to you. It would give you information about where to find characters in the park. You could learn wait times for certain rides and all sorts of insider information about everything related to Walt Disney World. They were expensive and popular. We sold them at gift shops throughout the property."

"Sold? You can't get them anymore?"

"No. Although they were popular, they were pricey. People liked them and there have been some new variations of the same technology. The technology was left on so they would still work, but eventually it will be phased out for new uses."

"How does it work?" Hawk wanted to know.

"The plastic nose has a sensor that's activated by transponders located throughout the parks and across Disney property. When you walk past one it activates Mickey and he vibrates, laughs, and talks to you. Come on Hawk, you're a big Disney fan, you surely have heard of Pal Mickey!"

"I guess I just didn't pay a lot of attention. How does he talk?"

Kiran reached down and snatched Mickey out of Hawk's hand. Fumbling with the stuffed animal for a moment, she held it between them.

"You're supposed to give him a squeeze and he'll tell you whatever the transponder has activated based upon where you are," she informed him as she gave Pal Mickey a squeeze.

The speaker mechanism inside the stuffed animal activated and the unmistakable voice of Mickey Mouse spoke to them.

"Gosh! It sure was dark in that old desk. Thanks for getting me out!"

Hawk's mouth fell open. He looked up toward Kiran and saw her amazement.

"That isn't something they would usually say, is it?" he asked.

She shook her head. The mouse started vibrating again.

"Ha-ha!"

"It has something else to say," she stammered. Holding it out unsteadily, she once again applied pressure to the stuffed middle of the mouse.

"We are going to be great friends. Together we are going to go on the adventure of a lifetime. Please take good care of me, Hawk!"

Kiran's hand opened and the stuffed animal fell. Hawk caught it and they both stared at it. Gripping the mouse, he held it away from his body.

Hawk spoke in a shaky voice. "Tell me that Mickey Mouse just didn't say my name." Kiran remained silent. "I thought I heard him say we're going on an adventure and that I need to take care of him. I did hear that, right? You heard that, didn't you?"

Kiran nodded her head in confusion. She pointed her finger at the archway leading to the Sorcerer's Hat. Clutching his newly discovered pal, Hawk stayed right at Kiran's shoulder as they briskly stepped onto Hollywood Boulevard. The entrance of the park lay at the end of the street.

After hours in the Disney Hollywood Studios is a beehive of activity. The park is cleaned from the traffic of the day's guests. In addition, lots of touching up is done, some fixing and repair work, and many preparations are made for the arrival of the crowds to come in the morning.

"Is it this busy every night?" Hawk inquired.

"Every single night."

"I suppose I never really thought about it before," he admitted.

"That seems to be a pattern with you," she replied with little emotion.

"What?"

"Not taking the time to give things much thought."

"Wait a minute, that's not true," he protested.

As they continued to walk Kiran turned toward him with a stone-cold look that served as a reality check for Hawk. It was true that over the last hour she had not seen him at his best. He decided it was better not to continue the conversation. Instead he again got lost in watching the buzz of activity. As they walked past Mickey's of Hollywood, a gift shop featuring character souvenirs, clothing, and assorted figurines, their escape was interrupted as a voice emerged from the shop.

"Good evening, Kiran!" came the bright greeting.

Pausing, Kiran turned and Hawk stopped slightly behind her so she could see who was calling her. Stepping out the doors of the shop was a young man with sandy blond hair. His name tag was imprinted with the name Sandy.

"Hi, Sandy, how are you this evening?" Kiran pleasantly returned his greeting.

"Great, are you enjoying your tour?" Obviously this was intended toward Hawk.

"Uh, sure, I've really enjoyed it," offered Hawk, remembering to follow Kiran's lead.

"Let me introduce you." Kiran took control of the conversation. "Dr. Hawkes, this is Sandy. Sandy, I'd like for you to meet Dr. Hawkes."

The two men shook hands. As they did Sandy studied Hawk more closely than Hawk had wished. Stepping back, Sandy smiled broadly.

"What have you seen this evening?" he asked Hawk.

Hawk smiled crookedly and opened his mouth to speak. Kiran injected the answer for him.

"This is more of a quick browse than a detailed tour, Sandy. The doctor and I are actually running a bit behind." She motioned for Hawk to begin moving forward. "I'm supposed to have Dr. Hawkes somewhere else already. Good night, Sandy!"

"Nice meeting you, Dr. Hawkes," Sandy called after they began moving away.

"You too." Hawk looked back over his shoulder and gave a partial wave.

He noticed as they left that Sandy did not move right back into the shop he'd come out of.

"You know he's still watching us," he whispered to Kiran.

"Don't flatter yourself. He's watching me." She smiled coyly. "Sandy is a good guy. He's asked me out a couple of times, and he's probably jealous that I'm giving you a private tour. If he only knew . . ."

 *Day Four*
Night

THE METAL SECURITY GATE silently swung open as a cast member provided Hawk and Kiran their escape from the Disney Hollywood Studios. Without saying a word they moved along the sidewalk toward the parking areas. After clearing and putting a safe distance between them and the last security checkpoint on the concrete path, they stopped. Hawk tried to read what Kiran was thinking as she looked off into the night sky. Having moved beyond the brightly lit confines of the theme park, they now stood under a magnificent Florida sky. The black velvet of the evening was enhanced by the twinkling glimmer of starlight. A poet would have called the sky romantic, but in this moment, with the events of the past few minutes, romance was not on Hawk's mind. He waited, knowing she would gather her thoughts and eventually tell him what she was thinking. The waiting gave him time to both process what had happened and try to anticipate her reaction.

Hawk realized he had told Kiran too much when she had caught him in Walt's office. Under pressure he had revealed far more to her than he normally would have. He'd rationalized that it was necessary to prevent her from calling security and having him arrested. With more time to think, he would have been more guarded in his disclosure. Hawk also wasn't sure what to conclude from her quick jump into his search. For Grayson Hawkes this whole evening had been one of high risk. In a matter of impetuous moments he had been willing to risk his integrity, his security, much of what he had tried to build professionally, and what he valued relationally. The thing he valued the most was not compromising his relationship with Jesus. Whether Jesus would have chosen to do what he had done this evening was something he would ponder later—and more than likely struggle with.

"I don't even know what to say," Kiran interrupted his thoughts.

"It has been quite an evening, hasn't it?"

"Look, Hawk, I'm not sure what to think of your story, your key to the kingdom, or your breaking into the attraction. I'm not sure why I didn't call security on you when I found you."

"Kiran, I . . ."

Kiran raised her hand for him to be quiet. He decided it was better to let her continue.

"I think I didn't call security because there was something about you that I found attractive." She hesitated and Hawk felt his face blush a bit. He hoped the dim lighting hid this from Kiran. "And I liked what you said when you were preaching. Perhaps I was hoping you were different than other people I knew. I think that's why I was hoping the story you told me about Farren Rales, the Dwarf Cottage, the key, and everything else was true. After we found the stuffed Mickey, I had about decided you were just another crackpot. Then it called you by name!"

"That was a bit odd."

"It was more than odd, Hawk! It was bizarre. This whole evening has been something out of a movie, or nightmare, or something. . . . I don't know what to call it."

"I'm not sure what to think about it either, but I'm glad you didn't call security," he graciously offered.

"Look, Hawk, like I said, I'm not sure why I didn't call them, but this is the end of the line."

"What do you mean?"

"This is it. I don't know why you ended up with that key to the desk. But you got a chance to open it and you got your souvenir. My advice would be for you to go home and figure out why your friend sent you on this scavenger hunt. If you ask me, we're both lucky we didn't get caught."

Kiran turned and stalked away toward the cast member parking area. Hawk watched her for a moment and then trotted after her. Cast member parking was the Television parking area of the Studios. As she passed underneath the pleasantly smiling face of Minnie Mouse, he drew close enough to get her attention.

"Kiran, wait," he called softly, and she turned back toward him. "I really appreciate your help tonight. Thank you so much. I need some time to figure out what really did happen and what it's supposed to mean."

"Hawk, didn't you hear me?" she asked tersely. "We were lucky tonight; it isn't that tough to figure out. There isn't any deeper meaning than that!"

"It's just that I need to get a little perspective on it, that's all. Let's figure out a time tomorrow to talk about what happened after we think about it awhile."

"Think about it all you want, I don't need to help you."

"I know you feel that way right now, but we were supposed to get together tomorrow night at seven o'clock. Meet me where we planned on Front Street," he attempted to convince her.

"No, I don't think so," she answered too fast. "I think the time we spent hanging out together tonight was memorable enough." She turned and again headed deeper into the cast parking area.

Hawk stood firmly planted in place as she left. She finally disappeared from his line of sight without looking back. Certain she was not returning, he began making his way toward his car, his footsteps echoing across the concrete. He tried to decipher the events of the evening. Stopping at his car door, he placed the Pal Mickey on the roof of his car, facing him. He slid his hand into his pocket and removed the skeleton key, the key to the kingdom, and held it up. Placing his elbows on the roof of his car, he leaned against it, staring at the key and at Mickey Mouse. Mickey had told him they were going on the adventure of a lifetime . . . whatever that meant.

 *Day Five*
Morning

IT WASN'T YET SEVEN THIRTY, and after a sleepless night, Hawk was the first to arrive in the friendly and familiar confines of his office.

Logging onto his computer he immediately put into action the plan born in the midst of his insomnia. Hawk had determined to understand better how Pal Mickey worked; his first stop would be at the Disney World Trivia forums. In moments his screen filled with a number of links loaded with information about Pal Mickey.

Relaxing and rocking back in his desk chair he reread what he found. The design of Pal Mickey began in the year 2000 as Imagineers began to flirt with ways that wireless devices could be used to enhance the guest experience in the theme parks. This technology would allow the guest to receive practical and helpful information but also allow the Imagineers to communicate some of the rich stories and details that were such an important part of the design of each unique park. Throughout the Walt Disney World Resort hundreds of hidden infrared transmitters emit information to the toy. The end result is a transponder network designed to keep the Pal Mickey constantly receiving and able to dispense information. The computer system that runs the emitters as well as the computing power inside the doll itself is one that builds and stacks the information so it becomes a genuine interactive experience. The small, protected transponder in the hard plastic nose acts as the receiver and behind the eyes is the speaker system that enables the user to hear all the information. Hawk also found that the Imagineers were only just beginning to experiment with the technology and that the future of what they could do was unlimited. Already prototypes of new receivers, transponders, and emitters were being tested. Pal Mickey had been the rollout of the first wave of this technology and it had worked. There would be more applications to follow, and as Karin had said, the Pal Mickey system would have to be turned off and shut down. But in spite of that, Hawk now possessed a plush pal that still worked. He reached into his bag and brought out the Pal Mickey he'd freed from Walt's desk last night.

Since this particular Pal Mickey had addressed him by name the night before, Hawk felt it safe to assume that this was one of the new prototypes he had read about. The technology behind it was impressive and obviously one that the Imagineers had mastered. It reminded him of Kiran's explanation of the technology behind the parades in the Magic Kingdom. Since Farren Rales had his hand in many things the Imagineers were working on, it would not be a stretch to think he could have his hand in this type of technology as it was developed and implemented. It was also fairly reasonable that Rales would be involved in whatever the next progression of this technology would become.

"Is it possible that Rales could have set up a system designed to communicate with just one receiver?" Hawk asked aloud toward Mickey.

It seemed to be the only reasonable explanation for the surprising sayings from the stuffed animal last night. Rales had wanted him to find the desk and the very special Pal Mickey. Rales also had intended for the interactive stuffed tour guide to talk directly to him. Beyond that, if he was thinking correctly about those things, then the key to the kingdom unlocked the desk and an even bigger mystery. This was something that Hawk hadn't been anticipating. His assumption was that the key itself would give him an answer to what the key to the kingdom was. Instead the key had merely served to open up more questions. Running his fingers through his hair he realized it was not over as Kiran had suggested. Instead he felt compelled to pursue this even further. If what he had done the night before was only the beginning, he shuddered to think what he might have to do next in order to solve the mystery.

The ringing of the phone shook him out of his cloak-and-dagger moment. Reaching to grasp the handle he hoisted it toward his jaw and spoke.

"Hi, this is Hawk."

"Hawk, this is Nancy Alport."

"Nancy, have you heard from Farren?" Hawk was hoping for good news.

"No, that is why I am calling," she said.

"I was hoping . . ." The statement was truer than he wanted to admit. Despite his suspicions that Rales had masterminded a grand mystery for him to solve, he was growing concerned. He could not ignore the way that Farren's disappearance, the key, and this puzzle all seemed to be interconnected. If Farren were around, perhaps he could shed some light on some of the things Hawk was thinking and of course bring some clarity to the mystery.

"The sheriff's department was just here. We couldn't find anyone who has seen Farren for the last three days. Since he doesn't have any family locally and he has never just missed work or meetings without checking in, this is serious."

"I agree, it is serious." Worry knotted Hawk's stomach.

"I wanted to give you a heads-up that I gave them your number and told them who you are."

"You did?"

"Yes, I hope that's okay. They wanted to know who his friends were and who he might have talked to before he disappeared. You're one of his best friends and you were one of the last appointments he had on his calendar when he met with you and your staff."

"Sure, that only makes sense." He was glad the late-night appointment they'd had was apparently not on Farren's calendar. "Not a problem at all. Did they say they would be coming by?"

"I don't know. They were here for well over an hour getting information. I'm sure we'll be seeing them again. I hope they find something out soon."

"Me too."

"Hawk, do you think something bad has happened to him?"

Hawk paused, thinking back to the night at Gamble Place. He had initially figured the person who had chased him off the grounds was a security guard. While that still made sense, the car he'd passed as he made his escape did not fit into the scenario.

"Hawk, are you there?" Nancy asked.

"Yes, sorry, I'm concerned like you are. If there is anything I can do to help, you know I will."

"I know you will. I was wondering if you could . . ."

"What is it Nancy? If I could . . . what?"

"I was thinking that maybe you could pray for Farren," she said almost apologetically.

"I promise you I already have been. And I have been praying for you as well."

"Thank you," she said softly. Her voice was choked with emotion. "Bye."

The connection ended and Hawk hung up the phone. If indeed the sheriff's department did come, he'd have to let them know about the after-hours trip to Gamble Place and the Dwarf's Cottage. If his disappearance was somehow related to the events from that night and the key to the kingdom, then Hawk must keep chasing the mystery. Perhaps if he could figure out what Rales had been trying to tell him, he might be able to find out where Farren had gone.

 *Day Five*
Afternoon

THE DECISION HAD BEEN MADE unconsciously.

The grumbling sounds emerging from Hawk's stomach reminded him he had worked straight through lunch. Over the last couple of hours he had managed to return e-mail correspondence, return a list of phone calls, answer a handful of letters, and clear out the bulk of the things on his calendar for the next few days.

His plan was unfolding similarly to his plan from the night before: a little action, mixed with a smidgeon of hope, and trust that he could make creative decisions on the fly.

The last thing he did was to leave brief voice mails for Juliette, Jonathan, and Shep on their office extensions asking them to hold down the fort because he was going to be "out" more than he would be "in" for the next day or so. He kept the message vague, telling them to call his cell phone if they needed him.

Hesitating a moment, he looked at Mickey sitting on his desk. Hawk was counting on some of his conclusions being correct. If they were, the Pal Mickey in his possession was a clue that Farren had placed for him alone to find. His limited understanding of the technology used caused him to summarize that either the system within his Mickey was loaded with very specific information Farren wanted him to have, or there was a unique set of emitters designed to send information to this unit exclusively. Somewhere in this complex combination of thought, Hawk decided the transponder system for his Pal Mickey was the best source to find more information. The data on the Web sites he'd researched clearly instructed him on how the miniature tour guide would work the best.

Hawk opened up his desk drawer and rifled through the jumbled mess inside. Rummaging through the clutter he found was he was looking for, a Velcro strap. The strap was intended to be used to hold together a cluster of computer cables, but he had a different use for it in mind. Grabbing the stuffed doll he spun it around, found the clip designed to attach to a belt or bag and went to work. In a moment he had successfully added Velcro reinforcement to the clip just in case he might need it. Now as he attached it to the waistband of his jeans, he could ensure its staying in place in an emergency with the Velcro wrapped around a belt loop.

He exited his office and climbed into his car to begin his journey back to Disney World. Since the key and the mouse had been found at the Disney Hollywood Studios, this would be the place to start. On the short drive to the park he was counting on his techno-tour guide to reset and update itself as he entered the park. If it didn't, he wasn't sure what his next step would be. He turned his car into the entrance and traveled with no other traffic as he approached the attendant distributing parking passes. When he flashed his annual pass, the attendant smiled and waved him through once again into the parking area. Following directions given by a series of waving arms and pointing fingers, he parked his car and made his way to the waiting zone for the next courtesy tram. Momentarily the late afternoon arrivals hoisted themselves aboard the rolling caterpillar-like transportation vehicle and listened as a host reminded them where they were parked and what time the Studios closed. Hawk leaned his head back and with eyes closed offered up a silent prayer that what he was doing was going to work and that he would have the wisdom to know what to do next. The tram arrived at the main gate and he exited with the other guests toward the entrance. Picking out the shortest line, he inserted his pass and pressed his finger on the biometric sensor. His fingerprint was analyzed and verified. The cast member at the gate handed him back his pass and he pushed through the turnstile.

 *Day Five*
Afternoon

IMMEDIATELY HAWK FELT A VIBRATION against his hip and heard a
cartoon voice say, "Ha-ha!" Based upon his research he knew that Pal Mickey
should have just reset itself as he entered the theme park. With his right hand
he unclasped Mickey from the belt loop and held him up by his right ear.
Squeezing the mouse, he listened to the information Mickey had to share.

"Welcome back to the Disney Hollywood Studios, Hawk."

Once again, although he was expecting it, the personalized greeting
from the interactive tour guide unnerved him a little. Before he thought too
much about this, the stuffed animal vibrated and laughed again. "Ha-ha!"
Hawk tightened his grip on the soft belly and listened.

"Oscar's Super Service Station is the only gas station in the Studios . . . but
you can't get gasoline here, pal. Oscar's is named for the statue given out at the
exciting Academy Awards Ceremony each year. Mr. Disney got a very special
Oscar for Snow White and the Seven Dwarfs. I love that movie, don't you?"

It had been a long time since Hawk had watched the movie, but over the
last few days he had a growing curiosity about it. The night at the Dwarf's Cottage, as Farren had told him about how the movie had inspired Alfred Nippert,
he'd decided he would need to watch the film again. The desk his key to the
kingdom had opened was once used to display the special Oscar that Disney
had been awarded. Now the name of the movie had been mentioned again. In
all that he had learned from Farren about the art of storytelling, he was certain
the repetition was not an accident. If this was some sort of story he was supposed to be hearing—and understanding—the mention of *Snow White* again
was not a coincidence. He had no idea what it meant, but knew it was something of importance. Looking absently toward Oscar's Super Service Station,
Hawk waited for another message, but the mouse was silent. Securing it back
on his hip, he moved down Hollywood Boulevard toward the giant Sorcerer's
Hat. The crowd flow in this area of the park was light and Hawk made his way

along the street alone in a bubble of space between himself and other tourists. The sun was still bright and he felt the blazing heat on his face. The warmth wrapped him in a glow of confidence and excitement as he anticipated what might happen next.

The first intersection on the main street finds Vine Street meeting Hollywood Boulevard. He paused on the corner of Hollywood and Vine, uncertain whether he should take a left along Vine Street or remain on his present course. The vibration on his hip, accompanied by the welcomed "Ha-ha" was about to make Hawk's decision for him. Freeing Mickey from his resting place, he raised him up to his ear.

"Hooray for Hollywood! This is a place where people can dream, wonder, and imagine. We have a lot to do, pal; we have to find the place where it all began. Hollywood and Vine is the perfect spot to do a little valiant detective work for ourselves."

Hawk stood looking at the mouse, waiting for him to say something else. The ensuing silence convinced him there was nothing else to hear. Standing in the middle of the street at Hollywood and Vine, Hawk slowly and meticulously spun in place, taking in his surroundings. If he had just been given a clue, it was one without much detail. Not knowing what he was searching for, he tried to absorb everything. He looked at the buildings, studied the signage, and even looked at the billboards creating the illusion that you had stepped into a Hollywood that had never really existed but was forever alive in the imagination of all who had been fascinated by the movie industry.

Street actors suddenly emerged on the street. Hawk was in the way as the actors began to engage a gathering crowd in an audience-participation event on the corner. Forced across the street, he moved away from the activity toward a less congested area. His mind whirring, he decided to buy a frozen shaved ice cola from Peevy's Polar Pipeline, the street kiosk set up in front of the Cosmetic Dentistry shop. *We have to find the place where it all began.* Drawing in a mouthful of the frozen concoction too fast sent a rush of pain into his brain. He closed one eye and cocked his head, waiting out the brain freeze. Out of his one opened eye he saw a door next to the kiosk which read, Holly-Vermont Reality Company. There was something about the name that he recognized; it was significant in some way. He allowed his eyes to glance up the side of the building. His gaze stopped at a sign in the second-floor window: Office Space For Rent. Suddenly his thoughts locked into place, sending another rush through his brain. This time it wasn't pain, but clarity. Standing under the street sign reading Keystone Street and Echo Park Drive, he remembered. Walt and Roy Disney had started their business in a garage until they saved enough money to rent their own studio space.

They rented a second floor office where they opened their studio. It was right above the Holly-Vermont Reality Company. Their first studio was a humble start, to say the least, but here in the Studios was a humble tribute to those beginnings. *The place where it all began.*

Stepping up on the curb he turned away from the previously unnoticed tribute back toward the direction from which he had come. Facing a restaurant now in front of him, he smiled. He made the short walk to stand directly in front of the building and studied it. The sign supported above the covered entrance featured an oversized street sign with the names Hollywood and Vine imprinted on each cross piece. The street sign was flanked by lit neon stars and surrounded by a silver oval highlighted with more neon. Wrapping the ledge of the entrance the words "Where Famous Stars Dine" glowed in blue neon to greet the diners. Since he had found the place where it all began, he was certain this must be the *perfect spot* the plush pal had mentioned. Hawk noticed something else barely visible from his sight line. Moving to his left he positioned himself where he could get a better view. Emblazoned on the second story window just to the left of the marquee entrance were the words:

Eddie Valiant
Private Investigations
All Crimes
All Surveillance
Missing Persons

The stuffed tour guide had said to do some *valiant detective work.* The window sign, which was a tribute to the detective from the film *Who Framed Roger Rabbit?* verified he was on the right track. Immediately the preacher moved toward the entrance of the appropriately named Hollywood & Vine. At the front door a hostess was waiting behind a check-in station.

"Do you have a reservation?"

"Actually I don't," Hawk replied. "But I'm only a party of one, do I have to have one?"

"I'm sorry, but we're booked solid for the rest of the day," the hostess said apologetically.

Hawk bowed his head and tried to feign disappointment.

"Since I can't eat, would it be all right if I just walked inside and took a look at the restaurant? I'm intrigued by the detail used in decorating around here."

Eager to please a guest, the cast member enthusiastically agreed, "Sure, that would be fine. Go right on in and feel free to look."

"Great, thanks," said Hawk as he moved into the restaurant. "I promise not to harass the diners," he added with a smile.

Stepping inside he vaguely recalled having eaten there at some point in the past. The buffet-style dining area was operating at near capacity. Because of a steady shuffle of people moving from their seats to the buffet line, there was greater activity in this restaurant than the others. This ebb and flow of motion allowed Hawk to move about without being in anyone's way. Looking to his right he saw giant painted murals covering the far wall. Gathering his perspective, he remembered that this restaurant connected to the 50s Prime Time Café through a series of corridors that provided bathroom facilities for both eating establishments. No detail of the murals stood out as valuable information to him. Spinning on his heel he looked toward the opposite end of the restaurant and saw another mural stretching across the length of the far wall. He strode across the room, noticing the outside of the mural was a map painted to include famous Hollywood landmarks. These landmarks were cartoon style drawings of buildings that were a part of the history of Tinseltown. The center of the mural was a full color painting of the famous Carthay Circle Theatre. Painted against a nighttime sky, the blackness was broken by radiating beams from floodlights capturing the excitement of an opening night. Just as he was glancing away, something drew his eyes back.

On the marquee of the theatre in the mural the featured film was *Snow White and the Seven Dwarfs*. Hawk instantly knew this was what he was looking for. The longer he stared, the more the theatre itself became surprisingly familiar to him. He remembered from his knowledge of Disney Trivia that *Snow White* had originally premiered at the Carthay Circle Theatre.

Like a fog lifting on a lazy sunny morning he knew he had seen the theatre before. Never having been there in person it must mean that he had seen something similar to it. Locking the image in his mind, he retreated and retraced his path to the door of the restaurant.

He wandered back toward Hollywood Boulevard. The street actors were no longer performing and the crowd had dispersed. Turning left on the corner he angled his way across the main street of the theme park until he came to the next street corner. He stood on the edge of the Studios version of Sunset Boulevard. The resolve Hawk had exited Hollywood & Vine with faded as he stood looking down the street. Glancing at the mouse on his hip, he waited, trying to will the techo-guide to speak. No vibration. The silence let him know it was up to him to figure out what to do next.

In the *perfect place*, the painting of the Carthay Circle Theatre had reminded him of a building he had seen. Could it be on this street? Much of the architectural work was patterned from classic Hollywood landmarks and design. One of the things Hawk had been fascinated by in his love for all things Disney was the amazing attention to detail hidden in plain view throughout the Walt Disney World Resort. Choosing to move straight down the middle of the street, he studied the buildings closely, straining to remember what had sparked the familiarity as he looked at the mural.

His walk slowed as he moved into the next block of buildings. A familiar design emerged from the architecture, and a grin broke out across his face. The building looming before him was unmistakably patterned after the theatre painted into the mural at Hollywood & Vine. The ornate sign above the entrance to the building confirmed this building was patterned after the very same theatre that *Snow White and the Seven Dwarfs* premiered in so many years ago. The sign read Carthay Circle. Inside the facade of the classic theatre was the Once Upon A Time character shop featuring clothing and items adorned with favorite Disney characters. His pace quickened as he moved toward the entrance.

"Ha-ha."

Hawk stopped short.

His pulse quickened. He knew Pal Mickey was going to confirm his success. Quickly releasing his speaking stuffed companion, he held the mouse to his ear and listened eagerly.

"Gosh pal, you're doing swell! The Carthay Circle Theatre was an important place for Mr. Disney. Once things got started here, there was no turning back! Now don't be scared, but if you need to you can always call for help! Be careful, pal!"

Facing the theatre facade he replayed the message again by pressing the little stuffed hand. *No turning back . . . don't be scared.* He was commited to this adventure no matter what. But who was he supposed to call for help?

With a few quick steps he was inside the store. Moving through the displays he saw nothing out of the ordinary inside the Once Upon A Time shop except for some vintage pictures of Walt Disney at the premier of *Snow White* displayed for viewing, not purchasing. The back of the shop held an exit onto Highland Street, which connected to Sunset Boulevard. Leaving the shop through this back exit, he briskly rounded the corner and cut back to his left. He once again found himself at the front entrance to the shop. Knowing he'd missed something, but not sure what, he moved back down Highland Street to reenter shop and retrace his steps. His peripheral range of sight noticed something just as he was about to enter the door. He stopped and took three steps backward without turning around. Affixed to the wall of the theatre, just to the right of the back door, was a box. It appeared to be vintage and right in place in the bygone era of greatness for the building. It was a police telegraph box. Painted-black steel contained the call apparatus used to get in touch with law enforcement in the case of emergency. This was certainly a way to call for help. He needed help figuring out what to do next; this call box had to be what his talking tour guide had wanted him to find.

Standing directly in front of it he placed his fingers on the edge and tried to open it. The front refused to budge. Testing to see if it needed more coaxing, he wedged his fingers along the edge again and tried to pry it open. Once again there was no movement. Trying yet again he strained to open it, emitting a groan from the effort. The box was locked. Lowering his hands and stepping away he examined it more closely. The words *Police Telegraph* were embossed in white. A fist grasping a handful of lightning bolts adorned the top of the box and the Gamewell Company from New York was the manufacturer. The identification number was 513 and there were two keyholes. One keyhole was marked Citizen's Key in the center of the box. A second keyhole was along the left side of the door; traditionally local law enforcement would have carried a master key for this lock.

"May I help you?"

The deep voice tore Hawk's attention away from the box. He jerked his head to the right, the direction from which the voice had originated. He turned so quickly he knew he must have appeared to be guilty of some mischief. A gentleman wearing a short-sleeved dress shirt, a blue tie, and a cast member name badge stood waiting. Obscuring his eyes, a pair of dark glasses rested on a nose so crooked it appeared to have been broken at some point, and it jutted out below a bald head ringed above the ears with neatly trimmed dark hair. Physically imposing at about the same height as Hawk, he showed no expression and waited for some type of response. Hawk wondered how long he had been standing there.

"Um . . . no, I don't need help. I was just curious and doing some exploring," Hawk replied as he dusted off his hands and walked toward this cast member.

According to the man's name tag, his name was Reginald. He wore a radio on his hip with an earpiece placed firmly in his ear. Offering a crooked smile, Grayson Hawkes waited for Reginald to say something. Reginald said nothing. The round face offered no expression whatsoever, and Hawk was convinced that the eyes behind the black shades were boring holes into him. He felt the strong urge to break the stare and look away, but he had learned a long time ago it was better to maintain eye contact. He continued to look back at his own reflection in the glasses. Still Reginald said nothing.

Shrugging and cocking his head slightly Hawk said, "Well Reginald, nice meeting you."

He moved past him back onto Sunset Boulevard heading toward Holly-wood Boulevard once again. Trying his best to be casual he sauntered along the sidewalk and nonchalantly entered the Planet Hollywood Super Store. It was only as he moved through the door that he dared a glance back to see if Reginald was still watching him. He was. Hawk quickened his pace and moved through this shop and into the next, since they were connected. The next shop allowed him an exit that had no direct sight line to Once Upon A Time. Stepping back outside he positioned himself where he could look back down to the Carthay Circle Theatre without being seen. Reginald was gone.

Hawk exhaled loudly. He had to figure out a way to get back to the call box.

CHAPTER SEVENTEEN

Day Five
Afternoon

GRAYSON HAWKES SAT in the Writer's Stop drinking a cup of coffee and sinking in an overstuffed chair, trying to relax enough to think. The Writer's Stop was a coffee shop and bookstore perched on the edge of the Streets of America. Over an hour and a half had passed since Reginald had discovered him at the police telegraph box. He was psyching himself to head back to try to open it again. The caffeine-stimulated brain cells had given Hawk the chance to formulate a more concrete plan. Shaking his head from side to side, he realized he was getting ready to break into another display here at the Studios. The box was not going to open easily. After trying to pry it open he was convinced it was locked. What he needed was a . . . key.

Patting his hand on his hip he felt the key to the kingdom hiding inside his denim pocket. Consuming curiosity compelled him to wonder if once again the key that Farren had given him would open something else inside the Studios. After rising from the chair he exited the building, tossed his empty cup in the trash, and headed back toward Sunset Boulevard. He walked at a relaxed pace, looking around like any other guest. The kingdom key would be in his hand and ready. He would simply insert the key and see if the key to the kingdom would work its magic again.

As he made his way down Sunset Boulevard, relentlessly studying the people in front of him and looking for the unmistakable figure of Reginald, his confidence faded. Once more Hawk entered the front of the Carthay Circle Theatre. He casually picked up items and looked at them for a moment, gradually making his way toward the back exit of the shop. Deciding it was time for action he pulled the key from his pocket and held it at the ready. He would step out of the shop and insert the key into the citizen's keyhole. If it failed to open he would try the second lock. If both of these attempts failed, he would retreat and move back to a safe distance and form another strategy to get into the box.

Inside the doorway next to the call box he stood motionless. He realized he was holding his breath and beginning to sweat and he silently reminded himself to breathe. With one quick step he was outside of the shop and next to the box. He looked to see if anyone was standing on the corner of High-land and Sunset watching him. Seeing no unusual gawking he slid the key into the center lock mechanism on the telegraph box. Twisting it to the right he felt resistance and the key didn't move. Shifting it back to the left he felt the lock give, click, and open.

He swung the door open. Inside was a thin package wrapped in plain brown paper. It was no more than eight inches long and five inches wide. The thickness of the discovery measured less than an inch. Grasping the package in one hand he steadily swung the door shut and relocked it. He removed the key, slid it back into his pocket, and moved immediately toward Sunset Boulevard. Rounding the corner in front of the Carthay Circle Theatre he saw Reginald standing in the doorway of the entrance. Hawk cringed and kept moving as he again perceived the stare coming from behind the shades. Casually raising the wrapped package in a wave, Hawk spoke.

"Hello again, I decided to do some shopping this time."

Not allowing his motion to stall he pressed on in an attempt to disap-pear into the masses moving along the boulevard. He glanced over his left shoulder and didn't see Reginald following. Sliding across the street to the far sidewalk, Hawk glanced down at the wrapped package in his hand. The nondescript brown paper wrapping bore no markings except for one word written in black marker in bold capital letters: HAWK. Just past Mickey's of Hollywood there was a memorabilia souvenir stand with some benches around it. This would be a good place to sit alone and open the package.

"Dr. Hawkes," said a voice to Hawk's right.

Turning toward the voice he saw the sandy blond fellow he had met the night before. He must have emerged from Mickey's of Hollywood.

"Uh, hi there . . . Sam, isn't it?" Hawk knew his name but he didn't want to let him know that.

"Close. It's Sandy. Did you decide to continue your tour today?"

"Sort of. I saw some things last night that I decided to see again." He paused and then carefully lifted the package in such a way as not to reveal the name written on it. "And I wanted to pick up some stuff."

"You can't see as much when you don't have a private tour guide," Sandy stated flatly.

"That's the truth, but since I had the time I decided to try mingling with the masses." Hawk smiled and began to lean as if to move on.

"So what did you come back to see again?" Sandy inquired.

JEFF DIXON

"Just a couple of things," Hawk responded, caught off guard by the directness of Sandy's question.

"What things?" Sandy asked without expression.

Within Hawk a warning alarm blared, telling him to get away because something about this cast member was just not right. Kiran had suggested he was jealous. Hawk only knew he was odd and that was reason enough to get away from him.

"Things," Hawk said with intentional vagueness. "Later!" Hawk ended the conversation abruptly and walked away. He didn't look back but knew Sandy was staring.

Refocusing on the task at hand he spotted Sid Cahuenga's One-of-a-Kind shop. The souvenir stop was bulging with autographed photographs of movie stars, movie posters, props, and even wardrobes that had been collected from stars both living and those from the golden era of the past. Of all the shopping stops inside the Studios this one was usually not as busy and hectic as the others. A series of benches surrounded it and its nearness to the front gate allowed him to sit in relative privacy hidden by the steady stream of guests entering the park. Hawk took a seat and studied the package in his hand. Folded paper neatly closed with clear adhesive tape sealing the seams. Nothing distinctive about the wrapping. He went ahead and tore off the brown paper. Before the contents were completely revealed Hawk realized it was a DVD case. Clearing the wrapping he flipped it in his hand so he could see the title. The top of the case read Walt Disney Film Classic and the title of the movie, *Old Yeller*, was written below.

"*Old Yeller?*" Hawk murmured.

Examining the case he saw there was no cellophane shrink wrap over it. He opened the case to see what was inside and found an *Old Yeller* DVD. Taking the disc off the safety spindle he found nothing outstanding about it. Carefully he clicked it back in. Snapping the case shut he looked off into the distance, trying to figure out what he might have missed.

"Ha-ha!"

The talking huggable toy vibrated and a glimmer of anticipation surged back through the puzzled preacher. He needed all the help he could get to unravel and understand this adventure Farren had designed for him. He squeezed Pal Mickey's midsection and the unmistakable voice was quick to respond.

"Gosh, didn't you cry when Old Yeller died? Maybe we should drop by and see if the man of the house is doing okay. I sure hope he is. He might even be able to help us. Hawk, if you can think outside of the box, you'll find exactly what we need."

It was becoming less strange to hear this talking tour guide call him by name. But Hawk had no idea what Mickey was talking about this time. Again he felt a vibration on his hip but he was still holding the stuffed animal in his hand. Perplexed he looked at the mouse but then realized on the next vibration that it was his cell phone ringing in his right pants pocket. He rustled past car keys to find and fish it out. Opening it without looking at the caller ID, he answered.

"This is Grayson Hawkes."

"Well, hello, Grayson Hawkes," came the familiar voice of Juliette Keaton. "I got your message that you'd be out for a few days, but I have a question for you."

"Sure, fire."

"Does your being out of the office for a few days have anything to do with the visit we just had from the Orange County Sheriff's Department?"

"Well, sort of . . . in a roundabout way, I think."

"What's going on?" she said in her usual discerning manner.

"I'd rather not tell you just yet," he told her. "I will, when I've figured a few things out."

"Did you know that Farren Rales is missing?"

"Yes, I know."

"The sheriff's department wanted to know if anything unusual happened at our meeting with him."

"What did you tell them?" He was curious.

"Nothing happened out of the ordinary from my perspective. Anything odd happen from your perspective?"

"You were there just like I was."

"Hawk, are you in trouble?" She attempted to carve away the vagueness between them.

"I don't think I'm in trouble."

"Is Farren in trouble?" Juliette asked. Hawk recognized her tone, it was the way she spoke when she locked into her problem-solving mode. As a leader she had the gift of being able to logically work through crisis and come up with sound and spiritual answers.

"I don't know."

"What can I do to help?"

"I don't think you can."

"Okay, Hawk, tell me where you are. I'll see if I can round up Jonathan and Shep so we can hook up with you. Whatever's going on, we can solve it."

"I'm all right for now. Really, I am . . . but thanks." He was genuinely grateful for her offer to assemble their team to help.

"So you really aren't going to tell me where you are and what is up?" She sounded a tad frustrated.

"No, I'm really not going to tell you." He laughed, desiring to calm her down. "I'll be fine and I'll let you know what's going on when I get a few more things figured out."

"I'm going to find Jonathan and Shep and tell them," she insisted. "You are being strange, Farren is missing, the sheriff is asking questions, and you are in trouble but trying to do something on your own that is only going to end up causing more trouble in the end."

"You're making quite a few guesses there," he teased.

"Sure I am." Her tone softened some. "Don't be afraid to call."

He knew her well enough to know that her insights were usually accurate. At this point he would agree with her summary of the events unfolding in his life.

 *Day Five*
Afternoon

GRATEFUL FOR JULIETTE'S CONCERN but not appreciating the distraction, Hawk refocused on the latest hint he needed to figure out. How could he go and see if the man of the house was okay? Studying the DVD case again he read the description as explained on the back cover. It had been years since Hawk had actually watched the movie. As a child he'd cried when Old Yeller had to be shot. In the film the dog was killed by the boy who was forced to become the man of the house while the father was away from their frontier home. His father had instructed him to be the man while he was away, and that was an underlying plot to the heartwarming story.

Rales had told him time and time again to remember a story and pay attention to details. As he read the back of the case he saw the oldest son was named Travis. This was the young man forced into being the man of the house. Remembering more of the story line he was growing more confident he was on track. *Maybe we should drop by and see if the man of the house is doing okay. I sure hope he is.* Dropping by to see the man of the house at the Studios was what Hawk didn't understand. He situated his guide back on his hip and started to walk toward the hub of the theme park, trying to break down the perplexing clue into logical segments. It made sense to him that if he was going to drop by and see someone, he would need to know where the person lived. If that was accurate, then the problem was to figure out where people would live within the Studios. The Hollywood Hotel housed the Twilight Zone Tower of Terror. People stayed in hotels for certain, but in the story line developed by the Imagineers for the attraction, the hotel had been struck by lightning and was now deserted.

When the Studios were first opened, there was an area of the park known as Residential Street. This street featured homes that could be filmed from a variety of angles to create outdoor neighborhoods for any time period. Over time a new attraction had forced the removal of the homes, so that was not the answer either.

Thinking and walking propelled Hawk down Hollywood Boulevard to the place where his trip this day had begun. He reached the corner of Hollywood and Vine and turned to walk past the Hollywood & Vine diner toward Echo Lake. Momentarily pausing to get his bearings he noticed the flow of people coming out of the 50's Prime Time Café. Adjacent to the café he saw the open doorway to the Tune-In Lounge, where guests of the café waited while their tables were prepared. The Hollywood & Vine diner was connected to the Tune-In Lounge, and the facade next to the buildings held some staging he had never paid attention to.

Getting closer he read the words above a black metal gateway protecting a set of stairs. Echo Lake Apts, it read. Behind the gate the stairs climbed skyward to a second story that from the ground appeared to be apartments. Of course, no one lived in the Studios, but if they could, this would be a place where they might. Hawk stepped to the gate and firmly placed both hands on it. He gave it a push. It didn't budge, and he noticed it was locked. He leaned with his back against the gate and forced himself to keep trying to work the puzzle. The DVD in his hand must hold another clue. Reading it carefully for the second time he allowed himself to travel down memory lane to the days when he had seen the movie for the first time. The description unfurled the frames of the film across his mind. The man of the house had been a boy named Travis. Travis had been played by a young actor who starred in a number of Disney movies and other feature films. The actor's name was Tommy Kirk, listed in parentheses in the description of the film.

If Tommy Kirk was the man of the house in the film, he would be the person to drop by and check on. Would Tommy Kirk be a resident of the Echo Lake Apartments here at the Studios? As Hawk's gaze fell to his left, he saw a bank of apartment mailboxes. Even in the most unnoticeable details of any Disney Theme Park, nothing was left to chance or done by accident. The preacher vaguely remembered from listening to one of the Disney podcasts that these mailboxes featured the names of people who had either helped construct the Studios or were related to people who had been instrumental in the construction. He was sure at some point he had heard the names mentioned, probably on the same podcast. Even if someone with the name Kirk would have been involved, he knew the odds that his name would be Tommy was incalculable. He sighed. If Tommy Kirk was supposed to have an apartment here, then his name would be on a mailbox. The twelve golden mailboxes indicated there were twelve residents in this small apartment complex. Scanning each box Hawk read the name and then moved to the next. A bottom box on the far right revealed the answer. According to the box, the resident in apartment 105 was none other than T. Kirk. What were the chances that there really had been a person who had helped to created the park with the first initial T and the last name Kirk? If there had been—and he decided to research this bit of trivia later—then Farren Rales would have been shrewd enough to figure that out. Amused and impressed at his luck he looked back at the steps, wondering how to scale them to find apartment 105.

He closed his eyes and listened to the cartoon voice replay the clue in his head. *He might even be able to help us. Hawk, if you can think outside of the box you'll find exactly what we need.* Think outside the box and find exactly what we need. There was something here, so he needed to think outside the box to find it. He looked back to the mailbox with the name T. Kirk on the label. Hawk realized with lightning clarity that he was thinking outside the box. Outside the mailbox!

He hurried to study the box closer. Bending over he saw it was similar to other apartment mailboxes built into a wall or multibox rack. When the mail was delivered the postman would use a master key to open the box and put the mail inside. Each resident would have a private key to his or her own individual box. Looking at the details of the golden box he knew that like most things at the Studios this had been intentionally aged and left for guests to see if they slowed down long enough to explore. Usually in a film set there wouldn't really be a mailbox behind the door. Still, the clue was clear and this could be more than just a decoration. Hawk needed to get in the mailbox. That particular task would require a key, and of course, Hawk had a key in his pocket. It wasn't the usual mailbox key, but up to this point it had opened everything he needed to open, so he figured it was time to try it again.

Removing the key, he looked to see if anyone was watching him. A quick scan of the crowd revealed nothing untoward.

The lock appeared rusted and unusable. Hawk felt confident that this was a visual trick created by Disney designers. He placed the key into the slot and pushed. There was some resistance and then the key slid easily into the lock. With a quick turn of the key, the lock and the mailbox door opened. Hawk's pulse quickened. He saw something folded inside. Reaching in and grabbing it, he withdrew his discovery and then closed and relocked the door. He unfolded the paper. It was a map of the Walt Disney Hollywood Studios. The map was a guest map that could be picked up by any guest upon entering the park.

Grayson Hawkes's focus on getting into the box had been so intent that he didn't scan the crowds very closely. If he had, he would have seen someone sitting inside the Hollywood & Vine diner looking out the window watching his every move. The observer had slid into the seat near the window after Hawkes had walked to the gate of the Echo Lake Apartments. The watcher had observed him as he leaned against the gate, as he looked at the golden boxes, and as he had turned his back to them and studied the box closely. The onlooker continued to watch him as he pulled a key from his pocket and prepared to insert it into the lock of the mailbox.

Inside Hollywood & Vine the spectator saw the preacher examine a theme park map. Trying to read the map and the face of the pastor through the window, the viewer could not tell whether the discovery meant anything to Hawkes. Abruptly Dr. Hawkes folded the map and placed it inside the DVD case he held in his hand. He walked away, never pausing to look toward the window where the watcher had been able to observe his most recent movements.

 *Day Five*
Late Afternoon

RUSHING ACROSS THE PARK, Hawk headed toward the Streets of America. The map in the mailbox was just a normal theme park map. Initially he hadn't noticed anything unique about it. Then he saw it, in the upper left-hand corner: a black star drawn by hand in black ink, on top of a small plane pictured on the map. Hawk was familiar enough with the contents of the park to know the plane and its location. He quickened his pace into something faster than a jog. Hearing his own breathing he reviewed what he knew about the airplane.

It was the small plane that had belonged to Walt Disney himself. This was the plane that Walt had flown in as he first surveyed the property he would purchase in Florida. Walt had been a man who enjoyed flying and had owned a number of planes. If Hawk remembered correctly, this was the last one he had purchased and was known affectionately as Mickey Mouse One.

Arriving at the back of the park he rushed toward the entrance of the Backlot Tour. Hawk knew the plane could be seen by passengers riding on the tour, and that was the way he hoped to catch a glimpse of it now—if he got there on time. But a barricade affirmed what he had dreaded. The attraction was closed for the day.

"Excuse me, sir, did you want to take the Backlot Tour?" Hawk looked over the barricade into the face of a smiling cast member. The man continued, "You still have time to catch the tram, but you've missed our effects tank demonstration. Follow me and I'll walk you over to the prop warehouse where you can catch the ride. But you'll have to hurry."

Hawk, out of breath, managed a nod as the cast member moved the barricade and motioned for him to follow. As Hawk walked behind him, the cast member briskly navigated past the huge water tank, down the ramps, and through a warehouse. Just as they emerged from the automatic double doors, Hawk saw the last passenger vehicle of the bright red and yellow tram was about to close. With a yell the cast member stopped the securing of the side of the vehicle. Hawk jumped aboard and slid across the backseat. He profusely thanked the cast member, and in less than a minute the tour was underway.

Time and expansion of the theme park had forced the tour to constantly change and not always for the better. Years earlier the Backlot Tour was a true behind-the-scenes look at what was happening around the studios. It lined up perfectly with the Walt Disney philosophy. The current attraction lacked the fun of the earlier editions. As the vehicle snaked along the roadway it drew closer to the Lights, Motor, Action! Extreme Stunt Show. The stunt show was an expansion that had radically changed the layout of the tour. This huge attraction needed a large stadium to house the crowds watching the unbelievable stunts. Stadium construction had decimated all of Residential Street and left the tour much shorter than before.

The tram crawled behind the stadium and Hawk saw the plane tucked behind the corner of the massive steel structure. Walt's plane had been moved here and placed on display for the Backlot Tour. The tram was on track to an area known as Catastrophe Canyon, a special-effects experience that unfolded around the vehicle. While the tram was shaken about, the riders could experience a carefully choreographed catastrophe from the safety of their passenger compartments. Hawk had been inside the canyon more times than he could remember. As the tram headed toward the canyon he was facing backward, turned around, looking back at the plane.

"Ha-ha!"

The tour guide was continuing her dialogue and the tram was rolling into its date with simulated destruction as Hawk grabbed the shaking mouse and held it up to his ear.

"Time just flies when you're having fun! Get it? Flies? See the airplane? Hee-hee. I can't believe Mr. Disney named this plane after me! He sure did spend a lot of time on this plane. We might have to call it like he did later, pal."

Hawk barely noticed the wall of water rushing toward the ride vehicle. While the passengers on board laughed and shrieked at the simulated destruction happening around them, Hawk was trying to figure out how he was supposed to call the plane like Walt did. Replacing his stuffed companion on his waist he readied himself to catch another look at the plane on the return trip. In a matter of moments the tram was passing the plane again. The empty back bench of the vehicle allowed Hawk to slide all the way across it to get as close as possible to see the airplane. This time as the tour passed the plane, the tour guide gave the guests some information.

"The plane we are passing is a Grumman G-159 multi-engine prop plane built in 1963. Walt Disney purchased this plane and it was the one he used to fly over the undeveloped property here in Florida that became Walt Disney World. This plane was also used by Disney executives until it was decommissioned in the 1980s and retired to the Disney Hollywood Studios."

The glistening white plane, striped in two-toned blue with gold highlights, looked like it would still fly today. The Disneyland and Disney World logos adorned the sides, and Mickey Mouse himself was on the tail along with the registration number of the plane. N234MM was clearly visible. If Hawk correctly understood the way the numbering worked, the N designated it as an aircraft. The numerals were numbers that Walt had chosen along with the MM, which stood for Mickey Mouse. As Disney, who clearly had liked to fly, retired one plane and bought another, he would assign it the same number. This number was the only one on the plane. The N234MM had to be important for something. What that something was, he did not have any idea. The journey through the park had been like a scavenger hunt. But his little helper had told him they would find *exactly what we need*. N234MM was what he'd found. It must be what they would need.

The tour came to an end and the passengers disembarked. Collectively they moved through the American Film Institute Showcase. Hawk glanced down at his watch; it read 6:00. The face of the watch jolted his brain with the promise of a potential appointment. In the excursions throughout the afternoon he had nearly forgotten he was supposed to meet Kiran at 7:00. She had been particularly pointed in her determination not to keep their date. Yet he had made the suggestion that they still meet. If he didn't show up it was a guarantee that she would. Life just seemed to work that way for Hawk.

The flowing tide of humanity moved him to the front gate without incident. Passing Mickey's of Hollywood as he moved down Hollywood Boulevard, he stole a glance through an open doorway into the shop. Inside, Sandy was helping a guest and looked up toward him as if on cue. The cast member's eyes bore into him with a disconcerting intensity. Hawk wished he hadn't looked into the store.

In order to make it back to Celebration in time he was going to have to hustle. Stepping into the shortest line to move through the exit turnstile he waited for the two people in front of him to push their way through.

"Ha-ha!"

He unclipped the mouse as he moved through the exit and squeezed its midsection gently.

"Hey, Hawk! Wouldn't it be swell if we visited the Magic Kingdom? I can hardly wait to get there . . . oh boy!"

There was no way Hawk could go the Magic Kingdom now. He was in a hurry to meet Kiran. Deciding to bypass the courtesy transportation tram, he jogged along the same path out of the park he had traveled with Kiran the night before. Freeing Pal Mickey from his waist, the preacher tossed the stuffed animal in the trunk before sliding into his car. Glancing again at his watch he knew he would be cutting it close but was confident he would make it. He hoped she would have thought about the events of last night and feel better about them today. If nothing else he wished that her curiosity to know more might win out over her doubts about him and get her back to Front Street.

 *Day Five*
Evening 7:00 p.m.

STANDING ALL ALONE on Front Street, trying to look nonchalant, Hawk waited for Kiran. The streets of Celebration were crowded with pedestrians shopping, finding places to eat, and enjoying the sights and sounds of this unique town. On any given evening the blending of both locals and tourists combined to create a magical mixture of humanity fleshing out the community in an environment igniting the nostalgia of yesterday against the hopefulness of the future.

Fifteen minutes passed, then thirty, and Hawk knew she was not coming. Taking in a deep breath and exhaling loudly he bowed his head and resigned himself to having lost the opportunity to get to know her. He rationalized that perhaps it was for the best. Now he could devote his attention to this kingdom key quest. Still, he could not quite so easily shake his disappointment. The preacher understood how fickle feelings could be. Too many people allowed their feelings to dictate their decisions in life. As a God follower he knew decisions were to be based on faith and the guidelines for life that God gives. Life always worked better that way. This was once again a chance for him to put his faith into action and allow it to win out over his feelings. Disappointment unchecked would lead to wallowing in self-pity. For Grayson Hawkes life was too short and too important to wallow.

Walking down Front Street he prayed, trying to sort through the things in his mind and heart. His destination was the coffee shop at the end of the street. One of his standing mottos for life was "Problems dissolve when you mix 99 percent prayer with 1 percent coffee." The clarity of prayer for Hawk was more than sufficient, of course, but the clarity of caffeine was a nice way to top it off.

Minutes later he emerged with a no-frills lightly creamed and sugared java. Aiming himself back toward his car, he planned on fulfilling the decision he had made waiting in line. He was going to the Magic Kingdom. His trusted plush comrade now locked snugly in his trunk said that was to be the next stop. During the afternoon something had happened. While the challenge had been laid before him by his friend, he had accepted it, and through the trek in the theme park earlier the quest was now his own. He would figure out what Farren was trying to tell him.

Popping open the trunk he shuffled the stuff he had hidden Pal Mickey under and pulled him out. As he closed the compartment he became aware of a car slowing behind him. Turning, he saw Jonathan rolling down his window and waving at him. He stepped toward the black automobile and leaned in to chat.

"Just coming back from getting groceries," Jonathan said.

Hawk waited, knowing something else was coming.

"I had an interesting call from Juliette this afternoon."

"You did?"

"Somehow I think you knew that." Jonathan smiled assuredly.

The truth was they all worked so well together they could almost anticipate what the other would do and even at times say. This was one of their strengths as a staff and at times a weakness, since they all were more predictable than they wanted to admit.

"Jonathan, everything is all right. I'm just involved in a little personal research project that's going to keep me busy for a few days."

"Do you need any help?"

"Not right now, maybe later, I'll let you know."

"Talked to the sheriff's department yet?"

"No, but I hear they're looking for Farren."

"Hawk, have you heard from Farren?" Jonathan sounded concerned.

"No. I wish I had." Hawk wanted to reassure Jonathan, but his concern for Farren was still growing as well. "I've tried to call him and even dropped by his house."

"Your research project have anything to do with him?" Jonathan probed.

"Perhaps." Hawk smiled. "It's a mystery more than anything else. It was something Farren was trying to tell me. Then he disappeared. I'm hoping if I can figure out what he was trying to say, then maybe . . ."

"Let me—let us help, Hawk," he said.

Hawk considered the offer. Over the years the staff had navigated crisis in the church, personal struggles, and managed to maintain their friendship, trust, and belief in one another.

"Tell you what, Jon, you're right. You guys have been my family since . . ." Hawk stopped himself from traveling down the trail laced with those memories. "I'd like you to know what's going on. See if you can get everyone together in the office first thing in the morning."

"Great, eight o'clock at the office!" Jonathan looked genuinely pleased Hawk had agreed.

"See you then." Hawk straightened up and stepped away from the car. Then as an afterthought he leaned back toward the car, placing his hand on the window.

"Let's meet at the Floridian." Hawk was referring to the Grand Floridian, a Magic Kingdom Resort.

"Where?"

"On the beach."

"The beach?" Jonathan's forehead creased.

"The beach." Hawk wanted somewhere they could talk in private, and away from the office just in case the sheriff's department dropped by. He wanted more information before he talked to them and wanted to keep his and Farren's late-night meeting at Gamble Place quiet for a day longer if possible.

"In the morning. Be safe!" Jonathan drove away and Hawk stood alone holding the stuffed animal in his hand. He turned the cute little face toward his and spoke aloud to it.

"Well, Mick, you wanted to go to the Magic Kingdom. Let's go!"

 *Day Five*
Evening

NIGHTTIME IN THE MAGIC KINGDOM is truly magical. The lights of Main Street USA, the twinkle lights illuminating the trees, the music, and sounds create an atmosphere that, once a person has been immersed in it, will never be forgotten. The entrance to the Magic Kingdom was carefully constructed and laid out to maximize the experience of each guest. A minimal crowd was entering at this time of the evening. The early morning rush had disappeared long ago and the mid-afternoon arrivers were all inside having fun. Hawk felt the familiar vibration on his hip as Pal Mickey reset himself as they entered the Kingdom. The motion was accompanied by the high-pitched "Ha-ha!"

Traveling through the tunnel that led into Town Square he listened to the mouse deliver the next message.

"Ooookay now, we're really getting somewhere, pal! We have a mountain to climb. I might be a little scared, but together we can scale any summit."

Hawk wedged his way between the people stacked side by side along Main Street USA anticipating the coming parade.

Carried along in the masses he tried to focus on the message from the mouse. There was the famous mountain range that formed the Magic Kingdom landscape. Space Mountain in Tomorrowland was the high-speed roller coaster ride through space. Big Thunder Mountain Railroad was the mine train that raced through caverns, mines, and an old western outpost town. Next to this mountain was Splash Mountain, a water ride experience that featured an impressive blend of animatronics with a huge plummet at the end of the ride. Hawk was a huge fan of all three rides and had been on them many times. *We have a mountain to climb.* Hawk decided to head toward Space Mountain first since the parade crowd would be strung along the streets through Frontierland. Tomorrowland was free of the parade crowds. It made sense this would be a better place to explore. Crossing the bridge leading into Tomorrowland he saw the spinning Astro Orbiter looming in front of him. This was the visual weenie that Imagineers built into the design of the parks to entice guests to move deeper into a themed area. The ride was similar to other spinning rides in the Kingdom, but this one was built on a platform three stories in the air. The added height gave the riders an amazing view of the park, especially at night. Drawing closer to it he allowed himself to drift left toward the gleaming metallic mountain. Hawk found himself in a slightly larger crowd of people who were converging to get in line for Space Mountain. The posted wait time for the ride was forty-five minutes, not surprising considering the crowds in the park this evening. Since the ride's opening it had remained one of the more popular attractions in the park. People loved the sensation of zipping through the blackness of space on the roller coaster adventure.

Suddenly Hawk felt a sensation of his own that caught him off guard. Studying the massive mountain he noticed a tug and pressure on his hip. Knowing the feeling to be different than the now-familiar vibration of Pal Mickey, he looked toward the plush animal. In the same instant he became aware of someone standing incredibly close to him, invading his personal space, and actually turning him around. This stranger had his hands on the stuffed animal and was attempting to tear it off the preacher's waist. The Velcro reinforcement was making the mouse snatch more difficult, but the stranger tugged so hard that he spun Hawk's body around. Hawk tried to pry the stranger's hands off the miniature tour guide. The Velcro gave way with a tearing sound.

The mouse was now in the grasp of the thief.

Hawk raised his eyes to see the larcenist: young, probably in his early twenties. Shaved head and pierced nostril was all the preacher saw as the young man darted away from him.

Without hesitation Hawk gave pursuit.

The smooth-domed, pierced criminal turned his head and saw he was being pursued. Running past the *Tomorrowland Arcade* the thief cut behind it. Hawk recognized the long trail of concrete that allowed guests a walk behind the *Tomorrowland Indy Speedway*. This seldom-used pathway lay inside the railroad tracks between the high-tech arcade and Fantasyland, on the far eastern border of the park.

Once again as they raced down the long pathway the shaved head turned and the eyes widened as though stunned to see the owner of the animal following closely. Hawk was gaining ground on the hairless dome bobbing in front of him.

The thief emerged from the path on a full sprint through the expanded Fantasyland experience. Emerging into the Dumbo Circus area and racing through Pixie Hollow, he stumbled as he tried to avoid parents and children moving out of the play area. His erratic trajectory caught the gaze of a Disney security guard. Stepping out in front of the running young man, the guard motioned for him to slow down. The young man sidestepped the guard, never breaking stride, and continued his flight away from his pursuer. The guard snapped a radio off of his belt and raised it to his mouth. Hawk, approaching fast, caught a barked alert. As the final words describing the young man who had nearly run him over cleared the guard's mouth, Hawk passed him at an all-out sprint. He heard the guard break into a run behind him as he called again on the security channel for help.

Cutting behind the Mad Tea Party, the pierced man broke into the Aurora and Winnie the Pooh area of the park. Hawk saw him hesitate behind the spinning tea cups, deciding which way to go next. The hesitation allowed the pastor to gain an additional couple of strides. Hawk feared his advantage in speed wouldn't be enough because the younger man would have better endurance. The sight of the stuffed Mickey in the thief's hand as he headed past the Cinderella attraction toward the castle wall doggedly inspired Hawk. He could not let him get away.

As the thief approached the Little Mermaid area, another guard stepped forward from behind a sugary-scented display of cotton candy, gesturing wildly in an attempt to get his attention.

The thief looked back over his shoulder at Hawk. Panic twisted his features. The uniformed guard stepped in front of him. Hawk saw the crash unfolding. At the last possible moment, perhaps by instinct alone, the young man lowered his shoulder and drove it into the security guard's chest. The guard was lifted off of his feet by the force of the blow and fell to the ground on his back. The impact had broken the momentum of the criminal and he stumbled toward his right trying to maintain his balance. Hawk now knew he would catch the young man. Closing in on the fleeing villain Hawk gobbled up the distance between them. The fleeing young man glanced back one more time and that last look was his undoing. Racing toward Cinderella's Golden Carousel Hawk got close enough to make contact.

Getting both hands in front of him the preacher shoved the young man forward. The speed and momentum caused the man to lose balance and stumble wildly out of control.

Hawk was now on top of the villain. Reaching out again the pastor grabbed the fleeing thief and their velocity carried them both thundering into the iron rail surrounding the carousel. Sheer speed and power lifted both men off of their feet over the rail, across the rows of shrubbery, and slammed them down onto the concrete on the other side. Bouncing on the unforgiving surface, the thief hit first with Hawk's full weight crushing down on top of him. The preacher regained his iron-fisted grasp of the pierced pilferer. Rolling dangerously close to the twirling carousel the thief looked up into the face of Hawk and screamed.

"Are you insane? Let me go!"

"You stole my Pal Mickey!"

"Take it—you're crazy!"

Hawk reached over and rolled away from the thief. As he did he snatched his stuffed prize out of the young man's hand.

Crawling away from the tackled thief, he gasped for air on all fours. Now that he had stopped so abruptly he felt the wave of exhaustion ripple through him as his lungs desperately tried to clutch every air molecule his panting would deliver. The bitter taste of leaves played across his tastebuds as he spit out the landscaping he collected when he flew across the shrubbery. A swarm of blue-shirted security guards and cast members rushed the two fallen men. Hawk felt someone grab him by the shirt and shove him back toward the ground. Turning his head he saw the thief had multiple people keeping him in place as well.

"Look, this guy stole my souvenir," Hawk protested, "I was just trying to get it back!"

"Just stay on the ground!" the security guard barked.

Hawk really didn't mind, it gave him a chance to catch his breath. More people arrived and momentarily two men helped to hoist Hawk to his feet and marched him away from the carousel. The tourists stared as both Hawk and the thief were led away. Again Hawk looked toward the shaved head of the man he had chased. He was bleeding from cuts to his face likely collected as he spiraled over the railing with Hawk minutes ago.

He looked back to the security guard that had been blasted by the momentum of the thief near the ride and saw the emergency medical personnel attending to him. The collision had been brutal and Hawk could image how it must have hurt. While the men were leading him away he gently placed the stuffed Mickey in his hand back onto his hip. Smiling at his success he suddenly felt his adrenaline begin to subside replaced by pain.

"Easy guys," Hawk pleaded as they led him across Fantasyland, past Snow White's Scary Adventures, through an unmarked door into a hallway.

The hallway was offstage and away from the eyesight of guests. Hawk and his escorts were in the hallway before the thief and his entourage followed. Behind him he heard the thief whine.

"I didn't do anything. That insane guy was just chasing me."

"Quiet!" The security guard was not yet ready to hear their story.

Hawk was led into a small room off the hallway. He was a bit surprised that the thief was not brought in as well but was thankful for the chance to sit down. Still breathing hard, he noticed for the first time that his tumble over the railing had skinned him up as well. Shirt torn off of one shoulder, scrape bleeding on exposed skin, and rash marks from the slide over the asphalt were growing more painful as he began to regain his composure and the intensity of the chase began to wane.

Over the next few minutes Hawk was brought a bottled water as three men, two in security uniforms and one wearing a clean white shirt and tie, listened to his story. He verbally retraced the chase and the eventual tackle across the railing at the carousel multiple times as the men listened and took notes. Hawk assumed there was a completely different story being told in another room somewhere in the behind the scenes hallways of Fantasyland. While he talked and answered their questions, the man in the shirt and tie was frequently on his radio and cell phone. Occasionally he would ask for clarification of something Hawk had said, and then he was back on his phone engaged in conversation with some unseen party who was trying to sort out the events of the evening.

An hour and a half later there were two empty water bottles on the table and Hawk had been bandaged by medical attendants, who then left. Only one security guard remained in the room with him as the last bandage was placed on his shoulder. The guard went to the door and ordered Hawk to remain in the room. The door closed behind him.

Hawk was now alone. Sliding in his chair he leaned his head back and closed his eyes. His body hurt. Completely drained and glad for the moment to rest, he wondered if the young thief had known the uniqueness of what he had tried to steal or whether it was just a random disastrous choice.

 *Day Five*
Night

TIME PASSED ACHINGLY SLOWLY in the cramped room. The door-knob turned and the door opened. Hawk sat leaning back in the chair, eyes still closed.

"I knew it." Kiran's voice unexpectedly filled his ears. "And by the way, you look terrible."

Hawk's eyes sprang open. Blinking away his exhaustion, he focused on her attractive frame standing across the room from him. He kept silent and watched as her eyes explored him. Kiran was gorgeous in Hawk's opinion, and he allowed that to pleasantly distract him. As his mind cleared, the distraction melted and he remembered his evening had started with waiting for her to meet him on Front Street.

"What are you doing here?" Hawk asked, surprised to see her.

"I wanted to see if it was really you."

"Really me?"

"I was on Main Street when I heard on the radio that there was one man chasing another through Fantasyland. They were fleeing security, which immediately put the whole park on alert. The chase continued with one of our security people getting run over, and then ended as both men go over the rail into the carousel. Then I hear that the reason for the chase is because a Pal Mickey had been stolen." She hesitated as though carefully choosing her words. "I thought to myself that must be someone who really doesn't want to lose his Mickey Mouse. I knew it had to be you."

Hawk stared at her, revealing no emotion. The silence hung between them until she broke it.

"Are you all right?"

"I'm fine. I just look terrible." he allowed a slight smile to sneak across his face before chasing it away. "What are you going to do with me?"

"I assume you're asking what Disney Security intends to do with you."

Hawk nodded in affirmation. Kiran stared at him for a moment. She looked as if she were getting ready to say something more but decided against it. Turning on her heel she opened the door and left. Hawk twisted his neck side to side feeling the tightness that would only get worse as the night went on. Eventually, the door reopened and Kiran returned, accompanied by the security man wearing the tie. His name tag read Kyle. Kyle sat down opposite Hawk.

"Dr. Hawkes, it appears that your story is accurate. The perpetrator has admitted to stealing your merchandise in Tomorrowland," he stated flatly. He glanced down at a sheet of paper he held in his hand. "Since you have gotten your merchandise back, on our end, this matter as it concerns you is closed. The sheriff's department is currently dealing with the thief since he recklessly assaulted one of our security people by running him over. Do you have any intention of filing a report with the authorities?"

"No," Hawk dryly responded. "I don't feel the need to do that."

"I suppose I should thank you for tackling the perpetrator."

"No thanks are necessary."

"Let me finish, Dr. Hawkes," Kyle continued. "I said I should thank you, but I won't. Your behavior and pursuit in the park put our guests and my staff at risk. Next time inform a cast member and let us handle it."

"Got it. I hope there is no next time."

"I trust there won't be." Kyle stood and motioned toward Kiran. "I understand you and Kiran are acquainted. She is going to escort you out of the park. I would ask that you follow her directions and she will make sure you get back to the gate."

Kyle turned and nodded at Kiran, then opened the door to leave. Pausing in the doorway he turned back toward Hawk with a nod and walked down the hall, leaving the doorway open.

"Are you ready?" Kiran asked.

Hawk straightened his legs under him and got to his feet. He wobbled as he stood. The unsteadiness surprised him and he placed his hands on the table to stabilize himself. The momentary pause gave him back his bearings and he stepped toward the door and walked past Kiran into the hallway. She motioned in the direction he had entered earlier. Moving down the corridor he pushed the door open and stepped back out into Fantasyland. The streets were empty, and although everything was lit up just as it was earlier, there were no people present. Hawk looked at his watch. The face was shattered.

"It's late and the park is closed," Kiran said.

She grabbed his arm just above the elbow with a firm grip. It wasn't an expression of affection as much as it was a practical attempt to be helpful. He was still shakier than he had anticipated; of course, sprinting as far as he had, without stretching, and minus the proper conditioning, was a formula for certain muscle fatigue.

"Are you sure you're okay?"

"Yeah, but I'm gonna be sore tomorrow." He grinned.

They moved silently toward the back of Cinderella Castle and walked through it. Normally Hawk would have taken the time to enjoy the colorful mosaics depicting scenes from the movie. Coming out of the castle they overlooked the length of Main Street USA all the way down to the back of the Train Station. Already the maintenance cast were washing down the streets, painters were scraping and repainting poles along the sidewalks, and there was an organized busyness happening all around them. Yet as they walked no one seemed to notice them, although Hawk was sure they were an unlikely sight.

His shirt was ripped and hanging open across his chest. His right shoulder was completely exposed, revealing the bandage covering his scrapes. The same arm of the shirt was in shreds and Hawk was sure there was more damage he hadn't seen yet. Kiran, on the other hand, was dressed impeccably in a tailored skirt, blouse, and jacket. With her radio on her hip she looked like she was escorting a transient out of the Magic Kingdom, but no one seemed to notice. Although sore, the further they walked, the steadier he grew. Apparently sensing this change she released her grip on his arm.

"What were you doing here, Hawk?"

"What does anyone do at Disney World?"

"You've already proven you don't do what other people do at Disney World. Last night you broke into an attraction after the Studios was closed. Tonight you endangered guests and cast members chasing someone who stole a stuffed animal you found in the attraction you broke into the night before. Now here we are, with me escorting you out of another theme park after it has closed." Her summary did put the situation into a different perspective. "I would venture to say that over the last two days no one has ever done what you have at Disney World."

Her face was expressionless except for her penetrating eyes staring into his, waiting for a response. She stopped and they stood in front of the *Partners* statue. Hawk continued for an extra couple of steps before he realized she had no intention of going any further without an answer.

"You know you are supposed to escort me out of the park?"

"You also were told to follow my instructions. So I am instructing you to tell me what you were doing in the park." She still did not move.

"Come on, Kiran. You know what I was doing." He walked back to where she was standing.

"No, I honestly don't know what you are doing. Last night you were going to leave whatever you were trying to do alone. Obviously you're up to something." Irritation crept back into her voice.

"You told me to leave it alone," Hawk corrected her. "I never said I would."

"So what exactly are you doing?"

"I've figured out a few more things since last night." He decided he was going to be a little slower to tell her as much as he had the night before. "I discovered that this is some sort of puzzle or scavenger hunt."

"Stop, let me get this straight. Farren Rales, the most recognized Imagineer in the Walt Disney Company, gives you a key that is the first clue of a scavenger hunt?"

"Yes."

"Yes? Just yes? So you think that gives you license to ramble around Disney property creating mayhem in your wake?" Kiran crossed her arms.

"I don't think I have license to do anything." Hawk turned and began to walk back toward Main Street. "But I am going to solve the puzzle."

Kiran trotted after him. "What did you just say?"

"I said I'm going to solve the puzzle."

"And just what do you think you're going to find?"

"I won't know that until I solve it."

"Have you found something else?"

"For someone who told me to let it go and that there was nothing to figure out, you sure do ask a lot of questions," he said.

His statement caused her to be at a loss for words as they continued to walk. As they passed the Plaza Ice Cream Parlor, a street cleaner was washing down the street. They waited for him to finish the area he was working on. Looking up and seeing them, he nodded and turned the pressurized nozzle in the other direction so they could pass unsplashed.

"So you really chased down the guy who stole your Pal Mickey from Tomorrowland to Fantasyland in an all-out sprint?" Kiran changed the subject.

"That's another question," Hawk pointed out. "But yes, I did."

"He was significantly younger than you."

"And significantly slower."

"Apparently." A slight smile laced her lips for the first time during their conversation. "I'm impressed."

"You know, for a minute I was impressed with myself as well," he said with a smirk. "Then I got up after sitting in the holding room in Fantasyland. I can barely move; my impressiveness is the real fantasy."

His statement drew a soft laugh. Hawk smiled back at her. They continued their walk down Main Street in an awkward silence, passing the Market House on their left.

"Ha-ha!"

The sound was followed by the distinctive vibration as the stuffed hip hugger sprang to life. Hawk stopped in his tracks, as did Kiran. She looked down to the mouse at his side.

Hesitantly Hawk unfastened Mickey from his side and held him out between them. Kiran studied the little mouse intently as the pastor applied pressure to his middle.

"You are doing great, pal . . . Now remember to keep your head up, Hawk. But let's be frank, we have to do something he never did . . . please don't drop me! That would be awful!"

"The stuffed animal called you by name again," Kiran said with the same expression she had shown the night before.

"I've kind of gotten used to it."

"Mickey talks to you a lot . . . by name?"

"Not always by name. He calls me pal a lot." He realized how silly that sounded.

"But it has been saying things . . . recorded just for you?"

"Uh-huh. Earlier tonight he said, 'We have a mountain to climb . . . and together we can scale any summit,' and now this." His mental gears were grinding. "I need to keep my head up."

Hawk was standing in the middle of Main Street looking up. He looked at lights, buildings, and windows. If there was something to see, he didn't want to miss it. A few minutes ago he was content to leave the park and go home; now he was trying to figure out the latest nugget of information and the one from earlier tonight. Kiran shook off her amazement at the personalized greeting from the mouse and was looking upward as well. Catching Hawk's eye she pointed skyward. He moved next to her, following the imaginary line stretched out from the end of her fingertip.

"What?" His eyes were darting across the third story of the building in front of them.

"Look at the window," she said softly.

The highest window in the merchandise shop was in the center of the building on the corner. It was the custom for the windows along Main Street buildings to contain tributes to the creators of the theme park. This was considered by cast members to be one of the highest honors an individual could ever be given within the company. You could read them like movie credits that rolled from the Train Station and down Main Street, USA. A quick look to either side gave Hawk the reason to conclude that the window they were looking at was the highest window to be found on the street. He read the window silently.

Seven Summits
Expeditions
Frank G. Wells
President
"For those who want to do it all."

"We have a mountain to climb . . . and together we can scale any summit." Hawk repeated the message from earlier. "That has to be it, Seven Summits Expeditions. But what does it mean?"

"Remember what we just heard?"

"Uh . . . 'Let's be frank, we have to do something he never did . . . please don't drop me.'"

They both performed mental gymnastics trying to understand the hidden meaning in the window. Frank Wells was the former president and chief operating officer of the company. He was loved and respected throughout the organization. His reputation as an adventurer who loved the thrill of mountain climbing and exploring had made him even more endearing to all who knew him. Tragically he had lost his life in a helicopter crash. The sense of loss had been overwhelming, and in the loss people realized how much heart and soul he'd brought to the company. Hawk knew who Wells was and some of the things that had been written about him. Still, he did not completely understand the secret message the window hid, but he was sure they had found the right window.

"Kiran, what does the window mean?" Hawk hoped she would be able to explain it.

"The window is one of the highest on Main Street, USA. It was an honor that the company wanted Wells to have for his leadership during the resurgence of the company after some of the rougher years. The seven summit reference is one that is familiar to mountain climbers. There are supposedly seven summits that any real mountain climbers will want to scale in their lifetime. Hence the name, Seven Summit Expeditions."

"Did Frank Wells climb all seven?" Hawk wondered.

"No, he didn't. He only managed to climb six of the seven. He never successfully scaled the seventh."

"Let's be frank . . . we have to do something he never did," he once again repeated the message. "Which mountain did he fail to climb?"

"Everest. He never was able to scale Mount Everest."

Instantly Hawk had the next move he was supposed to make.

Kiran studied his face. "What? What is it? You figured something out."

"We have a *mountain to climb, we can scale any summit* . . . the window clearly indicates seven summits or mountains. The other clue says we have to be *frank*—the reference has to be Frank Wells . . . and *do something he never did*—you just said it. He never climbed Mount Everest."

"So you have to climb Mount Everest?"

"No, of course not." He smiled. "I'm going to climb Expedition Everest!"

He turned and moved off quickly toward the exit to the park, listening for a sign the implication had hit Kiran. Moments later he heard her footsteps chasing him down Main Street, USA, and she fell in lockstep with him.

"You are out of your mind!" she whispered in his ear.

 *Day Five*
Late Night

EXPEDITION EVEREST HAD BEEN a monstrous challenge for the Imagineers to create. They had to figure out a way to bring the world's largest mountain to the state of Florida. Inside of the mountain, which was named Forbidden Mountain, they wove a marvelous maze of roller coaster track. The track would enable guests to ride aboard a steam train in, out, up, and down the mountain. Before the thrilling experience ends there is an up-close-and-personal encounter with one of the largest, fastest-moving robotic creatures in history. A twenty-five-foot-tall, 20,000 pound yeti waits to take a swipe at the riders in an attempt to protect the Forbidden Mountain. The entire attraction plays like a mini-movie for the guests.

Expedition Everest embodied all the elements of storytelling that Farren Rales had been emphasizing to Grayson Hawkes over and over again. As Hawk raced toward Disney's Animal Kingdom, where the Forbidden Mountain was located, he wasn't thinking about the details of the attraction; instead his mind was trying to design a plan for getting a closer look at the mountain. Sitting next to him in his car, Kiran was trying to derail or at least slow down the steam train of direction that Hawk was intent on riding.

She had followed him back to his car after they exited the Main Gate of the Magic Kingdom. Their walk beneath the monorail line along the red-bricked path was laced with short bursts of conversation as Kiran peppered him with questions about what he was planning. Arriving at his car, he popped open the trunk and stripped off his shirt. Throwing the remains of the shredded shirt into the vehicle, he pulled on a lightweight jacket, shoved the sleeves up to his elbows, and climbed into his car. Uninvited, Kiran had jumped into the passenger side and now they barreled together past the front of the Ticket and Transportation Center, leaving the Magic Kingdom area.

"Just slow down and think about this for a minute," she implored.

"I didn't ask you to come along," he reminded her as he drove along the roadways connecting the Walt Disney World Resort.

"I know that, Hawk." As they careened around a corner, she grabbed for the dashboard. "But I can't keep getting you out of trouble. What you're trying to do is—is—"

"Crazy?"

"I guess . . . a little."

"What do you mean a little? It is crazy on steroids!"

"Okay, you're right," she admitted. "However, you aren't crazy."

"I'm not?"

"No, you're passionate and believe you have to do what you are doing. You are on a quest. That's what scares me, because you aren't going to stop and let this thing go until—"

"Something bad happens," he finished.

"Right."

He braked and followed the signs that compelled visitors to come closer to the theme park.

"So what's your plan?" Kiran inquired.

"I told you." A smile crossed his face. "I am going to climb Expedition Everest."

"How?"

"Well, since you've decided to come with me, I'm going to let you help."

"I can't help you."

"Sure you can, you're my ticket into the park after hours."

Hawk drove toward the Animal Kingdom. As the road began to funnel toward the theme park he veered away from the main entrance and chose to drive toward the resort area next to the park. He was confident this would take him to the back side and cast member areas of the Animal Kingdom. Out of sight of the guests was a whole backstage area that kept the operations of the park going. For the last two nights Kiran had been his pass and license to wander through theme parks after hours, so her participation would make what he was planning to do easier.

Although he was pleased she had come along, he was dogged by the gnawing sense of confusion her presence brought. Over the last two days Kiran had managed to show up in just the right place at the right time. This was not a fact he could easily dismiss. On one hand her explanations were plausible. After all, his explanations as to what he was doing were extremely implausible, but still true. On the other hand she had become a piece of the very puzzle he was trying to solve. He couldn't figure out exactly how she fit into it, if she fit at all. He hadn't told her about the other discoveries he'd made. Perhaps later he would let her know.

"You think I'm going to get you in?" Her question emerged from his jumbled thoughts.

"Of course. I figure we're going to run into a security guard up here, and after all, you're a big cheese in the land of the mouse. I have confidence in you." He tried to be encouraging.

"Have you already figured out what I'm going to say to this security guard to get us in?"

"Nope, that's your area of expertise."

The car grew quiet as Kiran stared out the front window. Hawk knew the key to the kingdom, the opening of Walt's old desk, and the talking stuffed tour guide that offered personalized messages would intrigue anyone with a smidgen of curiosity. He believed that Kiran was curious. He made a right turn onto a roadway clearly marked for cast members only. Flanked by foliage on both sides, the street yielded into an opening, and a security booth blocked their progress. The time had come to see if Kiran was really going to help him. Braking as the security guard stepped out, Hawk rolled down the window. The guard leaned down and peered in the window as Hawk leaned back to allow Kiran to take the lead in the conversation. She cast an unsure glance at Hawk before looking past him and smiling at the guard.

"Good evening."

"Evening, can I help you?"

"We have a meeting with Gwen Black in Guest Relations." She passed her identification card across Hawk and handed it to the guard. "I'm Kiran Roberts."

"Does Gwen know you're coming?"

"Yes, we just found out we have some special guests coming in tomorrow so we don't have much time to get their itinerary set up," Kiran cheerfully fabricated her reason for the after-hours visit.

"Let me call her and let her know you're here." The guard stepped away and back into his station.

"Is this going to work?" Hawk asked after the guard was inside and out of earshot.

"How do I know?"

"What happens when he calls Gwen Black?"

"Nothing, I hope. She's gone for the day."

The guard exited his station and leaned back into the car.

"Kiran, Gwen didn't answer her extension," he said as he handed Kiran back her ID.

"I'm not surprised. Like I said, we're ramping up for these guests at the last minute. I'm sure she's busy." Pulling out her cell phone she continued, "If this is going to be a problem, I can call her on her cell." She began punching the numbers, feigning irritation.

"No, there's no problem, Kiran," the guard interrupted her number punching. "I suppose you can go on through. You know where her office is, right?"

"Sure do, thanks." She snapped the cell phone shut and put it back on her belt.

Accelerating away from the security booth, Hawk followed Kiran's directions.

"That was very nice."

"Like you said, I'm a big cheese in the land of the mouse. Pull in here."

The car pulled into the parking lot adjacent to some prefab buildings. The offices located within these buildings housed various departments that kept Animal Kingdom operating smoothly. Only two other cars were in the lot this late in the evening. As they got out Hawk looked across the top of the car.

"So what happens now?"

"Maybe you should tell me what you're planning," she demanded. "I've gotten you this far—before we go on I need to know what you're going to do."

"I told you, I'm going to climb Expedition Everest."

"And how will you do that?"

"Ah . . . that's the beauty of my plan," he said with a raised finger. "I have no idea."

"I could lose my job—not just my job, my entire career—for helping you." She stared at Hawk. "You know that, don't you?"

"Kiran, I know." He searched for what to say. Honestly he didn't know why she was willing to help him. But she had, and he hoped she was still willing to do so. "I'm not asking you to climb it with me. Just get me to the mountain. Please."

Hesitantly she started to speak. Then she motioned for Hawk to follow her. Kiran knowingly navigated between buildings and along a service pathway that was lined with various maintenance hubs. Moving through a gate, they suddenly found themselves within the guest portion of Animal Kingdom. The area was designed to resemble an Adirondack mountain retreat. Walking through the theme park at this time of night along the dimly lit pathways gave Hawk a chance to see things he normally would not see when the masses of humanity clogged the park.

On one of his visits in the past he had found out that often the cast members would create their own background stories as to why they worked where they worked in the Animal Kingdom. They were designed to perpetuate the story line of the park itself. The cast member Hawk had spoken to had described a shipwreck that caused them to be washed ashore. He pointed to the second story of a building and explained that was where he lived. The saga was told with a straight face and he never broke character. Hawk vividly remembered the moment. Walking past the same building the cast member had said he lived in, he found himself glancing up toward the window he said was their home.

"Do you know what you're going to do yet?" Kiran inquired as they weaved past the Tree of Life across a bridge over Discovery River.

"Not yet, but I'm sure I'm supposed to be here."

"So we're just going to Expedition Everest, and you're going to figure out what to do next?"

His lack of an answer was further evidence that he had no clear plan. They arrived at the mythical village of Serka Zong that had been brought to life by the Disney Imagineers. The village served as the home to Expedition Everest, nestled on the edge of the Discovery River. Moving through Serka Zong they passed a hotel, the Yak & Yeti Restaurant, an Internet café, and a hiking supply depot. All of the buildings and design in this area were based upon Nepalese culture and architecture. The village wrapped around the base of the Forbidden Mountain and tucked it away in a perfectly created illusion that become one of the most talked-about thrill adventures in the history and legend of the Disney Corporation.

"All right, Hawk." Kiran stopped as they stood alone in front of a sign that read Gupta's Gear, a climbing gear supply store that was a part of the exterior of the attraction queue area. "What now?"

"Ha-ha!"

Silently he looked down toward his waistband where he'd automatically clipped the stuffed animal as they got out of the car. Over the past day it had become a habit to take Pal Mickey with him as he entered a park. Now he was relieved he hadn't forgotten to bring it along. Holding it up between them, he glanced up at Kiran and offered a slight smile as he gave the midsection a squeeze to activate the message delivery system.

"Can you believe how big this mountain is, Hawk? I'm a little bit scared of what lives in the Forbidden Mountain . . . but if you take care of me, I'll be brave when we face it. Keep me close on the forbidden trail, okay, pal?"

The mouse fell silent and Hawk secured it to his hip. He raised his head to see Kiran looking toward the ground and shaking her head from side to side. When she looked up he saw a hint of concern in her eyes.

"So, you are ready to climb the mountain?"

"You heard Mickey. It sounds like he wants me to get up there and face the yeti."

"You realize what you just said?"

"Yes."

"You just said that a stuffed souvenir wants you to climb a mountain and face an animatronic creature." She didn't wait for a response. "I know you think this is some great search. And I'll admit I'm intrigued by what is going on."

Hawk opened his mouth to defend his case, but once again thought better of it as Kiran wasn't done yet.

"I'll agree that Farren Rales has gone to a lot of trouble to get you on this adventure, and I don't understand any better than you do what this whole key to the kingdom is, but Hawk, you get to a point where you have to admit this isn't realistic or even smart. You can't just wander into a multimillion-dollar attraction in the dead of night."

He pursed his lips and allowed her words to sink in. It became apparent that she had said her piece and now it was his turn to speak.

"Kiran, with all that has happened and all that I have found so far, I can't stop." He chose his words carefully. "Still, you're right. I am doing some things that are fairly risky."

"Oh, you think?" She jammed her hands against her hips.

"Look, you got me here, but I don't expect you to come with me. And you can't stand around waiting in the middle of the night." He reached into his pocket and fished out his car keys and handed them to her. "Wait for me in my car. Let me do what I need to do, and I can find my way back out."

She closed her eyes for a moment as though torn between choices.

"How long do you want me to wait?"

"Until I get back." He smirked. "Don't think I want you stealing my car."

Kiran held out her hand, palm up, and did not react to his attempt at humor.

"Give me your cell phone."

He pulled out the phone and handed it to her. She flipped it open and with rapid efficiency navigated the menu, then tapped several keys and pushed a button to store what she'd done. Shutting the phone she handed it back.

"I programmed my cell number into your phone. I'll go back and try to look like I'm doing something in the guest relations offices. Call me if you get in trouble or when you're on your way out. I'll meet you at your car. Don't waste time."

Standing on the street in Serka Zong they faced each other. Hawk sensed there was something else she wanted to say.

"What?"

"I hate to . . . ."

"Hate to what?"

"I hate to tell you something that's probably going to pour more fuel on your fire." She paused and then tilted her head toward the queue line. "If you were to look inside the Fastpass queue line, you'd find a picture of Frank Wells at a base camp on Mount Everest." Hawk smiled, realizing he'd successfully deciphered the clue. She frowned. "Why are you smiling?"

"Because I'm getting ready to do something that Frank never did."

"I knew I would regret telling you." Kiran walked away. Then she stopped and added, "Be careful."

He stood and watched her until she turned the corner. He was now completely alone. Slowly he turned to face the ominous Forbidden Mountain.

 *Day Six*
Early Morning

HAWK KNEW THAT BEING the only person in the area was a luxury that wouldn't last. His first impulse was to jump the rail and enter the ride where guests board the Steam Donkeys, as the train cars were called, and walk the track following the direction of the ride. As he made his way down a sidewalk toward a gate opening into the ride loading area, he stopped. The roller coaster was one of the most memorable attractions Hawk had ever ridden. As the train races over and through the mountain, the track unexpectedly comes to an end as though it has been destroyed by some type of creature. The train screeches to a halt, giving the riders just enough time to process what they are seeing, and then rockets backward into the dark recesses of the mountain. Eventually the train stops again and guests see the shadow of the abominable snowman. The last twists and turns of the ride whisk the adventurers up and down through the openings in the mountain until they come face-to-face with the yeti.

I'm a little bit scared of what lives in the Forbidden Mountain . . . but if you take care of me, I'll be brave when we face it. Keep me close on the forbidden trail . . .

Hawk thought back on the latest clue. Every clue contained just enough detail to keep him on course. He slowed himself and decided to take an extra moment to analyze the clue further before he continued. *I'll be brave when we face it . . .* Hawk assumed that meant they were going to come face-to-face with the yeti. *Keep me close on the forbidden trail . . .* The trail might be the way he was supposed to get there. It was an easy conclusion to deduce that it would be forbidden for him to be inside the ride area after it was closed, but the clue said specifically the forbidden trail. There had to be another trail inside the mountain. He couldn't think of finding the yeti from the perspective of a rider, because that involved moving forward and backward through the ride. Instead he forced himself to think like an explorer in search of the unknown.

Cautiously he moved away from the queue line and stepped back to face the mountain. Looking to his left he saw buildings that resembled a Nepalese village. To his right he saw the obligatory gift shop that guests must exit through as well as the rock formations and altars that were a part of the set design. Heavy undergrowth and foliage resting below a carefully placed tree line separated the guest area from the side of the mountain. He walked along the pavement toward a bridge that went across another portion of the Discovery River. From this angle he could see the track disappear inside the mountain, but the bottom of the mountain was obscured from his view by trees. At the edge of the bridge he noticed something he had never seen before: a fence. The fence ran from the edge of the bridge and snaked up the hillside, disappearing into the trees as it approached the base of the mountain. The fence couldn't be seen from in front of the attraction. Only after you got to the bridge could you see that it was used to block any access from the guest areas past the bridge along the river. Leaning over the bridge, he traced the line of fencing from the bridge toward where he lost sight of it. Eyes straining in the dark, he thought he spotted a gate. Looking further along the fence line he thought he saw a second gate, but it was too dark to be sure.

He immediately moved back across the bridge to where he had started and stepped off the path into the plush grass. The walk up the hill was easy but once he got into the trees, branches and twigs clutched at him from the low-hanging limbs. Eventually Hawk crested the slope and came upon the gate he had seen from the bridge. Something was clearly marked on it. Leaning in closely he read, Ride Access Control (RAC) Procedures must be followed prior to entrance. His hunch had been right. There was something significant behind the fence. If the area was restricted, then it was safe to conclude it was forbidden for him to be inside it. He tugged the latch on the gate. It was locked. Resting his palms on the wooden top rail, he hoisted his body up and across the barrier.

Halfway over, his body reminded him how much he still hurt from his tumble over the railing at the carousel earlier that evening. He flinched, and his legs slid out from underneath him, dumping him firmly on his backside. In a rising cloud of dirt he sat with legs extended toward the river and his back to the mountain. Standing painfully, he noticed something he hadn't seen in the darkness from his perch on the bridge. There were a series of dirt trails cutting through the grassy hillside. One of these must be the forbidden trail. His decision was practical; he chose the trail that took the shortest path though the trees toward the mountain. This trail carried him away from Discovery River and up to the tree line. The Imagineers had designed a line of stairs that ran alongside a great deal of the track length.

This enabled daily inspections of the ride and served as easy access for repairs and maintenance.

Emerging from the trees he had to decide the best direction. His only personal knowledge of the track came from when he was a rider, and he lacked perspective. The steps climbed upward and twisted alongside the winding track. Each aching step jarred his pain sensors, which fired in each joint of his body. Upward he drove himself inside the mountain, losing the ambient light from the park and plunging into darkness. He slowed his pace so he wouldn't misstep in the darkness. The route through the mountain followed steps that rose upward and then dove downward, melded with the placement of the track.

Hawk heard his breathing echo inside his ears as he approached another opening in the mountain. Dim lines of luminance made his pathway easier to travel. Rounding the corner, the preacher exhaled sharply. The shadow of a creature towered against the light of the gaping hole punched into the mountainside. Between the opening of the mountainous cavern and the preacher turned explorer was a monster towering over twenty feet tall in the darkness. It wasn't moving, but in the darkness it was imposing enough to cause Hawk to pause in his approach.

In order to get close to the huge creature, he crossed the track line and crept toward the mechanism that supported the mammoth beast. In the darkness Hawk began to navigate his way from a crouching position. By lowering his body he could quickly get his hand to the ground to provide extra stability as he drew closer to the abominable snowman.

The stooped perspective of the preacher made the twenty-five-foot height of the yeti loom even larger above him. Now that he was next to it he appreciated the sheer size of the creation even more than when he had rushed past it in a train full of screaming passengers. Hawk perched at the base of the legendary creature created from the nightmares of those who had claimed to have heard the howls drifting down from the mountains in Nepal. Looking up, Hawk saw a beam vertically attached to the back of the monster. Cocking his head sideways he could see this beam was attached to an actuator that ingeniously allowed the yeti a few feet of vertical motion. The support, hidden from the sight of any rider, allowed the creature to rise, towering over the roller coaster cars. Tracing the engineering of the mechanism, he saw the actuator connected to a sled mechanism that allowed the yeti to move out toward the track and then slide back. When everything worked together, the legendary snowman of the mountains could not only move up and down but also lunge toward the Steam Donkeys full of frightened riders. The enormous clawed arm of the beast would swipe down toward the engines on cue, making the most thrilling moment of the ride one each guest would remember and retell to friends for years.

Hawk was now face-to-face with the yeti. This was what he had been trying to accomplish, but to what end? In the light that snuck in through the opening in the mountain, he studied the sled mechanism at the base of the yeti. He noticed much of what one might expect to see. Finally his eyes were drawn to a metal box mounted behind the base of the creature's leg. At first glance it seemed to be nothing but an oversized junction box. Crawling closer to it Hawk saw something on the closed cover that caused him to widen his eyes in the darkness.

Shifting his weight so he could get his hand into his pocket, he once again pulled out the key to the kingdom. He inserted the key gently in the lock. It did not fit as easily as it had in other places. Hawk turned the key to the left. The lock mechanism released, freeing the latch and sending a burst of adrenaline through him. Carefully he opened the snug-fitting metal door of the box.

Darkness prevented him from getting a clear view of what was inside. It appeared there were several oversized circuit breakers, presumably part of the yeti's electronic control system. As he patted around the box he felt an oval piece of plastic. Removing it he noticed it was attached to something flat and rectangular. He flipped his discovery over and tried to angle it so the light would reveal what it was.

He had found the next piece of the puzzle. Although he was sure of what he had found, he could not comprehend what he was supposed to do with it. Hopefully there was more.

Once again he reached inside the box and tapped gently in the darkness. Feeling nothing else he rose up and rested his hands on both knees. To his left he caught a glimpse of movement in his peripheral vision. Something had cut through the darkness, but as he looked he saw nothing. Holding his breath he listened. All was quiet—and then he heard it. The soft faint sounds of someone whistling wafted up through the cavern toward him. Quietly closing the box he relocked it and removed the key.

If the whistler was walking along the same path he had taken then Hawk would not be able to see him until he rounded the last bend that placed him in the line of sight with the yeti. While this unexpected beast lunging around the corner frightened guests, it now allowed Hawk a moment of protection and seclusion. Still he knew that safety would not last. Calculating his limited options, he decided to follow the track past the yeti exiting the mountain. The steps should continue along the side of the coaster line and hopefully take him all the way to the exit of the ride, or, if he were lucky, there would be another place to get out of the attraction before the public exit. The whistling grew louder and Hawk shimmied off of the sled platform and cautiously stepped back over the track, finding the steps. Stepping quietly, he moved back into the light and now stood in the opening of the mountainside.

Significantly more light enabled Hawk to see the steps he must now descend. Moving below the opening in the mountain, he dropped below the sight line of the arriving whistler. His hope was to be around the corner of the ride before the whistler emerged from the opening. Not looking back, he continued his downward trajectory. Hawk kept moving as quickly as possible, trying to put distance between himself and the unexpected visitor inside the mountain. The steps wound wickedly toward the last curve of the ride. The guests would find this to be where the ride slowed down before they screeched to a halt in a blast of steam. Tonight there were no riders, just a lone man racing toward the bottom of the mountain. Reaching the lowest point of the track before it made its final turn for the unloading area gave Hawk a moment to glance back up toward the opening. No one had followed him.

Jumping across the gully between the steps and the track, he scrambled up into the exit of the attraction. He straddled the bars forming the barrier between the ride and guest areas, and was in the streets of Serka Zong once again. Without hesitation he briskly retraced the path he'd traveled with Kiran on the way to the mountain. The dimly lit path enveloped him in darkness, which provided a sense of security. The light threw shadows across the walkway and gave an eerie effect to the deserted guest areas in the early hours of the morning. Seeing no one, Hawk opened his cell phone and cued up the phone number Kiran had programmed an hour before.

 *Day Six*
Early Morning

RELAXING IN THE SAFETY of his automobile, Hawk began to breathe easier as Kiran drove past the security exit. She had met him seated snugly in the driver's seat with the engine running. Immediately after letting Hawk inside, she'd placed the Mustang in gear without saying a word. After clearing security she looked over at him with an inquisitive eye.

He offered, "All in all it was pretty uneventful, except for nearly bumping into another mountain climber."

"But no one else saw you . . . right?"

"If they did, I didn't see them."

"Did you find what you were looking for?"

"I guess. I don't really know what I'm looking for. I just keep finding stuff." Hawk tilted his head. "I'm hoping that when I put the stuff together it will all make sense."

He pulled the plastic oval out of his pocket and held it out so the green glow from the dashboard would illuminate it. Kiran glanced at it with a puzzled expression.

"It's an employee name tag."

"Apparently," Hawk responded. "The yeti was protecting it."

The white plastic badge is worn by all Walt Disney World employees. Emblazoned with the cast member's name across the center, each badge also reveals the hometown of the wearer. The reason for the mention of the hometown is to encourage conversation from guests who might be curious as to where a cast member hails from or even a common contact point to invite interaction between cast and guests. The tag Hawk had found in the box in the Forbidden Mountain featured his name, Grayson, and his hometown read, Celebration, Florida.

As Kiran drove she reached over and took it out of his hand. Bringing it closer to her she studied it and then passed it back.

"See the Mickey Mouse on the badge?" She turned the car toward the Magic Kingdom. "That's Sorcerer Mickey."

There indeed was a red-robed Mickey wearing a blue hat just as he had in the short film, *The Sorcerer's Apprentice*, a segment of the classic 1940 Disney film *Fantasia*. He did not understand why that might be important.

"Sorcerer Mickey is symbolic of Walt Disney Imagineering. The Imagineers see themselves as the devoted and loyal group that helps create the magic. Their inspiration is Walt himself. You have an Imagineers name tag."

"I see." Hawk nodded, although he hadn't had time to think through what he might be doing with this badge next.

"Is that all you found?" Kiran inquired as she pulled his car into the reserved parking area facing the Transportation and Ticket Center of the Magic Kingdom.

 *Day Six*
Morning

"SO WHAT DID YOU TELL HER?" Juliette demanded of Hawk later that morning.

Jonathan had done exactly as Hawk had requested. He had gotten in contact with both Juliette and Shep and they were all waiting on the beach at the Grand Floridian Resort when Hawk arrived at eight a.m. The early morning sun glistened off the water like a sheet of gold between the beach and the Magic Kingdom. Hawk's shoes sank shallowly in the sugar sand as he walked across the beach. He felt his face brighten into a smile in genuine pleasure at the sight of his staff. So much had happened, and he was much more eager than he'd thought to tell them the events of the past few days.

After settling into a tight circle of beach chairs and exchanging quick pleasantries, he began to unpack the saga.

"And that's all I told her," Hawk answered Juliette's question.

"But you found something else, didn't you?" She leaned forward, nearly falling out of her chair.

"I also found this." Hawk reached into his pocket and pulled out the flat rectangular discovery he'd found with the name tag below the yeti. He sat with the others and passed it over to Shep, who was sitting across from him in their beachside huddle.

"An employee ID?" Shep said.

"Yes, complete with my name, picture, and the department I work for within the Walt Disney Company."

Jonathan took the card from Shep. "Hey, you're an Imagineer!"

All three of them were studying the small card intensely. Juliette reached over and took the card from Jonathan, turning it over in her hand. A look of puzzlement crossed her face.

"You know, I've seen some of the cast IDs that folks at church have, but this looks different."

"Different how?" Hawk wondered.

"There is more to it. It's heftier, like a credit card." She continued to examine it. "This magnetic stripe on the back is different than any cast member ID that I've ever seen before."

Jonathan took the card from Juliette and concurred with her summation. Shep then examined the card again and nodded. After a few moments he passed the card back to Hawk. Replacing it in his pocket he exchanged it for the key that Farren had given him. Holding out the gift that had started his wonderfully strange scavenger hunt, he offered it for his friends inspection. They all examined it with the same thoroughness as they had the ID card.

"So what do you think happened to Farren?" Jonathan asked.

"I really don't know," Hawk said. "I initially thought he was just ignoring my calls while I tried to solve the mystery of the key. But when I couldn't find him and he didn't show up at work, I didn't know what to think."

"Do you think the person chasing you at the Gamble House had something to do with his disappearance?" Shep asked the very question that had weighed on Hawk.

"I've thought that. As far as I know he hasn't been seen since that night."

"Which means you were the last person to see him before he disappeared," Juliette interjected.

"Right."

"Now that he's missing and the sheriff's department is involved, I would imagine they'd be interested in hearing about your late-night excursion," Jonathan added.

"Maybe you should go ahead and talk to them," Shep said.

"I don't mind, but I was hoping that if I could solve the puzzle or whatever it is, I might be able to figure out what happened to him."

"Or at least know if the key and the puzzle are connected to his disappearing, right?" Juliette said.

"So maybe you shouldn't talk to them yet." Shep raised his shoulders.

"That's the problem, guys. I don't know what to do."

The question-and-answer session was similar to their weekly staff meetings. They occasionally poked fun at one another because each had such a strong personality they rarely bogged down when making a decision. However, in this situation silence settled across the group. Hawk found himself absently watching the early morning movement of a monorail snaking past the Grand Floridian to the Magic Kingdom.

"If you aren't ready to talk to the sheriff yet, what's your next move?" Jonathan asked.

"I don't know," Hawk restated.

"You don't actually have another clue to chase down," Shep said. "I suppose you could just wander around and wait for Pal Mickey to talk to you."

"You *do* have a clue to chase," Juliette corrected.

"I do?" Hawk asked.

"Sure you do. The *Old Yeller* DVD you found in the Police Telegraph Box at the Carthay Circle Theatre. You had to have it to figure out where to find the map to the plane, but you said the DVD wasn't factory sealed."

"But it looked like a regular DVD."

"Yes, and your Pal Mickey looks like a regular stuffed animal, and you don't look like a man who's been sneaking into resort attractions after hours."

Hawk cringed. "Okay, you made your point."

Juliette nodded and smiled a satisfied smile.

Jonathan was now plotting their next strategic move. "We need to watch the DVD. But Hawk, we can't go back to the office or your home, the sheriff's department might be there to talk with you."

"So we can go back to one of our houses," Shep reasoned.

"Eventually they might drop by those if they're actively working the case," Jonathan disagreed.

"Especially since we all saw Farren the day he disappeared." Juliette shook her head. "You can't go home and you can't go to the office."

"Why do we have go anywhere?" Hawk's eyes flickered with inspiration. "We're in the greatest tourist destination in the entire world. Let's get a room here at the resort and watch the DVD."

"That also gives you a place to stay away from the usual places," Juliette added. "After all, you did tell us you were going to be out for a few days."

"I'll get the room for you," Jonathan offered. "That way no one will be able to trace your name to it."

"Let's go." Hawk got to his feet.

Shep, Juliette, and Jonathan joined him and shuffled along the sandy shoreline. Reaching the concrete pathway, they knocked the sand off of their shoes. As they headed toward the resort, Hawk thought how oddly they must have looked dressed in casual work attire, sitting on a beach.

"This place is great. By the way, Jonathan, thanks for offering to pay for my vacation."

"Pay nothing," Jonathan retorted. "You're going to pay me back." They all laughed.

The four entered one of the side entrances to Disney's Grand Floridian Resort and Spa. The hallway teemed with people enjoying the luxury of the nineteenth-century-themed resort, and Shep got separated from the other three in a surge of people. The Victorian decor was meticulous in detail including the ceiling fans rotating throughout the interior of the massive complex. After glancing at the beautiful detailing, Hawk let his gaze drift to the faces of the people mingling about doing the things that tourists do. Suddenly his eyes ran across a face and then darted back, doing a double take. Locking onto his stare from across the expansive lobby was a round face he had encountered before. The preacher saw the same crooked nose holding up the same pair of dark sunglasses now worn indoors. He didn't need to see the man's name tag to remember his name was Reginald. The same official-looking, stern-faced cast member that had seen him at the Carthay Circle Theatre.

Although Hawk couldn't see through the lenses of the glasses, he was sure that Reginald had not only seen him but was intently watching him.

"We have a problem," Hawk informed the team.

"What?" Juliette whispered as she immediately looked around the lobby.

"Don't look, just listen." Hawk kept his gaze from straying back to Reginald. "There's a man watching us, a cast member named Reginald. He saw me when I found the DVD at the Studios. He wasn't very friendly and I don't think it's a coincidence he's here now." Hawk risked a glance and saw Reginald now headed their way. Shep, completely unaware of what was transpiring, caught up with their group as Hawk hurriedly gave instructions.

"Jonathan, you go and get a room at the Contemporary. Call me when you get checked in. Juliette, you and I are going to head up the grand staircase and move to the monorail landing. Shep, I want you to make sure the gentleman with the bald head, dark glasses, crooked nose, and the name tag that says Reginald doesn't stop us."

They immediately moved into motion. Jonathan peeled off and headed toward the resort's exit. Juliette and Hawk hustled toward the huge staircase that connected the entrance level to the next floor, where shops and the monorail station were located. Shep trailed a short distance behind them. By the time they rounded the first flight of steps and turned to head up the next flight, they'd broken into a run. Hawk glanced back as they crested the last step and charged to their left, headed for the exit doors past the shopping area.

Reginald broke into a casual trot, quickening his pace to a sprint as he avoided guests lost in the ambience of the Victorian resort. As he reached the top of the steps Shep grabbed him in a bear hug. Reginald's momentum knocked both of the men off balance. With both arms pinned at his sides, he managed to get his legs back underneath him and kept both of them from falling.

The monorail doors were open and loading guests as Hawk and Juliette exited the automated sliding glass doors that opened up from the interior of the resort. Moving through the doors Hawk ventured a last glance behind them.

Shep was grinning, pounding Reginald on the back as though the two were long-lost friends. If they weren't in such a rush to escape, Hawk would have stopped to watch the brilliant acting.

Heels clicking on the concrete, Juliette picked out an open car and veered off toward it. She reached back and clutched Hawk by the arm, pulling him toward the opening. They breathlessly hurtled into the empty passenger compartment of the monorail and sank back into the seat. It was only after they were seated that Hawk dared to look out the window to see if Reginald was still in pursuit. Seeing nothing, he looked over at Juliette seated next to him.

"You will never believe what I just saw!" Hawk said, trying to catch his breath.

The automated announcement warned, "Please stand clear of the doors," as the doors silently slid to a close and the monorail streaked out of the station.

"Uncle Reggie!" Shep exclaimed. "Don't you remember me?"

 *Day Six*
Morning

SILENTLY GLIDING ALONG THE TRACK, the monorail accelerated sleekly from the Grand Floridian toward the Magic Kingdom. The short journey gave Juliette and Hawk very little time to plot their next move. Each stop of the monorail involved a turnover of guests. The doors would open for passengers to disembark, then the doors on the opposite side of the car opened allowing new riders to climb aboard. Although extremely efficient and fast, when you were being pursued the moments of waiting could be excruciatingly slow. Hawk realized that if Reginald wanted them stopped, he could radio ahead and the monorail would be delayed until security arrived.

"Who was that?" Juliette asked.

"Like I said, he was watching me at the Studios."

"Security?"

"I assume so."

"So what do we do?"

"If he's security and radios ahead, they'll hold the monorail and we won't make it to the Contemporary."

The monorail they had managed to escape on was designated to make the resort loop around the Seven Seas Lagoon. The next stop along the rails would be the Magic Kingdom, then the Contemporary, the Ticket and Transportation Center, followed by the Polynesian Resort, and then once again at the Grand Floridian. The system was designed to get guests to their resort locations and allow them to navigate all of the Magic Kingdom Resort areas connected to the monorail line. There was a second monorail line running parallel to the first, making the same circle around the resort. The other track was the express track transporting guests nonstop between the Ticket and Transportation Center and the Magic Kingdom entrance. The express monorail ran in the opposite direction of the resort loop, giving guests the chance to see another monorail zipping past them going the other way.

As these monorails slid past there was just a few feet of clearance between them. Hawk was thinking about what to do next as a monorail passed going the other direction.

"We have to get off," he softly stated.

"And then?"

"Not sure, let's do one thing at a time."

The monorail slowed and pulled into the station in front of the Magic Kingdom. A ding signaled the opening of the door. As soon as the door slid open Juliette got up to exit as Hawk had said. He grabbed her wrist and pulled her back toward the seat.

"Wait!"

"I thought you said we needed to get off." She frowned.

"We do, but casually look out there." As he pointed, Juliette turned her head to the massive unloading area that dumped into a ramp carrying people toward the security checkpoints in front of the main entrance. "Have you ever seen that many security guards standing on the platform?"

She looked closer. "I count at least five." This was unusual because the security checkpoints were waiting for all of the guests at the level below.

Another ding signaled the opening of the opposite side door so passengers could climb aboard. These doors slid open and passengers began to make their way into the car. Hawk jumped to his feet and signaled for Juliette to follow. They moved against the flow of people surging aboard. Unusual movements in crowd flow always catch the attention of cast members and theirs was no exception. A cast member helping to load passengers headed to intercept them to see what was happening. The cast member smiled as she moved in front of the pair.

"Everything all right, Grayson?" The cast member smiled a friendly smile.

"Just great, Ashley, we're just getting a feel for how things are working." Hawk traded smile for smile, without hesitating.

Juliette turned toward Hawk with a puzzled look. Then her gaze slipped to the Imagineer's name badge he'd clipped to his chest. This, which had enabled the cast member to call him by name and Hawk to return the courtesy had also given them an official pass for going the wrong way.

"Take care," Ashley offered as she waved them on.

"You too, Ashley." Hawk nodded as they moved down the curved ramp. Trying to look nonchalant, they walked shoulder to shoulder as they searched for any possible obstructions to their escape.

"I didn't see you put the badge on," Juliette whispered in his direction.

It had been a last minute impulse as he and Juliette surveyed the security guards on the landing platform. His hunch was that while Reginald might have had time to get security to be there to meet them at the exit, they wouldn't be looking for them to exit through the entrance. He also knew that Reginald did not have time to launch an all-out effort to look for them, since it had probably taken him a few moments to get out of Shep's bear hug.

"We were lucky."

"Never hurts to have a little luck," she responded.

The pair moved to the bottom of the ramp and began to mingle into the movement of people heading toward the next stop of their vacations. To their right was the boat-docking area where passengers could travel in a variety of different directions. Ahead of them in the distance they could see the Contemporary Resort; above them the monorail they had been riding on passed over headed in that direction.

"Are we going to walk?" Juliette, like Hawk, was familiar with the resorts, transportation options, shortcuts, and how it all worked. Her family often relaxed and took advantage of all the entertainment choices Disney World offered. She knew it was just a short walk to the Contemporary along the pathway below the monorail line.

"Let's take a bus." Hawk moved toward the massive bus loading zone. "Buses don't make the short jump to the Contemporary, so we can go to Wilderness Lodge and make the connection there."

Finding the right bus was easy and in moments they were waiting in line for the bus to arrive. Hawk had removed the employee name badge, and they tried to blend in with other guests, occasionally risking a look for arriving security.

The bus arrived and the pressure of the brakes brought it to a halt. The click of the door being opened invited them to enter. They stepped on board and shuffled to the back. Collapsing into their plastic seats they looked toward each other and sighed.

"After we get to the Contemporary we can go around the back of the hotel to the boat docks. We can hang out there until we hear from Jonathan. That way, we don't get anywhere near the monorail stations and we aren't even in the hotel until we know exactly where we are going." Hawk unfolded his rapidly created plan as the bus began to move.

Juliette nodded. "I know you said Reginald saw you at the Studios, but why exactly would he be chasing you?"

"Not sure. Maybe I just look suspicious?"

"Maybe, but he would have tossed you yesterday if he thought you were up to something."

Hawk wondered if it was just coincidence that Reginald had been in the Grand Floridian. If it was coincidence, then his hurried escape had cemented his guilt in Reginald's mind. He needed to stay calm and not panic. If he was going to solve this puzzle, he couldn't afford to make mistakes. The ride was short and they quickly arrived. Juliette hesitated as Hawk began to move off to go around the building.

"Hawk, I'm going to have to run inside and find a restroom."

"You should have taken care of that before we were being chased," he jokingly scolded.

"*You're* the one being chased. I'm just curious enough to help my pastor figure out why before he gets tossed in jail. I'll meet you by the boat docks."

As they went their separate ways, Hawk heard his cell phone ring. The display read Kiran. She must have captured his cell phone number when he called her last night. He opened the phone.

"Have you gotten in any trouble yet today?" Her tone was playful and he wondered if somehow she knew about his escapades today.

She couldn't know. There would be no way.

"No, no trouble today . . . yet! What about you? Been helping anyone break any rules today?"

"Not yet, but it's early." She chuckled. "Someone kept me out too late last night. I decided to sleep in this morning. I have to work in a little while."

"Well, now that you mention it, I was out late last night too. But I managed to get to work early today."

"Awww," she feigned sympathy. "So seriously, what trouble do I have to get you out of today?"

"None, I hope."

"Really? Pardon me if somehow I don't believe you."

"I haven't figured out what to do next," he told her truthfully. "I don't have a clue or a direction to go any further."

"So you aren't going to do anything?"

"Well, not this minute. I don't have anything to do."

Silence hung for a moment. "All right, then, if you're sure you're going to stay out of trouble." She hesitated again. "Call me if you change your mind, something happens, or you figure anything out."

"I will." He didn't know if he was telling her the truth. It bothered him; lying was not something he did as a habit. In this case he decided it was best if she operated on a need-to-know basis. "Thanks again for helping me. I *will* call you later."

The call ended and Hawk again pondered the mysterious Kiran Roberts. It had been a long time since he'd met anyone who intrigued him as much as she did. At the same time there was that nagging sense that the timing of her walking into his life was not random. Still, she had done exactly the same thing he had. The more they had found and the more she knew, the more curious she became. Her knowledge and her position in the company, along with his Pal Mickey, had been his most valuable resource on this chase for the unknown.

Hawk's phone came to life again. This time the display read Shep.

"How did I do, boss?" Shep's voice rang with enthusiasm.

"Great." Hawk laughed aloud, remembering his last look at Shep grabbing Reginald in a bear hug. "Looked to me like you were a professional wrestler."

"You should have seen the look on his face when I called him Uncle Reggie."

"I'll bet." Hawk smirked. "Brilliant thinking."

"He informed me in no uncertain terms that he wasn't anybody's uncle and I was sadly mistaken. Apparently he's an only child, so no nieces or nephews." Shep was snickering. "But I did hear him radio someone telling them that he had to cover the Magic Kingdom monorail station."

"We saw some added security," Hawk told Shep. "We weren't sure if they were waiting for us."

"They could have been your welcoming committee. I take it that since we're talking, you managed to get away."

"Uh-huh. I'm out at the boat docks at the Contemporary waiting to hear from Jonathan."

"I'll head that way."

Looking up, Hawk saw Juliette coming down the sidewalk heading toward him. She waved as she approached, and then his cell phone rang again.

The name on the display was Farren Rales.

 *Day Six*
Afternoon

"ARE YOU GOING TO ANSWER IT?" Juliette asked.

Hawk opened the phone "Hello, this is Hawk."

Silence.

"Hello." He tried again.

Silence.

Pulling the phone away from his ear he saw it was dead.

"What happened?" Juliette looked intently at it.

"It died. I haven't had a chance to charge it."

"So you missed a call from Farren because you had a dead battery?" She reached into her purse passed her phone to Hawk. "Here, call him on mine."

"I would." Hawk slumped. "I don't know his number. It's stored in my phone."

"Which of course you can't get to, because your phone is dead."

"Right."

As if on cue Juliette's phone rang. It was Jonathan. She answered and Hawk eavesdropped as she got the details on where he was and what was happening. In short order they were on their way to the room Jonathan had secured. Soon they were all gathered in Jonathan Carlson's suite, pulling chairs close to the television. Juliette fished her phone charger out of her purse. While she finished hooking up Hawk's phone, he slid the *Old Yeller* DVD into the player. The usual fanfare loaded with logos filled the screen and the Old Yeller interface offered them a selection of choices. All four stared at the screen in contemplative silence, formulating which choice might be the best. Shep scrolled through the choices offered on the screen and each one changed color slightly as it was highlighted. Finally the BONUS FEATURES changed colors.

"Try that one!" Jonathan instructed.

The screen paused, faded, and then another series of menu selections appeared as the bonus features were presented. The film was an older film created long before the invention of digital video. Therefore the extras that are so prominent on more recent film releases were not available on this particular disc. The last bonus feature listed read *A Conversation with Walt.*

"What do you think?" Juliette looked toward Hawk.

"*A conversation with Walt* is as good as anything else." He didn't hold a great deal of expectation.

Shep highlighted the feature and pressed the enter key on the remote. Once again the menu screen faded and the television screen momentarily went to black. The emptiness was replaced by a brilliant flash of color and the cartoon image of Tinker Bell flying in a circle around the screen. She smiled and touched an animated wand to the center of the screen, and a dazzling splash of shimmering pixie dust exploded across the screen, opening into another image. This one looked familiar. It was Walt Disney's office, or at least the way it had been created as a set piece for the *Wonderful World of Color* television series. The series had aired from 1961 through 1969, allowing Walt to enter the homes of millions of viewers each week to be both the host and emcee of whatever wonderful adventure he had chosen to make come to life that week. It was this on-screen persona that had given Walt the familiarity so many felt comfortable with. Viewers felt like they knew him, could trust him, and he was a friend they looked forward to spending an hour with each week.

The four glanced at one another as the image of the empty office remained on the screen. Finally the sound of footsteps was heard coming from the speakers and Walt Disney himself walked into the image and smiled toward the camera.

"Well hello there." Walt spoke toward the camera in that familiar friendly voice, resurrecting memories of childhood within Hawk. Jonathan and Juliette had nostalgic looks on their faces. Shep was too young to have watched the Walt Disney–hosted shows; his fond memories would be connected to what he had seen on DVD or archived specials. "Sorry I'm late, I have been very busy, you know, working here at the Studio, keeping up with all that is happening at Disneyland, and working on our Florida project. These are exciting days to say the least." Obviously this had been filmed a short time before Walt's death. He looked to be in his sixties and his eyes twinkled above that familiar mustache. He wore a gray suit and white shirt, highlighted by a dark tie adorned with a golden tie clip with three initials: STR. He looked just like the classic images of him that graced the pages of books and the displays in theme parks, and most importantly the images blazed into the memories of children from the past. He continued, "I don't know who you are, but I wanted to take a moment to meet you. I wish I could see you in person, but since you are watching me like this, that just isn't possible now, is it?"

Hawk's eyebrows rose slightly. Juliette tilted her head. Jonathan leaned forward in his seat. Shep was the only one who spoke. "That sounded like he was talking directly to us!"

"Shhhh!" The other three replied simultaneously, keeping their eyes riveted to the screen.

"I guess I have always been a dreamer. Along the way I have been fortunate enough to have a lot of success. Oh, there have been failures, for sure, but I think the failures taught me some valuable lessons about how not to make the same mistakes the next time I tried to do something." Walt lowered his head and looked down for a moment, then returned his gaze to the viewer through the camera. "I've seen a lot of my dreams come to life, but mind you, I haven't done it all alone. I try to surround myself with great people, and together we make magic come to life. The one thing I want you to know is that no matter what we are working on, I am never afraid we won't pull it off. It sometimes takes a lot more work and imagination that I thought it would, but we always seem to make it. I suppose most people know that when we run into a problem, I try to find the best person to solve it." Walt sat back against the front of his desk and ran his hand along his tie, slowly straightening it. "Usually I head straight to Roy; that's my brother. I expect he will tell me we can't afford to do whatever I am trying to get done. But eventually I convince him, and he figures out how to get us the funding we need to make it happen. We've done a lot of things together, and . . . um . . . he is always watching over me, trying to take care of me, keeping us safe. Most people don't realize it, but going straight to Roy has kept me on track. You see, we've been partners in this thing from the very beginning."

Walt grew silent for a moment. As they watched him on the screen it appeared he was lost in a memory. His face took on a reflective demeanor and it was now even more apparent that this broadcast recording was a unique rarity. It was an unscripted dialogue that Walt was creating as he spoke it. The gaze of the legend on the screen looked back through the camera lens.

"I would imagine you are wondering what all this rambling has to do with you. I know I would be." Walt chuckled. "Like I told you, I have seen a lot of dreams come to life. I have learned some tough lessons along the way, and one of them is how important it is to protect and take care of your dreams. There have been a few people I could really trust to keep the magic we have made alive. That is why I am talking with you now. I'll bet you are wondering about this." Walt rose up from leaning on the desk, reached into his inside suit pocket, and pulled out a key, the very same key that Hawk had in his pocket now. Silent gasps rippled through the group of four gathered around the screen. This was the key that had opened some of the most unbelievable locks in the most unlikely of places. Holding the key in front of him toward the camera, Walt glanced at it then looked back toward the camera and ultimately the viewer once more. "This is what I call the key to the kingdom. You already know that, don't you? Of course you do, because this is the very same key that you have now. The fact that you have it means that you can be trusted to do the right thing for me. It means that you can be counted on to do whatever it takes to keep some of the dreams and plans that I have made alive. It also means I am not able to be with you or able to take care of things myself." Walt smiled a crooked smile as if admitting what he never wanted to admit. In that smile he acknowledged he had run out of time to live before he ran out of dreams. "I don't know who you are, but I do know that I would like you. And I am counting on you. The moment you were given this key, you really were given the key to the kingdom. What you do with it will affect the future of everything I have built and created. Since I don't know who you are or where you are, let me tell you what I do know. You are now holding on to the key that will unlock the future. So, my friend, now you are my partner. Be extremely careful and very wise. I am counting on you. I know you won't let me down."

Walt slowly replaced the key in his pocket and began to walk out of the camera shot. As he arrived at the edge of the filming area it dawned on Hawk that at no time during this film had the camera moved. There had been no zooming, panning, or any indication at all that there was someone operating the camera. Apparently it had just been turned on. This allotted for the extended time of the view of the empty office before Walt Disney had walked into the shot. Walt himself had turned on the camera. He was alone on this set, filming a very private and personal message to be seen by an unknown friend from the future. The friend had turned out to be a stunned Grayson Hawkes. Walt stopped before walking out of the shot and turned once again toward the camera.

"Thanks," Walt said with a wink and a smile. He then walked out of the shot. The moments that followed were filled with an empty office as before, and then the picture went dark. Hawk opened his mouth to voice his astonishment at this message from Walt Disney himself, but suddenly the picture faded from darkness into another scene. The blackness dissolved into the familiar face of Farren Rales. Hair disheveled, body enveloped in a comfortable cardigan, and beaming with a wide smile, he sat behind a desk that looked strangely familiar to the preacher.

"Well, Hawk my friend, you are in the middle of a pretty amazing adventure, aren't you?" The faces in the room all registered their surprise that this message was personalized for Hawk himself. "The very fact that you are watching this lets me know you figured out that I not only gave you a key but a few clues to get you started. I also know you have been pretty successful because you have managed to actually find the clues you need along with this one. I am proud of you, son, I knew you could do it . . . and I knew you were the right choice.

"I would love to tell you the quest is over and you are done, but you have much left to do before you find out what the key really unlocks. However, I am confident that you will figure it all out." Rales looked down and appeared to be studying his hands for a moment, contemplating what he would say next.

"If I were you I would be wondering why I just didn't tell you what the great mystery was. All of the hidden clues, puzzles, and secret messages make it far more complicated, don't they? I would come right out and tell you if it were as easy as that. But the story you are in the middle of is not that simple. The stakes are incredibly high, and part of being the keeper of the key to the kingdom hinges on your ability to figure it all out. I also have to be very cautious, just in case this little film project of mine should accidentally fall into the wrong hands. The circumstances don't allow me to help you any more than I have been able to. You must admit, your Pal Mickey is a pretty amazing creation, isn't it?" Rales beamed at the thought of his one-of-a kind creation.

"What I can tell you is this. Everything you have discovered up to this point is important. Think of each discovery as another piece of the bigger puzzle. Once you have the pieces, everything will come together in the end. I also have a feeling by now that some of the stuff you have been doing has probably caught the attention of a few folks. Just like any classic Walt Disney story, there are heroes and villains. It is up to you to figure out who is who and whom to trust. Be careful. While I can't tell you what you are looking for, I can tell you this. The value and importance of what you are doing goes beyond what you can imagine. After all, Walt himself told you he is counting on you." Rales again paused, and staring into the camera, chose his words carefully.

"You were not chosen by accident. You will understand if and when you unlock the mystery. I believe in you and know you can do this. Don't allow anything to distract you and get you off course. Hawk, remember the things I have told you. If you run into a problem . . . you'll figure it out."

In the background there was a faint indistinguishable sound. Rales paused and jerked his head to his right in search of the unexpected noise. He strained to listen, allowing time to make sure it was safe for him to continue. The silence screamed with a tension that spilled over into the room where the church staff watched and listened. Finally, apparently satisfied that it was safe, Rales turned his attention back to the camera.

"Now your journey with the key to the kingdom takes you back to the kingdom. Hopefully you have already been to the mountain. If you haven't, you need to get there. The next clue you need is a square; not just the square but what the square contains. You will solve it, you know how, just keep thinking. I wish I could help you more, but I can't. I wish I could contact you, but that wouldn't be right. So this was the only way for me to get you a message. I am proud of you, Hawk, and you would have made Walt proud also. You hold the key to keep his dreams on track. Bye!"

The ensuing silence was broken when once again the *Old Yeller* bonus features menu filled the screen. Shep turned the television set off. Eight eyes glanced between each other, blending a trace of wonder with loads of confusion. Jonathan stood and stepped in front of the television to face the group.

"Well?"

Shep turned to Hawk. "So what do you do now?"

Hawk sat with his head bowed. "I guess I'm heading back to the Magic Kingdom." He raised his gaze to the group, his heartbeat quickening with a desire to tackle the challenge Walt Disney himself had placed before him.

Juliette stood. Walking across the room she retrieved Hawk's phone.

"Didn't Farren call you a little while ago?" she asked.

In all of the intrigue and excitement Hawk had forgotten the call that had come in just before his battery went dead. He took the phone from her and powered it up.

"Rales called you?" Jonathan asked with surprise.

"Uh-huh, when we were waiting downstairs for you to get checked in. Just as the call came in my battery died. I saw the number and picked it up and had nothing."

While they talked Hawk punched back up his missed calls list and once again read the name Farren Rales. He held it out for all to see.

"We just heard him say he wouldn't contact you," Juliette reminded everyone.

"Maybe something changed," Shep offered.

"Perhaps he decided to do something different after he made the film," Jonathan added.

"Or maybe it wasn't Farren Rales calling at all," Juliette said. "It could be that someone has his phone."

"Who would have his phone?" Hawk asked. "And how would someone have gotten it?"

Jonathan jumped in. "It could be someone who found it somewhere, could be the police, could be anyone."

"Or it could be Farren Rales," Shep insisted. "You won't know until you call back."

The three staff members looked toward their pastor, waiting for him to decide what to do next. He looked from one to the next and finally looked back to his phone. Pressing the green phone emblem, Hawk dialed Farren's cell phone number. Anxiously they studied Hawk's face as he listened to the receiver. The phone rang four times and then sent him into Rale's voice mailbox. Hawk hung up without leaving a message. He snapped the cell closed and pushed it back into his pocket.

"No answer." he informed them.

Hawk stalked across the floor and glanced out the window toward Bay Lake, the massive manmade body of water that stretched out along the resort. Silence smothered the room as his mind raced across the possibilities of what they should do next. He had already told the group his next stop was back at the Magic Kingdom, but now he was attempting to develop some tactic to strengthen his searching ability. Seconds became minutes before he finally turned back to face the team.

"What are your schedules for the day?"

This couldn't be the first thing they expected their pastor to say. Still they quickly responded with their plans for the rest of the afternoon.

"I'm supposed to meet Tim in an hour," Juliette began.

"I have to finish up my stuff to be ready for band rehearsal later tonight," Jonathan said. "I can call everyone and cancel if I need to."

"I had some running around to get done, but I can do it later." Shep was the last to reply.

Hawk listened and allowed the last bit of the sketchy strategy to formulate. Turning his attention to Shep, he began to unfold his plan.

"Do you have your laptop?"

"Sure, it's out in the car!" Shep eagerly stood up.

"Go get it," Hawk instructed. "You're going to get to spend the day here, if you don't mind, at a luxury resort. That way I have Internet access through you if I need it."

"Do you want me to cancel rehearsal tonight?" Jonathan inquired.

"No, go ahead and do what you need to get done. Both of you have some pressing things." He nodded toward Juliette and Jonathan.

"Tim mentioned this morning that we might come out to one of the parks tonight for dinner, and the kids are at my sister's," Juliette said. "Maybe we can get out to the Magic Kingdom and see if we can help."

"You think Tim would be up for it?" Hawk asked, already knowing the answer.

Tim Keaton, Juliette's husband, had been a Disney animator who had been forced to form a graphic arts company when Disney shut down the Florida animation department. Hawk had instantly liked Tim and they had become the closest of friends.

"I think Tim would leave work right now if I told him what was going on." Juliette smirked. "Is it okay if I tell him what you told us?"

"No problem. Maybe he will have some helpful insight." Hawk trusted Tim and his judgment. He wouldn't mind if Tim got involved in his search with him. "If you come out here tonight, give me a call."

"I'll think about it." Juliette feigned disinterest. She quickly hugged her friends and moved toward Hawk last. Gripping both his shoulders and pulling him close, she whispered in his ear, "Be very careful!"

"I will," Hawk said.

"I mean it." Juliette stared at him sternly. "This is big. I don't know what it is or what you're looking for, but it is big. I mean, Walt Disney himself sent you a message. That sounds crazy! This is so big. Remember that, Hawk."

He nodded understanding. She turned and was gone. Shep moved out of the room behind her to accompany her to the elevators. She would jump on board a monorail and head back to the Grand Floridian to get her car. Shep would hike across the paved parking lot to fish his laptop out of the messy ocean of junk in his trunk.

"You sure you don't want me to cancel?" Jonathan asked, alone in the room with Hawk.

"No, meeting with the worship team is more important."

"We can survive without the practice."

"Call me later. Come back after practice if you can." Hawk knew Jonathan badly wanted to stay and help. "After all, this room is on your dime. You can visit anytime you want."

 *Day Six*
Afternoon

AFTER HELPING SHEP set up their command center, Hawk left the Contemporary Resort for the Magic Kingdom entrance. Shep, the church's technology expert, could find things online more efficiently and effectively than the rest of the staff combined. Armed with high-speed Internet access and awaiting Hawk's call, his job was to cyber-seek any background information that Hawk might need on the next leg of his journey.

At the main gate he exchanged greetings with the cast member and slid his annual pass into the slot on the turnstile. The pass was whisked into the mechanism and he placed his index finger on the sensor. These sensors had created an outcry from many organizations when they were introduced in the Disney theme parks. Privacy issues were called into question by groups concerned that using your fingerprints as verification to enter a theme park was too personal and too private. Hawk, like other guests, didn't think too much about the new system as it was introduced. Suddenly, the cast member moved forward and punched a few keys on the turnstile mechanism. A puzzled look came over her face.

"Everything OK?" he asked.

"Fine," she responded. "I'm going to need you to reinsert your pass and place your finger back on the sensor."

Hawk complied. Waiting with his index finger pressed against the blue glass bubble, he watched as his pass emerged on the other side of the mechanism. The electronic readout greeted him with a wish to have a nice day, and reclaiming his pass, he moved through the turnstile.

"Sometimes the sensor has trouble reading your print. Sorry for the inconvenience," the young woman apologized.

"Not a problem at all."

Stepping beyond the entrance gate, he casually strolled toward the floral garden below the train station.

The next clue you need is a square. Not just the square but what the square contains. The most obvious square to Hawk was Town Square that began the journey down Main Street USA. That square was just on the other side of the train station through the tunnels. He had to figure out what in the square he needed and what the square contained, if solving the clue could be that simple. He allowed his gaze to drift up the pristine landscaping until it rested on the train that was currently loading passengers above him at the station. The one short whistle blasted by the train was the alert that let everyone know the train would be leaving the station shortly.

The Walt Disney World Railroad travels on a mile-and-a-half loop encircling the Magic Kingdom. Statistically the railroad was one of the busiest in the country, transporting over 1.5 million passengers each year. The steam engine hit the whistle as it pulled away from the station. Hawk felt his cell phone vibrate in his pocket. Seeing the caller display information, he quickly answered.

"Hello, Shep."

"What is that noise?" Shep asked loudly.

"The train is leaving the station," Hawk informed him. "Hold on a second, it'll be gone and we can hear better."

In a matter of seconds the train disappeared around the corner toward Adventureland, taking its noise with it.

"I'm glad you're near the train station," Shep said.

"Why?"

"Well, boss, I've been thinking about what Rales said to you on the DVD. He said your next clue was a square. I think that might be the Town Square."

"I was thinking the same thing, but is it that simple?"

"I don't know if it's going to be simple, because he also said you had to find what the square contained."

"I'm with you, so what are you thinking?"

"Are you in Town Square?"

"Not yet," Hawk told him. "I haven't gone through the tunnels. I'm standing just below the train station."

"Don't move!" Shep yelled.

"Okay."

"Look up at the station."

Hawk looked up and studied the train station. "What am I looking for?"

"What does it say in the window at the top of the train station?"

Hawk's eyes focused momentarily on the sign that read Magic Kingdom, Elevation 108 Feet. Just above that sign there was a Railroad Office window surrounded by red bricks. The lettering on the window read Keeping Dreams

On Track . . . Walter E. Disney, Chief Engineer. Hawk read what he saw aloud to Shep.

"Rales said, 'You hold the key to keep his dreams on track,'" Shep reminded him. "I think he was talking about the railroad station. It's in the square. That has to be it."

Hawk had seen this window many times before. Yet he had not remembered it when he heard Rales say almost exactly the same thing on the DVD. After Shep had drawn his attention to it he realized that it made perfect sense. He was looking for the train station.

"Perfect! Whatever I'm looking for is in the train station."

"So now you just have to figure out what you're looking for," Shep said cheerfully. "So get moving and let me know how I can keep you on track."

Hawk groaned. "You already are. I'll call you when I find something."

Hawk moved into the tunnels below the train station. Instead of going straight through he veered off toward the center of the lower level of the station. This area had been used for a number of things through the years, including housing lockers for storage and for checking out strollers. As this lower level opened onto Main Street USA, there were displays and posters featuring information about Walt's fascination with trains, along with information about the Walt Disney World Railroad. Two wide, curving stairwells ascended to a large landing area that overlooked Town Square. Reaching the top of the stairway, Hawk emerged from the staircase and stepped across the landing heading toward the entrance of the train station. He entered the cavernous room and stepped to the center to look for a clue.

"Ha-ha!"

Unclipping Pal Mickey from his side, he firmly pressed the belly of his stuffed companion and held the toy to his ear.

"Hey, pal, if we're going to stay on track, finding the square is our ticket. When you see me you know you've got it!"

Hawk squinted as he slowly turned inside the station. Town Square wasn't the square he was looking for. He had to find something square. There were a number of square-shaped items in the station, but none of them caught his attention in a spectacular way. He moved to the edge of the room and slowly walked along the line of the walls. Nothing out of the ordinary gave him reason to pause. Avoiding people moving about the station he stopped, allowing them to pass. A train whistle signaled the arrival of another train full of passengers. Punctuated by a billowing hiss of steam, the train came to a halt. An energetic buzz of activity as people surged to get aboard distracted Hawk from his search for a moment. Realizing he didn't really know what to look for he decided to step back out onto the landing outside of the station.

He walked through the doors and once again saw the spectacular view down Main Street USA toward Cinderella Castle. Moving toward the rail at the edge of the landing he looked at the castle in the distance and mentally broke apart the most recent clue.

If we are going to stay on track . . . He didn't know whether that meant he needed to get on the train or *staying on track* was a generic staying on course. The next part of the clue also puzzled him: *finding the square is our ticket.* He and Shep had both concluded that the square and what was inside it had meant Town Square and the Train Station. Then the clue that his little tour guide had added unraveled that neatly woven thread of thought. Firmly gripping the rail he leaned against it and looked around Town Square at the steady flow of people across the red sidewalks and paved pathways.

Main Street USA is representative of the hometown people "remember" but most people never really knew. Created to capture the dawn of the Industrial Revolution, the street reflects an era in history where electricity began to replace gas lamps. It is a piece of Americana that oozes hope for a bright and exciting future. The castle marks the far end of Main Street, beckoning guests to move forward. The Train Station anchors the street and serves as the depot transporting you to lands waiting to be explored inside this Magic Kingdom. Some historians speculate that it was actually Walt Disney's love for trains that inspired his design and vision for his original theme park. An avid train enthusiast, Walt had needed a hobby outside of the studio, and trains became not only a distraction but a passion. This distraction in some ways had helped Walt himself to keep his dreams on track.

Now Hawk faced the challenge to keep his quest to solve the mystery on track. Turning his back to the castle and resting against the rail he looked back toward the entrance to the Train Station. *If we are going to stay on track, finding the square is our ticket.* Then he saw it. Tilting his head in doubt he wondered if the obvious might be the answer. He was staring across the patio at the ticket booth of the Train Station. If you needed a ticket, there was no better place to get it than in a ticket booth. He briskly covered the distance between the rail and the ticket booth and peered inside.

The interior of the ticket office was classic Disney design. Attention to detail made this look like a working ticket booth where customers would purchase tickets for destinations across the rail lines. Everything appeared period correct. Charts, maps, ledgers, papers, stamps, and items arranged neatly on shelves. On the left-hand side of the office was a three-tiered wire basket holding the railroad paperwork. Above the wire shelves were two wooden shelves attached to the wall. The lower shelf supported two stamps for inking documents, and above that was another shelf holding an old electric fan and a box. Hawk moved to the far side to peer through the glass, trying to find an angle with less reflection. Studying the shelf he saw a dark metal box. Not square, actually more rectangular, but the closest thing to a square in the ticket office. The box was aged to fit in with the decor of the ticket booth, but he wondered if what he was looking for might be inside it. Eyes dancing around the interior of the ticket office, he sought a way into the small room. The door at the rear of the booth was narrow and definitely the only way in or out.

The problem, of course, would be getting inside. Reentering the Train Station, he moved to the back of the booth and easily found the door that would grant him entrance. The door was locked, but if it was the correct door, he was confident his kingdom key would open it. Placing his hand on the doorknob he turned it just to see if it might be open. The knob turned but the door did not budge. The lock itself was placed higher up on the door.

"Can I help you?"

Hawk flinched.

"Uh . . . no." He turned to see who had spoken.

A cast member dressed as a conductor stood in the middle of the train station looking toward him. Obviously he had seen Hawk looking around over the past few minutes and had watched as he tried to open the door to the ticket booth.

"I'm just exploring," Hawk admitted. "I'm fascinated with the detail in every area of the park. Is there any way that I can look closer inside?"

"I'm sorry, I can't let you into the ticket office. Not allowed, you understand."

"Of course, I was just noticing some of the stuff inside and wanted to take a better peek."

"It is quite interesting," the conductor smiled. "This railroad station would have been a favorite for Walt Disney if he had ever seen this park completed. Trains were a favorite pastime of his—" A train whistle drew his attention away. On cue there was another surge of people moving into the station as the next train steamed in ready to exchange another load of passengers.

"I wish I could show you more, but your train has arrived." The conductor, whose enthusiasm for his role impressed Hawk, hurried back to help reload the arriving train.

Hawk guessed that in the movement of people he would have his best chance to enter the ticket office. The moment the conductor disappeared back through the doorway into the loading area, Hawk found the kingdom key in his pocket and pressed it into the lock. A slight turn to the right moved the bolt on the lock. In one motion Hawk swung open the door and stepped inside the booth, then closed the door behind him.

As people crested the stairs to make their way into the Train Station, some glanced toward the man standing very awkwardly inside the ticket office, surrounded by windows. He decided the quicker he could get out of this booth the better and was hoping to escape before the train left the station. If not, he would be far too easy to catch and he knew there was no way to explain why he was inside or how he had gotten there. Snatching the old metal box off the top shelf, he opened it to see its contents.

The metal lid hinged back, and resting inside was a shining silver box. Each side of the box measured four inches. Emblazoned on the cover of this silver box was the smiling figure of Mickey Mouse. *The next clue you need is a square.* It was Pal Mickey who had added to Rales's information. *Hey, pal, if we are going to stay on track, finding the square is our ticket. When you see me you know you've got it!*

This is what he was looking for. Then the message Rales had added came back to Hawk. *Not just the square but what the square contains.* Carefully opening the sterling box revealed four one-by-four-inch sections. Four pieces, identically shaped, fit in the sections within this box.

An uncomfortable feeling drew his attention away from the discovery, and he looked up as two children peered at him through the glass. Smiling, Hawk waved at them and the kids waved back. Hawk quickly closed and replaced the old metal box back on the shelf. He forced the other box into the oversized pocket of his jacket, a last-minute purchase at the hotel before he came back to the Kingdom. He needed to get out of the Train Station as quickly as possible. The familiar vibration on his hip returned with the distinctive *ha-ha!* Alerted that there was a message from Mickey, he held his breath, re-opened the door back into the Train Station and exited the booth as he heard "All aboard!" The train was just now getting ready to leave, meaning the conductor was finishing up his work.

Relocking the door behind him, he walked out of the Train Station back onto the landing and then casually moved off to his left to descend the winding staircase back down to Main Street USA. The stairs ended on a sidewalk opening toward the City Hall side of Town Square. Moving forward, he crossed back over in front of the Train Station and walked toward the Town Square Exposition Hall. Through the years this hall had been used for a number of different purposes but now housed a photo center and pin-trading location. The porch was Hawk's destination. The oversized rocking chairs that lined the front porch were one of the Magic Kingdom's easily missed charms. If you were fortunate enough to find an unoccupied chair, you could rock in the shade, watch as children greeted characters, and enjoy the smiles and excitement as people poured in streams from the tunnels below the Train Station catching a glimpse of Main Street for the first time. People moved past these chairs so quickly they easily went unnoticed by most.

Heavily sitting down and rocking back he reached down to release his plush clue-giver from his side. Pressing the midsection firmly he lifted Pal Mickey toward his right ear so he could hear. Allowing his eyes to search his surroundings he listened for the next message.

"Gosh, pal! You're doing terrific. Now we have to travel through time. When you find the fort at the monument, you'll know where to go."

Rocking, Hawk opened his cell phone and called Shep to describe the events of the past hour so they could decipher the next clue.

 *Day Six*
Late Afternoon

THE AFTERNOON SUN FELL from the Florida sky as evening began
to settle over the Magic Kingdom. Hawk had reluctantly given up his rocking chair when he and Shep had concluded that to *travel through time* must
mean a trip to Tomorrowland. However, the monument and fort portion of
the clue left them both puzzled. Shep decided to keep working on the clue
and Hawk would do some legwork to see what he could discover. Staying
on the move, Hawk had concluded, was the best plan since he never knew
when another specially created transponder would activate his personal Pal
Mickey. He moved from the Central Plaza hub across the bridge into Tomorrowland toward the Astro Orbiters. The height of this ride had made it the
one of the landmarks drawing guests to come deeper into Tomorrowland.
Walking, he wondered if one of the landmarks might be the monument
he was looking for. Both he and Shep had decided the best strategy was to
unravel the clue in parts. The first part was to travel through time. The most
obvious way to travel on a journey through time was to experience Walt Disney's Carousel of Progress.

Moving underneath the elevated transportation marvel known as the
Tomorrowland Transit Authority, he moved up the ramp to get in line
for the Carousel attraction. Via a television monitor, Walt introduced the
attraction. The Carousel of Progress was the centerpiece of an exhibit Disney designed for General Electric at the New York World's Fair in 1964. The
attraction showcased Disney's love for nostalgia with his own personal vision
for a brighter future that was ushered in with breakthroughs in technology
and innovation. The rotating theatre now stopped and the automated doors
opened. The crowd walked in and visitors began to seat themselves throughout the theatre. The size of the rotating auditorium allowed the sparse crowd
to spread out filling up only half the seats. Hawk found himself sitting on the
end of an aisle with ten seats between him and the family seated to his right.

Lights dimmed and the introduction began. Not certain what he was looking for, Hawk perched himself on the edge of his seat. This was a show that he was very familiar with and in his mind was the attraction that best captured what he believed to be the touch of Walt Disney. The audience would literally move around sets featuring four different generations of an American family as they shared the wonderful changes they had experienced in their lifetimes.

Through each scene Hawk tried to notice any detail that might be important. As the carousel continued to move, he arrived at the final scene and remembered the stories of how difficult it was for the Imagineers to keep updating the attraction to represent the family of the future. Eventually they had ceased trying as hard to keep up, because the future advanced faster than they could upgrade the attraction and it was beyond their ability to predict the changes. Even Hawk was amazed at how quickly things changed in the world around him. The last six days had blown past him with the force of a hurricane and there was no end to the wind in sight. As he sat in the theatre with the lights turned down, gently rotating around some very familiar scenes, the exhaustion of the mental and physical strains of the past few days enveloped him.

The future finale disappeared and the rotating theatre moved into the unloading scene. He had traveled through time and had not seen a monument, a fort, or anything else that helped him. He remained in his seat as the rest of the crowd got up and moved toward the exit. Realizing he needed to leave, he eased forward to get out of his seat.

Two hands grasped his shoulders and jerked him back down. He slammed backward, the shock leaving him unable to offer any resistance. Once he hit the back of the chair he quickly gathered his wits about him and once again moved forward to get out of the seat. With a click the automatic doors shut and the theatre began to move once again. The hands were still on his shoulders, but this time Hawk was ready. The grasp was not strong enough to keep him in place as he wrenched himself free and stood to face his assailant.

Standing as the theatre rotated back into the opening sequence Hawk had seen moments before, he was surprised as he stared into the face of Sandy, Kiran's friend from the Studios.

"Hello, Dr. Hawkes." Sandy spoke without expression.

"Just what do you think you're doing?" Hawk angrily spit back at him.

"Have a seat, Dr. Hawkes." Sandy made a sweeping gesture to the row of seats between them.

"I'll stand."

"Suit yourself."

"I said, what do you think you're doing?"

"Actually, that is what I want to ask you." Sandy jutted his chin forward.

"I'm not sure what you're talking about, but I'm certain I don't owe you an explanation for anything."

Sandy shook his head. "You do owe me an explanation."

Hawk studied him for a moment. The attraction played through the first scene and Sandy rose to stand facing Hawk with the barrier of chairs between them. Distracted by the events confronting him he hadn't noticed before that the attraction had not stopped to load in another group of guests. Suddenly Sandy reached out and grabbed Hawk by the shirt, jerking him toward the seats. Momentarily off balance, Hawk fell forward. He drove his palms into Sandy's chest. The thrust broke Sandy's grip and he started to fall backward. Hawk, stronger and now thinking more clearly, grabbed two fistfuls of Sandy's shirt and dragged him across the row of seats. He glowered at the cast member.

"I don't appreciate the way you kept me on this ride." Hawk breathed deeply, trying to regain a bit of composure.

"It is not a ride, you idiot! It is an attraction, a classic experience. Don't minimize it by calling it a ride!" Sandy was glaring back at Hawk with eyes wide.

"Do you have something you wanted to tell me?" Hawk had now regained control of his emotions. The shock of unexpectedly being grabbed and trapped now melted as he felt less threatened and more in control.

"Yes, I want you to stay away from Kiran!"

"Is that it?"

"Yes, stay away from her or I won't be responsible for what might happen."

"Are you threatening me?"

"No, you moron! I am warning you." Sandy's eyes narrowed and anger flashed even though Hawk held a distinct advantage in this encounter. "You have no idea what you are doing. Stay away from her or else."

Disgusted, Hawk shoved Sandy backward. He landed awkwardly in one of the seats and gave Hawk a look that was a blend of pity and frustration. He slid down the empty row of seats and walked to the front of theatre, which was now moving between scenes. Leaping on the front of the stage as it rotated he placed a hand on the wall separating the seating areas of each theatre.

"Remember what I told you," Sandy yelled defiantly as he slipped around into the next theatre. The dangerous maneuver paid off as the theatre stopped in front of the next scene, guaranteeing that Hawk would not be able to pursue him.

Hawk now stood alone in the empty theatre as the scene played. With Sandy gone he reviewed the confrontation. Hawk had been surprised, startled, frustrated, embarrassed, and angry in a matter of moments. Kiran had been right about Sandy; her fellow cast member was jealous. But this jealousy was more unhinged than Kiran had indicated. Now with nothing to do and no place to go, Hawk sat back down and once again watched the Carousel of Progress play out in front of him. As each scene played out, although he was sure he was alone, he kept glancing over his shoulder to make sure no one else had snuck into the theatre to grab him from behind again.

Twenty minutes later the carousel rotated into the area where Hawk was to disembark. This time there were no surprises and the door opened uneventfully. Hawk walked out of the theatre alone. The cast member watched as he exited and then looked in to see if any more guests were coming out behind him. When none did, the cast member's face registered a look of surprise.

"Small crowd this time around," Hawk said with a smile.

He moved down the exit ramp of the attraction as twilight began to unfold in layers over the Magic Kingdom. The dazzling twinkling of lights illuminated the buildings in Tomorrowland as Hawk realized that his efforts had not produced any new direction. Pausing with a glance back toward the Carousel of Progress, he wondered how Sandy knew where he was. Had Sandy followed him? Where had Sandy followed him from? If Sandy worked at the Studios, how had he managed to find him here in the Magic Kingdom? Only now after the adrenaline began to dissipate within his system was Hawk able to clearly wonder about this string of questions.

The questions dissolved as his cell phone went off. Rapidly searching for it he opened the unit without looking at the caller ID.

"This is Hawk."

"Hawk," came the familiar voice of Jonathan, "we've got a problem."

In his years of ministry Hawk had heard this phrase many times before. Within him it ignited a desire to solve and tackle the problem with swiftness and effectiveness. "What's wrong?"

"I just got a call from Tim Keaton. Juliette hasn't gotten home yet and he hasn't heard from her. He called to see what everyone had been doing today and when was the last time we saw her."

Hawk's chest tightened.

"She isn't answering her cell phone?"

"No, I told him what was going on and he tried to reach you on your cell, but it kicked him straight to voice mail."

"I was in the Carousel of Progress, probably didn't get a signal. Did you call Shep and find out where he last saw her?

"Sure did. He left her at the escalator in the Contemporary. She was heading up to catch a monorail."

Earlier in the day he had strongly felt the need to avoid any law enforcement involvement. Within him was a glimmer of hope that the disappearance of Farren Rales was part of an elaborate puzzle that Farren had created for him to solve. Now with the disappearance of Juliette he knew that neither could be an accident. Perhaps trying to put off contacting the sheriff's office had been a bad decision. If it was, then it was now time to correct it.

"Jonathan, call the sheriff's department and tell them everything that has been going on."

"Everything?"

"Yes, everything. Start by calling Al Gann and bring him up to speed. He'll know what to do and who to call."

Al Gann, a captain in the sheriff's office, had recently joined the church and had repeatedly extended an invitation for the pastor to call if he ever needed anything. This situation definitely qualified as need.

"I'm on it, boss!" Jonathan ended the connection.

Hawk had wandered absently while on the phone with Shep, and was now walking in front of the Tomorrowland Indy Speedway. He noticed a familiar figure in the distance. Immediately halting his walk he allowed the people walking past him to create a thickening human barrier between him and the person headed in his direction. The easily identifiable frame of Reginald was moving toward him. If Reginald had spotted the preacher he had given no indication, and this gave Hawk a moment in which to decide what to do next. Casually turning so as not to draw attention to himself, he leisurely strolled with the people around him. Now he was in front of Reginald, moving in the same direction. Not daring to look back over his shoulder, he kept pace with the quickest moving people near him. Walking outside the gift shop he veered around the corner to a path that would take him back across the bridge from Tomorrowland toward Central Plaza in front of Cinderella Castle. His heart pounded as he kept pace with tourists as they laughed, looked, and absorbed the sights and sounds surrounding them. He exited the world of tomorrow and continued toward the hub of the park. Drifting to the right he followed the street as it circled toward the castle. Once he walked past the castle he followed the street back around toward the bridge leading to Liberty Square. This gave him a chance to look back across the plaza toward Tomorrowland. The quick glance revealed what he had been hoping not to see. Reginald was in Central Plaza and making his way toward Liberty Square as well. Reginald was not looking directly at Hawk and there was more distance between the two of them. Still he was back there and moving in the same direction.

Crossing the dark wooden bridge into Liberty Square he subtly picked up his pace. On the other side of the bridge he slowed and moved toward Ye Olde Christmas Shoppe. Hawk again looked back across his right shoulder as he moved in front of the shopping area. His searching the crowd for

Reginald was interrupted as a hand grabbed his arm above his elbow and pulled him into the store. The gentle tug carried him inside and he found himself in the grasp of Kiran. Hand clenched around his arm she smiled at him suspiciously.

"Hi, Hawk, what are you doing?"

He hadn't expected to see her and he felt his eyes widen.

"Do you have another clue or am I supposed to believe you are just another tourist strolling through the park?"

Her dazzling smile disarmed him. She was dressed casually, just like any other guest in the park. She could have been just another guest in the park. He had told her he would call when he figured out what to do next. As the events of the day unfolded he had not considered it. Originally he had wanted to sit down and try to figure out the mysterious woman who had unexpectedly shown up in his life. It had been a long time since he had been attracted to someone. In Kiran he had seen glimpses of a person he wanted to spend time with and get to know better. Thinking about her had been crowded out by the twists and turns of the day. Now seeing her in person he was completely unprepared to deal with his feelings for her.

"Uh . . ."

"What is it?" Her smile faded as she studied his face.

"Someone is following me."

"Right this minute?"

He nodded and looked back out the door at the people passing. Reginald would certainly have made it across the bridge and would be right outside the door by now. Never releasing his arm, Kiran began to pull him deeper into the shopping area. As she led him inside, Hawk remembered her describing this store on the tour. Ye Olde Christmas Shoppe featured three distinctively themed stores interconnected. Kiran had pulled him into the Music Teacher's Shop adorned with period instruments that were being readied as Christmas gifts. The lights, smells, and look of the holiday shop were a detail that most people missed. One shop seamlessly opened into another as Kiran and Hawk weaved through the shoppers. They moved into the Woodcarver's Shop. This area featured the tools of a wood worker in various stages of preparing Christmas gifts. This store would open into still another, which was designed like the home of a family. Warm and inviting for the holidays, the last store created the third unique theme for a single store. Just before they entered the family home section Kiran pulled Hawk off to the left and out an exit door in the back corner of the Woodcarver's Shop, on the opposite side of where Hawk had entered.

Quickly they moved into an empty alcove behind the store. The glimmer of holiday lights radiating from the windows threw a dimly festive glow across the darkened walkways and foliage. They stealthily moved along paths that were lined with rock walls that surrounded natural landscaping. At the point farthest away from the Christmas Shoppes they stopped. Their new vantage point was isolated from the steady march of guests. No one could approach without being detected.

"Every time I run into you, something strange seems to happen." Kiran twisted her head, checking to make sure they had not been followed. "Who is following you?"

"Not sure," Hawk told her. "His name is Reginald."

"Reginald?"

"Yes, crooked nose with bald head. My height and tough looking."

"Reginald Cambridge," she said decisively.

"You know him?"

"If we're talking about the same guy." Kiran again glanced back toward the store they had exited. "Why is he following you?"

"He saw me snooping around."

"Hawk, he's a trouble shooter in our security division." Urgency crept into her tone. "Even though we're all supposed to be on a first name basis as cast members, he's always called Mr. Cambridge."

"Security you say?"

"Yes, security I say. But he's a rough customer. When he gets involved in a situation, it's serious business. Hawk, what have you done now? What have you found?"

"I guess I was just in the wrong place at the right time."

"And he just started following you?" Kiran's voice revealed a twinge of exasperation.

"I guess." Hawk smiled, trying to downplay her concern. Guilty as it made him feel, he didn't want to tell her about the events of the day involving Reginald Cambridge.

"You are leaving something out," Kiran said. "Mr. Cambridge doesn't stalk people without a reason. What are you leaving out?"

She wouldn't let it go. And he couldn't keep lying to her. "I have another clue."

"What?" Kiran's eyes grew wider.

"But something else has happened. One of my staff is missing."

"Because of your key?"

"Yes, Juliette is missing. Our entire staff was together this morning and I showed them the key. She left but never showed up at home."

"First Farren and now Juliette." She closed her eyes and lowered her head. "What is it that you're looking for that is so important?"

The sincerity of her concern reaffirmed Hawk's decision to tell her the truth. Kiran silently guided him back along the snaking, isolated path and then down a walkway that would take them toward the entrance of Adventureland. Looking over his shoulder, Hawk stole one last glance toward the Christmas Shoppes. Reginald was nowhere to be seen. He was certain Mr. Cambridge had spotted him and was probably still looking for him.

"Where are we going?" Hawk asked.

"Somewhere safe," she whispered. Their pace was brisk but not so fast they would draw attention to themselves. They slipped back among the moving guests as they crossed the bridge into Adventureland. The sound of drums drove the soundtrack that compelled them to enter this area of the theme park. Once across the bridge Kiran turned her head to speak in Hawk's ear as they walked.

"Do you have the name tag you found last night?"

"In my pocket."

"Good, put it on please." She nudged him to the right as she put on her own name tag.

Following her lead he stepped out of the fast lane of tourist traffic.

 *Day Six*
Evening

KIRAN AND HAWK STEPPED into an isolated backstage area of Adventureland, surveying the landscape for unexpected company. They saw no one, and she pointed for Hawk to walk in front of her toward a doorway a few feet away.

Once you step behind the scenes in the Disney theme parks, either the magic dissipates or you are even more intrigued by the way everything works. Grayson Hawkes appreciated both sides of the Disney show. On a different day, under different circumstances and with a different agenda, this would have been a moment he would have slowed down and tried to enjoy. This was not that day. Gripping his cell phone he dialed Shep, who picked up on the first ring.

"Did you get hold of Al Gann?" Hawk asked.

"I sure did." Shep was typing on his laptop as he spoke. "I told him everything."

"What does he want us to do?"

"He said he'll get started on the search for Juliette and contact whoever he needed to. And he'll call you as soon as he knows anything."

"Thanks, Shep," Hawk let his eyes cut directly to Kiran, who was listening to his half of the conversation with interest. "Did he have any advice?"

"He said for you to be very careful and stay out of trouble."

"I didn't need him to tell me that."

"Seriously, he said you were obviously into something a lot more serious than you thought." Shep paused. "He thinks we might all be in danger."

"You be careful too, then."

"Jonathan is coming back over here to meet me, and we're going to go look for Juliette."

"Do you have a plan?"

Kiran leaned in closer as if trying to overhear what Shep might be saying.

"We're going to retrace the path we think she took back to her car. Al's meeting us there."

"I'll come and help you." Juliette could be in danger. That trumped the urgency of finding Farren's clues.

"No, you need to get that puzzle of yours figured out," Shep said. "Juliette could be anywhere. If it's related, solving the mystery might help. Keep your phone on you, okay?"

"Sure thing." Hawk ended the call.

"No word on Juliette?" Kiran asked, concerned.

"No."

"I'm sorry." She laid a hand on his arm for a moment. "What are you going to do now?"

"I'm going to try to find the next clue; maybe it will somehow help Juliette."

"Let me help." Kiran reached over and grabbed Hawk by the hand, gently rubbing her thumb across his fingers. "I want to help you, please." She waited for some response or reaction. "You still need my help, right?" He couldn't make himself give her the response she wanted. "What's wrong?"

"Sure." His answer sounded hollow and unconvincing.

"Sure what?"

"Um . . . sure I need your help." Hawk tried to cover his hesitancy. He knew he was doing a poor job of it. "Nothing's wrong."

"You're lying." Releasing his hand and stepping back in stunned surprise, she whispered, "I don't believe your nerve! All I have done since we met is rescue you. On any number of occasions I could have had you arrested, but I didn't. I listened to your far-fetched story, and somehow you managed to convince me it was true and you act like you don't trust me. That's it, isn't it? You don't trust me? I have rescued you for the last time."

"Kiran, I want to trust you," he admitted apologetically. "These last few days have gotten pretty mixed up. Things are happening faster than I can figure them out."

She stiffened and her body language became defensive. They stood facing each other, not speaking. Hawk felt his stomach sink, leaving him queasy. Confrontation didn't usually bother him, but this time it did. He understood why. His attraction to Kiran threw him off balance, and he wasn't thinking as clearly as he normally might. The situation had become more urgent, and if Al Gann was right, the danger was real. Farren had warned him on the DVD to trust no one. Common sense told him not to trust Kiran. A few days ago she had been no one to Hawk; he hadn't even known she existed.

"I understand, Hawk," she said softly. Tears welled up and rimmed the bottom of her eyes. "Good luck."

He watched as she turned and left him standing there. She moved toward the door they had just walked through. Grasping the handle, she was about to push through, taking her back into Adventureland.

"Wait!" Hawk called. "I need your help."

Kiran paused with her back toward him. The preacher waited for what seemed like an eternity as she slowly turned back to face him. As she raised her head, Hawk saw her jaw tighten.

She shook her head slowly shook from side to side. "No, I'm done."

"Please." Hawk surprised himself as he said it. A few moments ago he wasn't sure he trusted her, but his options as he saw them were limited and the situation was desperate. Risk, although a quickly calculated one, dictated what he now heard his own voice saying. "Maybe if I can figure this out I can find Juliette and Farren. They're my friends. Actually they're my family. Please help me."

Kiran stared at Hawk, revealing no emotion. Her eyes took him in as if trying to determine whether she could now trust him. The steely gaze placed an invisible barrier between them. Hawk dared not breach that barrier. He didn't know if he had hurt her or made her angry. Perhaps both, but his rising fear made him willing to embrace any source of assistance. If he was making a bad decision, then he would deal with the consequences later.

"Kiran, I'm stuck," Hawk heard himself continue. "I have a clue that I can't figure out, I've got the meanest security guard of the company showing up everywhere I go, and I feel like I'm running out of time. I didn't mean to make you angry. I'm sorry. I just don't know what to do."

She spoke almost inaudibly.

"Excuse me? I didn't hear you."

"I said"—she raised her volume—"you didn't make me angry. You hurt me, that's my fault, my mistake." She blinked rapidly, and other than the glisten of tears, her face drained of all emotion. "What's your next clue?"

Hawk was once again caught off guard by the quick shift.

"Do you want my help or not?" Kiran repeated. "What is your next clue?"

Hawk cleared his throat. "My Pal Mickey gave me the clue. 'You're doing terrific. Now we have to travel through time. When you find the fort at the monument you'll know where to go.' Shep and I were trying to figure it out so I went to the Carousel of Progress."

"That makes sense." Kiran brushed a finger across her damp cheek. "Of all the attractions here, that one is a journey through time. I take it there was nothing to find."

"No, I didn't see anything that jumped out at me." Except Sandy. "And the fort at the monument doesn't fit at all, at least not at the Carousel."

"Did you have any other ideas you were chasing?"

"No, that was it. Right after I left the Carousel is when I got word about Juliette, and then Reginald showed up."

"So when I found you moving into Liberty Square, you were just trying to get away from Mr. Cambridge?"

"Right." He wondered if she realized she'd called Reginald by his formal name.

"Liberty Square is moving back in time," she offered.

"Could it be that simple? Then what about the fort and the monument part of the clue?"

"I don't know." She paced away.

"You know, Hawk, you might have been onto something moving into Liberty Square."

"How's that?"

"Liberty Square is definitely designed to be a step back into history." Suddenly her eyes widened in excitement. "You were headed in the right direction!"

"I was?"

"Yes," she motioned for him to follow her. Taking off her name tag and gesturing for him to do the same she said, "Let me show you, but keep your eyes open, we need to be careful."

"Where are we going?"

"Back out on the streets into Liberty Square!"

 *Day Six*
Evening

LIBERTY SQUARE IS WHERE a "new nation is waiting to be born. Thirteen separate colonies have banded together to declare their independence from the bonds of tyranny. It is a time when silversmiths put away their tools and march to the drums of a revolution, a time when gentlemen planters leave their farms to become generals, a time where tradesmen leave the safety of home to become heroes." This is the sign on the entrance to Liberty Square as you cross the bridge. It is a recreation of a place where the ideas of freedom were forged by the Founding Fathers of America. The stories of history that inspired this land were filled with adventure, danger, and great excitement as dreams came to life.

Now as Hawk entered Liberty Square the feeling of danger overwhelmed any excitement and adventure he might have felt. This was the very area that Kiran had rescued him from a short time ago.

Weaving seamlessly through the people, Kiran led Hawk toward the front porch of a gift shop between the Haunted Mansion and the Columbia Harbor House.

"Sit here and try to look inconspicuous." She pointed toward a corner of the porch.

They sat and she slid up next to him. With her hand linked inside his arm they tried to look like other park guests. Tilting her head toward his shoulder she spoke in soft tones.

"The Imagineers designed Liberty Square so the geography reflects a chronological transition through this area into Frontierland. I am thinking that might be your travel through time."

"Okay." The excitement in her voice gave him the sense she was about to impart important information. "Go on."

"So there's a detail of the park Grayson Hawkes doesn't know?" she teased. "See the Haunted Mansion?" She pointed back toward the attraction.

"It's designed after a home from the 1700s in the New York Hudson River Valley area. That's where it starts. Then look here at the Columbia Harbor House; all of this area reflects what Boston might have looked like." She waved her hand toward the buildings right in front of them. "These were intended to be from the mid-1700s."

She pulled Hawk to his feet with her arm still locked in his, and they moved toward the Hall of Presidents. In an upstairs window on the side of the building two lanterns were glowing.

"Do you remember anything about the Revolution?" Kiran asked.

"Lanterns in the window." Hawk thought back. "Sure, one if by land, two if by sea—the midnight ride of Paul Revere."

"Exactly. Now see the number on the top of the Hall of Presidents is 1787."

"That represents Philadelphia in 1787?"

"The idea was to allow the buildings, the architecture, and some of the design to provide a transition over the years from the 1700s and follow the push of exploration west. The Constitution was signed in 1787 as well."

Arm in arm, they walked from Liberty Square toward Frontierland. The journey with the Rivers of America on their right carried them past a building patterned after a structure style of St. Louis in the mid-1800s. Passing it Kiran reminded Hawk in her best tour guide spiel that St. Louis is known as the "Gateway to the West." The next buildings illustrated Kiran's narrative as she explained that Grizzly Hall, the home of the Country Bear Jamboree, was patterned after a mid-1800s building found in the Colorado Rockies. She also pointed out the 1876 on the Hardware and General Store as they walked making their way west. Pecos Bill Tall Tales Inn and Cafe is housed in a Saloon bearing 1878. Moving off to their right at the Town Hall, they pressed toward the only thing out of place in the trek west. The Splash Mountain attraction fit into the era, but would have been a detour south instead of west. The Imagineers believed strongly that the best fit for the attraction was in the Frontierland design.

"So we have managed to travel through time," she reminded Hawk as they stood in front of Big Thunder Mountain Railroad, having successfully strolled through the streets of Frontierland.

"I never knew any of that before," Hawk replied, genuinely impressed. "But if we've traveled through time, what is the fort at the monument?"

"I haven't figured that out," she replied. "There is no fort here."

"What is the monument?"

"It's right here."

"Here?" Hawk looked around to see what he was missing. "I'm not see- ' ing it."

Once again her tour continued. She walked Hawk past the entrance to Big Thunder Mountain and up the incline to the exit lines that allowed passengers to leave from both sides of the mine train. They stopped at a photo spot looking over the Rivers of America on their right and the mountains of Big Thunder directly in front of them. Stepping away from Hawk and turning to face him, she spread her arms wide.

"I give you Monument Valley," she said triumphantly.

Hawk looked across the brilliant design of the Big Thunder Mountain. In the evening it was lit, allowing the riders to have a much more exciting experience racing across the tracks at night.

They were no closer to helping Juliette or finding Rales, and the frustration of that was starting to make his head hurt. "I don't get it."

"Big Thunder Mountain is patterned after Monument Valley in California. The way the master design of the park is laid out, we have now traveled from the 1700s in New York to the late 1800s in Monument Valley, California. We have gone across the country and traveled through time."

"It makes sense." Hawk knew he never would have figured this clue out on his own. "I needed a tour guide to get me here."

"But your tour guide doesn't know what the fort and the monument are. As you can see, there is no fort here."

Hawk scanned the area surrounding him. There was nothing he could see that looked like a fort. Still he was convinced that Kiran's intuition had been correct. Her knowledge of Walt Disney World had managed to keep him on track. In this case she had found the track. His own best efforts had put him on a ride in Tomorrowland.

"It has to be here." Hawk continued to look around.

"I got you here." She drummed her finger on the rail. "But I have no clue what you're going to do now."

Hawk decided to explore. He wandered back down the path they had come up on, then meandered up the exit path of the attraction itself. Moving into the attraction backward he was met by a group of enthusiastic riders who had just gotten off the ride. He paused, waiting for them to move past. As soon as the path was clear he continued his search. A wooden crate lay to the side of the path, and he paused and crouched to get a closer look at it. He heard Kiran's familiar footsteps close behind him, and she stopped at his side. He looked at her and smiled, pointing to the writing on the crate: Ft. Dixon Depot.

"The fort at the monument," he said with satisfaction.

"Ha-ha!"

Pal Mickey alerted him that there was a new message waiting. Placing a knee on the ground Hawk steadied himself as he freed the stuffed animal from his waist. Kiran moved in close so she could hear the message. He pressed the midsection of the stuffed animal.

"You're terrific, Hawk; I just knew you could find it! Now you know where to go. I know you can do it . . . I know you can do it . . . I know you can . . ."

They looked at each other, bewildered. Looking back toward the stuffed Mickey Hawk squeezed it again to replay the message.

"You're terrific, Hawk; I just knew you could find it! Now you know where to go. I know you can do it . . . I know you can do it . . . I know you can . . ."

"Is it broken or stuck?" Kiran asked.

"I don't know, it kind of sounded like it." He shook his head. "But he said the same thing both times."

"Do you know where to go now?"

"Actually, I just might."

"So this isn't what we're looking for?"

"Yes it is, but we have to find it to find something else," Hawk explained. "That's the way the clues have been working."

"Where are we going now?"

"I have seen a crate like this before," Hawk said.

She swept her arm in a wide arc. "This whole area is decorated with crates."

"No, I mean I have seen a crate exactly like this one." He cocked his head. "At least I think I have."

"So now you know where to go?" Kiran prodded. "Just like Mickey said, right?"

"Let's find out." Hawk rose to his feet and led her through the exit ramp and navigated a course through the people around them. Approaching Splash Mountain he veered left along another path that gave guests a chance to watch the floating log rafts wind out of the water ride. The path ended on the main walkway in Frontierland. Beyond the railway another boat full of wet, laughing guests moved toward the end of the ride.

There was a wooden walkway that snaked along the Rivers of America, providing a magnificent view of Tom Sawyer's Island. Guests could take a leisurely stroll along this panoramic pathway that allowed them an escape from the crowds. It mirrored the street cutting through Frontierland, providing a bit of privacy from the pedestrian traffic.

"Look." Hawk pointed with one hand, grabbing Kiran by the arm with the other.

Reginald Cambridge was staring at them, heading their way. Hawk, now pulling her, quickened his pace across the wooden boardwalk along the waterway.

"Where did he come from?" Kiran asked, continuing to look back.

"I don't know, he just showed up."

"He's coming after us."

Hawk broke into a trot and Kiran sped up to keep pace. Again she turned back. Hawk increased their trot into a jog and then closer to a run. Moving along the pathway they passed a small wooden shack. Planting his right foot and cutting left he grabbed Kiran and pulled her with him. The sudden shift in direction threw her off balance and she stumbled, crashing into him. He caught her firmly in his arms and pulled her around the corner of the wooden outpost. They came to rest with their backs pressed against the wall of the shack now between them and the walkway. Catching their breath, neither said a word. Hawk scuttled along the back wall of the shack to peer around the corner, then ducked back. Cambridge passed the shack a few seconds later. The maneuver had bought them a few minutes. Crawling back toward Kiran, he sat back against the shack next to her. Leaning against this wall they could look out across the Rivers of America toward Tom Sawyer's Island. He was surprised to find her grinning at him.

"That was close." She laughed softly. "Is the coast clear?"

"For now." So far Reginald had been like a hound that had Hawk's scent. He didn't suppose they'd shake him for long.

"Hopefully he thinks we got off the path and raced into Fantasyland."

"We'll see."

"Now what?"

"We look."

"Where?"

"Right here." He pointed over his shoulder using his thumb.

Kiran twisted her head back toward the shack they were leaning against. Her puzzled look begged for an explanation.

"Did you see the crate sitting on the front side?" he prompted.

"No, I didn't see much of anything since I was falling when we got here."

Hawk grinned, remembering their abrupt but enjoyable arrival at their hiding place. "Well, if you had taken the time to notice the surroundings, you would have seen a crate marked Ft. Dixon Depot. It's identical to the one at Big Thunder Mountain."

"So this is it?"

"I think so." He crawled to the corner to once again peer back around it. "I'm about to find out."

He slid along the side and then the front of the shack.

The rustic structure perched on a dock along the water. Other than being a themed prop it served no function that Hawk was aware of. Looking in the window he saw what might best be described as a storage shed lined with wooden shelves. The Imagineers paid attention to detail here just like every-where else within the parks. The shelves were lined with jars, cans, and boxes that looked extremely old and fit perfectly into the decor. On the left of the window was a door. Hawk clutched the doorknob and turned it. It gave but the door remained in place. Just above the white knob was a lock. Reaching down into his pocket he found the kingdom key once again. Each time he had used it he was always surprised that it worked. This time he hoped it would work again; if it didn't, he'd be right back where he started.

The key slid into the lock and by the click Hawk knew that once again he'd interpreted the clue correctly. With the application of slight pres-sure the key turned left and the door unlocked. Pushing it open quickly he slid inside and pushed the door shut by pressing his back against it. He looked up and saw Kiran peering at him through the back window. She had a look of amazement and anticipation on her face. A slight movement of her head indicated her desire for him to start looking. The shelf was cluttered with the various storage containers. Hawk slid them around looking for something that he was not sure of. Finally he moved a can and behind it was another old-fashioned can held shut by a twist-on lid.

I know you can do it . . . I know you can do it . . . I know you can.

Mickey had said *can* three times. Although it seemed simple, it also made sense. The last piece of the clue was *can*. Hawk twisted the lid off the jar and tipped it over his palm. A chunk of metal landed in his hand. A fragment of light from a streetlamp glinted off it. Holding it up he surveyed the shining piece of silver metal. It measured nearly an inch wide and four inches long. The thin rectangle had something engraved into it. He tilted it for a better look.

"The way to get started is to stop talking and begin doing."

Hawk recognized it as a popular quote from Walt Disney, although he had no idea why it was significant. It was the only thing on the small metal bar. Flipping it over he read the quote again. As had happened time and again on this search he had found the unexpected. A light tap on the window star-tled him, when he looked up he saw Kiran, eyes wide in wonder. Waiting to inspect his discovery, she waved her hand, reminding him he needed to get out of the shack. Glancing out the front window to see if the wooden hiding place might be drawing unwanted attention, he saw none. Satisfied, he pulled back the door to exit the shack.

"Ha-ha!"

Halting immediately, he closed the door. It clicked shut once again. Slowly rotating toward the rear window Hawk saw a confused look wander across Kiran's face. Nodding toward her, he removed Pal Mickey from his waist and raised it toward his ear. Staring out the window at her he clenched his hand tightly across the stuffed midsection awaiting the next message.

"Gee, pal, you're doin' swell! Maybe you should go to a place where we can always check to remember the day we lost Mr. Disney."

As an automatic high-tech tour guide Pal Mickey had kept him on track. Wondering how long it had taken Farren Rales to prepare this hunt that he'd sent Hawk on, he took another peek out the front window of the shack, concluded the coast was clear, then swiftly opened the door and exited the depot.

Seconds later he reemerged around the corner behind the shack.

"What did you find? What was the next clue? Where do we go next?" Kiran fired question after question, leaving no time for Hawk to answer.

Smiling while motioning for her to slow down, he showed her the silver bar. Seizing it anxiously, she devoured it with her eyes before raising her head.

"What is this?"

"I assume it's a piece of the puzzle."

"This is what we have been looking for?" She once again studied the shiny silver metal.

He reached into his jacket and produced the larger square box he'd found at the train station. "It goes inside this."

The metallic surface of both the box emblazoned with *Mickey Mouse* and the bar were identical. Kiran's eyes widened. Hawk opened the lid of the box and reverently laid the metal bar into the top space. The bar slid perfectly into place as though it had found its home.

"So you're looking for three more pieces?" Hidden within the question was another question: what was it that they'd had actually found.

"I assume so." He put the lid back on the box and returned it to his pocket. "And I assume when I find all the pieces, then it will make sense."

Kiran cocked her head. He sensed she wanted to know where the box came from, but she did not ask—yet. Confident the question would come later he moved on.

"The latest clue said, 'Maybe you should go to a place where we can always check to remember the day we lost Mr. Disney.'" He gave her a moment to think. "Does that mean anything to you?"

"A place to check to remember the day we lost Mr. Disney," she mused. "You could go a lot of places to check when Walt Disney died."

Hawk held up his finger. "That's not what the clue said."

"What did I miss?"

"It is a place we can *always* check to remember the day we lost Mr. Disney." He thought aloud. "The *always* part of the clue is important, at least I think it is."

"Okay, then how does it connect to the day we lost Mr. Disney?"

"Walt died on December 15, 1966."

"How do you know that?"

"Farren Rales told our staff the story just a few days ago." He paused, wondering why he hadn't heard anything from Shep or Jonathan about Juliette.

"Did he tell you the date for a reason?" she asked. "Is it related to this clue?"

"I'm beginning to think that nothing Farren did or told me was by accident. After all, he's an Imagineer—the details matter. They help tell the story, they drive the story, they enhance the story. If you miss the details, you miss an important part of the story."

He shook his head from side to side, feeling like he was missing something.

"Are you okay?"

"Yes, I just wish I'd paid better attention and could remember everything he said. It would be helpful now, I think."

"So what now?"

"Let's take the clue apart. We know the date that Disney died, and *always check* has to tie into that somehow."

Kiran nodded. "Always check . . . always check . . . always check."

Suddenly Hawk reached out and grabbed her arm. The next instant the lights surrounding them began to fade. The evening parade was getting ready to come down the street, which would magically became a nonstop menagerie of twinkling lights synchronized to the musical soundtrack. People would stack up along the streets to watch the passing parades. Their hiding place would still be out of sight, yet they were now surrounded by masses of park visitors just a few feet away.

"We have to get out of here," Hawk urgently told her.

"Do you know where?"

"I have an idea," he grabbed her by the hand. "Let's go!"

They moved around the edge of the shack and headed back down the wooden walkway, now dark as the lights were extinguished. Silently Hawk led Kiran as they dissected the thick layers of people emerging from the crowd. A cast member waved them toward a pedestrian crossing and in mere moments they had crossed the street and rushed deeper into the mystery.

 *Day Six*
Night

THE CLANKING OF CRASHING SWORDS greeted them as they rounded the corner to Caribbean Plaza. Hawk dodged a backpedaling pirate but slammed into another, stumbling into the middle of a street show near the Pirates of the Caribbean. The Pirates attraction was not originally part of Walt Disney World. The planners didn't think guests in Florida would be interested in such an attraction due to the Caribbean's proximity to the state. But when the theme park opened, people would wander in and ask how to find the Pirates of the Caribbean. The original Pirates attraction had been such a success in Disneyland, it was assumed that it had to be a part of the new theme park. Public opinion ruled, and after scrapping plans for another adventure attraction, a new version of the Pirates was opened a few years later.

Noticing the short wait time to get on the ride, Hawk maneuvered them through the main entrance into the winding tunnels of the attraction. These lines would carry guests to the loading area where they would climb aboard boats and make their way on a search for Captain Jack Sparrow, the legendary pirate captain of the *Black Pearl*, introduced with the release of the Walt Disney Pictures Pirates of the Caribbean films. These motion pictures rejuvenated the popularity of the classic attraction for a new generation of guests. Imagineers had updated the ride to include some of the popular icons created by the stars of the motion pictures. Most of the crowd now was on the streets enjoying the parade, allowing them to enter the attraction with no other people in sight.

"Hawk, why are we here?"

The building housing Pirates of the Caribbean was modeled after a Cuban fort from the seventeenth century. Moving through the building they reached an opening in the wall lined with bars. Looking through the bars allowed the guests a view into a dungeon where two pirate skeletons were seated facing each other at a table playing a game.

"Look." Hawk stepped aside, allowing Kiran to look into the dungeon.

"Chess?" Kiran shrugged. "I've seen this scene hundreds of times. Why is this the clue?"

The pirates below had died sitting a table while playing chess, according to the story line. Now throughout time they remain just as they had been with nobody left alive to make the next move.

"The clue was *always check*," Hawk explained excitedly. "I remember hearing about this on podcasts; I've read it in books and often wondered about it. The game is in perpetual check. The only available move for either pirate leads them into a never-ending series of moves that leaves them right back where they started. They played until they both died—and they still sit in the same place with the same series of moves available. Always check."

"Incredible." Kiran studied the board, but soon returned her gaze to Hawk. "But what does this have to do with the day we lost Walt Disney?"

"We know the day Walt passed away, December 15." He thought. "What day did the Pirates of the Caribbean attraction open?"

"I don't know." Kiran fished her cell phone from her pocket. "But I can find out."

She pressed a key and they waited for the call to connect.

"I barely get a signal in here," she said, frowning. "We have an information line that can look up anything. Sometimes it might be because a guest asks a question, it might be for a staff meeting where someone is trying to get some—"

Hawk stepped closer, trying to hear both ends of the conversation. Kiran allowed him to place his head next to hers as they both listened to the man who answered the phone.

"Marquel, this is Kiran, I have a quick question for you. Please tell me when the Pirates of the Caribbean attraction opened."

As Hawk strained to listen he thought he heard the response, but wasn't quite sure. He stepped back a stride to look at Kiran, and the look on her face confirmed what he had guessed.

"Thanks, Marquel." Her mouth was opened in amazement as she ended the call. "The Pirates opened December 15, 1973."

"The day we lost Mr. Disney. 'We can always check to remember the day we lost Mr. Disney.'"

"How did you know?" She looked impressed.

"I guessed on the date," he said. "So I was hoping we had to get here. We found the place and what we're supposed to remember, but beyond that the clue didn't say anything else."

"Is there something we're missing on the chess board?"

"I don't think so; it's a series of moves that always repeats."

"Could that be the clue, something that always repeats?"

"Not sure."

After staring at the pirate skeletons for a few more minutes and running through the chess moves in his mind, Hawk hadn't come up with any new ideas. He motioned for Karin to move forward. The line descended gradually toward the loading area, where they found a small crowd waiting to climb aboard the passenger boats. Standing in line awaiting their turn Hawk felt the vibration on his hip.

"Ha-ha!"

Nonchalantly he once again released the stuffed mouse from his hip and held it between Kiran and himself. They listened closely.

"Hey, Hawk! Ha-ha, I sure am glad we're here together. There are lots of pirates hiding around here. Keep me close, won't you, pal? If you listen you can't hear them here, but they get bigger other places. Gosh, if you follow the trail to the letter, you can find it, by George!"

A cast member now stood before them, waiting to usher them aboard the waiting boat. Hawk pondered the newest clue as they took their seat. Sliding to the middle of the row they sat side by side, the only people on their row.

"Did you get all of that?" Kiran wanted to know.

"I heard it. I haven't figured it out, if that's what you mean."

"So is there another clue here in Pirates?"

"I guess so." Her questions weren't allowing him time to think clearly.

The boat jerked lightly forward as they set sail into a pirate adventure. Floating in the murky waters Hawk rummaged through the details he had accumulated. The stakes of the search, in his thinking, had been raised to a level of epic importance with the sudden disappearance of Juliette. His intuition had convinced him that in solving the mystery he would also figure out where she was. In some ways this mad search he was on didn't make much sense. Still, somehow absorbed into an Imagineers' plotline, he had faith there was an answer. The first moments of the ride carried them through a huge cavern toward a special-effects encounter with Davy Jones, another upgrade to the attraction based on the Pirates film series. As they moved through the cavern a voice echoed off the walls.

"Dead men tell no tales! Dead men tell no tales! Dead men tell no tales!"

The voice echoed through not only the refreshingly cool cave but also in Hawk's head. *Dead men tell no tales! Dead men tell no tales!*

The chant was distracting. Kiran was watching him intently as he thought and seemed to sense what he was thinking. Catching her gaze he smiled and motioned his head to the noise clanging off the walls of the cave.

"It would drive you nuts to hear that all day," she joked.

Nodding, he tried to ignore the repeating voice track. Eventually the endless sound loop would yield to the other sounds of the ride as you were carried down a waterfall into a pirate battle. Just as the boat crested the top of the waterfall in the darkness, Hawk had an idea. By the time the boat had plunged to the bottom of the falls, he was convinced he knew what to do next.

 *Day Six*
Night

BOUNCING WITH A STEADILY DRIVING VIBRATION, the boat broke free from the water-cushioned free float onto the moving rubberized track guiding the boat into the disembarking area. Stepping up out of the boat they moved with the other guests toward the inclined speed ramp that carried them back up to the exit into the shopping area of the Caribbean Plaza. Swarming shoppers filled the plaza, scooping up souvenirs of the ride. Immediately upon entering the plaza Kiran and Hawk began to weave through the visitors making their buccaneer purchases. Cutting around a display, Hawk stopped as he looked across the plaza at a man staring at them. The pastor narrowed his eyes and focused on the man's face. It was familiar, but Hawk could not identify from where. As he stared he realized he was not being paranoid; this person was watching him. Never breaking eye contact Hawk noticed a slight smile cross the face of the man. Just as the man took a step toward them, the preacher pushed Kiran in the other direction and quickly led them out of the plaza.

"What's wrong?" Kiran turned her head to look back at the plaza.

"We have company," Hawk muttered.

"Who? Where?"

"Keep moving."

Once they'd cleared the plaza they moved toward the entrance of the Jungle Cruise. The streets of Adventureland were starting to clear; it was about time for the park to close. Prior to reaching the stairs down to the cruise they moved off to their left between the Enchanted Tiki Room and the Magic Carpets of Aladdin. They continued to move through the rapidly emptying section of the park until reaching a narrow cut-through to Frontierland. Moving between the buildings they emerged in Frontierland right outside Grizzly Hall, the home of the Country Bears. It didn't appear they had been followed.

"Who did you see?" Kiran demanded.

"I'm not sure." He swept his gaze around them again, alert to pursuers. "But his face was very familiar. He didn't try to hide the fact he was staring at us. He started heading in our direction."

Hawk led Kiran with a sense of urgency along the street through Frontierland. Drifting to their left in front of Grizzly Hall they headed toward Pecos Bills once again.

"Where are we going?"

"Pecos Bill's."

Stepping onto the porch of Pecos Bill Tall Tales Inn and Cafe, Hawk grabbed the door only to find it was locked. Surprised, he looked back toward Kiran. Saying nothing she stepped off the porch and traced the wall of the restaurant through an outdoor seating area and headed toward another entrance. Continuing to peer backward over his shoulder he followed her. Kiran stepped to the second set of doors and found one of them open. Motioning for him to follow her she stepped inside.

"Normally the food areas close down as it get closer to park closing." She glanced at her watch. "The Kingdom closes in a few minutes, so they're done serving for the night. Sometimes you have to look for a way inside."

Now inside Hawk began to navigate the empty restaurant. Stepping through the main dining hall and past the ordering and serving areas, they returned to the spot they had been talking in earlier. As he halted abruptly, Kiran bumped into him. Hawk surveyed the room slowly and deliberately, allowing his eyes to search for details.

"Hawk, tell me what you're doing. Why are we here?"

"Remember the clue?"

"Sure. 'If you listen you can't hear them here, but they get bigger other places . . . follow the trail to the letter, you can find it, by George.'"

"Right." He began to unpack his thoughts. "Think about the first part of the clue. 'If you listen you can't hear them here.'"

"I'm sorry, I'm not following you."

"You gave me the idea, remember what you said would drive you nuts?"

"Sure, dead men tell no tales."

"Exactly." He nodded at her, willing her to figure it out. "Dead men don't tell them—in other words, you can't find them here."

"Dead men tell no tales—*tales* is the clue?"

"Part of it. Dead men don't tell them, so we couldn't hear them at Pirates. But they get bigger other places. If the clue is *tales*, and they can be found bigger somewhere else . . . where else could we go?"

"Pecos Bill's?" Karin asked without much confidence.

"Right!"

Her forehead rumpled. "I don't get it."

"Where are we?"

"Pecos Bills."

"No, where are we? The actual name of this place."

"Pecos Bill Tall Tales Inn and Cafe."

"And dead men tell no tales, but they get bigger other places. In other words, the tales get taller . . . bigger . . . tall tales!"

"Oh!" Her eyes flew open wide with recognition. "Of course, I never would have figured that out. Fantastic, great job."

"Thanks," he smiled without trying for humility.

"What now?"

"Still working on it." The moment of success now melted away in the heat of trying to solve the next part of the clue.

Immediately Kiran started searching the room as well. The Imagineers had based Pecos Bill's on the legend of Pecos Bill, a character in a featured segment of the Disney animated feature *Melody Time*. The story featured the song "Blue Shadows on the Trail" sung by Roy Rogers and the Sons of the Pioneers. Later the segment was released in theatres as a featured short film. The dining establishment was created around the story line that Pecos Bill opened up an inn and café and all of his legendary friends from the wild frontier had donated memorabilia for his new business. Throughout the restaurant there were displays that featured some of the most famous legends of the West. Details were what made creations by the Imagineers so special, and it was in the details that Hawk sought once again to discover answers.

Kiran repeated the next part of the clue aloud. "Follow the trail to the letter and you can find it, by George."

Hawk thought deeply. "We have to follow the trail to the letter."

"This is a western-themed restaurant, so following the trail west—"

"Happy trails to you," Hawk injected.

"Wait, that might be it!" Kiran brightened.

"Happy trails?"

"Maybe. Didn't Roy Rogers sing 'Happy Trails'?"

"Did he?"

"Roy Rogers also sang the song in the *Pecos Bill* cartoon."

"I'll have to take your word for it."

"I'm sure he did." She nodded vehemently. "I don't remember what the song was, but I am certain it was Roy Rogers."

"Great, then we're on the right track."

"Or the right trail, as it were."

"So now we follow it to the letter."

"We are closed!" The voice caused Hawk to turn with a start.

The source of the voice was a brown-haired woman dressed in street clothes wearing a name tag that read Patricia.

"Hi Patricia." Kiran stepped to meet her. "Kiran Roberts, guest relations, we're on a tour."

Hawk noticed Kiran had put her name tag back on.

"I wasn't told to expect you." The woman eyed Kiran's name tag. "We closed thirty minutes ago."

"I'm sorry; I actually just came through the open door. We are exploring some of the details and themed elements of the restaurant."

"Well, there sure are a lot of them." The woman held out her hand to Hawk, and shook his. "I'm Patricia. Pecos Bill Tall Tales Inn and Cafe is one of the best themed, best-kept secrets of the Magic Kingdom. Of course, I am partial to it since it is my area of responsibility."

"I don't blame you." Hawk smiled pleasantly. "Do you have a minute to show me some of the secrets?"

"Is that okay with you, Kiran?" Patricia asked.

"That would be great. I appreciate it, and I am sorry we just wandered in."

"Glad to do it." Patricia beamed with pride.

"I'll catch up with you, I need to make a call." Kiran stepped away from them as Patricia guided Hawk toward a wall in the restaurant.

Hawk watched Kiran use her cell phone as Patricia began to show him around. The name Annie Oakley was printed on a plaque beside a large glass display featuring a Western handgun and five playing cards. Each card had a hole in the middle. By the layout of the display it was clear to Hawk that according to legend, Oakley would have shot through the five cards with a single shot. Patricia also explained the boots they had placed in the restaurant from Annie Oakley were intended to mimic some of the celebrity-themed restaurants across the country featuring displays of memorabilia. This was the idea the Imagineers were trying convey in their design. Momentarily Kiran returned and joined them as Patricia's cell phone rang.

Kiran smiled at Hawk as Patricia conversed briefly on her cell. Upon closing it she looked apologetically at the two of them.

"I am so sorry, I have to go." She seemed genuinely disappointed. "Pressing matter waiting for me."

"Thanks for taking the time to show me around." Hawk shook her hand.

"Glad to do it," she enthusiastically responded. Turning to Kiran she continued, "You can let yourself out?"

"Sure can," Kiran assured her. "We'll only be another minute."

"Take your time. There is much to see." Patricia headed back in the direction from which she had first appeared. Kiran and Hawk watched as she exited through a door that led her off set and back into the hallways leading to the kitchen and storage areas.

"I am her pressing matter," Kiran murmured.

"What?"

"I called and tracked down her supervisor and phoned in a request from our department that we need an immediate answer for."

Hawk grinned. "Because we can't have her standing here as we snoop around."

"So hurry up and get snooping!"

Hawk allowed his mind to replay the last part of the clue over and over. *Follow the trail . . . to the letter . . . you can find it, by George.* They moved in opposite directions, examining the displays. Hawk heard Kiran's footsteps as she moved on the other side of the dining room. He moved toward the back of the restaurant, into a smaller dining area. On the wall he noticed Old Betsy, the rifle of Davy Crockett. Standing and staring at the rifle he remembered watching the adventures of Davy Crockett on the old Walt Disney television shows. He recalled what a surprise hit the television episodes and the movies had been. There were fan clubs, raccoon-skin caps, and Fess Parker dressed as Davy himself had helped to open Disneyland. The memory of the images of Fess Parker with Buddy Ebsen as his sidekick carried Hawk back to Sunday evenings as a child sitting in front of the television. Turning away from the rifle he saw another display fastened to the wall. It was a heavy dark wooden shelf. The aged, ornately designed single shelf was thick and worn. It held a variety of items that caused Hawk to stop and then he knew.

The first nameplate on the wall below the shelf read Casey Jones. Hawk remembered this cartoon legend as a train engineer who vowed to make sure his train arrived on time. It was the other nameplate that excited Hawk. The name George Russel adorned the marker. George Russel was Davy Crockett's sidekick and friend. Hawk slid a chair over so he could stand up on it and see what rested upon the shelf. A metal can, a metal pot, and a rolled piece of leather that at first glance held paper. A brown leather saddlebag along with a piece of paper that had writing on it was wedged in the center of the items. Being at eye level with the contents Hawk was able to read what was on the sheet of paper.

I remember the day Davy entered his shootin' match against the meanest and nastiest man on the mountain, Big Foot Mason. He claimed to be the best shot in Tennessee. Old Davy, he wasn't scared. He was sent to challenge Big Foot and that he did.

The letter supposedly had been written by George Russel. It was a letter *by George.*

Follow the trail to the letter and you can find it, by George.

The trail to the letter by George was just what he was looking at. The letter was inside an open leather container. It was made to be rolled and buckled shut. Obviously the leather roll was a letter carrier. As he reached out to attempt to remove the letter, he discovered it was attached. Not wanting to tear it away from the display, he picked up the entire leather letter carrier. It was about the size and weight of a rolled-up newspaper. He stepped off the chair and set the package down on a table. Fumbling with the buckle, he was about to loosen it when Kiran came back across the restaurant. When he explained what he was doing, instead of scolding him, she grinned with satisfaction. He unrolled the leather wrapping, it opened, and inside there was another piece of paper in the same print as the letter on the shelf.

> Davy was most at home in the frontier. He never met a stranger and tried to be a friend to all he met. One day he showed me a present he was given by an Indian warrior. I could never say the real Indian name he had been given by the tribe, but Davy always called his friend Hawk. One of the most prized possessions Davy had was a small saddlebag his friend Hawk had made for him. He always used it to keep important things inside.

Kiran pointed to the shelf. "That is Hawk's saddlebag, and there is no way it's an accident that the friend in the letter is named Hawk."

"Let's take a look." Hawk stepped back onto the chair.

Removing the saddlebag from the shelf, he stepped back off the chair and returned to the table. He slid the letter to the side with his hand and gently opened the saddlebag. Reaching inside he found what he was looking for: a shining silver bar identical to the first one he'd found. Kiran crowded next to him and simultaneously they leaned in to read the writing engraved into the metal.

"All of our dreams can come true if we have the courage to pursue them."

"Another quote from Walt Disney?" Kiran asked.

"It is."

He set the silver box on the table and once again opened it. Hawk gently placed the silver bar into one of the open spaces inside. Once again it was a perfect fit. Two silver pieces were now in place; there were two open spaces left. He closed the box and returned it to his pocket.

"I guess we should get out of here." Hawk wrapped the leather letter carrier closed and climbed the chair to replace it and the saddlebag. Satisfied that all looked as it had before, he stepped down from the chair and returned it to the table. As he was cleaning up, Kiran peered out the windows of Pecos Bill's, looking into Frontierland.

"Hawk, I have a feeling that our search is either going to get very easy or extremely difficult. Go ahead and put your name tag back on."

"Why?" He stepped to her side and looked out the window.

"The Magic Kingdom has closed for the night," she answered. "We can't disappear into the crowds. It'll be easier to get around as cast members, but if someone spots us . . ."

"We're in trouble."

 *Day Six*
Night

HAWK AND KIRAN STEPPED OUT onto the wooden porch outside the restaurant into the now empty streets of Frontierland. Lamplight illuminated the street and even in the darkness the details of the magical land seemed to shine even brighter minus the loud surging crowds that normally filled it. From the doorway Hawk cautiously probed the darkened recesses of the Western-themed area with his eyes, looking for anyone who might be hiding trying to observe them. Convinced there was no one watching, he stepped off the porch.

"Let's move in front of the shops and try to stay in the darker areas."

Kiran kept pace with him. "By the way, where are we headed now?"

The familiar alarm sounded on his hip.

"Ha-ha!"

"Timing is everything." He smiled.

Freeing Pal Mickey from his belt had become second nature. They found a dark nook alongside Grizzly Hall and huddled over the Pal Mickey to listen.

Gosh . . . Isn't exploring fun? I can't think of anyone I would rather be with than you, Hawk. Thanks for taking care of me with all those pirates. But now we are going to need a little luck to find the unlucky lights . . . I'll be talking to you real soon!

Hawk clipped the toy back to his belt. "We need luck to find the unlucky lights."

"So what is an unlucky light?"

"A light that doesn't work . . . or a light that goes out just when you need it?"

"Do you have an idea?"

"Not yet." His neck tingled as though he were being watched. "I've got to tell you though, I wish we were somewhere a little more out of sight."

"I know what you mean." Kiran stepped out of the alcove onto the walkway. "I promise you that Cambridge hasn't quit looking for us."

"Don't you figure he thinks we slipped out with the crowds?"

"Let's see." Her tone dripped with sarcasm. "He spots you numerous times acting suspicious on property, he spots me with you, and since he already knows who I am, my guess would be that he decides to call it a night."

"So the entire security force is looking for us."

"Correct." No sarcasm.

"Tremendous."

"You don't have any idea where we're going next?"

"To the unlucky lights."

"So that would be a no. All right, then, let's keep moving." She looked at him, waiting.

He joined her back on the walkway, eyes sweeping the park for anything unusual about the lights.

Nonchalantly moving along the Frontierland store fronts they headed back in the direction of Liberty Square. Their footsteps emitted a steady clunk along the boardwalk as they moved past the Frontierland Shootin' Arcade, bringing them to the edge of the Western-themed area. Now arriving back in Liberty Square they moved past the replica of the Liberty Bell and the Liberty Tree. Their walk carried them between the Liberty Tree and Ye Olde Christmas Shoppe. Slowing to see if they were being watched, they decided to sit on the wall surrounding the Liberty Tree. The tree and the decorative hedges around it provided a small amount of privacy, preventing them from being seen as easily. The dim light provided by the lanterns suspended from the tree cast a soft glow over them.

"We have to figure this out," Kiran whispered.

"I'm trying. The new clue sounded simple, but where do we find unlucky lights?"

"What makes something unlucky?"

"Well, if you believe in luck, I guess a lot of things. Broken mirrors, walking under ladders, spilling salt, stuff like that."

"You don't believe in luck?" Kiran quizzically leaned toward him.

"Not really." He shrugged one shoulder. "I'm a man of faith, so I really don't look at life as lucky or unlucky."

"So how do you see life?"

"I believe I have been called to follow Jesus. So I live my life based on trying my best to be a God follower. If I am serious about doing that, I have to trust that the things that happen fit into God's plan."

"And that leaves no room for luck?"

"I guess not. Whatever happens good or bad, I remind myself God is in charge, and because He is in charge, I don't spend a lot of time asking why. Instead I focus on what I should do or how I should react."

"So all of this . . . this puzzle, Farren, Juliette, being chased, and even meeting me . . . ?"

"Somehow fits into God's plan," he said softly.

Kiran hunched her shoulders. "I wish I had life figured out that way."

"Don't get the wrong idea, it isn't always easy. And I am really not as good at living that way as I would like to be."

"Tell me." Her voice was filled with a gentle sincerity.

"Think about it like this. Here we are in Liberty Square under this tree. This represents the historical background that our country was born in. You have to know that as our founding fathers made decisions they weren't always sure they were doing the right or best thing . . . but most good historians realize that these founders had a belief in God and that there was a divine reason to do the things they were trying to do. It had to have gotten pretty ugly, messy, and confusing, but history has proven our founders did an amazing job at setting us on course as a country." Being here made Hawk feel something of the enormity of that responsibility. "I think that sometimes God's plan is like that—ugly, messy, confusing—and sometimes you don't understand it until you get the chance to look back at it later."

"Your life and direction are a lot different than mine," she admitted.

"God has been good to me, better than I deserve, kind of like the lights in this tree; even when it's dark, there is just enough light to see." Hawk shifted, causing Kiran to move away and give him some space. "Kiran, tell me about this tree."

"Didn't I mention it on the Keys to the Kingdom tour?"

"If you did, I don't remember. I was distracted by my tour guide."

"All right." In the darkness he couldn't tell whether she was blushing, but she sounded like she was. "The Liberty Tree is a huge oak tree that was originally found on the property in the initial phases of construction. When it was moved it made history as one of the largest trees ever to be relocated. The reason it was placed here was to continue a tradition established in Colonial America where each town would choose a tree as the symbol of its fight for independence. It was more than symbolic though, it also became the town's meeting place. History talks about these liberty trees as the place the Sons of Liberty would gather."

"What about the lanterns?"

"They automatically come on at dusk. And there's a lantern tied to the tree for each of the original colonies."

"And how many original colonies were there?" Hawk asked with a smile crossing his face.

"Thirteen." Kiran's voice conveyed her excitement.

Standing to their feet they both turned to face the tree. Hawk moved his lips, whispering the numbers as he counted. One, two, three . . . Kiran jabbed the air in the direction of each lantern. Nine . . . ten . . . eleven . . . Now Hawk was up and physically circling the tree to complete his count. He ended up on the opposite side of where he and Kiran had been sitting moments before.

"Twelve and thirteen," he whispered with more volume. "Thirteen is certainly an unlucky number. Thirteen lanterns would be unlucky light."

Hawk now stood under the tree in front of a bronze marker explaining the significance of the tree and the history behind it.

"Ha-ha!"

Kiran quickly moved around the tree to meet Hawk.

"I suppose Jesus and not luck caused us to stop right here," she teased as she waited for him to free Mickey.

"Believe what you want. I don't believe in luck." He winked as he applied pressure to activate the voice of the mouse.

"You're doing terrrrrific! But we have to keep looking because we have more to find. So watch out, don't pout, and don't cry. Let me tell you why! Walt's grandfather has left you a gift. Find it quick, but be careful. I imagine there are a lot of people chasing us by now, and that can be a *huge* problem. But don't worry, I once got seven with one blow; I'll be here to help you, pal."

Kiran's eyes were dancing with excitement. Hawk saw the look on her face and had no idea what she was reacting to. Eagerly she waited for him to put Mickey back into place before she grabbed his arm, jerking him around toward the gift shop side of the Liberty Tree.

"Have you figured it out?" Hawk asked.

"Maybe!"

"What does it mean?"

"It is the one thing you didn't learn on the Keys to the Kingdom tour."

"I think . . ." Hawk stalled, trying to think of a detail she hadn't revealed on the tour. "It was a very thorough tour, I can't think of anything you didn't tell us."

"Oh, come on!" Playfully she slapped him on the arm. "What was the very last thing you asked me about that day?"

Suddenly the memory came to him. "Kepple. You didn't tell me about the name Kepple!"

"Right." She brimmed with enthusiasm, " Kepple is the name on Ye Olde Christmas Shoppe. The name is on the section that looks like a home."

The entrance was directly across from where they stood beside the Liberty Tree. From this vantage point Hawk could see the small blue wooden heart fastened to the wall beside the door. The name in white letters read Kepple: the unanswered bit of trivia from the tour where he had first met Kiran.

"So tell me, why was the name Kepple chosen for the shop?"

"You really don't know?"

"If I knew, would I have asked?"

"I'm just surprised. You seem to know a lot of Disney history, and I just figured—"

"Will you please tell me what is important about the name Kepple!"

"Sorry," Kiran apologized. "Kepple is the name of Walt Disney's grandfather."

Suddenly the newest clue began sliding into place. *Walt's grandfather has left you a gift.* Now he knew that the grandfather's name was Kepple. *Ye Olde Christmas Shoppe* would be an obvious place to find a gift. *Watch out, don't pout, and don't cry . . . let me tell you why* was a reference to Santa Claus, meaning the next clue had to be inside the home portion of the shop. Kiran had already moved to the doorway of the shop. Hawk quickly moved over and stood next to her.

"Now all we have to do is get inside."

After the park closed, the doors to the gift shops were closed and locked. During the course of the night maintenance crews might move in and out, occasionally doing the necessary cleanup from the previous day's business. Kiran twisted the doorknob of the shop and it didn't give.

"Locked."

Hawk smugly stepped forward and took the key to the kingdom from his pocket. Sliding it into the lock he found it didn't fit just right and it would not move once he had managed to finagle it into place.

"So the magic key isn't always magic." Kiran suppressed a laugh.

"It isn't a magic key," Hawk corrected her, feeling deflated. "It's a king-dom key."

He moved off toward the left and headed around to the back of the building. This was the same area he and Kiran had managed to hide from Reginald in earlier in the evening. Silently he moved to the door on this side. It was also locked. Once again he tried his key and the results were the same. Kiran had followed him and moved past to check a door further up.

"Hawk!" Kiran whispered loudly as she motioned for him to join her. "We just found our way in!"

Through the glass panes of the door he saw a cast member wearing a maintenance uniform entering on the front side of the building.

As they cautiously moved back toward the main entrance of the shop, Kiran whispered, "Still don't believe in luck?"

"Nope, I still don't believe in luck."

As they confidently strolled through the front door, the unsuspecting custodian saw them. She jumped and yelped.

"Don't mind us," Kiran said enthusiastically. "We're running a bit later than we had planned, but we won't be in your way."

"Nobody's supposed to be—" The custodial cast member's gaze settled on the Imagineer name badge Hawk wore.

"We'll only be a few minutes," Kiran continued her bluff. "We're supposed to be looking at a few props and some theme details."

"Do you want me to come back when you are done?"

"No." Hawk waved off her concern. "We'll let you know when we leave. We just need to take a quick look, sorry to be in your way."

"Not a problem." The woman smiled and moved aside so they could pass.

Hawk and Kiran stepped into the home-styled section of the Christmas shop.

"Watch out, don't cry, don't pout," he whispered to her as they looked around. "Lets find the next clue and get out of here."

On a normal day Hawk would have spent a great deal of time looking at all the Christmas decorations and gifts crowding the shelves and tables here. As far as Hawk was concerned, Christmas was, as the old song stated, the most wonderful time of the year.

So watch out, don't pout, and don't cry. Let me tell you why!

The clue was obviously a portion of the phrase from the classic Christmas song "Santa Claus is Coming to Town." Hawk guessed there was a Santa Claus connection to the clue and searched the room for it. Of course the difficulty was in the fact that the room was bursting with Santa Claus souvenirs. Kiran drifted toward the far end of the room where the checkout counter was located. Allowing his eyes to follow her while she searched, he realized he had quit looking for clues and had settled on looking at her. She paused behind the counter. Her glance his way took a moment to register and then he knew he had been caught. He shyly smiled back at her.

"Keep looking," she mouthed to him with a smile.

His mouth went drier than a stale Christmas cookie, and he had to force his attention back to the search.

Behind Kiran, mounted to the back wall of the room, was a shelf loaded with the stuff that might be found in the home of a Pennsylvania German family. The brown wooden shelf had pegs on the bottom where items could be hung for safekeeping. A pair of cutting shears, a whisk broom, a dress, and bonnet were suspended from the wooden holders. The shelf itself contained other items used for day-to-day life—clamps, a candle in a candleholder, and wooden spools of thread lined up like soldiers standing at attention keeping guard across the shelf. Yet there was one item on the shelf that did not belong with the other items. It was easy to miss, as it blended into the theme of the shop. On the right-hand side of the spool soldiers stood a simple statute of Santa Claus. It was as if Walt's grandfather, Kepple, had left him a gift nestled among the family necessities tucked away on the shelf.

Hawk hurried across the room and jumped onto the counter. Startled, Kiran joined him and immediately began searching for what he'd spotted. He leaned out and stretched his arm to retrieve the Santa from its resting place. Lifting it gently he saw it had something tucked inside. Knowing exactly what it was, Hawk slid the small rectangular silver bar from inside Father Christmas. Turning it in his hand he found the words engraved on it and read them loudly enough for Kiran to hear.

"It's kind of fun to do the impossible."

"Another quote from Walt himself." She smiled with satisfaction.

Hawk crouched down and stepped off the counter. Opening the square silver box he placed this new discovery in its slot. "It fits into the box just like the other two. Now there's only one space left."

"Then I suggest"—she nudged her head toward the shop's entrance— "we get busy finding it."

Kiran led the way back through the shop. Pausing for a moment inside the doorway they thanked the cast member who was still cleaning. Hawk searched the streets for any suspicious activity as they stepped back out into the dim glow of Liberty Square. The Hall of Presidents rose up in front of them and they moved across the street, stopping underneath the covered porch adjacent to the building.

Creeping through the Magic Kingdom at night made the theme park seem even bigger than it did during operating hours. "I think we'll be less noticeable if we stay close to the buildings," he softly said.

"Where do we go now?"

"I don't know," Hawk answered. Reaching down reflexively, he released Pal Mickey from his resting place.

"Did he signal you?" Kiran asked.

"No." The minister looked toward the stuffed creature. "He didn't. But it doesn't seem to me like we finished the last clue yet."

Walt's grandfather has left you a gift. Find it quick, but be careful. I imagine there are a lot of people chasing us by now, and that can be a huge problem. But don't worry, I once got seven with one blow, I'll be here to help you, pal.

The grandfather's clue had been in the Christmas Shoppe. But the rest of the things that Pal Mickey added had to be the next part of the puzzle. Standing in the darkness with Kiran next to him, he explored his mind for the thought that would continue their journey. In the silence of the moment she ventured away from him and peered around the corners of their hiding place to scan the walkways to ensure they were alone and safe. Her movements were slow and methodical. He watched as she moved from one side of the covered porch to the other. Taking her time she gave Hawk extra precious seconds to think through what they should do next. Apparently satisfied they were very much alone for the moment, she returned and stood close to him. Still she said nothing.

Hawk gazed toward the Liberty Tree and for a moment drew a mental image of the Sons of Liberty gathered under the tree discussing what they should do next. There was no script or outline for them to follow; their quest for freedom wrote the pages of history as they went. Indecision was not an option for the founders of America. Surely they didn't always know if they were doing the right thing, but they did do something. Hawk knew he had to do something as well. The mystery had brought him too far to end now. There was something else to do, something he was missing.

"We can't just stand here!" Kiran finally caved in to her compulsion to say something.

"You're absolutely right. You can't just stand here!"

Hawk and Kiran jerked their heads toward the startling voice coming from the darkness just beyond the porch.

 *Day Six*
Night

OUT OF THE SHADOWS, the man slowly materialized. His expressionless face was intensified by the unrelenting glare he cast toward Hawk and Kiran. The preacher wondered where he had come from. They had heard no one approach and Kiran had checked to make sure the coast was clear. The stranger's first step had brought him out of the darkness where they could see him. His second step carried him close enough to invade their personal comfort zone. Reflexively Hawk slid in front of Kiran. The man now stood close enough so he could be heard as he spoke in a menacing whisper.

"You're behavior has been extremely unacceptable, Dr. Hawkes."

Grayson Hawkes was at a disadvantage. This man knew who he was. By identifying him as Doctor he revealed he knew exactly who Hawk was and what he did, and there would be little hope of bluffing their way through this encounter. Allowing his eyes to narrow Hawk studied the man who now stood threateningly close. He looked familiar but the preacher could not recall where he might have seen the man's face before. Kiran pressed up against Hawk from behind as the man leaned even closer to speak again.

"You did far more than play 'what if?' didn't you, Doctor?"

Hawk plowed through his memory trying to figure out who this person was. What he said had a familiar ring to it. It was a phrase that someone had used recently in conversation with Hawk, but in the firestorm of activity over the past few days he could not find anything beyond a flicker of familiarity.

"What if?" Hawk retorted with an edge that he hoped would defuse the intimidation he was feeling.

"Yes, what if?" A patronizing expression crossed the man's face. "What if Walt were still alive? What if he had seen Disney World completed? What if he were still running the Disney Empire? What if you could sit down and chat with him?"

The words he had just spoken were words that Hawk had heard recently. Hawk knew that for certain. Not wanting to acknowledge he was trying to connect the words, the man, and the moment, he nudged Kiran to give them room to move slightly away.

"However," the stranger continued, taking back the space the pair had just created, "you just couldn't stop with those questions. You didn't just gaze like other people at Walt's office and wonder what it would be like to sit in there with Walt. You decided to go in and have a look around. You broke in and made yourself at home in Walt's office. Didn't you, Dr. Hawkes?"

Instantly Hawk remembered. His name was Jim; he had spoken to Hawk at One Man's Dream at the Studios as Hawk had been looking through the window into Walt Disney's office. The conversation and the look on the man's face now reconnected. He had been nervous and trying not to look too suspicious when Jim engaged him in what he had thought was just a cast member interaction. But Jim knew who he was and on some level why he had been there. Apparently he also knew that Hawk had broken into the display at the attraction.

"You remember me now, Hawkes?"

"Jim, if that's your name," Hawk answered. "Why are you here?"

"What I want is simple." A smile now creased Jim's face. It was not a pleasant look. "I want you to give me what you found in Walt's office."

"I didn't find anything in Walt's office." He wasn't being untruthful; the search in the office had produced nothing, since he had been looking in the wrong place.

"Come now," Jim growled. "Let's not play games. Give it to me and I'll be on my way."

Pal Mickey had been found in Walt's desk. But not the desk that sat in the office display. Perhaps Jim did not know that and was not sure what Hawk had found.

Jim pressed in closer. He grabbed the front of Hawk's shirt with one hand. His other hand moved down toward Hawk's hip where Pal Mickey was attached. Apparently he did know about the treasure Hawk had found.

When Jim's hand reached the high-tech mouse, the preacher drove his forearm across the chest of the other man and with legs churning shoved him backward. Hawk's move was not intended to be a punch; instead he intended to force Jim away from Kiran and put him onto the ground. The initial move caused Jim to lose balance and rock back on his heels. This was the momentum Hawk had been hoping for. Like a running back driving across the line of scrimmage toward a first down, Hawk's knees moved up and down like pistons. Jim still held onto Hawk's shirt, which stabilized him momentarily before he finally yielded and lost his balance. Falling backward off the porch and collapsing onto the asphalt ground, Jim fell with Hawk forcefully following him. Jim hit the pavement. Hawk intensified the impact by allowing his forearm, still planted across Jim's chest, to become a battering ram. An audible expulsion of air from the fallen man's lungs left him stunned and unable to move. Something clattered to the ground in the darkness as the men tumbled.

"Run, Kiran!" Hawk rose up and crouched over the downed man.

Kiran leapt off the porch, momentarily paused, stooped looking for something, and then ran toward the Liberty Square Riverboat. Taking a right turn upon reaching it she ran past the Haunted Mansion and toward Fantasyland.

Standing up and seeing where Kiran had gone, Hawk moved to follow. His first step was cut abruptly short as Jim grabbed him on the ankle and pulled sharply on his leg. This time it was Hawk falling toward the unforgiving ground. It rose up to greet him. Stumbling in a vain attempt to keep his balance he only increased his speed as he floundered out of control onto the ground. A paralyzing bolt of pain traveled through his body, reminding him of his tumble in the theme park only a day ago. He felt his body bounce and then finally stop in an aching heap on the path between Frontierland and Fantasyland. He looked in the direction Kiran had taken; he could no longer see her. Hopefully she was now safely hidden. Rolling over to get back to his feet, he was assisted by Jim, now looming above him. Hawk's legs scrambled, trying to find the footing he needed. Between Jim's tugging him upward and his finally finding footing, Hawk was able to jump back to his feet.

Twisting his head, Hawk saw Jim draw back his hand to swing. The punch was a wild roundhouse of a blow that the preacher ducked easily beneath. Jim flew off balance as the blow became nothing but a gust of wind swirling over the intended target's head. Hawk knew instinctively that Jim was not proficient in pugilism since his first attempt was a typical playground punch that rarely worked. Uncoiling from his crouched position Hawk tightened his fist and threw an arrow-straight jab targeting the chin of his adversary. Although he had not been in many fights during his adulthood he remembered enough to know that experienced fighters could strike with power and clout without wasted motion. His fist found Jim's face with a thick thump, snapping his head back. The combination of the punch and the wildly off balanced roundhouse a heartbeat before sent Jim thundering back toward the ground once again. Landing with a crunch on his side, he moaned in agony, moving his hands to his jaw.

Hawk walked toward him before freezing in the awkwardness of the moment. Dr. Grayson Hawkes would defend himself, fight for a cause, champion a battle for those that couldn't, and would fight for anything that threatened his faith or those he loved; both Juliette and Farren were missing, and he wanted answers. There was no more fight in Jim because he was not in the habit of fighting. He had proven that with the one punch he had thrown.

"Hold on there!"

Hawk looked up to see two men trotting their way. They were maintenance cast members. He regretted causing this rare sight in the Magic Kingdom, two men fighting on the streets in the middle of the night. Sadly a little bit of the real world had managed to break into the magical setting of the theme park.

Frustrated, Hawk released Jim and painfully eased back into the darkness. Joints and muscles screamed as the adrenaline surging through his system only moments ago had now ebbed and the aftermath released a blast of pain he doggedly tried to ignore. Knowing he needed to put some distance between himself and the scene, he loped beneath the second level of the Columbia Harbor House. The second story formed an overpass above the street that served as the dividing line between Liberty Square and Fantasyland. The sign for the Columbia Harbor House Restaurant featured a U.S. shield with an eagle crying and clutching arrows in its right claw. Hawk knew the sign represented that the country was at war on its own soil. Unraveling this mystery was becoming more like a war with each passing second and with each action that pushed the boundaries of what he knew to be right. There were a number of things he needed to do. His mind formatted the checklist. Getting out of the street, tracking down Kiran, and finding somewhere to rest for a few moments were the ones that topped his priority list.

Emerging from beneath the overpass he entered Fantasyland. Hawk imagined Jim would create whatever fable was necessary to relieve him of any guilt in their fight, and add fallacies creating an additional layer of trouble for him. Seeing the Swiss ski chalet to his left, he settled upon his destination and chugged through the brown wooden A-framed entrance and up the walkway leading to the loading area of the now defunct Skyway to Tomorrowland. The Skyway no longer existed and this loading area was isolated and off the beaten path. The entrance had been converted to a stroller storage area and was ignored by most people.

Hunkering down in the shadow of safety created by a sidewall, Hawk listened for sounds emanating from the path below. Silence wafted up toward his hiding place. It wouldn't be long before security heard whatever report Jim concocted that would send them scurrying to find him.

Darkness smothered him as he strained his ears to hear any detectable signs of being followed. Flattened against a wall in the structure, he plotted his next course of action. Kiran was somewhere near but exactly where, he didn't know. The last clue had been discovered in Ye Olde Christmas Shoppe but Pal Mickey had not offered any more information. He allowed the animated voice to rewind and play again in his mind.

You're doing terrrrrific! But we have to keep looking because we have more to find. So watch out, don't pout, and don't cry. Let me tell you why! Walt's grandfather has left you a gift. Find it quick, but be careful. I imagine there are a lot of people chasing us by now, and that can be a huge problem. But don't worry, I once got seven with one blow, I'll be here to help you, pal.

Since the clue was the gift left by Walt's grandfather, he needed to figure out what was still missing. *Find it quick, but be careful.* Hawk could find no hidden meaning in that line. *I imagine there are a lot of people chasing us by now, and that can be a huge problem. But don't worry, I once got seven with one blow, I'll be here to help you, pal.* He was being chased and it was a huge problem. If there was a clue in those lines, it were still hidden. *Seven with one blow* sounded familiar, but he didn't know why.

Muffled voices drifted through the air, snapping Hawk's focus from the clue to his surroundings. Lifting his head over his Skyway barricade allowed him to see two workmen walking down the street. They moved past him along the street without pausing to search in any of the alcoves or darkened corners along the path. If they were looking for him, they were not searching diligently, and their voices soon disappeared into the background noise of the evening. Hawk knew he couldn't stay where he was. If he didn't find the next clue, the mystery would remain locked away and his efforts in finding the whereabouts of Juliette would be wasted.

I imagine there are a lot of people chasing us by now, and that can be a huge problem. But don't worry, I once got seven with one blow, I'll be here to help you, pal.

The familiar voice of the mouse played again in his imagination as he closed his eyes and thought about each word. Slowly exhaling he allowed his eyes to reopen with new insight rekindled by the possibility of understanding. On aching legs he rose to his feet, peered around the corner to check for any motion, and then moved away from his place of refuge. Crossing the street he moved under the alcove to Peter Pan's Flight.

"Ha-ha!"

The sound stopped Hawk in his tracks and he whirled around to see if there was anyone around him that might have heard the noise. No movement could be seen and he crept into an opening that offered guests a Fast Pass to ride the attraction. Back pressed against the pass distribution machine he slid down until he rested on the ground. Releasing the stuffed travel guide he gave it a tight squeeze to hear the next clue.

"You're here too early, pal. It's not time yet."

Craning his neck he looked back at the attraction. Peter Pan's Flight was where he had been when the alert sounded. He was there *too early* . . . it wasn't *time yet*. He didn't realize he needed to be there at all. Thinking about time gave him pause to glance at his watch. Hawk had no idea what time it actually was. Twisting his wrist so light would fall across the face of his watch, he noticed for the first time that it was cracked. A spiderweb of fine lines danced across the crystal. Slightly changing the angle of the wrist he could see the sweep second hand of the watch lying dormant in the wreckage of the timepiece. This was the second watch in two days he had managed to trash. This time he blamed Jim.

Instinctively the preacher knew Jim still had to be close. His ability to find Hawk and Kiran in Liberty Square had been troubling. If they were discovered there, then Jim was capable of discovering them again. Except Hawk was alone now, and where was Kiran? He had told her to run during the fight but now in the aftermath he was surprised she hadn't reemerged. He wondered if she'd been caught or had to hide as well. He was isolated and full of questions with few answers, and caught in the most unlikely of all situations . . . hiding in the Magic Kingdom in the middle of the night.

With this latest installment of information he wondered whether he should stay and wait or keep moving forward. Waiting, he concluded, was the worst option since he had no idea what he was waiting for. He would move forward into the streets of Fantasyland. Pausing at the edge of the attraction he looked across the concrete pathway toward Sir Mickey's. Sir Mickey's was a souvenir shop located behind Cinderella Castle.

As guests traveled through the interior of the castle they would emerge into Fantasyland. To their right they would see the shop Hawk was looking at now. If they went left they would find Cinderella's Fountain. The fountain itself was an amazing piece of Imagineering that Farren had once shown Hawk. To the casual observer it was nothing more than a fountain featuring Cinderella dressed in the rags she wore before she was a princess. However, from the perspective of a child, you could look up into the face of the princess and there would be a crown sitting on her head. This optical trick allowed the crown painted on the back wall of the fountain to be seen through the hopeful eyes of children in the place it belonged, on the head of Cinderella. Farren pointed out that seeing beyond what others could see was the difference between just moving through life and really living life. When you really live you can see the impossible and the incredible. It was that kind of detail to storytelling that Grayson Hawkes was hoping would help him now. The first time Farren explained the fountain, Hawk had told him that the story of Cinderella was really about transformation. Cinderella was always a princess, she just didn't know it. It was only when she believed that she became what she had been created to be. The fountain reminded Hawk that Jesus had said to follow Him with a childlike faith. Only a child could clearly see that Cinderella was a princess at the fountain. Those observations had sparked some serious conversation about spiritual things that crackled with creativity and had drawn both men closer in their friendship.

He was tempted to head in the direction of the fountain when he glanced back toward the gift shop. Sir Mickey's was a shop in which Imagineers had blended two classic Mickey tales to create the look of the shopping haven: *The Brave Little Tailor,* created by Walt in the late 1930s, and *Mickey and the Beanstalk* from the *Fun and Fancy Free* feature created nearly ten years later. The sign to the shop hung crooked, and upon closer observation the casual viewer could find the reason. The post the sign was hanging on had been surrounded and choked by a vine. This vine had snaked its way around the sign and moved the sign askew.

Hawk remembered from seeing both of those films that in each one Mickey had faced a *huge* problem. In each of the cartoons the brave mouse had come face-to-face with a giant. In *Mickey and the Beanstalk* he had faced a giant named Willie after he had traded the family cow for magic beans. The beanstalk had grown out of control and was now meshed into the architecture of this unique little shop. The giant he had faced in *The Brave Little Tailor* was similar. Mickey ended up facing this huge problem due to a misunderstanding. He had said something that was taken out of context, and then as the story line progressed, everyone assumed he was a giant killer. Sir Mickey's had blended these two cartoons together and created a themed shopping experience where Mickey still faced his huge problem.

 *Day Seven*
Early Morning

THE GUEST ROOM Jonathan had secured in the Contemporary Resort had now become a command center. Al Gann had covered the table with notes he had written as Shep and Jonathan recounted the story that had been unfolding in the life of their friend, Grayson Hawkes. Shortly after midnight, Tim Keaton had arrived. Juliette still had not been found.

"Tim, you say Juliette called you while she was on the way to her car leaving here?" Gann asked, reviewing something he had written down earlier.

"Yes, we were going to meet at the house and then come out here for dinner." He paused, slumping in his chair. "She said I wouldn't believe the mystery Hawk had been drawn into. From what I've heard here over the past couple of hours, she was right."

"Al, do you still think Juliette's disappearance is tied to what Hawk is involved with?" Jonathan asked.

"I'm sure." Al rested a hand on Tim's shoulder. "Tim, we haven't filed a report. I'm here unofficially trying to help some friends. We can make it official and get my department involved."

"What do you think has happened?" Tim inquired as Jonathan and Shep leaned forward.

"This whole thing is unbelievable. Hawk gets a message from Walt Disney, you are getting chased through resorts, there is some mystery woman who arrives in Hawk's life just as this starts unfolding, then Juliette ends up missing. The only thing that the department is working on is trying to locate Farren Rales. When he didn't show up for work, a woman named Nancy Alport—she works with Rales—reported him missing. Apparently Hawk is one of the last people to have had contact with him."

"You know Hawk doesn't know where he is or what happened to him!" Shep's voice rose anxiously.

"Relax," Al tried to calm him, "I know that. Hawk is my friend too. But I did find out one of our investigators has been trying to get in touch with him."

"Hawk was trying to avoid that conversation," Jonathan reluctantly admitted.

"Of course he was. I would have done the same. As a matter of fact, curiosity alone would have had me doing most of the things Hawk has been doing."

"Do you think Juliette is okay?" Tim sat upright.

"I don't know, because I don't know what we're dealing with here." Al shrugged. "Shep and Jonathan found her car in the parking lot, so she didn't drive away. As far as we know, Hawk never left the Magic Kingdom. We can't reach either of them on their cell phones, which means they might not be getting a signal or they're unable to answer."

"What do we do?" Shep stood up eagerly at the promise of a plan of action.

"For starters we keep trying to reach them on their phones." As Gann completed that line both Tim and Shep began punching the keypads of their cell phones. "I have a contact that works in Disney security. I'll wake him up and see if he's aware of anything happening on property out of the ordinary. I also am going to have to get some of the sheriff's department involved. We can low-key it, but there's too much going on now not to have them included."

"Juliette's phone went straight to voice mail," Tim informed Al.

"So did Hawk's," Shep added.

"Keep trying." Mike picked up his own phone and began searching through the electronic phone book for a number. "If Hawk is going to figure out his puzzle, he's running out of time. By morning we'll have a whole new wave of people involved."

CHAPTER THIRTY-EIGHT

Day Seven
Early Morning

I IMAGINE THERE ARE A LOT OF PEOPLE *chasing us by now, and that can be a huge problem. But don't worry, I once got seven with one blow, I'll be here to help you, pal.*

The huge problem could be a giant problem. At least that is what Hawk was thinking as he continued to stare toward the entrance to Sir Mickey's. He had nearly been spotted by a two-person team moving through the area with a power washer blowing grit and grime off the walkway. Scurrying backward, the preacher disappeared into a dark alcove and waited until they were gone.

The sound of the power washer faded around the corner and Hawk crept back to view the entrance of Sir Mickey's again.

But don't worry, I once got seven with one blow, I'll be here to help you, pal.

As Hawk stared at the vine-entwined sign on the building it came to him. Mickey, in *The Brave Little Tailor*, was bragging about killing seven flies with one blow, and it was misinterpreted by the people of the village. They thought he meant giants; as a result he was expected to go giant hunting. The huge problem was a giant and the clue was designed to draw him to Sir Mickey's. Smiling, he realized how lucky he had been. A huge giant had gotten him moving in the right direction; what should have been relatively simple Mickey Mouse trivia had confused him. This had to be the right place and should bring him another step closer to solving the puzzle.

Racing across the open walkway, he paused at the front door of the shop. He firmly turned the doorknob. It gave but did not open. It was locked. Crouching down he looked in the window and saw his favorite detail of the gift shop. The roof was being lifted off by the giant just like in the cartoon. Looking to his left and then back to his right he saw no other access into the building. Studying the door, he decided to try the key that Farren had given him. The key reluctantly slid inside the lock mechanism. In one quick twist the key loudly released the lock and the door swung open into the gift shop. Swinging the door shut behind him, he crouched and looked out the window to see if anyone had been watching him. Seeing no one, he turned his attention to the interior of the shop.

Willie the Giant lifted the roof to the shop and could be seen peering in toward the far corner. In that corner a statue of Mickey Mouse stood on a piece of wildly grown beanstalk. Over his shoulder were the supplies needed by the brave tailor, a variety of cloths and threads all neatly placed on the shelf behind him. Hawk decided to get a closer look. Climbing awkwardly up onto the display and grabbing the beanstalk he pulled himself up toward the shelf behind the mouse. Keeping one foot resting on the shelf, using one arm to hold on to the beanstalk, he rifled through the spindles of multicolored threads. Using his hand to search he found a shape similar to the other clues previously discovered. Gripping it with his fingertips he lifted it up and watched it emerge from the threads that had hidden it. With a swing of his arm he began his descent from this makeshift perch when his foot slipped. Wildly off balance he tumbled to the ground and the fourth silver bar clamored across the floor. He righted himself and crawled on his hands and knees to retrieve the bar. Engraved into the stunning silver bar was another phrase.

"If you can dream it you can do it."

This was perhaps one of the most recognizable Walt Disney quotes of all time. Mr. Disney was known as a dreamer and the words adorned posters, paperweights, and almost anything else that marketing companies could make a profit on. Seated in the center of Sir Mickey's, Hawk removed the silver box from his pocket and opened it. Glistening in the dim light of the shop the three previously discovered silver bars were cradled in the box waiting for the set to be completed. Gently the preacher placed the final piece of sterling into the box. Finally the four bars were in place, each one bearing a thought spoken by Walt Disney.

> The way to get started is to stop talking and begin doing.
> All of our dreams can come true if we have the courage to pursue them.
> Its kind of fun to do the impossible.
> If you can dream it you can do it.

Each quote was a powerful reminder of both the genius and insight the founder of the Walt Disney Company had left as a legacy to the dreamers and doers that followed. Hawk reflectively thought of his missing friend Farren, his missing friend Juliette, and wished a little bit of the genius and insight Walt possessed would inspire him to figure out whatever he was supposed to understand. He closed the mirrored lid on the box. It clicked shut.

"Ha-ha!"

Anxiously he reached down and in one motion had retrieved the stuffed wonder and given it a firm squeeze to activate the next message. Holding up the small creature as if it were real, the preacher looked into the face of Mickey Mouse, waiting for him to speak. He didn't have to wait long.

"I knew you could do it, pal! Let's fly to where it is always past my bedtime. Gosh, even though it's late and I should be asleep, I'm sure Mr. Disney wouldn't mind. Oh, ha-ha, I almost forgot . . . remember the pixie dust!"

Another clue! Hoping the last silver bar was the final piece of the puzzle, Hawk had convinced himself that his latest discovery would bring clarity to the entire mystery. Now he was presented with another piece of information. Something else to be figured out, somewhere else to go, something still to find; and having no clear-cut answers stirred a wave of frustration within the usually steady preacher.

He fell to his knees and slammed the Pal Mickey to the ground. Tightening his hands into fists around the toy he let out a subdued groan born of disappointment. Angrily exhaling he wrestled with the reality that he still had more to find.

The mental journey ended abruptly as tapping on the glass of the door startled him. Rolling on his side and shoving Pal Mickey back to his hip, he spun in the direction of the light tap. Kiran's inquisitive face stared at him through the glass. Staying low, Hawk crawled to the door and cracked it open enough for her to enter. He reached up and grabbed her hand, pulling her down out of the sight line of the windows as he closed the door behind her. They sat with their backs against the wall.

"Are you okay?" Kiran leaned close. "I was coming through Cinderella Castle and I saw something out of the corner of my eye. It was you, falling off a beanstalk, I think."

Hawk laughed softly. "That was me."

"You're all right?"

"Sure. I got away before the giant got me."

"Funny." She waited a moment. "Did you find another clue?"

"I did. I found the last silver bar. It was another quote from Walt Disney."

"And?"

"When I put it in the box my Pal Mickey gave me another clue."

"So finding the last silver bar wasn't the end?" Kiran's disappointment was palpable.

"No, I have to go to where it's always past Mickey's bedtime."

"That's the next clue?" Kiran slid away from the wall and turned toward him.

"And I'm supposed to remember the pixie dust."

"Well, pixie dust is important I guess."

"It must be." Hawk was shaking his head and smiling in spite of the circumstances. How silly this conversation would be on a normal day. Falling off a beanstalk, following the clues of a stuffed mouse, and remembering pixie dust were pretty indicative that this was anything but a normal day.

"So what do we do?" Kiran rose to her knees.

"I haven't had time to figure that out."

"Then you're going to have to follow me." She peered out of the glass into the streets of Fantasyland.

"Follow you where?"

"While you were trying to get away from our visitor in Liberty Square, it dawned on me we needed a safe place to hide and think. I found the perfect place."

Hawk joined Kiran looking out the window. The isolated streets glowed, the nighttime lighting casting eerie shadows.

"Are you going to tell me where this perfect place to hide is?"

"Cinderella Castle!" Kiran beamed as she pulled out a plain white key card with a stark black magnetic strip crossing it. "I found out there were no guests staying in the Cinderella Castle Suite tonight. No one will ever look there, and I got us a fresh set of clothes to change into."

"Clothes?"

"Have you looked at yourself lately?" She was laughing as Hawk took inventory and for the first time noticed how grimy he was after his evening of adventure. "I think I guessed right on the sizes. We can clean up, and you can figure out where we go next."

"Won't someone know we're there?"

"I don't see how. This is a master key. It's not in the system. There's no concierge assigned to the suite tonight because we have no guests there. I picked up the clothing from wardrobe and have already put it in the room. It gets us off the streets where we can be seen easily and—"

"You've convinced me," Hawk interrupted. "Let's go."

Carefully the pair cracked opened the door. Seeing nothing, they moved from the safety of Sir Mickey's back into Fantasyland. Kiran stepped out and led them to a route that veered off the back of the castle. Ahead they would find a path to the secluded unmarked doorway that would carry them to their hiding place.

She froze in her tracks.

An instant later Hawk stared in horror as he saw the unmistakable Reginald Cambridge approaching them on the path that wound toward the back of the castle. Moments after being spotted by the pair, he saw them.

For a few painful seconds no one moved. Finally Hawk grabbed Kiran's arm and pulled her back away from Cambridge's direction.

Instantly breaking into a sprint, Hawk ran toward Fantasyland. Kiran ran alongside him but couldn't match his speed. Reginald was fifty yards away when they spotted him. Their quick retreat bought them a few additional yards, but they were running blind.

"This way!" Kiran tugged his arm from behind.

Hawk turned back to his left as Kiran headed for an unmarked door. Swinging the door open he followed her into an undecorated hallway. Still in a dead sprint she surged ahead with Hawk right behind her. Yanking another door open they both stepped into a stairwell and began a steep descent. Somewhere behind them Hawk was certain he heard the door they had stepped out of Fantasyland through open as well. Reginald was right behind them. Feet dancing lightly over each step, they twisted around a landing and continued their downward race. The steps came to an end. Never breaking pace Kiran hit the next doorway and shoved it open. Together they ran through it.

 *Day Seven*
Early Morning

KIRAN AND HAWK CHARGED into one of the best-known and least seen legends in the Magic Kingdom: the utilidor. Most guests of the Magic Kingdom don't realize they are actually walking on the second floor of the theme park. Underneath the streets, the flowers, the trees, and the water is the underground portion of the Magic Kingdom known as the utilidor. This massive infrastructure, a network of offices, massive storage areas, and administrative space, woven together by a one-and-a-half-mile color-coded tunnel system, expands out over nine acres. The unique construction allows the Magic Kingdom to create an extra sense of magic with cast members and characters traveling from one place to another unseen by guests.

Beyond the convenience of moving cast members from place to place, the utilidor serves as the control and command center for the park. Rooms off each side of the tunnels lead to employee areas containing video games, locker rooms, dressing areas, and places to watch television and relax. Cast members can find a cafeteria, barber shop, wardrobe headquarters, paycheck center, utility hubs, and the controls that run the entire theme park. This windowless creation is one of the most creative portions of the Magic Kingdom, which, although extremely functional and practical, helps create the onstage magical world that all of the guests experience.

Kiran ran to her left through a tunnel that began to wind away off to their right. Hawk followed her closely, glancing behind him to see if Reginald was in pursuit. In a full sprint, their footfalls reverberated in the utilidor.

The pair wildly ran along the concrete corridor. In a full-bore sprint Hawk could feel the fatigue of the last few days sapping the spring out of his step. Realizing his current pace would momentarily exhaust him, he willed his conscience to create some kind of plan. The utilidor formed a complete circle below the Magic Kingdom. A long corridor down the middle of the oval ran below Main Street USA and stretched back below Fantasyland. Hawk was trying to get his bearings, but it was assumed that if you were in the utilidor you knew where you were going. The assumption did not always hold true and he'd heard many new cast members, confident they could navigate the passages and find the correct stairwell, would easily get lost in the loop of the tunnel. The corridor Kiran and Hawk were in came to an intersection and they both hesitated.

"Hawk! Let's go left and we'll end up back near the main entrance of the park."

"No, let's go right." Away from the entrance. And somewhere down here, if he could find what he was looking for, was his way out. "Reginald might not expect that."

"Do you know where you are?" Kiran whispered.

"Where I am exactly . . . I have no idea," he admitted. "But I don't have time to ask for directions."

"I'm giving you directions. Follow me and let's get out of here."

"I think we should go this way," Hawk gestured in the opposite direction.

"Go where?"

Hawk settled the conversation as he grabbed Kiran's hand and tugged her in the direction his instincts had chosen. They ran again and in short order the utilidor veered sharply to the left. Making the turn they came to yet another intersection. This was the corridor Hawk had been looking for. They stood at the opening of the main hallway that divided the underground oval of the utilidoors. The pipes streaming sideways along the walls and roofline mixed with the shadows created by the fluorescent tube lighting made the corridor look like it stretched toward infinity. Still holding hands they paused and looked down the utilidor.

"We go that way." Hawk sighed and got ready to run once more.

"No!" Kiran pulled back against him, causing him to turn toward her.

"It's deserted this time of the morning, let's go!"

"No, we can still get back to the main entrance of the tunnel." Kiran strongly leaned in the other direction. "At the end of the main utilidor is the wardrobe area, dining room, DACS, and where any traffic would be this time of night."

"I have an idea," Hawk urged her. "Trust me."

"I'm telling you, Hawk, if we go back we can get out of the tunnels and sneak back down Main Street to the castle."

"Reginald is right behind us," Hawk said. "Don't you think he will be expecting us to do what you just said?"

"I—" Her eyes danced back and forth as though she expected, as he did, Reginald would come racing around the corner at any minute.

"Follow me." Hawk began moving down the long passageway.

Hesitantly Kiran followed as she glanced back over her shoulder to see if they were being followed. The preacher's greatest fear now was that in this long, straight corridor they would lose their ability to stay hidden. Running around the oval had allowed the bend in the hallways to constantly break the line of sight between them and their pursuer. Now that luxury was gone and an all-out sprint through the utilidor risked exposing them. Hawk had a destination in mind, he just didn't know if they had time to get there.

Cambridge thundered to a stop as the corridor abruptly came to an intersection. He looked to his right as the sweat soaked through his shirt and ran down his temples. Turning his head to the right he knew this direction would take him past a large cast member break room, then to a series of tunnels that would all provide access back into the theme park. Hawkes and Roberts had been moving through the theme park all night and he was confident they would go back there. Reflexively he reached toward his waistband for his radio. The cameras in the utilidor were monitored in a security station. In a moment he might have known where the two were, but in his haste to get back into the park, his radio was still in his office. He would have to trust his instincts. He headed to his left to find a stairwell back into the theme park.

Halfway down the never-ending utilidor Hawk and Kiran were still alone.

"He isn't behind us," Kiran panted.

"Where is he?" Hawk broke down and slowed his pace. "Where did he go?"

"I don't know, maybe he went the other way."

Following Hawk's lead Kiran began to slow and they both settled into a brisk jog. Three people rounded the corner from the direction they were heading. The cast members had been talking but quit as they saw the unexpected sight of two people running toward them. Silently staring as the pair trotted in their direction the three men took their places in a golf cart that was sitting along the wall in the tunnel. The tires squealed on the concrete as the black rubber gripped and jolted the cart forward. Kiran and Hawk drifted to the right side of the corridor giving the cart room to meet them. Just as the cart was in front of them the driver broke into a broad smile.

"It would have been easier to have grabbed a cart!" Jovially he waved and the other two men smiled.

"Now you tell us!" Hawk returned the wave as the cart headed past them.

"Obviously they weren't looking for us," Kiran commented.

"But we did look a little odd running down the corridor."

"You think?"

"Just keep jogging, we're almost there." Hawk moved back into the center of the utilidor.

"Almost where?"

"Almost here." Hawk stopped at a doorway.

"What are you doing?"

"We're going in." Hawk pulled his employee ID card out of his pocket and swiped the magnetic stripe through the lock on the door. The time had come to reveal the discovery he hadn't shown her after his climb through Expedition Everest.

"Where did you get that?" Kiran asked as she saw the card for the first time.

"A yeti gave it to me," Hawk responded and placed it back in his pocket not giving her a chance to take a closer look.

The door opened and Hawk smiled as they entered the Character Zoo.

 *Day Seven*
Early Morning

THE CHARACTER ZOO is the place where many dreams begin to come alive for kids although they never realize it. Below the streets and attractions of the Magic Kingdom is the place where "friends" of all the famous Walt Disney characters gather to pick up wardrobe, make minor repairs to outfits, and transform themselves into the famous celebrities created by Disney through the years. Mortal everyday people walk into the zoo and exit as a legendary character designed to bring delight and smiles to people of all ages.

In many ways this is the one place many dream of seeing but deep inside don't really want to. There is something magical about suspending belief and imagining you are meeting the one and only Goofy or Pluto. Inside the Character Zoo a little of the magic unravels. Unlike many other areas of the Magic Kingdom, this large area is wildly disheveled.

Hawk thought that describing it as a zoo was appropriate. There were large oversized heads of the characters given birth in animated dreams of artists through the years. Hanging in row after untidy row were the various pieces of each outfit and costume necessary to bring the famous cartoon celebrities to life. Hawk and Kiran moved deeper into the zoo, twisting through the maze of crowded clothes racks.

"Hawk, we shouldn't be in here!"

"Why not?"

"Because night is when they have a crew in to do costume repair. Someone will see us."

"I don't see anyone here." He gestured toward the oversized head of Minnie Mouse resting on a shelf above a clothes rack and lowered his voice. "I don't hear a creature stirring, not even a mouse."

"Not funny."

"Relax, we're going to be okay," he reassured her.

Kiran held his arm as they went deeper and deeper into the zoo. She reluctantly followed and at times Hawk had to pull her along to get her to keep moving forward. The further they went the more cluttered the zoo seemed to get. This was surely an area that had trouble keeping up with the high volume of activity that took place on an hourly basis. Soon they moved beyond the clothes racks near the back of the zoo. The hanging costumes were replaced with massive piles of costumes, costume pieces, and other items. There seemed to be an organized plan in place as each of these items were stacked on top of each other, but the clothing piles formed a mountain range along the back section of the Character Zoo.

"So do you have a plan?" Kiran whispered directly into Hawk's ear.

"We're going to hide in here until the day shift comes in." He climbed between two hills of costumes. "When the park gets ready to open, we're going to put on a couple of outfits and walk through the tunnels, right into the theme park."

"You have lost your mind!"

"Maybe, but then we'll find a place out of sight up topside to dump the outfits and get lost in the park crowd. Reginald Cambridge and park security will never know any different."

"You really think that no one will notice a couple of Disney characters going rogue and just wandering off with guests in the park?" Kiran shook her head in disbelief. "These costumes are treated like gold. They're valuable and closely guarded; no character leaves the zoo and walks into the theme park without being led by a cast member. Even if we got out of the zoo, we'd be mobbed by guests. Are you planning on wandering through the park, ignoring people as they follow you, taking off the outfit, and tossing it in the trash?"

"I didn't say the plan was foolproof," he admitted.

"More like fool fueled." She smiled back at him. "Let's get out of here, Hawk."

Realizing he would need a better strategy, Hawk relented. Tilting his head in the direction from which they came, Kiran began to retrace the path they had used to discover the costumed mountain range. She stepped back between the hanging racks of cloth. Hawk watched as she walked away and then moved to follow.

He heard a muffled sound from the far corner. The stacks of clothing in the back corner were even higher than the ones he stood between. Hawk paused and strained to discern what he had heard. Lightly taking a step toward the deepest corner of the room, he again stopped to listen. Silence beckoned him to take another step, then another, and he found himself in the deepest part of the costumed mountain range. A footstep behind him startled him, and he spun in the direction of the new sound.

"I thought you were behind me," Kiran said.

"I heard something." He raised a hand for her to be quiet so he could listen.

"Let's get out of here!" She tugged his shirtsleeve to get him moving. He allowed her to nudge him into motion as he continued to look at the heaps of costumes. Turning to follow her back out of the zoo, he again heard the same muffled noise he had heard before. This time he was positive he had heard something distinct and the sound was out of place for a deserted dressing area. Spinning on his heels and this time moving to the back of the zoo with purpose, he rounded the largest of the clothing mountains.

There, nestled in the costumes at the base of the mound, was Juliette.

Waves of relief rushed over Hawk. Seated in the mountain of cloth, she was bound with both feet together, her hands tied behind her back, and a wide strip of duct tape across her mouth and wrapped around her head. Juliette craned her neck to see who was approaching her. Her eyes excitedly widened as she saw Hawk, who rushed toward her and knelt in front of her.

"Are you all right?" He wrapped his arms around her and gently pulled her upright.

She nodded affirmatively as tears flooded her eyes while he began untying her ankles.

"Hawk, where are . . ." Kiran rushed in and began to untie Juliette's wrists.

"Mmm. Mmmm," Juliette tried to speak through the tape wrapped across her face.

"Hang on." Hawk worked at the knots. "Juliette, I'd like for you to meet Kiran, Kiran, this is Juliette."

"Nice to meet you," Kiran joined Hawk in grinning. "I've heard a lot about you."

"Mmmm. MMMM!" Juliette's eyes widened again.

"Give me a second," Hawk said, releasing the last knot at Juliette's ankles. He stood and began to work at gently pulling the tape from her neck below her hairline.

Juliette grabbed Hawk by the wrist, forcing him away from the tape and pushing him back. Her gaze had turned to one of fear, and she was looking past him, trying to get him to do the same. On one knee he turned and looked up and saw the man who had just come around the corner.

Jim stood over the group with a disgusted expression across his face. Scowling, he held in front of him an electronic device about the size of a deck of cards. This black box crackled to life as he threatened the group. An arc of electricity surged between the probes on the box as he took another step toward them.

"You really have become a problem for me, Dr. Hawkes. This time I will take what I want, and sadly there is little you can do about it." Jim pushed the button that ignited another spark from the Taser. "Now for starters, toss me the Pal Mickey on your hip."

Hawk glanced at the stunned faces of Juliette and Kiran. Slowly he reached down and unclasped the stuffed animal from his waist. Methodically he rose to his feet and stepped away from the two women. Then nodding toward Jim he pulled back his arm to toss the small electronic wonder to him. He threw the mouse slightly off course. Jim reached for it but the Pal Mickey flew just beyond his fingertips, falling to rest at the base of a clothing rack. Jim smirked at Hawk as he bent to retrieve it.

Hawk sprang to his feet and hurtled into Jim just as he reached the stuffed animal. The collision of bodies threw Jim off his feet and the momentum of the flying pastor drove both men airborne through the curtain of costumes.

Juliette and Kiran stared slack-jawed as the men disappeared as if swallowed by the clothes. Kiran hastily went back to work removing the tape from Juliette's mouth as they anxiously stared toward the wall of clothing. The distinctive tearing sound of duct tape releasing its grip echoed between the women as Kiran unwound the loops of tape encircling Juliette's head. Juliette stretched her jaw to restart the stifled blood flow as the final loop fell free.

"All right?" Kiran asked helping Juliette to her feet.

"Yes, thanks," she softly replied.

The wall of clothing, which at one time draped vertically from the rack, was now alive. Movement of clothes shaking, falling, and vibrating, urged on by the battle behind them, could be seen.

"Quickly. Follow me." Kiran began moving.

"Wait," Juliette said.

"Hawk would want me to get you out of here."

"We aren't leaving without him. We wait."

A dull thud, followed by another, and then yet another was accented by a painful groan. Bodies colliding, clothes hangers straining with untested pressure sprang off the rack as forces raged against them. An unmistakable crackle sizzled in the stale air of the room as the Taser fired again. An agonizing scream accompanying a much heavier thud indicated that someone was about to emerge victorious. As the scream subsided another arc of electricity popped, causing an additional groan before silence wafted from behind the clothing.

Hangers screeched over the metal rod supporting them as the costumes opened like a curtain revealing a behind-the-stage look at some grand show. Grayson Hawkes emerged from the other side of the clothing, shoving himself through the opening. Grasping the Taser in his right hand, he stepped over the scattered clothes and back toward Kiran and Juliette. In a quick grasp he hugged Juliette.

"I was so worried," he got out.

"I am so glad to see you." She exhaled with relief. "I wasn't sure what was going to happen."

"How did you end up here?" Kiran asked her.

"Him." Juliette gestured to the semiconscious form of Jim lying askew over the costumes. Looking closer she noticed his face had disappeared inside a massive wolf head. "What did you do to him?"

"I hit him with the head of the costume." Hawk looked over at Jim. "It seemed appropriate."

"Very appropriate. The Big Bad Wolf here, minus his head of course, approached me on my way to car as I was leaving the Contemporary. He asked if I was Juliette Keaton and said he had a message for you from Farren Rales I was supposed to deliver." She rubbed her jaw as she felt the tingle of where the tape had been begin to dissipate. "He hit me with the Taser, and the next thing I remember I was here, buried in that pile of stuff. Hawk, I was beginning to think I would never see Tim, my kids, you, Jonathan, or Shep ever again."

"What do we do with him?" Kiran walked toward Jim, cautiously making sure he was still suffering the effects of the Taser.

"Tie him up and leave him here," Hawk stated. "Someone will find him, security already knows we're running around down here, they'll know we did it to him, and by then it won't matter. We're going to have him arrested for kidnapping."

Juliette picked up the ropes that had been used to restrain her. Kiran reached over and took them from her and moved off to tie up Jim. Hawk handed the Taser to Juliette, wrapping her hand around it and guiding her finger to the power switch.

"The sheriff will probably want this," he said as she took it from him inquisitively. "Do you want to pop him with it one more time before we leave him?"

"Is he going to get away?"

"No, but if you wanted to make sure, I would completely understand."

"Maybe," she pondered the possibilities of a little payback. "But who's afraid of the big bad wolf?"

"Not me." Hawk smiled.

"Me either." She returned the grin.

"Well, that makes three of us." Kiran joined them, dusting off her hands with a flourish. "He's not going anywhere, and someone is sure going to be surprised when they find him."

"Perhaps it will keep Reginald Cambridge busy for a while," Hawk offered.

"Reginald!" Juliette jumped in. "Is he still chasing you? What have you been doing? Have you figured this thing out yet? And what are you doing here—where is here—and how did you find me?"

Her questions were coming in rapid bursts as the tension of being terrified melted into trying to make sense of all that had happened and catching up with all she had missed. The expression on Dr. Grayson Hawke's face was one that Juliette had seen many times before. She knew there were answers for all her questions and they would come over time, but there was something else that had to happen first. As she had done ever since she had gotten to know Hawk, she would trust his instincts and follow his lead.

"You have a lot to catch up on." He put his arm over her shoulder and turned her toward the endless line of costumes.

"That's an understatement," Kiran confirmed for her. "Aren't you forgetting something?"

"What?" Hawk raised his eyebrows.

"Your Pal Mickey!"

Hawk quickly stepped over the mess and picked up a stuffed Mickey Mouse.

"Where are we . . . and where are we going?" Juliette began to take in her surroundings.

"We're in the Character Zoo, underground, in the utilidor below the Magic Kingdom," Kiran said, helping Juliette get her bearings. "But we need to decide where we are going."

"What time is it?" Hawk asked.

"About 4:30," Kiran replied.

"Morning or afternoon?" Juliette had lost all track of time since she had been taken.

"It's 4:30 a.m. and we've been running around the Magic Kingdom in the middle of the night, trying not to get caught but running out of places to hide," Hawk summarized their current state of affairs.

"I almost forgot," Kiran turned to face them. "We have reservations."

 *Day Seven*
Early Morning

"SO IF YOU HADN'T KEPT TRYING to solve the puzzle, you never would have found me?" Juliette smiled at Hawk.

"If I hadn't been playing junior detective, you wouldn't have been taken at all." Hawk slowly shook his head.

"You didn't create this mystery. Farren started the whole thing, but then something went wrong."

"I'm just glad I found you," he sighed. "And you're safe."

"I'm glad you didn't quit looking."

"Juliette, I just couldn't."

"I know, that's what I was counting on."

"I kept hoping if I could figure this whole thing out, I'd be able to find you and find Farren."

"It sounds like you're getting close."

Hawk and Juliette sat opposite one another in Cinderella's Castle Suite. Their escape from the Character Zoo had been easy and surprisingly uneventful. After a brisk walk along the utilidor they had accessed a stairwell and reentered Fantasyland behind Cinderella Castle. The three had made it to the castle undetected. Kiran's card had given her access to the elevator that lifted them to the fourth floor of the castle. The opening of the elevator doors deposited them into a foyer adorned with original movie concept art created by the famed artist Mary Blair. It also featured a display case holding the legendary glass slipper of Cinderella herself.

The Renaissance-style suite combined old-style luxury with digital-age technology. The usual attention to detail by the Disney designers had turned this castle suite into a once-upon-a-dream experience for guests fortunate enough to be chosen to stay there. Bathroom sinks created to look like washbasins, faucets that looked like hand pumps, and a hand-cut stone floor made the bathroom a place of luxury. Hawk cleaned up, trying not to spread dirt and water over his pristine surroundings, and changed into the clothes Kiran had hidden in the suite earlier.

Immediately upon their arrival they'd found their elevated castle room allowed everyone to receive a clear cell phone signal, which rarely happened for guests in the theme park. In the midst of the madness of the night a clear cell signal was perhaps the best feature the suite had to offer, at least from their perspectives.

Juliette had gotten in touch with Tim for a tearful reunion over the phone. As she talked, Hawk and Kiran had moved into the foyer to allow her some privacy. Hawk then had the chance to talk to Tim, who promised he would take his pastor to any restaurant, anytime, for the rest of his life in appreciation for finding Juliette. Hawk admitted he really had found her by accident, but they all understood the preacher's dogged determination had worked in their favor. Hawk also spoke with Al Gann, who would be entering the Disney tunnel system very soon, rounding up the man in the Big Bad Wolf head, also known as Jim. Gann had been in touch with Disney security, and the sheriff's department was officially involved. Al was the lead person on the case, but Hawk was out of time. He was going to have to come in and answer some questions about the missing Imagineer Farren Rales. Hawk was not surprised by this but had been shocked when Al told him the rest of what he had to say. Gann promised the department that he personally would bring the preacher into the office for an interview. He had promised to have him there by 2:00 p.m. Al had managed to give Hawk a few more precious hours to solve the mystery. Juliette was safe, the person who had abducted her should be picked up momentarily; the Disney security force and the sheriff's departments were now both involved, so everything was getting ready to change. Gann said the gift of a few hours and not giving a full disclosure to the Disney people quite yet were the best he could do for his friend. He urged Hawk to figure it out and wrap it up.

The strategy Hawk, Gann, Tim, Juliette, Jonathan, Shep, and Kiran had devised would have them hide out in the Cinderella Castle Suite until the Magic Kingdom opened in the morning. Once the park was open and the first wave of people had made it down Main Street USA, they would leave the castle. Juliette would exit the park and board a monorail to the Contemporary to be reunited with Tim and go home. Hawk and Kiran would follow as many leads as they could through the park, hoping they wouldn't be stopped by Disney security. At 1:00 p.m. Hawk would head over to the Contemporary and rejoin Jonathan, Shep, and Al to let them know what he had found and what needed to happen next. From there Al Gann and Hawk would head to the interview at the sheriff's office to unpack the entire story and hopefully find out what had happened to Farren Rales.

It was still shortly before daylight when everything had been decided. The Magic Kingdom was not scheduled to open until 9:00 a.m. There were snacks to eat for breakfast in the room and turns to be taken in the luxury bathing facilities, giving Juliette and Hawk time to talk privately. Standing up and walking near the bathroom door Juliette confirmed that Kiran was still bathing and she came back to join Hawk.

"So Kiran is good?" Juliette asked with a quizzical look on her face as she sat down.

"What do you mean good?" Hawk's mind went uninvited to the shower, and his face flamed. Juliette laughed.

"I mean, she's one of us—one of the good guys—and you trust her?"

"I didn't have any choice. She rescued me when Cambridge was after me, she helped me solve clues, and she's managed to get me out of more than a few jams over the past few hours."

"And?"

"I probably wouldn't have been able to survive the night in the park without her, and I wouldn't have been able to find you."

"So she's good?"

"I guess . . ."

"And she's gorgeous."

"I hadn't noticed." Hawk replied, thinking Snow White's stepmother would kill her in a heartbeat.

"You lie," she teased.

"She is pretty," Hawk yielded.

"And you trust her?" Juliette pressed the last question between them, instantly serious. Hawk hesitated and thought of Kiran dressing behind the bathroom door before looking back at Juliette. She asked again slowly, "And you trust her?"

"I want to . . ."

"But?"

"You heard the DVD when Farren told me to be careful about whom to trust. Like any classic Disney story, there will be heroes and villains."

"From what you've told me she sounds fairly heroic."

"She has been pretty terrific," he admitted.

"Look, Hawk," She leaned forward and lowered her voice to a whisper. "A lot has happened over the past twenty-four hours. It sounds like she's risked a lot to help get you this far. The problem is, you're starting to really like her. Be wise, trust her with as much as you can, but in the end remember this is your quest, your puzzle, your mystery to solve. The people who really love you understand that and want you to figure it out . . . because they love and trust you. Kiran sounds like she is one of those people. So figure this thing out—"

The bathroom door clicked open and Kiran walked out looking refreshed and radiant. At least those were the adjectives that crossed Hawk's mind when he saw her. Stepping into the room she stopped and playfully stepped back as though sensing she may have interrupted a deep conversation between the two old friends.

"I'm sorry, I could come back later, but I don't have anywhere to go." She flashed a smile.

"Come over." Juliette motioned for her to join them. "Hawk is trying to catch me up on his escapades. I'm sure he's forgetting some of the details."

Over the next hour they relived and retold the events of the previous night. Hawk would tell a portion of the story and Kiran would take over and fill in the gaps. Juliette laughed with them as they recounted the events that, although serious, seemed a little less intense in the safety of the castle. They ended up with the final clue Pal Mickey had offered at Sir Mickey's.

I knew you could do it, pal! Let's fly to where it is always past my bedtime. Gosh, even though it's late and I should be asleep I'm sure Mr. Disney wouldn't mind. Oh, ha-ha, I almost forgot . . . remember the pixie dust!

"So that's your next clue?" Juliette tilted her head.

"There are a number of attractions in the Magic Kingdom you can fly on," Kiran offered.

"The secret may be in the next part of the clue," Hawk thought aloud. "'Even though it's late and I should be asleep I'm sure Mr. Disney wouldn't mind.' That seemed to make sense in the middle of the night. But in the light of day it's tougher."

"What do you mean?" Kiran asked.

"Well, we need to find a place where it's past Mickey's bedtime."

"And don't forget the pixie dust!" Juliette said.

"So we fly, it's late, and we need pixie dust," Kiran recapped.

"Of course! We head to Peter Pan's Flight," Hawk announced triumphantly.

"Are you sure?" Kiran slid forward in her seat.

"Positive, it makes sense," Hawk reasoned. "Think about it, the ride takes place at night after the children are supposed to be asleep. They fly out the window after they get sprinkled with pixie dust, and they follow Peter Pan."

"After all good kids should be in bed," Juliette pulled the line of reasoning together.

"And after all good little mice should be in bed as well," Kiran playfully added. "Mickey was always portrayed as Walt Disney's creation, almost like a child; Walt was a good parent, Mickey would have an early bedtime."

"It's just around the corner." Hawk began tapping his foot. "We can be there as soon as the park opens."

"Not to be a party pooper, but I'm going to let you two go fly with Peter Pan." Juliette yawned. "I am going home to my family, and my own bed. After all, I had a long day and didn't get to play in the park all night."

CHAPTER FORTY-TWO

Day Seven
Morning

GRAYSON HAWKES STOOD LOOKING through the window of the Cinderella Suite and saw the first strands of sunlight push against the twinkle of nighttime illumination. Chasing the darkness, a new day burst into dawn over Walt Disney World. Juliette stepped next to him as the brilliant scene unfolded. This moment was a once-in-a-lifetime event and Hawk silently allowed the daylight to flutter across his eyes as the two friends watched the beginning of a new day.

"Wow," Juliette said after a few silent minutes.

"Pretty spectacular." Hawk felt almost sad that the moment had ended.

"Are you ready to finish this?"

"I hope so. I have to. I'm out of time."

"How much more can there be to find, Hawk?"

"I'm not sure." He resigned himself to the reality of how little he knew. "I'm not sure what any of the pieces I have found mean—if they mean anything."

"I think"—she paused, measuring her words carefully—"I think when you find the last piece, everything will fall into place. I also think you have to be getting close to the end."

"I want to believe you're right." Hawk shook his head. "All I know to do is keep looking."

"You'll figure it out." She grabbed him by the arm and steered him toward the table. "Come get something to eat, this place is stocked with goodies."

A short while later the gates to the Magic Kingdom opened and the crowds flooded Main Street USA. Guests ran down Main Street and funneled through the interior of the castle, filling up Fantasyland. Others strolled more leisurely, content to let the eager attraction seekers move ahead. It was now time for Hawk, Kiran, and Juliette to exit the castle. The three took a deep breath as they pushed open the door and reentered Fantasyland.

Juliette wished them luck and was off through the castle headed toward the exit. Kiran and Hawk used the corner of the castle as cover as they surveyed any obstacles that would block their path toward Peter Pan's Flight. Assured the coast was clear they briskly stepped out, mingling with a crowd of wide-eyed tourists.

Peter Pan's Flight was created in the image of the original. In 1955 the attraction had been built by Walt in Disneyland. He had desired to give his guests a chance to experience firsthand scenes from the 1953 film *Peter Pan*. The ride was a mainstay of the Magic Kingdom, and the wait time could exceed an hour. Since Hawk and Kiran were early there would be almost no wait at all for them to board the ride. Walking casually toward the entrance they both kept a sharp watch for anyone that seemed unusually interested in them. At the corner of the entrance Hawk remembered a moment from the previous night.

"Kiran, when I was here hiding last night, Pal Mickey gave me a message."

"Right here?" She frowned at him, and he regretted not telling her before.

"Yes, I was hiding before I made it over to Sir Mickey's. The message was, 'You're here too early, pal, it's not time yet.'"

"It probably would have made the clue easier to figure out if you had remembered that," she jokingly scolded.

"I guess in all the excitement, I forgot."

"I hope it's time now."

"Me too." His time to figure this puzzle out was running out.

Weaving their way through the queue line were three other groups waiting to board. The attraction's operator waved them through as Hawk and Kiran took a seat in their own private flying ship. The ride wound them through the bedroom of the Darling children. Peter Pan beckoned them, and every other rider, to come with him to Never Land. With a quick sprinkling of pixie dust the boat, suspended on a track above them, lifted them through the bedroom window, over the Darlings' backyard as their dog Nana barked, and through the nighttime sky of London.

Hawk recalled the first time he had ever flown in this attraction as a child. Surprised to see all of the scenes from the movie below him, he'd been nervous and excited. He hadn't realized he would be flying above the action. Kiran nudged his arm and pointed at Big Ben. The clock was in front of them as they flew.

"See what time it is?"

"It's 9:06—way past the bedtime of little children," he confirmed.

The shaking of the stuffed tour guide on his hip was expected.

"Ha-ha!"

Hawk momentarily thought of the disaster it would be if he accidentally dropped the mouse out of the boat into the streets of London below. The nervous thought caused him to hold it just a little bit more tightly and in doing so activated the voice mechanism inside. Kiran and he both leaned in closely to hear the message, their faces side by side. Unexpectedly Kiran kissed him on the lips.

"For luck!" She smiled.

Smiling back at her he hoped she wouldn't notice his blushing in the darkness of the ride. His face was warm and his mind swirled before Pal Mickey interrupted the moment.

"Hiya, Hawk! You're fantastic! Now it's time, this is your last clue. You know Walt Disney's story but you don't know the last chapter. That's what you're gonna have to get to the bottom of now. Hey, pal, thanks for being my partner. The best thing about being partners is you always have someone that will point you in the right direction."

The message played out as they flew over Never Land. The boat passed over an island of mountains, flowers, and a volcano. An epic battle was now being waged as Peter Pan and Hook were dueling for the freedom and safety of the prisoners.

"Now we have the last clue," Kiran finally spoke. "That's a good thing, right?"

"Oh, it's good . . . we just have to figure out what it means." Hawk was trying unsuccessfully to shift his thoughts from Kiran's kiss back to the puzzle.

"Help me, Mr. Smee, help me!" Captain Hook called to Smee from below as the pirate straddled the ticking crocodile's menacing jaws. This signaled the ride was coming to an end and the flying boat would be landing momentarily.

Stepping off the boat, they moved through the exit back into the streets of Fantasyland toward the carousel. Blending in with the motion of the park guests, they moved back toward the castle. Hawk checked often that they weren't being watched, and led them on the pathway around the castle to the right. Deciding it would be less noticeable than moving directly through the castle they made their way around the waterline near Liberty Square. Pausing about halfway down the path he guided Kiran to a bench that offered some protection behind surrounding trees and shrubs. They took a seat, looking about to see if they'd remained undetected. Seeing no one except park guests, Hawk leaned in to speak quietly to Kiran.

"We're getting ready to be very visible."

"So you know where we're going?" Her excitement spilled into her voice.

"We're going out to the hub in front of the castle."

"Why?"

"The *Partners* statue is there."

"I know the *Partners* statue is there. Remember I showed it to you when you took my tour?" Kiran paused and then her eyes widened. "But Mickey called you his partner, that's why we're going there."

"Partially," Hawk informed her. "But there's more."

"Are you going to tell me or not?"

"It is something that Walt said," he said reluctantly.

"Walt—you mean Walt Disney?"

"Of course." Hawk smiled reassuringly.

"You're going to have to help me here, Hawk, because I don't have this piece figured out yet."

"Not only did Mickey call me his partner"—he paused longer than he intended—"but Walt called me his partner."

"Walt Disney called you his partner?"

"Yes, he did." He realized how odd that sounded when he said it aloud.

"You've spoken to Walt Disney?" Kiran's tone became wary.

"Not actually spoken to him," he corrected. She said nothing and it became obvious she was waiting for him to continue. "He sent me a message and told me that his brother, Roy, was his partner—and that I was his partner."

"He did?" Kiran's forehead wrinkled in puzzlement. "Hawk, Walt Disney is dead." Her words were carefully measured. "He died December 15, 1966, and you know this fact. So how did he send you a message?"

"It was on a DVD." He quickly added, "Obviously DVD technology wasn't around in 1966, but he filmed a message for me. He didn't know it would be me that would eventually see it. It was a message for whoever would end up with the key."

He noticed her jaw had fallen, and he gently reached over to her face. Taking a finger and placing it tenderly below her chin, he applied enough pressure for her to close her mouth. The action caused her to snap back to the moment.

"Where did you get this DVD?"

"I found it in Tommy Kirk's mailbox at the Studios. It was a bonus feature on *Old Yeller*."

"Do you know how insane what you just said sounds?"

He laughed at the disbelief in her voice. "I hadn't thought about it."

"On a copy of *Old Yeller* that you picked up in Tommy Kirk's mailbox, Walt Disney left a message for you because one day, years after his death, you would have a key and be trying to solve a mystery," Kiran scoffed.

"That pretty much covers it."

"Why didn't you tell me about this message?"

"I was afraid you would think I was crazy!"

"You're kidding."

"You have to admit, it's hard to believe."

"I have no trouble admitting it, but you didn't tell me because you didn't trust me . . . correct?"

"We have already been down this road." He searched her face. "I didn't tell you then, but I've told you now, haven't I?"

She nodded. "Yes, you have. And I guess it should make sense. Preacher, if God talks to you, then I shouldn't be surprised that Walt Disney can talk to you as well."

"I've only heard from Walt Disney once," he corrected. "I hear from God on a regular basis. I pay more attention to Him."

"Then let's go see your partner."

 *Day Seven*
Mid-Morning

THE PLAZA IN FRONT of Cinderella Castle served as the connection point where all of the various lands of the Magic Kingdom converged. The centerpiece of the hub was the statue known as *Partners*. The rendition of Mickey Mouse holding hands with Walt Disney was a favored picture spot of most guests to the park. Kiran and Hawk arrived as people had formed an informal line waiting to take a picture. Trying not to be in the way, they positioned themselves strategically to the right side of the life-sized statue, looking up at it.

"Is the clue the statue, something hidden beneath the statue, or something around the statue?" Kiran asked eagerly.

"There's nothing different about the statue, is there?" Hawk asked.

"Not that I see." She studied it more closely. "Do you think something has been changed?"

"No, but I just want to be sure." Hawk was thinking aloud, trying to reason out the clue. "I would imagine the clue is something on the statue that could never be noticed without the information we have."

"I'm not sure what the information is, Hawk."

"Think through it with me," he invited. "Mickey called me his partner, the statue is called *Partners*, Walt called me his partner in the message, and twice in his message he said that his brother Roy was his partner. The clue has to be right here."

"Roy was Walt's partner, Mickey is Walt's partner, and now you're Walt's partner, and we're right here with Walt and Mickey," Kiran tried to reason out the solution.

"So all of Walt's partners are here except—"

"Roy," Kiran finished the thought. "There's a statue of Roy in Town Square at the other end of Main Street USA, but we can't move it. How else can we get Roy here?"

"I don't think we're supposed to move Roy's statue. The clue has to be here." Hawk continued to study the statue closely. "Kiran, what does STR mean?"

Hawk's gaze had come to rest on the tie Walt Disney was wearing. The tiepin on the center of his tie was made up of three letters: STR. Although he had seen the statue on many different occasions he had never really noticed these letters. They seemed to stand out a little too much and perhaps were too noticeable. The creator of the statue wanted these letters to be clearly seen by those who viewed it.

"STR means Smoke Tree Ranch," Kiran answered, her gaze following his to the letters on the tie. "Walt Disney had a cottage there in Palm Springs, California. When he moved in, the community wasn't thrilled with a Hollywood type becoming their neighbor, so Walt spent a lot of time investing himself in the community. He loved his home there and would often be seen wearing the pin with the initials."

"Smoke Tree Ranch," Hawk repeated. "STR, Smoke Tree Ranch, STR, I wonder . . ."

"Wonder?"

"I wonder if it could mean something else." He turned toward Kiran. "Doesn't it seem odd that these three letters that very few people would identify with Walt Disney be featured as boldly as they are on this statue?"

"I suppose, but he did wear a pin like that one."

"Sure, but whoever designed this statue made sure the three letter details really stand out. Maybe Disney did wear that kind of pin all the time, but I never remember seeing it in pictures of him, except one time.

"So Smoke Tree Ranch is the clue?"

"No, the clue isn't Smoke Tree Ranch," Hawk concluded. "Maybe it means something else. Maybe the STR is our clue."

"I'm lost," Kiran admitted.

"In the message Walt left me he said a couple of things about Roy. The film had Walt dressed pretty much like the statue has portrayed him. Believe it or not, he was wearing the STR pin, I remember noticing it. On two different occasions he said the same phrase. He said he would go straight to Roy when he was in trouble, and he would go straight to Roy to keep him on track."

"And that's the clue?"

"Couldn't STR mean Straight To Roy?" Hawk looked back at the statue intently. "After all, we're in a little bit of trouble and we could use some help getting out of it, and we definitely need someone to help keep us on track . . . and Roy is the only one of the partners who isn't here."

Kiran looked at the statue of Walt and Mickey and then slowly turned her gaze down the length of Main Street USA. Pausing she allowed her eyes to return to the *Partners* statue. Hawk had done the same thing Kiran had but had walked around to the back of the statue. Kiran saw the movement and followed him, giving them a view down the length of Main Street toward the Town Square and the Railroad Station at the far end.

"STR, straight to Roy." Hawk smiled. "And notice his hand; he's pointing the way . . . straight to Roy."

"So we need to go down Main Street to the statue of Roy Disney?"

"Because that is what Walt would do, it's what he told us to do, it's where the next clue is."

"You're sure?" Kiran didn't sound convinced.

"Remember what Mickey said?" He looked away from Main Street toward Kiran. "'The best thing about being partners is you always have someone that will point you in the right direction.'"

Without giving her time to answer he grabbed Kiran by the hand and took off down Main Street USA. Bobbing and weaving through groups of people, Hawk and Kiran eventually got to the end of the street next to the Emporium. Stepping off the curb under the covering of the Emporium they moved across the street to the statue of Roy Disney.

Unlike the statue of his brother, Walt, the life-sized statue of Roy was much less dramatic in its design. Roy is seated on a bench, legs casually crossed, holding hands gently with Minnie Mouse. In life where Walt was the charismatic and powerful point man of the company, Roy was working behind the scenes and content to stay out of the spotlight. In many ways this statue managed to capture the difference. Farren had described to Hawk how Roy had come out of retirement to complete Walt's dream and make sure that Walt's plans stayed alive. *Sharing the Magic* was the name of the statue, dedicated twenty-eight years after Roy had dedicated the Magic Kingdom. It was an unassuming tribute to the lesser-known partner and brother of Walt Disney.

While Kiran stood guard, Hawk stepped in front of the statue and crouched down in front of where the bronzed Roy was seated. Studying Roy and then looking over at Minnie he examined the intricacies of the creation. Hawk moved in closer to the statue of Roy Disney and looked directly in the spectacled face.

"You find something, Hawk?"

"Just noticing something," he replied, not looking back at her.

"What is it?"

"Not sure." Hawk rose to his feet and stepped back away from the statue until he'd put eight feet between himself and the seated figure. The preacher gazed into the face of the less famous of the Disney brothers and again knelt down, never breaking eye contact with the crafted eyes of the statue. He rose to his feet once again and stepped in toward the face of the statue, maintaining eye contact.

"Check his eyes." Hawk stepped away so she could see.

"He's looking at Minnie," she said as she began to examine the statue.

"Not really," Hawk said, leaning back in. "He's sort of looking at her, but his gaze is somewhere else."

"Hawk, it's a nice, sweet statue." She stood and now studied the preacher. "It's a well-crafted piece of art. So his gaze might be off a little, what does that mean?"

"Don't know." Hawk moved away from Kiran and the statue and circled behind it. "It might mean nothing or it might mean a lot."

Hawk now was standing behind the iron railing that encircled the landscaped garden of flowers and shrubbery that fanned out behind the statues seated on the bench. He stood up straight and then crouched down once again. She stepped over and placed herself directly in Hawk's line of sight just on the other side of the statue.

"Will you move?" Hawk raised his palms in frustration.

"You're not doing a very good job of blending into the crowd," she warned him. "You're stalking the statue."

"Come over here, please," he said politely.

"Have you found something?" Kiran quickly moved toward him.

"No, not yet, but I did get you to move out of my way." He smiled, satisfied. "Dork!"

Now they both stood behind the statue, looking over the head of Roy back toward the entrance to the Exposition Hall. The Victorian building was a single structure with three separate entrances. The first entrance featured a ramp that went up to a set of entry doors. The next entrance was the main doors to Exposition Hall, and the last set of doors was an entrance to Tony's Restaurant. The long porch, dotted with rocking chairs under the cover of shade, was already collecting a smattering of tourists needing a place to rest.

"Let me ask you something." Hawk gazed over Roy's head. "What do you think ol' Roy here is looking at?"

"Minnie Mouse?" Kiran said, looking over the statue's head.

"No, he really is not," Hawk corrected. "Sure, for the sake of the statue it looks that way, but this is Walt Disney World, the details matter."

"Okay," she tried again. "The direction of his head is really pointed more to the corner of the building. I guess he's looking to the south side of it."

Hawk realigned his gaze to match the direction Roy's head was tilted. Directly over the statue's top he saw a long, garden-flanked entrance area with a set of four steps that connected it to the corner of Main Street USA.

He pointed toward the steps as Kiran moved in closely next to him to align her sights to match his direction.

"The steps?"

"Yes." He nodded with satisfaction. "The steps, Roy is actually facing the steps. His head is facing in that direction. His gaze seems to be looking down toward the ground, but he is facing that way."

"So he's really not looking at Minnie?" Kiran asked. "And this is important?"

"For all practical purposes he's looking at Minnie, but when you look at the details of the creation, maybe he's looking at something else."

"Keep going." She quit looking toward the steps and turned to Hawk.

"In Walt's message, along with his telling me that he always went straight to Roy, he said something else. 'We've done a lot of things together and um . . . he is always watching over me, trying to take care of me, keeping us safe.' I think that's a clue."

"Roy is watching over Walt keeping him safe?"

"No," Hawk corrected her. "Details, Kiran. Walt said Roy was always watching over him, trying to take care of him, keeping *us* safe. I think the statue, placed here on the anniversary of Roy's keeping Walt's dream alive when he dedicated the Magic Kingdom, is somehow symbolic of Roy's keeping Walt and the dreams they had as partners safe."

"You've lost me." She shook her head.

"Put on your tour guide hat for a minute," he encouraged. "What is Roy looking toward?"

"The edge of the building?"

"Yes, but what's in the building?"

"The main area of Exposition Hall is a gift area. You can enter Tony's and can find the exit to the character greeting area."

"Wow," he playfully complimented her, "you know your stuff."

"Gee, thanks."

"But what was there before?"

"Before?"

"Before the character greeting area." He raised an eyebrow.

"The last attraction that was there was the . . . Walt Disney Story!" Kiran remembered with a brilliant smile.

"Right," Hawk said. "I remember seeing that first as a kid. If my memory is serving me correctly, that was the first and only attraction ever in this building."

"It was open nearly twenty years off and on," Kiran added.

Hawk's memories of the place came flooding back through the recesses of his mind. He remembered walking down a long hallway with his father that was loaded with Walt memorabilia. There were letters from famous people, pictures of Walt taken around the world, models from the movies and the actual submarine from *20,000 Leagues Under the Sea*. He remembered the attraction ended with a film about Walt Disney's life. Walt himself provided the narration. His dad had told him that one day he could bring his children here and introduce them to the dreams created by Walt Disney. The memories grew darker; Hawk had never gotten the opportunity to do what his dad had suggested.

"The attraction was adapted from time to time," Kiran said. "Occasionally the film piece was changed to highlight something special, like the opening of Epcot, the Studios, or an anniversary of the park. Hawk, are you with me?"

Kiran's comment snapped Hawk back from the brink of being overwhelmed by his thoughts.

"Yep."

"Where were you? What were you thinking?" She placed a concerned hand on his forearm.

"Just remembering what used to be, I'm sorry. I'm listening."

"But the company closed the attraction for good in the early nineties," she concluded. "Does it matter?"

"I think it does." Hawk nodded. "We followed Walt's directions and went straight to Roy. Here sits Roy doing what he always has done, watching over Walt and keeping their dreams safe. The dreams were placed on display in the Walt Disney Story attraction for the whole world to see."

"So now Roy is watching over Walt's dreams," she summarized.

"I think."

"Hawk, this statue is fairly new. The Walt Disney Story was closed long before Roy was ever placed here. Most of the things in the old attraction were improved in One Man's Dream . . . you remember it, right? You broke into Walt's office, I believe."

"Never heard of the place." He deflected the verbal jab. "Maybe the statue was placed here because Walt's dreams were in danger, or Roy needed to protect or help him again."

"Seriously? You think this whole mystery is about protecting something that Walt and Roy had dreamed up?"

"Why not?" Hawk explained, "I've been given the key to the kingdom by an old, old friend of Walt's. Walt Disney has left me a message recorded before he died and explained how important this key was."

"Walt mentioned your key in the message?"

"Yes." Hawk paused. "He held it in his hand as he was talking about it."

"You forgot to give me that detail."

"Sorry," he continued. "This mysterious adventure we're on has been loaded with clues that relate to the way Walt Disney told a story, or taught others to tell a story."

"So we're going into the Walt Disney Story?"

"Or what's left of it."

"Is the secret in there?"

"We're about to find out."

 *Day Seven*
Mid-Morning

KIRAN AND HAWK WALKED UP the steps and entered Exposition Hall just off Main Street USA. Immediately upon stepping inside the door Hawk's cell phone vibrated, startling him and stopping his forward motion. Kiran continued on for a few more yards before realizing Hawk was no longer beside her. Turning, she watched him open his phone to take the call.

Hawk looked at the caller ID; Shep's name had appeared. He answered quickly.

"Did Juliette make it out?"

"Sure did. She and Tim headed home."

"Good." Hawk took in a deep breath and exhaled.

"We've got a problem, boss . . ."

"Problem?" Hawk narrowed his eyes and turned away from Kiran.

"A little while ago Al went into the utilidor with some folks from Disney security."

"And?"

"There was no one in the Character Zoo."

"That can't be!" Hawk exclaimed. He felt Karin's hand touch his back for a moment and then she drew it away.

"Everything fit the description and details you gave perfectly. There were signs of a huge struggle, piles of clothes, and even a cracked Big Bad Wolf head, but there was no person there."

"Shep, we left the guy there. He was tazed and tied up."

"He was gone."

The deep sound of a man clearing his throat caught Hawk's ear, and he turned back into Exposition Hall. Kiran's eyes were open wide and staring straight at him. Standing behind her, with an arm over her shoulder and across her throat, was the man missing from the clothes pile in the zoo. Jim had pulled Kiran against his body. His other hand, pressed firmly to Kiran's side, was holding a small, glistening blade.

"Why don't you hang up the phone, Dr. Hawkes?" Jim was not making a suggestion, he was uttering a command. "Let's step inside Tony's Restaurant, it won't be open for another hour and we can . . . talk."

Jabbing his head in the direction of the restaurant, Hawk followed his lead and closed his phone. Walking in front of Jim and Kiran he moved slowly, pausing to look over his shoulder at them. Kiran was rigid, breathing in short shallow bursts of air.

"Don't worry, Kiran," Hawk said to her. "It will be all right."

"Hawk—"

Jim tightened his grip across her throat and pressed the blade against her side for emphasis.

"There is no reason for you to be talking, sweetheart," he sneered in her ear. "Keep moving."

They entered the restaurant and Hawk wheeled to face Jim. The assailant had allowed some distance to form between himself and Hawk. The tip of the blade made a deep indentation in Kiran's blouse. He motioned with his head for Hawk to take a few more steps back. Now Hawk stood opposite Jim and Kiran with two tables between them. It was too far for Hawk to jump across. Hawk noticed Jim's face for the first time; he was wearing souvenirs from the previous encounter in the character wardrobe area. Slightly bruised and cut, Jim had not gotten the chance to clean up, but still had managed to escape. Someone had helped him; Hawk wondered who that might have been.

"You have caused me considerable inconvenience and . . . pain."

"That is a shame," Hawk smartly retorted.

"It has been a long night and I am tired. So, the time for games and negotiating has passed. You will give me what I want." Jim jerked Kiran back against him, shoving his forearm harder against her neck. "Or I will take from you what you want."

Hawk made a calming gesture with his hands. He tried not to look at the knife. His pulse raced. "What is it you want?"

"Come now, Dr. Hawkes, don't insult me." Jim's nostril's flared. "I want the key, the silver box, and the Pal Mickey. You can set them on the table and then leave the restaurant."

Hawk was stunned that he knew about every single clue. The preacher stood staring at Jim, trying to figure out what to do. He couldn't get to Kiran and didn't believe Jim would let her go.

"Hawk, don't!" Kiran gasped. Jim increased the pressure on her neck, and she whimpered.

"Obviously." Jim smirked at Hawk. "Ms. Roberts is giving you some very bad advice. You leave the items on the table in front of you, leave Tony's, and make your way to the front gate. Once you have left the park, I will let her go."

Hawk tried to formulate a way to get to Jim without hurting Kiran. There wasn't one. But if he gave Jim what he had asked for, there was no guarantee he would let Kiran go.

"You are such a fool!" A new voice boomed from the other side of the restaurant.

Hawk twisted quickly to see who entered. Jim did the same, dragging Kiran around in front of him, lifting her off her feet with the arm braced across her throat. She gasped at the motion, and Hawk's heart wrenched in his chest.

"Who are you?" Jim demanded of the newcomer to Tony's Town Square Restaurant.

"I told you to stay away from her!" Sandy ignored Jim and spoke directly to Hawk.

Sandy had emerged from the kitchen side of the dining room. Dressed in street clothes, he was slightly disheveled and extremely agitated.

"Who are you?" Jim barked again in Sandy's direction.

"His name is Sandy," Kiran managed in a whisper.

"If you didn't notice," Hawk addressed Sandy, "You've arrived at a bad time."

"You know"—Sandy laughed and took a seat at the nearest table nonchalantly—"you really should have listened to me. I told you to stay away from Kiran. I really thought you would have had more common sense than you actually do."

"We can talk about this later." Hawk grew fearful that Sandy's presence might cause Jim to panic and hurt Kiran. Calling upon all his counseling skills, he tried to use a calm tone to defuse the situation. "Sandy, you and I may have gotten off on the wrong foot. I know you have strong feelings for Kiran and I do as well. We can talk about those later."

"So you have strong feelings for her?" Sandy glared at him.

"He has strong feelings for me," Kiran whispered aloud to no one in particular.

"Be quiet," Jim hissed at her. "Sandy! It would be best for everyone if you just got up, turned around, and left. Nothing that is happening here is any concern of yours."

"But it is a concern of mine!" Another voice echoed across the dining room.

Hawk now whirled back in the opposite direction toward the windows lining the restaurant along Main Street. Jim dragged Kiran backward, moving them into a more strategic position with an escape from the increasingly crowded dining room. Sandy looked up from his table, unimpressed at the newest arrival to the conversation. Reginald Cambridge closed the door leading out to the tables along Main Street and locked it behind him. Quickly glancing across the room and taking inventory of all the parties involved, he spoke into the radio he held in one hand.

"Hold everyone back," the security man commanded.

Hawk wondered how many people *everyone* meant and where they might be. Glancing out the window he saw nothing out of the ordinary on Main Street USA. Now with the addition of Reginald Cambridge there was a four-way standoff in the dining room of Tony's. The preacher was concerned that Jim would hurt Kiran, he knew that Cambridge would have backup out there somewhere close, and he wasn't real sure what Sandy would do if the situation escalated. Cambridge, Sandy, Jim, and Hawk all eyed each other warily as if trying to figure out who might actually have the most advantageous position.

"Here is what is getting ready to happen," Cambridge blustered. "Jim, you are going to let Kiran go and relinquish your weapon. Threatening a cast member is a violation of company policy, but of course you already know that. And I should inform you that right outside I have some people that urgently want to talk to you about abducting a park guest and attempting to hold her hostage. It appears you were trying to gain some leverage to use against Dr. Hawkes here, and clearly it didn't work. You are complicating things by threatening Ms. Roberts." Cambridge kept watching Jim, waiting for him to ease his grasp on Kiran. "Ms Roberts, you have been a very busy lady these past few days. I am anxious to hear an explanation as to why you have been blatantly disregarding every security procedure we have on the books while acting as a personal tour guide for Dr. Hawkes." He turned slowly toward Sandy, who was still seated at the table farthest from him. "And as for you—I believe I heard your name is Sandy—I need for you to march yourself right back out the door you came in through. Nothing that is happening here involves you, but rest assured, I will find you and we will talk later." Finally he turned toward Hawk. "Dr. Hawkes . . ."

"I'm not going anywhere, you overstuffed company goon," Sandy yelled to Cambridge.

Reginald blinked. "Excuse me?"

"Aw, did I hurt your feelings, Reggie?" Sandy taunted. "You'll get over it."

"I hate to interrupt this annoyingly over-crowded meeting." Jim turned back toward Hawk. "But Dr. Hawkes, I asked you to do something for me, and the extra people with us in the room don't change that." Then looking over at Cambridge he added, "If I see anyone come near me, the young lady here will not be able to explain why she has broken your precious security rules. Do I make myself clear?"

"Don't give anything to him, Hawkes, he won't hurt her." Sandy rolled his eyes.

"You are mistaken, young man," Jim responded threateningly.

"Go ahead, cut her then," Sandy challenged.

"NO!" Hawk yelled toward Jim as he saw his eyes tighten at the challenge.

Cambridge reflexively took a step toward Jim, as did Hawk. Jim jerked Kiran off her feet with the blade jabbed against her. The tip poked a hole through the cloth of her blouse. With very little pressure Jim would puncture her side.

"Relax, you two." Sandy spoke with sudden calmness to Hawk and Reginald. "He won't hurt her, they're working together."

Kiran's eyes remained wide in terror. They darted from Hawk to Sandy and then back to Hawk.

"They've been working together the whole time, Hawkes."

"You lie!" Hawk's jaw clenched in fury.

"Why do you think I told you to stay away from her? I warned you, but you just didn't listen."

"Don't be deceived," Jim growled. "The words of a babbling fool will cause this to end badly."

"Ah, you sound very convincing," Sandy mocked Jim. "Go ahead, let us see it end badly. Cut her, strangle her, show us what you've got."

"Don't do it, Jim!" Hawk took another step toward Jim and Kiran.

"Calm down, preacher. Jimmy boy won't hurt her, he's gutless."

Hawk stopped, fist clenched, and turned toward Sandy.

"What did she tell you?" Sandy continued. "Did she tell you I was an ex-boyfriend? Or maybe a crazy stalker who just wouldn't leave her alone? Did she tell you I knew who she was and what she was up to? No, I'm sure she didn't tell you that . . . . did she, Hawkes?"

"Don't believe him, Hawk," Kiran managed to gasp from behind Jim's stranglehold.

"Oh, I would believe him, Grayson," said a man who stepped into the restaurant behind Kiran and Jim.

The sixth person to arrive at Tony's had a face Hawk recognized. He had seen this man look directly at him the night before in Caribbean Plaza outside of Pirates of the Caribbean. He and Kiran had gotten away from the man then. The face had been familiar but Hawk had not been able to place it. Suddenly the features of the man's face fell into place inside Hawk's mind. Hawk had seen him in the train station. He had been the conductor Hawk had spoken with as he was looking for the silver box.

"Do you recognize me?" said the conductor to Hawk. "You met me in the train station."

"Yes, and I saw you another time," Hawk added.

"In Caribbean Plaza." The conductor smiled genuinely pleased that Hawk remembered. "You were with Kiran when I saw you there. Why don't you listen to what Sandy has to say."

"Let's hear him out, Dr. Hawkes." Reginald Cambridge eyed the new arrival and then looked back toward Sandy. "Jim doesn't seem to be in that big of a hurry to hurt Ms. Roberts. As a matter of fact, I thought I saw him loosen his grip on her neck so she could speak a moment ago."

"You're crazy!" Jim said, holding Kiran in front of him.

"Perhaps." Cambridge nodded toward Sandy, urging him to continue.

"Did it ever bother you that Kiran kept showing up and finding you every time you were in a theme park?" Sandy accepted the invitation to speak. "She was tracking you. Every time you placed your finger on a biometric print reader, she was notified. I know it's commonly believed that we aren't really looking at people's prints, but if we really want to find someone, we can. Hawkes, every single time you entered a park she knew you were there, then she just had to find you."

Hawk looked from Sandy to Kiran, who was staring directly into his eyes, pleading for him not to believe what Sandy was saying. For a brief moment Hawk didn't want to tear his eyes away from hers. He wanted to believe and trust her, she was his friend, but still . . . he listened as Sandy continued.

"Did it ever dawn on you that she was being too helpful? When did she show up in your life, Hawkes . . . after Farren Rales disappeared?"

At the mention of Farren's name, Hawk broke his gaze away from Kiran and whirled toward Sandy.

"You know where Farren is?" Hawk questioned.

"No." Sandy rocked back in his chair. "But I know Kiran wants to know just as badly as you do. She wants to figure out the little puzzle you're working on so she can find the prize for herself. As long as she kept batting her eyes and holding your hand, you kept her around for the adventure."

"It's not true," Kiran desperately whispered from Jim's grasp.

"He did it again!" Cambridge roared. "He loosened his grip on her neck so she could talk! Unbelievable!" One side of his mouth curled upward ever so slightly. It might have been a smile. "Continue, I'm enthralled."

"I don't know where Farren is." Sandy's chest puffed out. "She doesn't know where he is either, but she wishes she did—don't you, sweetheart? Ol' Jim here has been watching you for a long time, Hawkes. He has been following you, keeping track of where you go and who you talk with. He especially has been interested in the time you were spending with Farren Rales. Once Farren was gone, you were in their sights and they had to get their hooks in you. With Farren missing you were the only one who would be able to learn the secret."

"What is this secret?" Cambridge slowly asked.

"Ah, now that's the problem, Reggie. Only Farren knew it, and Hawkes here is the only one who has a chance at figuring it out." Sandy scowled. "I told you, Hawkes, Kiran is bad news. She played you, and you fell for it."

The room fell silent as Sandy's words hung in the air. All in the room had their eyes fixed on Hawk. He stepped back, deflated, like he had been punched in the pit of his stomach. Kiran somehow effortlessly slipped out of Jim's grasp, shoving him backward, and raced across the room to Hawk. She stopped in front of him and stared into his face quizzically. Reaching out she took both of his hands in hers.

"He is a liar, Hawk," she began. "Look at me, look in my eyes, think about all we've been through over the past few days, the things we've talked about, the time we've spent together." She smiled her gorgeous smile. "I have no idea why he's saying these things . . . but you have to believe me."

"Oh, please!" Sandy muttered.

"Quiet," Cambridge threatened Sandy.

"You trust me, don't you Hawk?" Kiran pleaded.

Hawk studied her, trying to look behind her eyes into her soul. The look on her face peacefully pleaded with him to trust and believe her. He tightened his grip on her hands and she responded in kind. He turned his head back to Sandy, who rolled his eyes again. Hawk inhaled deeply and swung his gaze to Cambridge. Reginald's slight smile was now gone.

"No." Hawk exhaled. "I want to, but it just doesn't make sense. You show up for the Keys to the Kingdom tour after I sign up to take the tour at the last minute. You just happen to eat lunch with me that day. You accept my invitation to come to church and you ask me out on a date. Later you just happen to be leading a private tour and catch me after hours hiding out in Walt's office. But you don't turn me in; instead you help me, and after finding something unexplainable, you tell me to let it go and forget about it."

"Exactly, if I were some monster trying to find some treasure, why would I tell you to let it go?"

"That's what I was thinking too, but then you showed up when I got attacked in the Magic Kingdom and my Pal Mickey was stolen. You showed up there, but you didn't show up for our date."

Sandy scoffed. "She probably hired the guy to steal it from you. After all, she knew the minute you hit the park. She was tracking you by fingerprint at the admission gate!

"I'm not telling you again." Cambridge's voice blasted like a cannon toward Sandy, causing him to shrink back in his chair.

"That isn't the way it happened." Kiran tightened her grip on Hawk's hands. "You snuck me into Animal Kingdom, you showed up unexpectedly when I was in the Magic Kingdom; you helped me get past every obstacle I was facing."

"Listen to yourself, you wouldn't have gotten this far without me." Tears formed in the corners of her eyes and rolled down her cheeks.

"When we tied Jim up and left him in the Character Zoo, there is no way anyone would have known he was there. I called my friend at the sheriff's department, and Juliette called Tim; who did you call, Kiran?" Hawk paused then remembered. "You tried awfully hard to keep me out of the Character Zoo to begin with. Did you know Juliette was there?"

"I can't believe you are saying this." Her tears flowed freely now.

"Hawkes, let me ask you something." Sandy spoke again despite Cambridge's threat. "Do you have Farren Rales's phone number?"

"Of course."

"Then how about giving it a call. Farren's phone was in his office. We found it after he disappeared, but unexplainably the next day his phone was gone too. Go on, Hawkes, try the number," Sandy urged.

Hawk wrestled his hand from Kiran's circulation-stopping grip and found his phone in his pocket. He rifled through his electronic phone book and found Farren's name. He hit the green call button. Silence filled the room as he pulled it to his ear to listen. After a slight delay "When You Wish Upon A Star" played across the room. The song was Farren's ringtone. The sound was coming from Kiran's pocket. Hawk reached down and shoved his hand into her pocket, freeing the phone he found there. It was Farren's phone receiving the incoming call from his own.

"When I was fighting with Jim in Liberty Square, something fell on the ground. You picked it up. Jim had Farren's phone and you knew it."

Kiran opened her mouth slightly, then released her grip on Hawk's other hand and tossed him away. Looking toward Sandy, the conductor, Cambridge, and then back to Hawk, she spun on her heels and ran for the exit. Jim had already silently slipped out of the room during the exchange. Hawk stood there numbly with a cell phone in each hand watching her run away.

Reginald Cambridge again picked up his radio and placed it to his mouth. Expressionlessly he looked at the remaining people in the room and motioned for everyone to stay in place.

"This is Cambridge," he spoke evenly. "You should see two of our suspects trying to get out of the building. Kiran Roberts and Jim Masters. Stop them, take them to lockup. I will be there momentarily." He looked up at the rest of the group. "They won't get far. We have people waiting for them at every exit to this place both above and below ground. It will only take a moment to get them."

The conductor walked over to Hawk and gently removed each cell phone from his hand and placed them on the table beside them. He motioned for Hawk to have a seat. The preacher quietly sat down and the kindly conductor motioned for Sandy and Cambridge to come and join them.

"What I am about to tell you will be hard to believe." The conductor paused and studying Hawk's face concluded, "or maybe not. Sandy, myself, and a few others are a part of a select group of Disney cast members who are very loyal to the dreams, imagination, and values that this company was built upon. Those ideas were the same ones that Walt and Roy believed in when they started the company. Farren Rales has chosen you to hold something that is very important, something that we do not understand. Farren Rales has chosen us to help protect you and keep you safe. You are the keeper of the key to the kingdom."

"What key?" Cambridge asked.

"The key to the kingdom," the conductor continued. "As I said, we have no idea what the key is for, what you have found, or what you have been doing. Our task is simple. We were to watch over you, watch out for you, and help protect you if we could. What you know and what you are trying to find is something that we are not entrusted with. We believe in what Disney stands for, what it means to people, what the brand means across the globe . . . and you, Dr. Hawkes, have been chosen to hold the key to all of that."

"Kiran and Jim are a part of a group that wanted to possess the key for their own personal gain and power," Sandy said. "They figured out the key was not enough. What you have discovered, the knowledge you now have, is necessary for the key to work. That is why Kiran decided to stay so close to you. They realized they would need more than the stuffed Pal Mickey to find the answer. They needed you."

"I'm so sorry, Dr. Hawkes." The conductor again spoke kindly to the preacher. "I know finding out you were being used must be painful."

"So what happens now?" Hawk looked to the conductor and Sandy. "What do I do now?"

"Whatever you were doing before!" Sandy blurted incredulously.

"What he means," the conductor helped, "is that our job is to help protect you. It became apparent that Kiran and Jim were getting too close. We have no idea what you have found or what you are trying to do."

"Do either of you know the whereabouts of Farren Rales?" Cambridge addressed the conductor and Sandy.

"No," they replied in unison.

"I must admit I am intrigued and fascinated by this entire scenario. Farren Rales, as the last of Walt Disney's personal Imagineers, makes him a very precious and valued part of this company. The fact that he is missing and there is reason to suspect foul play leaves me with very few options." He paused and drummed his fingers on the table. "We are going to have to talk; I need to know what has been going on."

"Of course," the conductor replied, "we will be happy to help, but we don't really know what is going on."

"Let me determine that," Cambridge said as he turned his face toward Hawk. "As for you, Dr. Grayson Hawkes, I have grown weary of you turning my theme parks upside down. I want it to stop and I want you out right now."

"But—"

"Let me finish," Cambridge continued briskly. "I have a friend who has called me on your behalf, Al Gann. He has filled me in on some of the things that you have been managing to do right under my nose." He cleared his throat. "I also have found out, much to my surprise, that you are suddenly listed as a cast member of this company, a cast member with access unrestricted to every area, even places that I cannot go. I don't completely understand this, but I do want answers and I want it resolved."

Suddenly Reginald Cambridge pushed away from the table and got to his feet. He motioned for Sandy and the conductor to accompany him as they headed toward the doors to step back onto Main Street USA, leaving Hawk seated at the table alone. As the trio exited the restaurant, Cambridge closed the door behind them and turned back toward Hawk.

"Dr. Hawkes, I do not like that which I do not understand." He narrowed his eyes. "However, I do understand from Gann that you have an appointment with him early this afternoon. I suggest you finish your business in my theme park and keep that appointment. Then I suggest you and I sit down to help me understand the things that are not yet clear to me."

"I would be happy to do that, Mr. Cambridge," Hawk said. "And thank you for your help."

Cambridge nodded to the pastor and turned to leave. Hesitating, he turned back to Hawk.

"I hope you find what you are looking for, Dr. Hawkes," Cambridge said stoically.

"Thanks, and call me Hawk . . . please."

"Very well . . . Hawk," he again turned to leave. "And if you don't mind, you can call me Reg. All my friends do. I have a feeling we are about to become friends." Reginald Cambridge shot Hawk one last glance and flashed a very pleasant grin, which immediately disappeared as he stepped through the door and back onto Main Street USA.

 *Day Seven*
Late Morning

GRAYSON HAWKES SAT in the quietness of Tony's Town Square Restaurant. The muffled noises from Main Street shoved their way through the windows only to fade into the background of his thoughts, which were very far away. The numbness that he felt had enveloped him as Reginald had closed the door to leave. The six of them had all converged on this place. Sandy had proven to be ally instead of an enemy. Reginald Cambridge was simply a man who took his job seriously and carried it out with pride. He wasn't an enemy either. Jim had proven to be an adversary who was willing to stop at nothing to get what he wanted. He had been willing to kidnap Juliette, he had been willing to attack, and been willing to deceive the preacher. Then, of course, there was Kiran. Hawk knew she was the real source of his pain. He had been suspicious of her but had convinced himself he was wrong. It was his lapse in judgment that opened the door for her to get too close. He should have known better, he did know better, he had just hoped for better.

Time was running out. He forced himself to rise from the chair and get moving. The end of this quest had to be near. He had never considered what would happen if he couldn't solve the puzzle. Slowly leaving Tony's, he stepped back into Exposition Hall and walked to his left. This carried him to an area where guests could meet and greet Mickey Mouse. After Mickey's Toontown Fair had been removed, this area was created for guests to meet their favorite character. Mickey, according to Roy Disney, became the closet thing anyone had left of Walt. Here, where people could always meet Mickey, the preacher was trying to find something that Walt wanted him to find.

Open daily in the Magic Kingdom, this attraction did not open for another hour. Moving through the various greeting areas he noticed a curtain toward the middle of the attraction creating a barrier. Pulling it aside he slid behind it. Certainly off-stage; he observed boxes, clutter, and other things stored away from the sight of guests. It was boringly plain and nothing caught his inter-est—until he saw an unmarked wooden doorway.

He moved toward it. Opening it he found another place to store things, too big to be called merely a closet, but not large enough to be a room. This area housed stacks of boxes, each with a tag indicating what was inside. The storage closet was much better organized than the open backstage area. Clos-ing the door, he looked to the opposite side and saw another door, identical to the one he had just entered. He guessed he would find another storage area, but since he was trying to find anything that might be helpful, he decided to take a look. Grabbing the handle and turning it, he was surprised to find it was locked. He bent down to look at the doorknob and noticed a keyhole beneath the knob.

Every locked door holds something behind it.

Hawk stood, remembering all the doors that had magically opened as he used his key to the kingdom. Once again, like so many times before, he took out the old key and attempted to place it inside a lock that to an observer would not be a good fit. Feeling resistance he almost stopped trying; then the key slid into the lock with a soft click. Turning the key to the left, he felt the lock mechanism open, and the knob was released to turn freely in his hand. Behind the door was a stairwell, its steps descending away from him. Hawk stepped forward to see where the steps were going. As he did the door shut behind him, plunging him into darkness. Retreating to the door he reopened it, allowing light to fill the stairwell. There was no light switch to be seen on the wall. Scoping out the area visually, he saw no light fixtures. He didn't want to take the time to go a buy a flashlight and wasn't sure which gift shop would have one. Time was running out; if he were going to go down the stairs, it would be in the dark.

 *Day Seven*
Late Morning

EACH STEP DROVE HIM DEEPER into the stifling blackness, blindly spiraling downward, and the steep descent felt as if it were taking much longer than it should have. He tried to judge how far down he might be going and guessed he must have descended at least three stories if not more. Each tread dropped him down another foot deeper, then another, and yet another.

His journey abruptly halted when his foot hit a solid mass in the blackness and his face pushed up against a cool surface. Placing both hands on the unyielding barrier he blindly searched for a doorknob. His hand traced what felt like a lever. Gripping it tightly he pushed it down. It did not move. He muscled up on it and shoved it down with more force and felt it slowly slide downward. A muffled click echoed up through the stairway as the latch released. Without releasing the handle he pushed against the heavy bulk of the door.

The hinges creaked as the massive door cracked open, flooding Hawk with blinding light. Blinking away the sudden brightness he reoriented himself. The stairs dead-ended into this door with the width of a step serving as the landing facing the doorway. Whoever had designed this stairwell had not designed it to meet the code of any inspector. It was clearly a private passage that very few ever traveled. The door opened into a small space, leaving enough room for the door to open and for a person to step inside. Directly opposite him was another door. The preacher stepped completely into the space and allowed the stairway door to close behind him. Facing the next door he was able to inspect it closely as his eyes continued to adjust to the light.

Eight feet high, four feet wide, and made of stainless steel, the door literally formed the entire wall of this small alcove. The door had no handle and no visible hinges. It had a lock mechanism unlike anything Hawk had seen before. A blinking light was the only reasonable point of interaction with the lock.

Dropping down to one knee he leaned in and carefully inspected the complex locking unit. Like the door it was stainless steel. It had a keypad with an intimidating number of keys. Six rows, each containing six keys, featured a corresponding key for each letter of the alphabet along with ten numeric keys beginning at 0 and ending with 9. Above the keypad was a narrow display screen. Below the keypad were two rows of slots each measuring one inch wide. Two slots in each of these rows surrounded a classic keyhole that sat in the center of the four slots. The entire mechanism was stainless steel like the rest of the door with a red light flashing a steady cadence at the bottom of the shoe-box-sized interface.

Hawk wondered if this was what he had been looking for. Could this be the end of his adventure? He had to know what was behind this door. He immediately reached for his key to the kingdom and placed it in the opening for the standard key. It fit perfectly and the blinking of the red light sped up. He tried to turn the key. It didn't budge to the right or the left. Pulling the key back, Hawk was consternated when the key refused to be extracted. Applying steady force to make the key release had no effect. It was now securely fastened into this massive lock. The red light continued to blink an accelerated rate, creating a sense of urgency within Hawk that may have been necessary or imagined. He didn't know what to do, it was the only key he had.

Bending over and inspecting the slots around the key, he noticed something about them that was familiar. Perhaps it was the smooth silver with the red slivers of light reflecting off of it in rhythm with the blinking bulb above. Reaching into his pocket he removed the shiny silver box and reverently opened it. Taking great care he removed the first metallic bar containing a phrase Walt Disney had once uttered.

"The way to get started is to quit talking and begin doing."

Turning it in his fingers he leveled it out flatly and lined it up on its edge with the opening of the slot up and to the left of his key. Carefully he slid the bar into the slot and felt it click into the mechanism. He tried to reverse what he had just done and just like the key it was now locked in place. He pulled the second bar out of the box.

"All of our dreams can come true if we have the courage to pursue them."

Gently he placed the bar into the next opening, and exactly like the first one it slid into place. He discovered this one could not be retrieved either.

"It's kind of fun to do the impossible."

The words on the third bar disappeared into the slot as Hawk pushed the bar found in the Kepple House into place. The light continued to blink and he quickly grabbed the final bar that had been found at Sir Mickey's.

"If you can dream it you can do it."

The final bar slid into place as Hawk realized he had been holding his breath. Exhaling loudly, he was startled as the red light began blinking even more rapidly. The key and all four bars were now in place inside the mysterious lock. There was no lever and no latch. The only apparent way to open the door was to find the right combination for the locking apparatus. The red light served as a steady reminder he had not yet managed to open it.

Hawk turned his attention to the thirty-six-key pad, the only part of the lock he had not yet tackled. He wondered what combination he would have to key in to satisfy this level of security. Randomly he placed his fingers on the keys and typed the letters *D-I-S-N-E-Y.*

Each letter displayed itself on the screen above the keypad as he typed. They flashed on and off, and then disappeared. As the screen went blank the red warning light increased its rate of blinking. Hawk wondered if typing in the wrong code would cause the lock not to open at all. He again glanced down at the key and bars now all resting in their places. Each was a discovery he had made on his travels through Walt Disney World. If each piece of the puzzle was a piece of this lock, then what else had he found that might be the code necessary for the keypad?

The strobe effect of the light cast a quickly bursting crimson glow across his face as his mind replayed his journey of the last few days. His finger brushed across the keypad carefully as not to punch a key in error. Allowing his finger to come to rest on a letter, he pushed it, uttering a quick prayer to be correct. The letter immediately lit up on the display screen.

N. Moving to the numbers he pressed in 2-3-4. Committed to finishing his hunch he completed the call letters and registration numbers he had been sent to find on Walt Disney's airplane. *MM* for Mickey Mouse. The entire display glowed back at him once again. N234MM . . . the letters flashed once, twice, and then went blank. This time the red light also disappeared and then in a deafening silence the light turned green.

The green light was accompanied by a metallic click and the door automatically swung open, leaving the locking mechanism attached to what Hawk now saw to be the stainless steel door frame. The door stopped, leaving enough room for Hawk to enter.

The preacher paused and reached down to the lock once more. He grabbed each of the silver bars, which now slid effortlessly back out of their slots into his hands. The Key to the Kingdom came out of the lock as if it had never been held there. Placing all of these back in his pocket, Hawk stepped in and peered around behind the opened door.

JEFF DIXON

 *Day Seven*
Noon

THE ROOM BEHIND THE DOOR was a reception area. Plush carpet covered the floor, and in the center of the room an oversized chair faced a wall of thick glass. The glass wall reached from floor to ceiling and stretched twenty feet across. The reception area was well lit but what lay behind the glass wall was cloaked in darkness. Hawk stepped behind the chair in the center of the room and looked into the murky blackness behind the glass. He was sure he saw something moving, but could not make out what was in the shadows of the room. His own reflection kept getting blocking his field of vision. The lighting contrast between the two areas sufficiently kept him unable to see what was behind the glass. Apparently that had been the idea.

"Please have a seat, Grayson," came a familiar voice from a set of speakers embedded into the ceiling.

Hawk moved cautiously around the chair, trying to distinguish why the voice was so familiar. He had heard it before many times, he was sure of that, but his name sounded strange as the voice said it. Taking a seat in the chair, he sank into the cushioned back as the chair engulfed him. Staring toward the darkness he waited for what was to happen next.

"We've been waiting for you," the same familiar voice said again as the lights softly began to pierce the darkness behind the glass.

Hawk leaned forward slightly as the lights began to warmly radiate from behind the now transparent barrier. The voice had been familiar but now as he sat staring he knew what he was seeing was impossible. The voice speaking to him was Walt Disney's.

Rising to his feet from behind his desk was the creator of the things so familiar to Hawk. The dreamer, the doer, the man himself; Walt Disney smiled as he stood, giving the preacher a chance to absorb what he was seeing. Mr. Disney was in his office, just like the one Hawk had broken into at One Man's Dream.

Suddenly Hawk's gaze shifted to the right as he noticed someone seated in the office facing Walt. This man now rose to his feet and turned to face the stunned preacher on the other side of the glass. This too was a person very familiar to Hawk; it was his friend Farren Rales.

The old Imagineer was beaming as he turned to face his dear friend. No one uttered a word as the reality of what he was seeing rippled through his brain cells. Hawk sat in disbelief as his eyes flitted between the two legends, Walt Disney and Farren Rales.

"Hello," Farren said, smiling excitedly. "I knew you would find us."

Slowly Walt turned and looked toward Farren as he spoke and then sat back down behind his desk. Walt's hair was mostly white yet his facial features, the distinct mustache, and the familiar frame were exactly what Hawk had seen time and time again on television, DVD, and in pictures. This Walt Disney was an older version of the man who had spoken to him on the *Old Yeller* DVD. The genius turned his head back toward Hawk as Farren sat back down, spinning his chair toward the massive glass wall to face his friend.

"You know," Walt Disney said, "I'll bet you have a million questions. Now that you've made it here, you can have those answers. But before I let you and Farren talk I just want you to know that I'm glad you finally made it."

"I got here as soon as I could," Hawk softly said and then realized how dumb it sounded. His mind was a blazing racetrack of activity. What he was seeing was impossible; Walt Disney was over one hundred years old. There is no way he could be here talking to him right now. Farren Rales hadn't disappeared, instead he was hiding, and they had been waiting for him to come and find them. It didn't make sense.

"I suppose all of this is pretty difficult for you to understand right now," Walt continued. "Believe me, Grayson, all of your questions will be answered, and I think you are going to be pleased with what has happened."

"Pleased?" He couldn't seem to string together an intelligent set of words.

"It hasn't been easy for you to get here, I understand that." Walt smiled as he spoke. "But I think you will agree that all of this mystery must be for a good reason. The problem is you don't know the reason . . . yet. While you have been looking for us you have had a chance to go on a bit of a treasure hunt. You have discovered some of the history of how we do things here at my company. Actually you have discovered some of my history. I hope you have enjoyed that part of your adventure." Walt chuckled. "I know I enjoyed living it."

"How can this be happening?" Hawk interrupted.

"Hold on, Grayson." Walt held up a hand to stop the question. "My friend Farren here is going to tell you everything you need to know, but first let me finish."

"Sorry," Hawk apologized.

"No problem." Walt laughed. "I'm sure you have quite a few stories of your own to tell about all that has been going on. But now that you are here, you have to know how important it is that you found us. You did exactly what we hoped you would do and now my kingdom will be safe. Thank you."

"You're welcome," Hawk said softly. "But I don't—"

"Farren, you have made a good choice." Walt did not give Hawk time to finish his thought or ask the question that had to be coming.

"Thanks, Walt." Farren was absolutely bursting with pride as he looked at his friend. "I knew he could do it and I knew he wouldn't let us down."

"Okay, Grayson." Walt grinned. "I know you are anxious to get a few answers. I know I would be. I'll be quiet and let Farren explain anything you want to know."

Walt looked toward Farren, who stood and approached the window. Hawk also rose to his feet and stepped to the glass. They were close with just the glass wall separating the two of them.

"Well?" Farren said with a sparkle in his eye.

"Uh . . ." Hawk had so many questions he didn't know where to start. "How can this be happening?"

"You are at Walt Disney World," Farren said matter-of-factly. "Magic happens here all the time, you know that. This is a place where dreams come true."

"But Walt Disney is over one hundred years old. How can he be sitting there talking to me?" Hawk looked at Walt then back to Farren. "No disrespect intended, Mr. Disney, but how can you be here?"

"It's a good question," Walt agreed. "I'll bet you feel like Alice getting ready to step through the looking glass. You'd better go ahead and tell him, Farren."

"Walt is not here, Grayson." Farren studied Hawk's face and he looked over toward Mr. Disney, who looked entirely present to Hawk. "Walt Disney is dead."

 *Day Seven*
Afternoon

"I AM DEAD," Walt Disney said. "I died in December of 1966."

Hawk closed one eye and looked at Walt. The conversation had turned from unbelievable to surreal. He turned away from Walt, who was now smiling and obviously pleased with the impossibility that Hawk was dealing with, and looked back toward Farren, who was nodding in gentle understanding. The preacher was at a loss for words.

"Would you like to step into the office and have a seat in here?" Farren offered.

Hawk nodded and then walked alongside Farren on the other side of the glass partition as they made their way to the end of the room. The Imagineer stepped out of the very same door that Hawk had used to enter the recreation of Walt's office and momentarily disappeared. Instantly the one remaining door in the reception area opened and Farren stepped through, embracing Hawk in a huge bear hug.

"I am so pleased you got here," Farren whispered as he held Hawk tightly.

"I'm glad you are all right," Hawk uttered, realizing for the first time that his friend was really safe.

Keeping an arm wrapped tightly around the preacher's shoulder the Imagineer lead him through the door into a hallway and then back through the door in Walt's office. Gesturing for Hawk to take a seat, Farren waited for him to sit down before taking a seat next to him. They both faced the desk as Walt Disney looked back at them.

"Dr. Grayson Hawkes," Farren said formally. "I would like for you to meet the one and only audio-animatronic Walt Disney."

Walt Disney nodded. "That's me. You have to admit I look pretty good for an audio-animatronic creation. Pretty amazing what they can do now with technology."

Now that Hawk was seated close to the entertainer he began to notice the slight hints that he wasn't a real person. Yet he was amazed at the realism that had been captured in this recreation of the legend. Farren gave him a few moments to gaze closely at the magnificent lifelike image before him. Amazingly as Hawk stared at Walt Disney, Walt smiled and looked back at Hawk.

"Back in the 50s Walt was traveling and purchased a mechanical bird," Rales began.

"I was on vacation in Europe actually," Disney added.

"After he got back, Roger Broggie and Wathel Rogers started working on what they called Project Little Man. They developed a miniature figure that would tap dance. It was primitive but it was the starting point for what would later become known as audio-animatronics."

"The first true audio-animatronic technology was used in the birds we designed for the Enchanted Tiki Room and for the figure of Abraham Lincoln in Great Moments with Mr. Lincoln," Walt filled in the history.

"Hawk, you are familiar with how much audio-animatronics have helped to create the magic in Disney theme parks. The A-100 Audio-Animatronic figure was debuted as the Wicked Witch of Oz on the Great Movie Ride at the Studios. This technology was groundbreaking; the movements and gestures were so lifelike and complicated. It took eight hours to animate one second of movement." Rales looked from Hawk to Walt and then back before continuing. "We kept dreaming and engineering and the technology allowed us to keep getting better and better. Meeko from *Pocahontas* became our first portable audio-animatronic figure. Lucky the Dinosaur was another breakthrough for us when we were able to create a free-roaming audio-animatronic figure. Each time we created something better we amazed ourselves."

"We sure have come a long, long way from the first birds we created, that's for sure," Walt injected.

"The biggest A-100 creation is the yeti in Expedition Everest. Over eighteen feet tall, he is quite an accomplishment," Rales continued.

"Yes." Hawk decided to join the conversation. "I met the yeti up close."

"Ah, but of course you have." Rales knew exactly what Hawk was talking about. "The beast is pretty intimidating, isn't he? The most closely inspected A-100 was the Captain Jack Sparrow figures we added to Pirates. The most complicated is Mr. Potato Head in Toy Story Mania."

"The potato is so advanced that he removes and reattaches his ear. His lips move and he is able to look our guest in the eye as he speaks," Walt explained, looking directly into Hawk's eyes as he said it.

The irony of what he was hearing—and whom he was hearing it from—unnerved the preacher. "But that is what you are." He pointed toward the audio-animatronic Disney.

"Not exactly," chuckled the rich voice as Walt looked once again toward Farren.

"A lot of people didn't realize we made a decision that for some was controversial," Rales began to explain. "In 2007 we decided we would start outsourcing some of the design and creation of our audio-animatronic figures. Some people screamed that we were hurting the company and that Walt never would have done it this way." Both Rales and Hawk looked to Walt, who remained silent with a mischievous expression on his face. "The reason we outsourced is so we could take some of our most creative designers and put them to work on the next level of audio-animatronics."

"The next level?" Hawk asked.

"Yes, we wanted to create the first walking, talking, lifelike audio-animatronic man. It was a big, daring project, but we wanted it to be done in secret so we could really experiment and test it. We wanted to get it right."

"So, how do you think we did?" Walt grinned at Hawk.

"I think you pulled it off!" Hawk responded quickly, which seemed to please Walt.

"The goal was to blend our previous technology with new experimental designs and then even add to the mix artificial intelligence, which would allow a level of realism and interaction we had never achieved before." Rales paused and looked at Walt Disney. "Walt here is the result of that work."

"I'm what they call around these parts an AI-1000 Audio-Animatronic." Disney smiled as he said the words. "I can roam anywhere I want in this office, I can interact with and you verbally and can sense most of your gestures. I'm almost real."

"Indeed he is." Rales beamed. "Hawk, you are the first one outside of a few of his designers to ever see him."

"So did you design him for an attraction?"

"Not really." Farren paused for a moment. "Walt was created for a different reason."

"Farren, that's enough about me," Walt said casually. "Grayson, obviously I'm not real. But my creation does have something to do with you and why you are here now. Farren, I think it is time you should tell my partner what is really going on."

"Of course, you're right." Rales said. Looking at Hawk and standing he made a sweeping motion with his arm back toward the door. "It is time to show you something."

Hawk stood and followed. As he and Farren got to the door, Walt called out to them from behind his desk.

"If you need me, I'll be right here." He saluted with two fingers placed near his forehead and smiled as the preacher and Imagineer walked out the door.

The pair stepped back into the hallway Hawk had been in for just a few seconds before. To the right was the door that would have placed them back in the reception area Hawk had entered earlier. The hallway did not extend beyond that point in that direction. Turning to the left Hawk looked down the length of a massive hallway. Mentally he was trying to figure out exactly where he was in relation to the utilidors. Before he could figure it out Farren had guessed what he might be thinking.

"You have entered through one of the two entrances to this tunnel," he stated as he pointed his finger behind and then forward. "It was created especially for what you have seen and are about to see. There is no access into this tunnel from the utilidors and to get in here you have to know the way or you will never find it."

"Farren, I thought something had happened to you!" Some of the shock of seeing Walt Disney had worn off, and now Hawk's presence of mind began to return. "The police have been looking of you!"

"I know, I'm sorry to have put you through all of this, but it was the only way to get you here. There are so many people who would do anything to have the key to the kingdom and solve the mystery. I knew you could do it and it was a mystery that could only be solved by someone who was passionate and really cared about Walt Disney, his dreams, and what he lived his life trying to create."

"You mean, this is it? I've solved the mystery?"

"Yes, my friend, you have solved the mystery."

"The mystery was finding the AI-1000 Audio-Animatronic Walt Disney?"

"No, Hawk, the mystery was unlocking Walt Disney's Kingdom and becoming the keeper of the key to the kingdom."

As the two walked side by side down the long hallway, their footsteps echoed in a hollow refrain. The offset lighting lining the ceiling gave the passageway a warm and cozy feel. Momentarily they came to the end of the passage and stood in an intersection where they had to choose to go right or left. Without hesitation Rales guided them to the left where they came face-to-face with another stainless steel door. The cold metal door stood in stark contrast to the decor of the hall. The lock was identical to the one Hawk had entered earlier gaining access to the reception area of the audio-animatronic Walt's office. Rales looked at Hawk, waiting.

"You know how to open it," he said reassuringly.

Hawk slid the old key into the opening.

"I'm glad you didn't lose the key I gave you," Rales kidded.

"If I would have known all the trouble it was going to cause . . ."

"I know, that's why I didn't tell you all it would open."

The key was followed by the four silver bars and then the N234MM punched into the keyboard. The light turned green and the door unlocked. Pushing it open Hawk once again retrieved the key and the bars from the lock. Rales nodded for Hawk to enter first. As Hawk finished pushing the door open, they both stepped through into the next room.

 *Day Seven*
Afternoon

THE ROOM WAS LINED with workspaces. Counters and consoles containing flat screens blazing with images, twinkling lights, whirring computers, and monitoring systems engulfed them. A sudden drop in temperature made Hawk feel as if he could actually see his breath as the wave of cold air hit him. The extreme chill, he realized, would allow the equipment to run smoothly, preventing overheating. In the center of the futuristic space was something that appeared as if it could have been snatched right out of Tomorrowland. It was a tall silver cylindrical tube that resembled a rocket ship loaded with gauges and dials. The entire area appeared to be designed around this ten-foot-tall hub, just as the rest of the theme park was designed around the hub of Central Plaza.

"Where are we?" Hawk asked.

"This is a command center." Farren spread his arms. "You can actually sit in this room and monitor everything that is happening in the park."

"Everything?"

"Everything," Rales repeated. "I have been able to watch your progress as you got closer and closer to finding me."

"So you watched me getting chased and beat up?"

"Well, almost everything." Farren patted his friend's shoulder. "But you are good; there were times I couldn't keep up."

"So this is a security center?"

"No, no, no . . . this is a unique command center designed for controlling the entire park. Security can only do what it was designed to do based on the plans of our security teams and designers. This place can see things that security can't. It can override every other control in the park; it is a base of operation that gives access to every area and can protect the park even better than security. However, there are limitations."

"Limitations?"

"Yes." Rales shook his head. "For example, I didn't know that Juliette was being held in the Character Zoo or I would have gotten her out. I didn't know she was missing until you were looking for her and didn't have any clue where she was until she emerged in the utilidor with you and Kiran after you freed her." Rales punched up a view of the utilidoors and the entrance to the Character Zoo. "I could have seen her being taken in there if I had been looking for her, but I didn't know she was missing or even in the Magic Kingdom. This command center is designed for more specific tasks than just general security. I spent most of my time tracking you as you moved through the park."

"Can you track activity in other parks?"

"No, just this one.".

"Farren"—Hawk titled his head—"I don't get it."

"I'm sure." He smiled. "Hawk, remember I told you I was giving you the key to the kingdom and if you took that key and did what Walt did when he left the Dwarf's Cottage . . . your imagination . . . your ability to understand a story . . . and how you touch the world will never be the same?"

"I do remember that." Hawk nodded.

"I know you do," Rales added. "Because you could understand the story, you were able to start figuring out the puzzle, the mystery, you cracked the clues I left for you. Now, I'm sure you had some help from Pal Mickey. By the way, what do you think of my interactive clue giver?"

"Amazing," Hawk patted the mouse's head.

"There has never been another one like it!" Rales beamed. "It was created especially for you. After they took the little creature out of the gift shops, it became easy for me to tweak, adjust, and add to the technology we already had in place. I figured if I couldn't be with you, then you needed someone to keep you on track. And now you have followed the trail, solved the clues, and have unlocked the kingdom, Walt Disney's kingdom!"

"I'm sorry." The preacher wrinkled his forehead. "I still don't get what I've unlocked."

"My dear friend." Rales's smile grew bigger. "You have unlocked the kingdom and it is now yours!"

"Walt Disney's Kingdom is mine?"

"Yes, the kingdom is now yours!"

Hawk looked thoughtfully at his friend. He slowly allowed his attention to drift to the command center they were standing in. He wandered away from where Farren was standing and began to study the room more closely. Walking, he made a complete circle through the room, around the silver cylinder, before returning to where he began.

"I guess you still have some questions." Rales quizzically raised his eyebrows.

"I would say more than just a few."

"Have a seat." Farren laughed as he pointed to one of the command stations. "Let me tell you the story."

"I knew there had to be one." Hawk sat, glad to be talking with his friend, who was safe and unharmed.

"There is always a story." The old Imagineer chuckled. "This one began a long time ago. In the sixties when plans were being designed for Walt's Florida project, some of us began to notice a change in Walt. His health wasn't as good as it had been. Part of it was age, surely part of it was from the stress and pressure of being Walt Disney, but something else was wrong."

"His cancer," Hawk knew.

"Yes." Rales slowed. "Walt didn't know he was as sick as he was, but he began to think about his legacy. What if something went wrong? What if something did happen to him? What would become of his plans and dreams? All of those became troubling questions for Walt. One night in the summer of 1966 a few of us gathered in Walt's office for a meeting. We didn't know why we had been asked to come; with Walt you never really knew, you just knew he had an idea . . . and this one shocked all of us!"

"Was it something about Walt Disney World?" Hawk slid forward in his seat.

"Oh no, something very different. I arrived at Walt's office, and Roy was there, and two other trusted members of Walt's creative team."

"Who?"

"You'll learn soon enough." Farren patted Hawk's arm and went back to his story. "Walt and Roy had a plan. It was a contingency plan, an emergency plan, in case anything ever went wrong. Walt wanted to make sure that no matter what happened, there would always be someone who could take his dream, his vision, his passion for all the things he had poured his life into . . . and keep them alive."

"That's what Roy did."

"Yes, Roy really did take care of Walt; they were partners in this great adventure. But that night was different. The rest of us in that room became partners in this amazing plan Walt had designed to make sure the Disney dream would never die. That night Walt and Roy gave the three of us the biggest project any Imagineer would ever tackle. Bigger than building a theme park and bigger than creating any resort. They entrusted us to create the Key to the Kingdom."

Hawk pulled the key out of his pocket and sat it on the counter. "This?"

"That actual key was ultimately a big part of it. But we designed the plan that would ensure that the story of Walt Disney, his life, the dreams that inspired him, and the imagination that gave him his passion would never die. We would make sure that no matter what happened, Walt would always have a voice in the direction of the Walt Disney Company. Whoever was entrusted with the Key to the Kingdom would be the one and only person who would speak for Walt in the Disney organization."

"Wait." Hawk raised a hand. "You said I had been given the Key to the Kingdom."

"That's right; you are now the keeper of the key." They sat silently before Rales continued. "Walt and Roy explained that no one could predict the future but they believed you could shape the future. The three of us the Disney brothers had invited were to create the story line that would protect Walt's dream in the years ahead. We were given total access to Walt and Roy, any plans, any discussions, and any decisions that were made. Although we were familiar with the brothers we became experts on the family history, the company, the directions, the plans, and all things that were related to Walt and Roy Disney. The message that Walt left for you on the *Old Yeller* DVD was given to me right after Walt died with the instruction to get it to the one who would be the keeper of the key. When Walt recorded it on film he had no concept we would convert it to a digital copy for storage through the years."

"Why me?" Hawk slowly looked around the room, collecting the questions churning through his brain cells. "What does this all mean?"

"After the Magic Kingdom was opened and Roy suddenly passed away, the three of us who had made our promise to Walt and Roy had to put our plan into place. Roy had helped us get everything ready over the years, as always he was working behind the scenes and watching out for his younger brother. The company floundered a little bit in the years after Roy's death. Walt and Roy both knew these would be difficult times and had cautioned us not to panic but be vigilant. The three of us—"

"Who are the other two people involved in this plan?"

"You will find that out in the days ahead." Farren leaned forward, clasping his hands together. "Let me answer your other questions. The three of us had great positions of influence within the organization. Yet no one knew that our influence and leadership really was something the Disney brothers had counted on us having. As a result we were able to be influential voices when the company needed an outsider to step in and give leadership to Disney."

"Outsider?" Hawk shifted his weight to the arm support of the chair.

"Yes, someone who really had no ties to Disney through family or history. Michael Eisner was one of our best strategic moves. In the Eisner years the Walt Disney Company went from being a ten-billion-dollar company to a sixty-billion-dollar company as the Disney Decade became a reality.

A changing economy and changing culture made us realize we needed to make some changes. So we used our influence again to start the movement that would have Michael exit his position and allow us to bring in Bob Iger. Iger was a fantastic move for us. He immediately inked the deal with Pixar that allowed Disney to become the uncontested leader in animated storytelling. The Pixar partnership also invigorated the Imagineering department and allowed me to have the freedom to put into place what was going to happen in our next transition . . . which you are a part of, Hawk."

"Me?"

"Yes, you." Farren stretched out his hand. "Do you have the cast ID card you found?"

Hawk produced it and handed it to Farren. He swiveled in the chair he was sitting in and slid the card through an electronic card reader. The sound of a computer processing information clicked and Farren pointed to a video screen.

"Cambridge told me I was a cast member with unrestricted access," Hawk told his friend.

"You don't know the half of it." Farren nodded to the screen. "Like I said, you have the Key to the Kingdom."

The screen blinked and flashed the image of Grayson Hawkes. There was a series of lines containing personal information about him. As Hawk read the information and eventually got to the bottom of the screen where Farren's finger was pointing, the lines that followed left him speechless.

Chief Executive of Walt Disney Imagineering
Unrestricted and Unlimited Access All Areas
Fantasia Security Clearance

"What does this mean?" Hawk asked in disbelief.

"Ah, well let's see . . . you are the new head of Imagineering for the entire company. So you now have a creative voice in leading, guiding, pushing, and telling all of the Disney stories in whatever way you think they need to be told. You have access to every single area of the company, theme parks, movie studios, and you can travel where you want, when you want, however you want."

"Fantasia . . . ?"

"That means you have a security clearance that allows you behind the scenes to all of the magic of the park. It is the highest level that exists. In other words, you are now my boss, you are everyone's boss, and you answer to no one else in the company. You don't have to run anything or you can run everything . . . that, my dear friend, is up to you."

Hawk sat there taking in what Farren had just said as Rales handed him back the ID card. He felt his heart thumping in his chest. He furrowed his brow and got ready to say something but his mouth felt like it was full of cotton. Gulping, he allowed the silence to speak for him.

"Let's see . . ." Farren kept unloading information. "I think you wanted to know why you were chosen. We needed someone who could handle the responsibility in a way that Walt would have handled things. You know all about Disney history, you are a fan of all things related to Disney, you appreciate the image of the company, you value the attention to details, and the most important thing is you know the value of a great story and why it is important to tell it well. As a preacher you are telling the greatest story ever told. If you can handle that, then you can surely be entrusted to tell Disney's stories. While they are not the greatest ever told, they are pretty good, and they have a global audience."

"But I'm a preacher." Hawk opened his hands, palms upturned, as he leaned deeper into his chair.

"Of course." Farren nodded slightly. "You are an extremely good one. Your passion is what first got me thinking that you might be the one to be the next keeper of the key. You have a good moral compass, you care about right and wrong, you will do business guided by your heart and what you know is right. Walt used to do business that way. Roy always worried about the business side but Walt brought the heart and passion. The company has lots of people who know good business . . . but you will bring a heart and passion to the areas you decide to get involved in. You keep on being a preacher, but when you aren't preaching you can influence and have access to the biggest and best storytelling company ever created."

Hawk breathed deeply and slowly exhaled. "I don't know what to say!" A bead of sweat rolled in front of his ear to his jawline.

"I'm not surprised; you have had one tough week. You have been living out a Disney story at its finest. You are a hero and you have had to face some villains. I have been watching you use your knowledge of Disney, his stories, the theme park, and your care for me, and doing the right thing. I knew you were the best choice. I can't wait to see how you will bring your insight, imagination, and creativity into Disney's world and make it even better."

"So all of this has been a test?"

"Partially. It also allowed us to find out who was out there trying to discover the key."

"Us? You mean the three of you?"

"No, by 'us' I mean a group of loyal cast members who have pledged themselves to keeping the theme parks and the company on a track that Walt would have liked. We call them Warriors of the Kingdom. The conductor from the train station, Sandy, and there are others . . . you will get to know them in the days ahead."

"Is Reginald Cambridge a Kingdom Warrior?"

"They are called Warriors of the Kingdom."

"Sorry."

"No problem." Farren waved his hand. "You will learn it all eventually. And the answer is no, Reginald is not a Warrior of the Kingdom. He is a good man and has been extremely loyal to the company. If you decide he can be trusted, then you have the responsibility to choose any new members of this very exclusive group. They will become your most trusted allies. Although they will be loyal to the company, their real loyalty will be to keeping one man's dream—Walt's dream—alive and protected."

"Why have you chosen to tell me this now?"

"Honestly the answer is simple. The time is right. Rapidly changing culture, quickly developing new technologies, entertainment is changing, digital on demand, different delivery systems, new networks, this is a different world. It isn't the world I understand. Walt knew things would change, he just didn't know how. He also knew that he had to have someone who could understand how to navigate through the future. I could see the time was now, so I decided it was time to give you the key."

"What if I hadn't figured it out and solved the puzzle?"

"I had confidence in you," Farren reassured. "I'll admit the longer it has been since Walt and Roy have been with us, the tougher it has gotten. We even designed the AI-1000 Audio-Animatronic Walt Disney thinking that one day we might be able to make him so lifelike that we could film Walt proposing bold new ideas, kind of like a bunch of previously undiscovered Disney films, or something like that. We have the technology to fool people into thinking that Walt had left some marching orders for us."

"So why didn't you go with that plan?"

"Well, it was dishonest for one thing, but the other is that Walt left us with a plan. Again, Walt always knew that the times would change. He had enough imagination—we see it in Tomorrowland—to know that the future was going to be incredible. His plan guaranteed that we would have a person who understood the culture, the world we live in, and the Disney way enough to speak for the genius. That, my friend, is you!"

Hawk sat silent as a slight smile twitched across his lips.

"I know it has to be overwhelming," Rales agreed. "But there is something else you need to know."

"More?"

"Oh, yes . . . much more!"

 *Day Seven*
Afternoon

"HAWK, I WOULD LIKE for you to meet Walt Disney!"

Hawk looked blankly at Farren. A quick glance around the room confirmed that the AI-1000 Audio-Animatronic Walt Disney hadn't slipped into the command center. The preacher and the old Imagineer were still the only people in the room.

"I'm sorry?" Hawk widened his eyes and leaned forward.

"I said, I would like for you to meet Walt Disney," Farren made a sweeping gesture.

Hawk followed the gesture of his old friend and saw it whisk across toward the middle of the room. Again the preacher turned head Imagineer confirmed they were alone. Then with startling clarity it hit him. There was only one thing in the entire command center that was out of place and yet to be explained. The large metallic silver cylinder standing in the center of the room glistened in the room's lighting. Hawk turned back toward Rales to see his face smiling as he realized that Hawk was beginning to understand.

"Inside this cylinder is Walt Disney." Farren paused, allowing what he said to sink in. "He is in a state of cryonic suspension."

"No way," Hawk lunged from his chair toward the cylinder.

"History tells us that the first cryonic suspension took place about a month after Walt's death. The man was Dr. James Bedford, a seventy-three-year-old psychologist from Glendale, California. He was suspended January 12, 1967. Now, it is reasonable to think that Walt would have had the technological savvy to be aware of this process, since he was always looking to the future. Beyond that he knew he had more dreams than he could cram into one lifetime and he dreaded the thought of death. He wasn't afraid of it as much as he just didn't want to miss out on living. So, the truth is, Dr. Bedford's was really the second cryonic suspension ever to take place. Walt's was the very first. With the ongoing development of new forms of technology, in particular nanotechnology, the manipulation of individual atoms and molecules, eventually it may give medical technology the knowledge to build or repair virtually any physical object, including human cells and biological tissue. One of the projected applications is the repair of damage to human tissue created by freezing at liquid nitrogen temperatures, along with the ability to repair and eliminate cellular and organic damage caused by disease and aging. When the day comes that medicine finds a cure for cancer, then perhaps Walt Disney will reemerge from his current cryonic state."

"I always thought it was just an urban legend." Hawk circled the silver container. "I've heard for years that Walt had his body frozen and was being hidden somewhere under the Pirates of the Caribbean."

"Now, that's silly. You've seen Pirates of the Caribbean—where would we have hidden Walt there?"

Hawk looked over to read Farren's facial features. He could see clearly that Rales was delighted with sharing this latest piece of information with his friend.

"We figured there was no better way to keep this a secret than to go ahead and start talking about it. So the urban legend was actually created and repeated originally within the company itself. It didn't take long and then someone told a friend, who told a friend, who knew someone who worked for Disney that knew for sure. Once it was an urban legend, no one would ever believe it was true."

"So Walt Disney is really in here?" Hawk respectfully touched the cylinder and leaned in, looking at the dials.

"Yes, he is." Rales rose from his chair. "This is a self-powered facility. Even if everything else in the park goes down, this area does not. It can run on its own power source for up to six months. Hawk, this is now your command center. No one else knows about this—not the Warriors of the Kingdom, no other Imagineer but myself. I am the last one who knows this secret and now I have shared and given it to you."

Hawk continued to listen and at the same time studied the container. It was then he noticed the locking mechanism. It was the same elaborate multi-lock he had encountered twice before. There was a place for the key, four distinct slots to contain the metal bars, the keypad, and the flashing lights. He turned back toward Rales.

"Yes, Hawk, you have the key to the lock. Everything you have found to get you this far, you will need to open the cylinder. You might say this is the lock that unlocks the rest of the kingdom . . . and once again, you have the key."

Hawk turned to face his friend. Sighing deeply, he measured carefully what he was about to say. As Hawk faltered, Farren motioned for him to take a seat. Together they moved back to where they had been before. Heavily dropping into the chair, the preacher looked up toward the Imagineer who was waiting and ready to speak.

"Hawk, you are now the keeper of the key. You have the Key to the Kingdom. Whether you ever open the cylinder is entirely up to you," Rales stated slower than normal for emphasis. "Another reason you have the key is because I need to know there is someone that will have the wisdom and insight to know when and if the cylinder needs to be opened. Your moral compass, your understanding of what is right and wrong in the eyes of God, is an important part of the decision that has to be made on the day this becomes an option. Walt understood that. It is the way he wanted it."

"You mean he didn't want to come back from the dead?"

"Not necessarily." Farren shook his head side to side. "Walt loved life and he loved what he did. He really believed he made the lives of people better. There was always a need to put a plan in place to protect what he had worked so hard to create. Coming back himself was a last resort. He understood better than anyone that just because you can do something doesn't mean you should. It should only be done if there is a real need. Hawk, listen to me." Farren locked eyes with him. "You know what it is like to lose someone you love. If you had the chance to turn back time, to bring them back, to put things back as they were . . . would you if you could? Should you do it? I know you have wrestled with that and would do the right thing."

Hawk felt his eyes begin to burn with tears. Farren had done this before; he had brought Hawk to the edge in conversations. He knew the preacher's past. He knew the secret pain very few were aware of and that Hawk had chosen to share with a select few. Now he realized why Farren had taken their conversations to the brink of this emotional canyon so many times before. He blinked and studied his friend's face that was now smiling gently. The preacher lowered his head and felt the sting of tears escaping the corners of his eyes. Breathing deeply, he stopped as he felt Farren's hand on his shoulder.

"Hawk, you will know whether to bring Walt back if you ever can. He wanted that to be an option in case we ever needed him to keep his dreams alive. Life and death is a decision made best by those who know God. You know God intimately and you follow Him passionately. That is your life story. Who better to help Walt Disney tell his!"

 Six Months Later

THE FIRST WAVE OF PEOPLE scurried down Main Street USA as the Magic Kingdom opened for another day. Music drifted into his ears as Dr. Grayson Hawkes peeked out the window from his second-floor apartment over the Fire Station on the corner of the Town Square. The apartment was patterned after the one built by Walt for use by his family in Disneyland. Farren had given it to Hawk on that life-changing day six months earlier when he had become the Chief Executive of Walt Disney Imagineering. The pair had entered the apartment on that day using a hidden stairwell that connected directly to the private command center where Walt Disney waited in cryonic suspension. Shortly thereafter Hawk had the apartment remodeled and set up for him to stay in. Now at least three nights a week he stayed in the theme park after the guests were gone. He strolled up and down Main Street, enjoying the music and watching the night shift prepare the park for the following morning. Immediately Hawk had become a favorite of the night crews, often opening up Casey's Corner and distributing soft drinks to them as they worked. Some evenings he was even known to open up the ice cream shop and scoop ice cream for the cast members to enjoy on their break.

The major remodel he had made to the apartment was his favorite feature. He had a fire pole placed in the apartment so he could slide down the pole from his apartment, land in the gift shop below, and then walk out into Town Square. The idea had come from Walt Disney himself. In the original design of the family apartment at Disneyland, Walt had used the fire pole to leave his apartment and enter the park. One day a curious guest climbed the pole, pushed against the trap door, and poked his head into the Disney apartment. Later that day Walt had the door sealed to prevent any pranksters from breaking in. Hawk had heard the story and decided his apartment had to have a fire pole exit. If he chose to use this route when the park was open, as he did this particular morning, it always amazed and startled the guests who had dropped in the station to shop. The cast members working in the Fire Station had grown accustomed to his unexpected descents and had taken to calling him the Hawk .

"Morning, Hawk!" a cast member gleefully greeting him.

"Good morning!" The Imagineer Preacher walked out of the Fire Station.

The crowds moved past him, eager to begin a day of adventure. Hawk thought back over the journey he had been on the last six months. Since he had become the one with the Key to the Kingdom, his life had been a whirlwind of activity. Farren had given him a crash course in Imagineering and the Disney Corporation. Hawk had been in meetings with all the top-ranking officers in the company, and although confused about the sudden emergence of this new member of the Disney family, most had been receptive to him. As one board member had said when trying to understand who Hawk was, "Just another day at Disney!"

After Hawk had honestly confessed to Farren that he knew just enough to be confused, the old Imagineer decided Hawk knew enough to get started. He left Orlando and was spending the next year working with the Imagineers at the Disney theme park in Paris. Farren had suggested that Hawk decide who he was going to surround himself with as new Warriors of the Kingdom. For Hawk it had been an easy decision. He climbed the stairs of the Main Street Station where a couple of them were seated on the balcony overlooking Main Street.

"Morning, boss," Shep waved as Hawk crested the stairs.

Hawk smiled, greeting both Shep and Jonathan, who were there waiting. "Hi. Juliette coming?"

"She called this morning," Jonathan informed him. "Was hoping it would be okay if she and Tim spent the day playing with the kids in the park."

Hawk laughed, thinking about the changes in their lives over the past few months. His staff members were his new Warriors of the Kingdom. He trusted them and they were family. Although he still preached each Sunday, the day-to-day operations of the church were now being handled by the staff. They had also all moved on to the payroll of the Disney Corporation, which freed up valuable financial resources at the church. Their full-time occupations were as ministers; they paid the bills for their occupation with the funding from their new vocations working for the Disney Company. As they looked over Main Street, the three saw Reginald Cambridge standing below them, wearing dark glasses, and looking up toward them.

"Uncle Reggie!" Shep yelled, recalling for Hawk the first unexpected meeting Cambridge had ever had with the student minister.

"Everything okay?" Reginald directed the question toward Hawk.

"Good." He leaned over the rail to answer. "You good?"

"Indeed, thanks for asking. Need anything today?"

"No, got a development meeting later, anxious about seeing some of the new stuff!"

"If you need me before then, call."

Reginald waved at the three and moved off down Main Street. Hawk had also made Cambridge a Warrior of the Kingdom. He now worked as the Chief Security Officer for the entire corporation. He was assigned to be in the same general location as Hawk at any given time. As Reginald walked past the statue of Roy Disney and Minnie Mouse, the preacher smiled. He took a moment and followed Roy's gaze back to where the old classic Walt Disney Story attraction had been. It was just another day at Disney World, and Roy was still watching out for Walt.

"Hawk, I've got something to tell you." Shep interrupted Hawk's thoughts.

"What's up?"

"I was watching the *Old Yeller* DVD. I listened again to Walt's message to you and was just goofing around."

"And?" Jonathan leaned toward Shep curiously.

"Well, I found an Easter egg," Shep informed them.

"An Easter Egg?" Hawk slowly straightened and leaned forward.

"A hidden surprise, an unmarked bonus feature. Usually you have to figure out some combination of pushing arrows and hitting buttons, then all of the sudden, boom, you find the Easter egg."

"And you found something?" Hawk was now intrigued.

"Yes, it was a riddle, I guess. It was a picture of something, not sure what . . . had a riddle written over it on the screen."

"You mean like a clue or a puzzle piece?" Hawk's pulse quickened. "Did you bring the DVD with you?"

"Of course." Shep produced the DVD from his backpack.

"Let's go take a look at it. We can watch it at the Fire Station." Hawk got to his feet.

"Oh, no," Jonathan moaned. "Not another mystery."

His words fell across the now empty chairs as his friends were both already up heading across the street toward the Fire Station.

"Here we go again." Hawk stopped on the steps and followed Jonathan's gaze to the castle. "Just another magical day at Disney World!"

He turned and raced down the staircase, his friends close on his heels, to begin a new quest.

A Story That Will Never Be Completed . . .
(Author's Afterword)

WALT DISNEY ONCE SAID about Disneyland, "It will never be completed. It will continue to grow as long as there is imagination left in the world." The same can be said for Walt Disney World or any other of the growing number of Disney theme parks as they are constructed across the globe.

The story you have just read springs out of the imagination ignited within me as a child wandering through the Magic Kingdom before it ever opened to the general public. In the days prior to Walt Disney World's opening, people would flock to the Walt Disney World Preview Center. (Today that building is known as the Amateur Athletic Union Headquarters.) As a wide-eyed kid I would look at the huge model of what the park was going to look like, I would watch Walt on film talking about his dreams for building the theme park, and then wander through the Disney merchandise. I remember thinking how amazing this place would be, but nothing really prepared me for the day I got the chance to walk down Main Street USA for the very first time. From that moment on I was a fan.

Eventually I would work in the theme park, I would become a collector of Disney memorabilia, I would find occasions to travel to the park and visit, and spending time at Disney World through the years has become a part of my DNA, the experiences have become a permanent part of who I am.

In Key to the Kingdom I have written not as much about the Walt Disney World that is, but instead about the Disney World that exists in the imagination of Disney fans all over the world. It seems fitting since Walt Disney as a storyteller always was igniting the imagination of his guests. I have taken a great deal of time to research the things I have written about and you can go on your own quest to find the Key to the Kingdom. I strongly encourage you to do so. Obviously at some point your journey would take you to places that the general public doesn't have access to, whether these off-limit places exist or not, I will leave to your own imagination to decide. Moving the inaccessible places aside, there is enough to keep you hunting and searching for clues that will satisfy any treasure hunter with a love for mystery and Disney trivia.

On purpose I have given an almost mythical quality to the Imagineers of the Disney Company. The people who make up WDI are regular people just like the rest of us, except that they have a wildly creative slant on the world. Imagineers are the ones who ask "what if" and "why not" when most think something is impossible. Having met with and chatted with Imagineers, I have also discovered they take their art very seriously and they get to paint stories against the most unique canvas in all the world, the Disney theme parks.

Last but not least, you have heard it said that art imitates life . . . and vice versa. Someone asked me if the story I have written is true. I respond with, "It contains as much truth as *The Da Vinci Code*!" Somehow I think that pretty well sums it up. I hope you have enjoyed the story. On some level it is every Disney fan's dream come true. What happens next? Remember what Walt said: "It will never be completed. It will continue to grow as long as there is imagination left in the world."

Jeff Dixon
Tree House Villas
Saratoga Springs Resort
Walt Disney World

The following resources were invaluable in understanding the background, history, operation, and attractions within Walt Disney World.

Birnbaum's Walt Disney World and *Birnbaum's Disneyland 2007.* New York: Disney Editions, 2006.

Canemaker, John. *Walt Disney's Nine Old Men & The Art of Animation.* New York: Hyperion, 2001.

Eisner, Michael and Tony Schwartz. *Work in Progress.* New York: Random House, 1998.

Gabler, Neal. *Walt Disney: Triumph of the American Imagination.* New York: Knopf, 2006.

Gordan, Bruce and Jeff Kurtti. *Walt Disney World: Then, Now and Forever.* New York: Disney Editions, 2008.

Green, Katherine and Richard. *The Man Behind the Magic: the Story of Walt Disney.* New York: Viking, 1991.

Hench, John. *Designing Disney: Imagineering and the Art of the Show.* New York: Disney Editions, 2003.

Holliss, Richard and Brian Sibley. *The Disney Studio Story.* New York: Crown, 1988.

————. *Snow White and the Seven Dwarfs & the Making of the Classic Film.* New York: Simon & Schuster, 1987; Hyperion, 1994.

Imagineers. *Walt Disney Imagineering: A Behind the Dreams Look at Making the Magic.* New York: Hyperion, 1996.

Jackson, Kathy Merlock. *Walt Disney: Conversations.* Jackson, MS: Univ. Press of Mississippi, 2006.

Kurtti, Jeff. *Imagineering Legends and the Genesis of the Disney Theme Park*. New York: Disney Editions, 2008.

Marling, Karal Ann. *Designing Disney's Theme Parks*. New York: Flammarion, 1997.

Miller, Diane Disney and Pete Martin. *The Story of Walt Disney*. New York: Holt, 1957.

Mongello, Louis A. *The Walt Disney World Trivia Book (Volumes 1 and 2)*. Branford, CT: The Intrepid Traveler, Vol. 1, 2004; Vol.2, 2006.

Neary, Kevin and David Smith. *The Ultimate Disney Trivia Book*. New York: Hyperion, 1992.

————. *The Ultimate Disney Trivia Book 2*. New York: Hyperion, 1994.

————. *The Ultimate Disney Trivia Book 3*. New York: Hyperion, 1997.

————. *The Ultimate Disney Trivia Book 4*. New York: Disney Editions, 2000.

Peri, Don. *Working with Walt: Interviews with Disney Artists*. Jackson, MS: Univ. Press of Mississippi, 2008.

Ridgeway, Charles. *Spinning Disney's World: Memories of a Magic Kingdom Press Agent*. Branford, CT: Intrepid Traveler, 2007.

Smith, Dave and Steven Clark. *Disney: The First 100 Years*. New York: Hyperion, 1999; Disney Editions, updated 2002.

————. *The Quotable Walt Disney*. New York: Disney Editions, 2001.

————. *Disney A to Z: the Official Encyclopedia*. New York: Hyperion, 1996; updated 1998, 2006.

Snow, Dennis. *Lessons from the Mouse*. Sanford, FL: DC Press, 2009.

Surrell, Jason. *The Disney Mountains: Imagineering at Its Peak*. New York: Disney Editions, 2007.

Thomas, Bob. *The Art of Animation.* New York: Simon & Schuster, 1958.

———. *Walt Disney: An American Original.* New York: Simon & Schuster, 1976.

———. *Building a Company; Roy O. Disney and the Creation of an Entertainment Empire.* New York: Hyperion, 1998.

Thomas, Frank and Ollie Johnston. *The Illusion of Life: Disney Animation.* New York: Hyperion, 1995.

Vennes, Susan. *The Hidden Magic of Walt Disney World (Over 600 secrets of the Magic Kingdom, Epcot, Disney's Hollywood Studios, and Animal Kingdom).* Avon, MA: Adams Media, 2009.

Wright, Alex. *The Imagineering Field Guide to the Magic Kingdom at Walt Disney World.* New York: Disney Editions, 2005.

WEBSITES

These are some of the author's favorite Disney fan sites that helped provide information and resources beyond the printed page.

The WDW Radio Show, http://www.wdwradio.com/.

Inside the Magic w/ Ricky Brigante, http://www.distantcreations.com/.

Jim Hill Media, http://www.jimhillmedia.com/.

Theme Parkology: 2719 Hyperion, http://www.2719hyperion.com/.

Resort Information, http://www.mouseplanet.com/.

Disney News and Information, http://www.laughingplace.com/.

Walt Disney World News, http://www.wdwmagic.com/.